KINGDOM'S BONES

By

H. Sylver

Instagram: @8thandrolle

Instagram: @kingdomsbonesbook

Website: www.8thandrolle.com.

Table of Contents

Dedicated to the Loving Memory of

Mr. Deen President.

Chapter 1:

What Remains

The door to the chambers where they gathered opened, and all eyes remained on the object the servant was carrying. Miguel, having only heard of this gathering in stories, was met in the middle of the aisle by the concerned and troubled face of one of the leading five chairs of the Assembly. As he drew closer everyone near enough grabbed hold of their noses, as a searing stench began to gradually permeate the open space. With his face wrapped, Miguel bowed without raising his head, presenting the chest with a note sealed and wrapped in a manner that was recognized by all. The 40-chaired chamber was overflowed with decorated uniforms adorned by as many generals and royal guards as the eye could see. Some whose kingdoms were at war at that very moment. Yet their weapons were collected and stored. They sat vulnerably next to each other, at least today, as brothers.

The Chairman accepted the chest and lowered it to the ground. He took up the letter and broke the seal. Taking a deep breath through his lip surrounded by his snow-white beard, he peered around the room looking at those struggling to keep their eyes from leaking a silent sorrow shared by all who were present. He began to read aloud:

18th Day of Octobre 1806

My Brethren,

I bid you great salutations from the unknown. It is my most dire of wishes that this letter finds you and the ears of my brothers in arms. I will saunter on no further in my words, as these last of my orders must be carried out as stated without delay.

I order that the Assembly immediately disband, voiding all current and future contracts as these words are being read. No reason will be given. No explanation bestowed. Failure to heed my word will constitute swift swings of the Candiru's blades, and so it stands. All accounts are to be divided amongst the counsel and each Candiru member. Abandon all symbols, all artistic and literary accounts. Destroy all ledgers and speak never of our existence until my song returns. Preserve the Minister's line.

My time has come. Death is upon me. Evident in this trunk.

The threat has befallen my unknown legacy.

If you revere me as you pledged, execute my direction.

And so it stands.

3

-Mayer the Formidable.

The room's silence were daggers in the ears of the members who wanted more context to the letter.

"What does he mean to disband?!" screamed one the generals, as the Chairman opened the box to reveal a still decomposing skull. The chatter continued as he peered at the head of not only a mentor and teacher, but one of the fiercest warriors to have ever lived. He could not be dead. The quarrels became louder.

"Has this document even been examined to be sure these are the words of Mayer?" asked another.

"This must be a trick of the Templars! We must be vigilant and strike them before they attempt something like this again! Mayer cannot die!" exclaimed another.

"Brothers! There will be order!" yelled a gavel-swinging member of the five. Adjusting his black robe as calm once again returned to the dander filled space they operated. "There is only one way to verify the authenticity of the letter and the remains. Bring in the minister."

A side door to the chamber opened, and an elderly woman gracefully walked in wearing the white soldier's uniform, golden buttons, with the insignia of the Assembly stitched perfectly on the chest piece. Lowering her red hood to reveal her comforting wrinkled face, with her chalk white hair draping her slightly hunched back. She made her way to meet the chairman, who was now on the verge of tears. She rested her palm on his cheek, as a tear seeped out of his lower lid. He brushed it away as his eyes met her sharp stare. She smiled and took the trunk from him. Instantly the smile disappeared as her hands trembled. She looked around and smiled again, laying the trunk graciously on the ground. She knelt over it and pulled a vial from her pocket. The violet-colored substance glowed as she shook it before opening the top.

"This day was to be," said the old minister as she poured the contents out onto the skull. "Extinguish all the lights in the room!" she commanded.

All eyes watched as the liquid seeped into the crevices of the frontal bone, into the nasal cavity, down into the mandible that had dead flesh still hanging from it.

"No reaction," said the old woman, as she struggled to make it to her feet. As she stood, the trunk began to rattle violently. The oily substance reversed from saturating the wood floor, back into the bottom of the box. The dead flesh began to rejuvenate from the chin up to the teeth, as gum began to form.

"What madness is this?" yelled another chairman, leaving his seat to join the others as they went to witness the phenomena.

An audible choking sound came from the skull, the vocal cords forming, as the healing of skin followed. Suddenly, the flesh began to rot away again.

"Why have you left me?" said the parched voice that escaped

5

the grizzly skull rattling violently. Then silence. Back to its original decomposed state. The men of valor and the Candiru that protected and enforced the law of Mayer were all exasperated. Some born to battle and others having seen atrocities that aged their eyes and battle scarred faces were silent. Nothing could prepare them for such a sight.

"This is truly Mayer," said the minister. "The great leader has fallen."

Chapter 2:

Generals

6 Years Earlier

1799, Saint-Domingue/Hispaniola

The cause was noble. At least that was the thought he kept reciting in his head as the unusually warm night air brushed repeatedly against his dry, dark skin. More disturbing was the calm of the sea, the moon's reflection dancing on its surface. As Mayer stood at the foot of the boat, he smirked, realizing that the men he saw the night before at sea gave a valid description of what he saw in front of him at that moment. Rightfully so, for the past hour upon his approach to Hispaniola, the embers and ash filled the air.

"It will be the one on fire!" they said in a shaky but warning tone.

It smelled like the battles he'd seen countless times. The setting was different, but the mix of gunpowder, wood, blood, and human flesh burning was no stranger to his nose. No fear could be found in his expression, no tremble in his posture. Any other soldier would have thought of avenues to run away from this haunting conflict. Especially those without an alignment to any side, on a one sail propelled boat. He adjusted the engraved ring on his finger, taking a final look at the two chests that lay at his feet. The harbor was finally in view.

"Two minutes until we dock, patron" said Miguel, his attendant, as his paddles became more strategic as to not draw too much attention to their vessel. They approached the dock, dismounted, and tied the boat to an available post. Surveying the harbor generated another look of delight on his face. Another one of Napoleon's great battalions were retreating to their post; battered, broken, and carrying what was left of their dying and dead. He pitied the poor soul that had to give "Little Boney" the bad news. Decapitation was never a fate you gleefully walked into.

He then dug into his coat for an object wrapped in cloth. Carefully undoing the knot, revealing a broken piece of curved wood. With a gaze of emotion and care that had not rested on his eyes since his departure from the ship, it was clear that the most valuable thing to him was best kept hidden until it was time.

Being cautious, Mayer and his squire took a path away from the heat of the fight. As they made their way further into the woods, Miguel couldn't help but be curious.

"Patron, are you sure you know the way?" asked the young pupil carrying the chest on his shoulders.

"Yes Miguel, the directions we asked for were simply to find out where the French post was and their exit strategy to their ships. That way, we can leave without drawing too much attention. Any fight should be avoided, especially those that do not provide a challenge, bare purpose, or improve one's skill", said the teacher as he wrestled with the brushes and branches overhead.

As his student opened his mouth to compliment the sage advice, the all too familiar clicks of riffle hammers cocking back, encompassed them. They were surrounded but were not rattled by the unseen danger.

"Six men, 3 guns, all with machetes. Stay calm, we must wait for one of them to speak. Our attire doesn't exactly scream ally," said Mayer, slowly raising his hands. His student followed suit.

"Are you a spy!? Are you a spy?!" yelled one of the militia appearing with his gun pointed at them.

In their language, the Formidable replied, "I seek Jean-Jacques, or Toussaint, please take me to them."

The militia mumbled to each other. Some wanted to kill them where they stood, some did not want to kill men that directly asked for their commander, let alone looked like them.

"I assure you I am no spy, my allegiance is not with the

French, British or Spain. I only have my sword and it is locked in its sheath. We are on official business," pleaded Mayer.

"What is the call?" yelled another gunman.

"What are they saying Patron?" asked a curious Miguel.

"What is the CALL!?" he demanded again.

"Koupe tet, boule kay (Cut off their heads, burn their houses.)!" yelled Mayer with emphatic resolve.

Silence fell on the soldiers, looking at each other as they came out from the shadows.

"Follow me," said the leader of the militia. They were led to a camp a few miles inland. As he walked, it became clear that the defeat of the French was imminent. The Revolution's soldiers were not only well prepared but showed no mercy. History was unfolding before his very eyes. Eyes that had seen moments that shaped the fabric of the world.

"Commander Toussaint! We have a visitor!" announced the militia's leader.

"What is the meaning of this?! Why are we being interrupted as we plan our next move?" grilled Toussaint L'Ouverture.

"I am a friend. May we please speak in private?" requested Mayer.

"I do not know who you are, friend. You are very brave to have made it this far into our camp. But I will have to have you escorted out. Resist? I would have no choice but to order your execution right where you stand," said the well-respected general.

"Perhaps a demonstration is in order! To prove I am worth your time, send me 5 of your best swordsmen. If I defeat them, I get five minutes of your time."

"Five? Haha, these are men that are not afraid to die. A force so feared for having killed the best that Europe has to offer. Are you sure?"

"Ten then"

"As you wish," replied Toussaint as he grabbed the nearest seat.

"Patron, are you sure this is wise? I have never seen you engage ten men at once." asked Miguel.

"I'll be fine Miguel, just safeguard the chests until I am finished." spoke a confident Mayer.

The Formidable removed his jacket and handed it to his pupil. He then unhooked his sword from his strap without removing it from its sheath. He wanted to make it clear that he had no intention of killing his opponents. Toussaint was floored by this but was intrigued. Slowly, men armed with machetes and French issued swords surrounded him. He took a slow, deep breath, and gradually the ash in the air moved as slow as molasses, blurring to reveal a focused vision of a soldier darting towards him. Assessing the speed, height, and weight of the assailant in a matter of milliseconds, he chose to counter the attack with a swift kick to the leg. His attacker went down quickly. Two others came at him. Now assessing the nerves and pressure points of their bodies, he threw two quick punches to the neck and rib cage of one. Then grabbed his sword and disabled the other with three hits to the left side of his body. They both fell in unison. Toussaint was brought to his feet. Excited yet stern.

"Next! Go! He may have the color of our skin but do not let this man make a mockery of this revolution!"

Motivated by their leader, the men now wanted blood. They all ran towards him, without a thought of what was getting ready to happen. The men's feet kicked up dust, clouding the rapid succession of strikes, kicks, sweeps, and cries of pain. When the dust settled, one of Toussaint's men stood with his hands raised. The whole camp cheered, but it was soon short lived after the men took a closer look. Behind the man was the soldier's own hand-musket pointed at the back of his head.

"Your men have fought valiantly General; they are a force to be reckoned with. I am glad to know that what I have heard about your army has exceeded my expectations." complimented Mayer.

"Thank you. I would hope that my men would speak nothing of this little exhibition." Toussaint said in a warning tone.

The defeated men got up dusting themselves off, but quickly saluted their leader in agreement. General L'Ouverture welcomed Mayer into his tent. Both taking a seat at the table.

"May I offer you something to drink Monsieur....?" began Toussaint.

"Forgive me, General. I cannot believe I have disgraced your hospitality. Allow me to introduce myself. My name is…"

"Mayer! I must admit old friend, if it hadn't been for me recognizing your fighting style, I would have shot you from where I was watching," said another General entering the tent.

"Jean-Jacques! It is great to see you again." said Mayer, embracing him.

"You are friends with Mayer the Formidable?!" gasped Toussaint.

"The word "friend" does not describe him. This is the man that bought my freedom. He gave me a name free of bondage. Taught me almost everything that I know."

"Almost Jean?"

"I knew how to fight long before you came along Mayer," Jean-Jacques shot back playfully.

"And I vaguely remember a few lessons that helped you hone those skills. Your mother would have been proud to see that you have grown into a mighty warrior, leading your people!" applauded Mayer.

"I have heard many great things about you Mayer. It is great to have you here with us. I trust you have come to aid in our efforts against the French." peered Toussaint.

"As much as I would love to stick it to the little man, my presence today warrants a greater cause." said Mayer as he took a seat. "I have come to enlist your protection. In exchange, I will provide you with funds to continue your campaign." Mayer motioned to Miguel to bring forward the two chests. He opened them and the air was quickly sucked out of the room. Jean-Jacques' eyes opened widely as he moved closer to the small wooden caskets that held gold pieces and coins. Some he recognized, some inscribed with symbols he had never seen before.

"Who is after you Mayer?", asked Jean-Jacques as he examined the treasure closely.

"And is this worth the trouble? We are in the middle of a war." Toussaint added. "You are a legend, Mayer, but I have heard the whispers of your international conquests. You are not only feared, but the church wants your head. Housing you may start a bigger conflict before we have fully formed our nation."

"I understand your reproach Toussaint, and I will not insult your intelligence. Yes, I am aware of the Assembly's reputation, and as its leader, it would be futile to debate otherwise. However, the asylum that I seek, is not for me, it is for this." Mayer pulled out a wrapped wooden shard and unveiled the small object to a disappointed audience.

"You have risked your life for this piece of withered wood?!" snarled Toussaint. "We are in the middle of war in case you haven't noticed! You have cheated us out of precious time we could have dedicated to planning our final campaign to take the island."

"Cheated? This from a man that thinks sitting at the table with Napoleon after slaughtering his whole garrison will be a civil transfer of power. You cheat your people!" snapped Mayer.

Toussaint jumped up from his seat and drew his sword. Jean-Jacques stepped between them.

"How dare you come into my camp and besmirch our efforts!" exclaimed Toussaint as he readied his sword to strike.

"You speak for yourself. Jean-Jacques and every general with a brain can see that your planned meeting with him is suicide." said Mayer as he stood up leisurely, calmly wiping his lips with a cloth from Toussaint's table.

"How about I cut yours out of your skull?!" barked Toussaint as he advanced towards the warlord.

"I'll be glad to add you as the eleventh man to fall to me in less than 20 seconds!" said Mayer as opened the side of his coat, revealing the numerous blades hanging from chains sewn into his garment. This baffled and enraged Toussaint, as he knew of the stories and legends around the bloody massacres involving Mayer and his abilities. Yet, he could not show weakness. He continued his pursuit only to be met with the halt of Jean-Jacques' hand on his chest.

"Gentlemen!" interceded Jean-Jacques. "I can't believe that I am playing peacekeeper here, but we all know that we cannot afford for our men to see such division. Toussaint, hang up your sword my comrade. You're a formidable swordsman, but even I know how this will end. Trust me, it's you that will end up on your ass."

Toussaint, angered by the lack of faith his brother-in-arms had in him, advanced further.

"My apologies Toussaint," interrupted Mayer. "Again, I mean no malice upon your character or a man of your stature. I am just concerned for your wellbeing and your cause. I can tell you that men of war from the motherland to the edges of Asia have heard of and respect you, as do I. Please sit, let us not quarrel any further; allow me to explain my proposition."

Toussaint, taken aback by the world knowing of his conquest to raise up the Western Hemisphere's first free African Nation, assertively slid his weapon back into its holster. A grin flashed across his face, and malice left his eyes.

"We are men of fortune Mayer. Fortune that makes Europe and all its allies tremble in fear. Forgive my outburst, you are our guests," said Toussaint as he again took a seat at the table. Mayer approached the war table to take a seat when suddenly he was halted by Toussaint raising his hand. "Before you take a seat, I do have one favor to ask of you, Mayer."

"Name it." Replied the reluctant warlord.

"Transform into the demi-god that few have lived to see. If death is as sure for me as any warrior on the battlefield, then grant me the rare observation. I have heard of the claims that you are a man capable of wielding 100 swords at once." said Toussaint. Jean-Jacques took a seat next to his fellow general with an equally curious demeanor. Mayer pondered as his vision darted between the two generals.

"Ok my friends. But please be warned, you may want to take a few steps back" relented Mayer. The men stood and did as he said, bracing themselves with their hands on the handles of their weapons.

"I call!" fired Mayer before a flash of light illuminated where they stood. The wind picked up in speed and might, as all that were near covered their eyes to avoid the dirt and immaculate blare of the shining attire appearing to knit itself to Mayer in a rapid haste. A golden symbol of spheres and three swords mimicking an instrument of time rested on his chest. Multiple blade endings swayed in peaceful unison just shy of the bottom hem of his chalk-colored garb. The sputtering sound of energy seized the ears of its witnesses.

"Satisfied?" inquired Mayer.

"Ecstatic!" replied Toussaint, clapping in amazement. Jean-Jacques, still taking in the scene, cracked a smile. He lifted his chin, with pride and honor, as his claims of his teacher's abilities were no longer legend, but truth amongst them.

Chapter 3:

FREE

It was that time again. Sitting in his cell, looking at the ceiling for what he presumed to be his last time. Judson couldn't help but rethink the steps that got him there. He had done it all. From dealing narcotics, to running an underground fighting ring that saw the likes of men that wouldn't dare step foot outside the shadows. The predicament of "Ti Swayze" began with events that were not important at this time. Not to him at least. His thoughts drifted from how quick he could get to the nearest strip club with a sack of God's chosen green, to getting his 1975 Chevy Impala donk back into pristine condition. Footsteps echoed through the cell block as the school of guards approached his cell. The ashy, muscle-bound inmate sat up to wash his face. His beard was nappy with a few droplets of water that clung stubbornly. The wife-beater stretched across his protruding belly, indenting into his dark skin emblazoned with Miami's best ink jobs. The Haitian coat of arms on his chest was a great conversation piece, while simultaneously striking fear into anyone who was close enough to observe the details.

The guard standing at his cell door was relieved as he was joined by his supervisor and fellow COs. The "free-man-elect" sat up on his cot with his patented grin which evolved into a slight chuckle, then a short spurt of grand laughter.

"You know you didn't have to bring all of them, right?" snared Judson, as one of the COs opened his cell's sliding door.

"Only for our safety Mr. Jean-Baptiste. I assure you; we are no match for what is waiting for you outside these prison walls. We truly want no parts of the karma you have coming!" said the Warden who would join the escort.

"Warden McMillan. So glad that you would take the time out of your dominatrix time to walk me to freedom. Tell me, has she used the large dildo yet? Or are you still being groomed?" laughed Judson. The slight clearing of throats came from the group of officers struggling not to laugh.

"I have dreamt of this day Baptiste. It's like a wet dream you have no shame waking up from in front of everyone with your cock swinging," the seasoned warden shot back.

"That is very aggressive sir!" said Judson, as he was being shackled for the long walk to the release building. "I will say that you have been nothing short of a gracious host. I will miss this. This cell. This building. Your donut eating orgies the female COs

19

would tell me about when I would knock 'em down in the shed behind the pantry."

"Are you confessing to a crime, Jean-Baptiste?" asked the Warden as he motioned for the procession through the cell block to begin.

"Not at all pumpkin spice. I know nothing, I see nothing. I fuck nothing. No matter how fat Officer Patrice's ass is." replied Judson, as he winked in the direction of the female officer who quickly turned the corner to avoid any further embarrassment. They reached a door that was buzzed open from the other side. The loud inmates knew that someone was getting out and had a ticker tape like parade ready. Complete with toilet paper, empty toothpaste tubes, magazine cutouts, and sheets soaked in all kinds of bodily fluids that would make the freedom walk a biohazard.

The quadrant of the jail erupted in yells and taunts as the 7-man team of officers entered the cell block. The inmates were prepared until Judson's bald head made an appearance from behind them. The cell block fell silent as if every man went night-night while standing up. The paraphernalia in their hands dropped to the ground. Some in fear, some in restrained anger, most in satisfying disbelief.

The curiosity of one of the rookie officers could not be contained as he was expecting a barrage of waste raining down onto them.

"Why is everyone so quiet? What happened to the confetti? They scared of this clown?"

"Ayo. shut the fuck up!" whispered the senior guard.

"It's okay Simon, let me further school the young piglet," interrupted Judson, as he continued to nod to some of the most feared men in the world. Some respected the gesture; some were elated that the undefeated fighter was now on his way out of their collective space. These were murderers, rapists, and some of Florida's most violent criminals who all subscribed to the joint silence.

"Do not return. If I see your face again, I will put a 12-gauge to your mouth and do the Lord's work myself." called the warden to Judson as they were being buzzed through the next door that led them through a series of exits.

"I'll miss you too, sir! Or is it ma'am today? I can't keep up with your costume changes." Laughed Judson as he exited the first of a series of tall, barbed wire gates of the prison for the first time in a few years. The bleached-over smell of human and rodent waste faded away as his walking cadence quickened. The rays from the sun felt different on his skin as he made his way to processing. Breathing was like a forgotten skill with each step. Judson tried his best to bottle up the joy. Rubbing his wrists to massage away years of handcuff cuts, bruises, and indentations. Judson shook off another yearning to show any emotion other than his regular cocky demeanor.

Chapter 4:

Reunion

Judson was given a bag of his belongings. From what he could gather, there were items missing. Had it been years ago, he would make a stink about the jewelry. At this point, buying a new watch and chain would be more of a reward than a loss after getting out the pen. The clothing was wrinkled with dirt and blood stains, and smelled like mildew. None of it bothered Judson, as he could already smell the air of freedom on the other side of the three layers of barbed wire fences and concrete. It was time to get back to the grind. No one was going to hand him anything, and he expected no one to do so. Now dressed, he was escorted out to the last and final gate that was between him and the outside. Before he could bask in the sight of the last fence finally opening after the loud buzz, he noticed a black car. A woman leaned against the passenger door. Apart from the annoyed look that her sunglasses couldn't hide, she was dressed in clothing that screamed power and authority. The black pants that hugged her hips caught the eyes of the guards. The white button-up, complete with a jacket, made them think twice about whistling.

"Well, well, Baptiste, already got a bitch waiting for you, huh?" asked the guard standing next to him.

"That bitch, will bite the nose of your face, chew it, then force feed it back to you like a vulture! Besides, that's my little sister. Now apologize for disgracing her honor," requested Judson.

"My apologies," yelled the guard in her direction. He wanted no part of the smoke with Judson, not even in the slightest.

Judson made his way towards Sonya with a smile on his face. Sonya turned around and opened the door of the black sedan and got into the driver's seat.

"Well damn. Nice to see you, too, little sister." Smirked Judson as he walked around to the passenger's side.

"You smell," said Sonya, as she started the engine and put the vehicle into gear.

"Thank you, it's from my new line called "Fresh out". Coming soon to a Macy's near you."

As much as Sonya was annoyed, and disgusted, she was happy to see her brother out of jail. She had to be stern and cold to him to make sure he realized that this was a major inconvenience. A junior agent of the CIA wouldn't dare call in

23

the favors and back door deals to get an inmate serving 10 years out after a year and half. Family was everything to her, at least the family she had left. Sometimes, it was all she needed. Other times the void of their parents overcame the young, sweet, but fierce Air force vet.

"So, where is the old man? I thought he would have shown his face this time. It's been months since his last visit." said Judson, as he attempted to scratch at the small patches of mildew and dust stained into his shirt.

"Why would he come down here again, Judson? To see you locked away again for the same ol' dumb shit?! He has better things to worry about."

"Like what?! That stuck-up ass church he parades in a dress in front of every Sunday morning?"

"Have some respect and grow the fuck up, Judson! I can't believe after all these years; you still have the complex of a 13-year-old class clown! Priesthood is not a joking matter. He has seriously given his life to it, and the least you can do is support and not mock his path," said Sonya. The beaming of the sun did not last as she adjusted the visor.

"One of many Sonya, which one is he? Preacher? Stupid father figure? Assassin? Or a pain in my ass? He's a jack-of-all-trades, but a jack ass at life." Judson waited for a negative reaction and got one: Sonya slammed on the breaks and slapped him.

"It's been fucking decades Judson, get over it!" yelled

24

Sonya, as she used her index finger to repeatedly mush his head against the glass window. Hairline cracks formed from the impact. "He couldn't save them! He did what he could to save our lives and help us control the pain, and anger."

Judson rubbed his temple, marveling at the marks left by Sonya's nails. "By training us to take muthafuckas heads off but get mad when I use it for my own gain? What type of backwards doctrine is that?"

"Backwards?! You want to talk about…" Sonya stopped mid-sentence to realize her assumptions were true. They were being followed. The same three cars that changed lanes with her in a synchronized fashion also came to a quick halt. Whoever they were, they were professionals and the concern started to sink in. They weren't just cops waiting for dispatch to OK the tags on Sonya's vehicle.

"Buckle up!" barked Sonya. She hit the gas pedal so hard the force almost threw Judson into the backseat.

"Ok, ok, I get that you're mad but…." began Judson, as he adjusted himself in his seat, looking back at the grill of a black SUV as it smashed into them.

"Who did you piss off Judson!? Who do you owe?!" Sonya regained control of the wheel.

"Nobody important." Judson contemplated the list of his possible enemies that had the resources to ambush him.

"Well, they were important enough to hire hitmen Judson!"

The cars gave chase as expected. On a hot summer day in

Dade County, the chances of a high-speed chase being ignored by bystanders were slim. Sonya put her com in and called her trusted analyst and best friend Jesse.

"Jesse! We are southbound on NE 4th Court, making a right on 62nd." snapped Sonya into her com unit. "We are being tailed by 3 hostile vehicles. Requesting alternate route and extraction!"

"Umm...isn't today your day off?" Jesse asked in confusion.

"J, I swear if I get shot, I will shoot you as soon as I clock in! Get me a route!" she demanded.

"Alright, alright, I'm on it!" responded her best friend slash handler. For years, Sonya dreamed about being out in the field. Any rookie would have crashed by now, or even worse. Yet, she had a level of control and calm that came from years of discipline and training at the hands of Elam. The man that saved and raised them. The windows rolled down on the vehicle closest to them, and two handguns began firing in their direction.

"Shit! It's the Russians!" yelled Judson. "Give me a strap!"

"I really should not be putting an assault weapon in the hands of a convicted felon. But hey! If I lose my position over this? I will come after you and finish the job!"

"Quit your babbling woman!" Judson said sarcastically as he took the M16 rifle she handed to him. He rolled down his window and returned fire. He took out the gunman in the passenger seat, then made quick work of the driver. The car swerved onto the sidewalk, into a strip mall. The thrill of gunshots was the perfect welcome for a gangsta. At least for an elite marksman like himself.

A second car approached aggressively. All the windows were rolled down. An assortment of weapons from AKs to submachine guns tasted the humid Miami air. Seeking to devour glass, metal, and flesh.

"Jessie, get us out of here!" yelled Sonya. She rolled down her window and fired a few shots of her own, right before that back window blew out.

"Two intersections ahead. Make a sharp right, do it fast! I have tapped into the traffic lights, and directed all of Liberty City your way. You have to neutralize the threat, or we are looking at civilian casualties!" Jesse frantically stated as he tapped away at his keyboard.

The siblings sped through the first intersection before a bombardment of cars and trucks came from both directions. The first car narrowly escaped before the car holding more henchmen behind it was crushed by the onslaught of vehicles. Making the right turn as instructed, the car behind them took time to reload while the driver attempted to get next to Sonya. Suddenly, from an alleyway, came a masked man on a motorcycle. The wind kicked up every strand of dreads on his head. Revealing the most piercing and focused eyes that were latched onto the hostiles in the remaining car. He revved the throttle, gaining even more speed but maintaining control. In a swift motion, he reached down and pulled out a custom-made machete blade. The Japanese steel reflected the sun, further exposing the sharpness and grandeur of its design.

"Do you see that?" yelled Sonya to Judson, while he attempted to reload.

"You didn't think I was going to just let you guys have all the fun now did you?" said a familiar voice through her com.

"It can't be. Ronel?! How did you..." began Sonya.

"Baby sister, tell my dumb ass little brother that he can stop trying to reload. Looks like he's a little rusty, I got this!" said Ronel. Sonya was speechless, as was Jessie. He was trying to figure out how another voice was able to tap into their conversation. The biker sped up to the side of the henchmen. They extended their weapons for another barrage. With a swift swing, Ronel cut off the arms of both the front and backseat passengers. The men yelled out in terror but were both shot in the head by a defiant Judson. The biker swung his machete, blowing out the front and back tires. The remaining driver panicked as the car drifted from side to side. Losing traction and slamming into a parked car. Ronel stopped and jumped off his bike and ran towards the vehicle. The driver, still conscious, began to fire in his direction. He was confused by the rapid deflection of the bullets as they ricocheted off of Ronel's machete. Keeping his momentum, Ronel leapt from the ground. He flipped forward onto the top of the vehicle while driving the sword through the sunroof. Into the skull of the driver.

"This nigga and his theatrics. Does he always gotta show off?" scoffed Judson, as he envied the acrobatic ability of his

28

shorter, leaner, older brother.

Ronel forcefully removed his machete from the roof, stained with brain matter. He jumped down to the asphalt. He shook his sword to get as much blood from it as possible as he walked towards his siblings.

"You were the last person I was expecting to see. I thought you were still in Barcelona," said Sonya as she opened the door to embrace him.

"I was, but a new mission came up. This one brought me home," said Ronel as his delight quickly descended into anger.

"You know you could have gotten her killed, what is your problem? Who were those guys?" yelled Ronel to Judson, who was exiting the car.

"So, it's fuck Judson Day, huh? Nigga I just got out. If you hadn't gotten here when you did, I would have killed the rest without your help."

"Out of jail for just a few hours and already gotta have someone pull your ass out of shit." rebutted Ronel.

"Like you have the track record of saving me when I needed you the most?! Fuck you and fuck the old man too! You try to be so much like him, and it makes me sick!" yelled Judson, walking away.

"And where do you think you are going, jackass? You are still in my custody." belted Sonya.

"I'm taking the bus," Judson replied, holding up a middle finger.

"With what money?"

"With the 20 dollars I found in your wallet. Thanks, lil sister, I will pay you back." Judson walked into the busy intersection, narrowly being missed by unsuspecting drivers. "You know I'm more than good for it!"

"Muthafucka! They are going to send more goons after you!" fired Sonya.

"Follow the body trail then, you will know where to find me."

"Let him go, Sonya, I will catch up with him later. There are only a few places that he is going to be at. A free man needs the essentials. Weed, Ass, and Booze. I'll find him," said Ronel, attempting to comfort his baby sister.

"You didn't deserve that, Ronel. He just knows which buttons to push with everyone who still gives a damn about him."

"I understand his anger, and unfortunately, he is going to become more of a handful after we speak. There is something that I have to tell you both."

"What, what's going on?"

"I will let you know in due time, but there is a reason I am back," said Ronel as he shook his blade one final time to remove the excess bloody residue.

"And it's not a what. It's a who. Be patient, I will let you know soon enough."

Chapter 5:

The Commander

He couldn't help himself. As much as Judson loved being an asshole, the tears that began to well up was a testament to how much he loved his siblings and hated disappointing them. But there was no time to dwell on it. He shook off the thought and kept on his path to the nearest cell phone store to get a burner phone. Arizona green tea, pickled eggs and hot sausage mushed together in a baggie made a great snack. He hurried to catch the Tri-Rail north to Broward County. Home.

He made a few calls. All but one wasn't disconnected. It was the one that mattered most to him. She didn't answer the first time, so he called again.

"Hello?"

"Daddy's home, baby," said Judson. "Can you pick me up near the RaceTrac?"

"Which Daddy are you?" Shona asked sarcastically.

"This is Judson! Your man?!" yelled the hurt free man.

"Oh, you mean the nigga that left me with every snake in the city that he owes money to? The nigga that was fucking my sister, and my cousin?!"

"Yeah....so you found out about her too, huh? Look, I will make it up to you. Please just come pick me up."

"I can tell you what you can do nigga, call someone else to come get yo ass! Hit up one of your lil hoes."

"You going to keep throwing that shit in my face for real?! That's what I can't stand about yall fe-" began Judson before being interrupted by a click..

"Hello? Hello! Fuck that bitch!" conceded Judson. But he still loved her, and ultimately understood her animosity. Deep down, he knew he wasn't worthy of her. He knew it from the time they met; through his cheating spells, the court dates, and violent life he chose to live. Before he could finish reflecting on how he had wronged her, the burner phone rang.

"Look, I will come get you, but that don't mean we back together. I got a man now. Your car and your stuff is at Jacmel Auto in the East." said Shona.

"Ok, I'll be here waiting for you,"

After twenty minutes, Judson noticed the silver Camry that belonged to the woman who still had his heart. He smiled and got into the passenger seat. He went in for a kiss but was blocked by her hand.

32

"I told you, I got a man,"

"But you came to get me though, that alone says you love me."

"No, that alone says you owe me! You owe me money; you owe me for the years I had to look over my shoulder. My mama house getting shot up. You owe me your life!"

"Ok, ok, damn girl, I got you. You look good. Did I tell you that already?"

"Don't fuck with me today, Judson. I'm just doing you this favor in hopes you can run me what you owe me."

As he stared at her caramel skin. Her left side, emblazoned with tattooed red roses from her neck down to her thick thighs. He longed to rid her of the short-striped cotton dress and have his way with her one more time.

"Who is this nigga anyway, and why didn't you wait for me?"

"Those are questions that I don't feel like answering right now, Judson. Just get back on your shit, and fix the shit you broke in the city. Niggaz want your head." She stopped the car, and unlocked the doors. "We are here."

"You big mad, huh?" asked Judson, holding her there longer than she wanted to be. Shona looked ahead without acknowledging him. "Ok, I'll hit you up."

"What about my money? That's all I better get a call about. And please take a shower! You smell like jail."

He reached in to give her a kiss but met her cold cheek as

she looked forward. Judson, knowing that it was futile to try to swoon her further, got out of the car. She sped off, leaving him in a hot dusty mist. He knew it was just a matter of time until she got past it and forgave him. He gave no thought to the new guy she mentioned. Maybe a little bit. As he walked up to Jacmel Auto, he was greeted by one of the mechanics.

"Look who it is y'all, my nigga home!" said Jimmy as he pulled in Judson for a pound and a slap on the back.

"What's good fam?" asked Judson. Jimmy stepped back abruptly as his nostrils took in Judson's stench, but business was business. Judson was one of his best customers.

"Good to see you back out here in the real-world Jude." Jimmy handed Judson a cluster of keys. He pointed him in the direction of one of the locked garages. "As always, thanks for the business. It took some work, but we got you looking clean."

He led Judson over to the rail door. Judson was curious as to what he meant. He thought that they probably just washed and waxed it to keep the blue, marine candy paint from chipping at the point of impact. After the raid, he was told that his car was stripped of its rims, sound system, and leather interior. Judson unlocked the sliding door and raised it to find that his Impala was covered. Miscellaneous bags were neatly stacked in the corner of the garage. That didn't hold his attention long. He noticed the Impala was sitting on all black 26-inch rims. He looked at the owner, as if to get some sort of silent approval that this was indeed his beloved car. He removed the covering. The once candy blue paint was now a dark glossy crimson paint job. New cream leather covered the interior, with dark red piping all throughout.

"Who did this? How did you know to do this?! And who paid for this? I know you don't do work for credit!" said Judson as he tried to contain his excitement.

"Some dude with dreads dropped a bag and left the instructions for the repair and work. He came by two days ago just to make sure it was done. He dropped another bag for storage and legalities. Plates are clean and the paperwork is in the glove compartment. You have this storage space until the end of the year. It's all been paid for. " said Jimmy. "I just have one request though Judson. Don't bring no drama to my place of business. Other than that, we good."

Judson couldn't help but admire the work. He told Shona time and time again about how he wanted to overhaul his car, but this exceeded his wildest dreams. He snapped out of the euphoria to try and grab Jimmy's attention who walked away.

"Hey man, the man that paid for all this, does he ride a motorcycle?"

"Yeah. Matter fact, he just pulled up."

Judson looked outside to see his big brother kicking the kickstand to set his bike to rest.

"You didn't have to do this Ro."

"You were coming home man. I had to make sure my little brother shine out here," said Ronel.

Judson pulled his brother close for a hug. "Look bro, I'm sorry, I'm so sorry." Judson started.

"No need to do that bro, we good. I just need you to keep a level head now that you out. Most of your debt in the streets has been settled. I had no idea you had dealings with the Russians, but Sonya is working her channels to dead that shit."

Judson's gratitude quickly went south as he realized that he was giving his older brother too much slack. As much as he appreciated everything, he did not want to let go of the adolescent nature of holding something over his brother's head.

"Imma pay you back, for everything. I still don't like how you came at me earlier."

"Same ol, little bro." said Ronel. "what do you say we take her out and slide through the city? You hungry?"

Judson, whose stomach has been smacking him in the face for the past hour, obliged.

"Let's ride," said Judson as they made their way to the car. He started it up. Instantly, he melted into the seat as the growl of the engine took him back to the time he first fell in love with donks. Ronel jumped in the passenger seat and buckled his seat belt.

"Really?" asked Judson. "You still a square ass nigga, huh?"

"A square ass nigga that want to live," replied Ronel

The brothers were off into the streets. Judson cranked the system, as Trick Daddy's "Can't Fuck with the South" intro began to play through the new, sharp speakers. The Florida brothers nodded their heads. They anticipated the part of the song that everyone from South Florida rapped aloud. They began to recite the lyrics in unison before breaking out in laughter.

"Damn it feels good to be home!" yelled Judson, as they ripped through the avenues of Lauderdale Square.

"Good to have you on this side of the wall bro. Wanna go to Sunrise Bakery then stop and get some weed?" Judson immediately slammed on the breaks.

"Ok, out with it." demanded Judson

"Out with what?"

"Nigga, I'm not that 12-year-old fat boy you use to bribe with *patte* and *tablets* so I would take the fall for shit. Second, who says 'get some weed?', your square ass don't smoke Ronel!! Why are you doing all of this for me?"

"Pull up behind the bakery, we gotta talk" said Ronel in defeat. He knew he couldn't keep up the ruse any longer. His brother may have been a hot-headed, narcissistic asshole, but what he had to tell him, was going to affect him the most.

"Naw, we can talk right here! What the fuck is going on?!"

"Look, I will tell you. Can you please wait until we can sit and talk this out?"

"Let me guess, you and old man Elam got plans to put me in a program or some shit, huh? I bet he got something to do with this buttering up session. What are y'all hiding from me?"

"The commander is alive." answered Ronel softly. "There, that's what I needed to talk about. So right about now, your feelings for the old man are mutual. Elam lied to us. I don't know why, but I get the feeling he has known all this time."

Judson's eyes drifted off as the sound of his brother's words became muffled thumps to his eardrums. The word "rage" could not fully explain the fast buildup of emotion that was now bubbling into his bloodstream. His eyes cut like jagged spikes as he looked at his brother, who was now trying to get his attention, but the words were still not audible. The memories came rushing into Judson's mind. He gripped the steering wheel so tight the wood grain began to crack. He could only muster a few words through his tensed jaw.

"Where is he?!" exploded Judson. Ronel reached to try to calm his brother down as he realized that nothing he was saying was registering.

"Bro, you have to listen to me, I know that-" began Ronel, as he placed his hand on the now trembling shoulder of his younger brother. Judson smacked his hand away and grabbed Ronel by the neck, adding pressure by the millisecond. Ronel, now coming to grips that he must defend himself, drove his fingers into the pressure points of his brother's wrists. Judson quickly let go of his grip and swung. Ronel dodged, narrowly missing the punch. He grabbed Judson's wrists again, then his fingers. Bending them back in a direction that human anatomy was not built for. The excruciating pain caused Judson to yield reluctantly. Although he had the strength to pummel his older brother in a straight up fist fight, Ronel had him beat in close quarters combat experience.

"Are you going to listen to me now?"

"Let me go. Tell me where that cocksucker is so I can kill him myself! Then I'm snapping the old man's neck!"

"I need you to listen, Judson. You have to listen! I'll let you go if you hear me out and not take off. Hand me the keys."

Judson took the key out of the ignition and threw it at Ronel, hitting him in the chest before they landed in the mid console. He released the fingers back to his brother. Judson rubbed them in relief and asked again.

"Where is he?! How did you find out?! Why is this muthafucka still breathing if you, of all people, know he is still alive?!"

Chapter 6:

Alive

"*I was in Toledo when I got called for a rescue contract.*"
Began Ronel. "*Some high-powered attorney's mother went back to Haiti to live out the rest of her years and was kidnapped by a gang from Cite-de-Solei. Because she was Haitian, and not a citizen of the United States, law enforcement agencies gave him and his family the typical diplomatic answer. 'Pay the money and hope they don't kill her.'*

The gang asked for 1 million dollars, which they did not have. A week later, they shipped the attorney her ring finger with the ring still attached. The gang continued to call him, increasing the ransom by a million each time. He found me through some of his contacts and hired me. Confidence was slim that she would still be alive, but I took the job. Not only to bring the family closure, but to slaughter the assholes who took her to begin with.

With some back channel tapping and tracking of the calls, I was able to find their hideout. To my great relief she was still alive. However, she was dying from an infection of the severed finger and malnutrition. I waited until it was dark and took out the gang and their defenses. I managed to capture the ringleader. He confessed that a partner at the attorney's firm concocted the plot for the kidnapping out of jealousy. Unfortunately, the mother died enroute to the hospital. The family requested to extradite the ringleader to the United States. Not only to stand trial but testify against the mastermind. The family oddly requested that the kidnappers attend the funeral in Gonaives, Haiti. I did not plan on staying throughout the ceremony, but I did. Something did not sit well with me. One of the politicians who attended was always looking for a photo op. That face. His features. He looked so much like the Commander who killed our parents, except younger and taller. It couldn't have been him. That is, until I noticed the frail man leaning his shaky hands on a cane. He embraced the politician after his spirited speech against the gangs and kidnappings.

The older man's face was reconstructed with plastic surgery, but one telling scar remained there. Right between his eyes. It was Charles. Not a dead Charles. An alive, living, breathing, smug smiling Charles! And yes, my first instinct was to kill him on site. However, the funeral was no such setting. So, I waited. After the funeral, I followed them until I noticed they were heavily guarded by Haitian officials. I stayed for a few days monitoring *his every move. Eventually, he boarded a private jet destined for Miami where his son is preparing his campaign to become President of Haiti. What made me hold off was something extremely odd that stood out to me the most. The ring that he wore on his finger. It had a symbol that was very familiar. The same symbol that the old man has tattooed on his back. We need to talk to Elam."*

Judson was caught off-guard. Wondering how it was possible the man that was responsible for so much of their pain was alive right under his nose the whole time.

"Does Sonya know?"

"No. She is not equipped to handle news like this. You know how much she loves Elam."

"So, hand me my keys. Let's run up to that church and find out why Elam lied to us this whole time! I have been looking for a reason to finally kick his ass!" snared Judson.

"How do you plan on just running up on the man who taught us everything we know about combat? About our abilities and how to control them? This must be handled with a little finesse," said Ronel. "I am just as mad and disappointed if he knew all this time. He must answer to all three of us."

"Then after he gives you his patented deep and wonderful answer, then can I knock his ass out?" asked Judson, balling his fists.

"Then, yes. Knock yourself out, literally. Because that's what's going to happen."

"You may have no confidence in me, but I have improved. I can take him on."

"I've watched you improve; you were able to grab me by the neck before I knew it. You're getting faster, and stronger. Now if you were to just lay off the weed, you can-"

"God damn it Ronel! Shit, you can't go two sentences without criticizing me? After what you just told me, I'm going to need one hell of a fat sack to mellow me out." said Judson as he finally began to release some tension.

"This weekend is his 15-year anniversary into priesthood. We should go to mass; it's been a while. We can confront him there after the service when everyone is gone,"

"Ok, let's do this your way. But for now, I'm hungry, sober, and I need to be throwing some bands on some booty meat. You down?" asked Judson.

"Well, you're not going to use any more of my cash for that. I was able to salvage the money you had during the raid. It's in the trunk. Let's go eat, then you can take me back to my bike. We will meet at the church on Sunday."

"Aight, just to let you know, if he says something I don't like, I'm knocking him out in front of his church folk,"

"Make sure you have a suit. For once in your life, dress the part. You will be amazed at the money you could make with me if you were a little more disciplined and civilized." Ronel said.

"This coming from a nigga with dreads, wearing a leather biker vest with a Haitian flag on the back, that just diced up some niggaz a couple hours ago? Civilized?" asked Judson.

"Shut up, and let's go get some of these patties." shot back Ronel. "And don't worry, we are going to get that muthafucka. For mom and dad...."

"For mom and dad." Judson echoed, as they made a pact with a pound of their fists.

"One more thing Judson, there is something else I should bring to your attention." said Ronel, as he looked toward his feet.

"Man, you sure are doing a bad job at unwrapping your story. What other bad news you got for me?"

"It's Sonya...."

"What about my annoying ass sister?" laughed Judson.

"I wish it was that trivial bro. She has been keeping something from us that I'm surprised you haven't picked up on."

"She is just her regular bitchy little self, what has she done? Did you just find out that she lost her virginity, and she didn't tell you?" laughed Judson while slapping the back of his older brother's head.

"She popped her cherry alright, except the blood that's been spilled is not hers," said Ronel regretfully. "She has killed more than once, and I think she has developed a taste."

"So what?" asked Judson. "I don't remember what happened when Elam put her in that trance. Hell, I'm still struggling with my own memory. Elam said that he locked away her abilities and the fact that it seems to be unraveling doesn't surprise me. He isn't as wise as you think. He makes mistakes just like everyone else."

"I am aware that Elam needs to come clean about a lot of things." said Ronel looking into his reflection on the chrome piping that protruded from the back of the donk. He looked up at the stars, taking in the downtown Fort Lauderdale skyline. The sea breeze tickled the roots of his dreads. "Her eyes have changed, and the wind blows differently around her now. We must protect her."

Chapter 7:

Special Girl

The clock seems to have stopped. It hadn't really. It was just the way Sonya was looking at it after hours of briefings. She was the second female in the room other than the Lead Agent conducting the overview. Special Operations Officer Lauren Tanner distributed the tasks to the freshman class of 7 men, and one woman. Sonya gave no thought to her fellow agents. What stole her attention was the next tick of the dollar store-bought clock that hung on the wall. Each tick bringing her closer to freedom from the CIA's newest remote branch overseeing Brickell Avenue. The slow cadence of every movement around her, from physical to sonic, fueled the insatiable desire to finally do some real work in the field. Although scanning and organizing paperwork was on her schedule for the next couple of months, the young Air force Sergeant had another plan.

"Jean-Baptiste! Your report from yesterday was due at 0800 hours, where is it?" yelled Agent Tanner.

"It's on your desk Ma'am, right below the two red folders. I made sure to color code the errors and questionable filings. I also created an additional report on how the current system could be streamlined to increase turnover times of reports and actually get us out into the field doing the real work," explained Sonya.

"Your real work is whatever I say it is Jean-Baptiste. Are you trying to show me up?"

"No ma'am, not at all, I was just trying to be proactive," Sonya responded.

"Well take your proactive ass into one of these offices and continue to file the documents as stated by command. Do I make myself clear?!" Tanner dropped a stack of fresh binders of reports that shifted the table in front of Sonya slightly.

"Yes Ma'am, I understand," Sonya assessed the page count. It was clear that it would take her another two hours to sift through, sort, align, and repeat all the reports until they met Tanner's desk. Sonya realized she had to act as if the procedure would be difficult, so she asked for permission to work on the reports at home. The last thing she needed was to make an enemy out of a superior.

Later that day....

"Girl, why are you carrying all that paperwork? It's Friday.

47

Doesn't that new job of yours care about your personal time?" asked Manouchka, as she watched her best friend struggle with her laptop bag and multiple file folders, all while trying to balance on her agency approved heels.

"No they don't, and obviously neither do you Manny. I can use your help here instead of you leaning up on your car like you trying to pull your next husband," snapped Sonya.

"I'm sorry Sonya, I got you. You know I gotta keep em looking. I just made one of your co-workers do a double take when I leaned over to grab my bag out of the seat. He was looking like a total snack," said Manny as she cracked a smile.

"I swear your whore-moans is on 10,000 today,"

"Speaking of men that I would love to be a whore for; you said Ronel was back in town? When will he be coming by your house?"

"He should be coming by real late tonight but by that time, you and Jesse should be stuffed with popcorn and wine after finding nothing else on Netflix. Besides, he don't want you. He's still stuck on Rosa."

"Oh the mystery Bitch that's keeping me from my man? Whatever! It's funny that you mentioned Jesse though. I mean for a big boy, he is kind of cute don't you think? He is funny too."

"What's going on with you and your standards? First, random guys at my job, to my brother, now Jesse? Besides, I thought you didn't like big guys and don't y'all hate each other?"

"I don't care for Jesse like that. He talks a lot of shit but he cool peoples. He seems to fancy you though, Ms. Too-focused-on-my-career-cuz-my-punani-don't-work."

"Jesse? Naw that's the homie. He never made it known that he was into me. I mean, he's been there for our anti-Valentine's Day parties, where we eat ice cream until our stomachs hurt. Then our weekly blerd-out time where we watch anime and Game of Thrones." explained Sonya.

"Both examples are of you and him, together, by yourselves. Are you fucking him and don't want to let me know? He's a great guy, girl. I won't hate on you getting some maintenance even if it's from mid-career Rick Ross," laughed Manny.

"No, none of that is happening. Jesse doesn't want me like that, and knows where I stand with relationships right about now."

"No relationship doesn't have to mean a no-dick policy. Anyways girl, are you coming out to Gouyadville next week? It's been awhile since we danced all night." Gouyadville was the hottest Haitian party of the year and Manny was not going to miss it.

"I'll let you know Manny. You know I can't do my hair the way I used to, or my nails. But you know me, if the DJ is on point, you know I'm gonna turn up," said Sonya.

They both laughed, and entered Manny's vehicle.

As they drove off, eyes were on them from the top floor of the field office. Agent Tanner rocked her small sturdy frame. Years of special forces and agency missions engraved the mild wrinkles surrounding her death scowl.

"Two weeks in and we already have four dead Russian gangsters, the local police department poking around, and a bullet riddled government vehicle! You want to explain to me how she made it through our extensive vetting process? She has the gall to tell me how to run my field office!" asked Agent Tanner, as she paced back and forth in front of the conference room desk.

"I can understand the frustration, Agent Tanner. By no means does it make me or anyone who respects your service to this organization; feel great knowing you are playing this babysitter role. But, rest assured, this is all going according to plan." said the raspy Director Preston Lee, whose voice brimmed from the conference call device.

"Sir, she is beginning to ask questions. The kind of questions that she has the means to get answered with the level of clearance you asked me to give her. Not to mention, she has a former intelligence analyst that knows how to hack his way through the Kremlin."

"All for a greater goal, Agent Tanner. Forgive the hesitance of information, but there is a reason for everything. I feel that it is time that we fill you in on a few details regarding our interests in Sonya. I sent you a document. Please display it on the conference screen." advised Director Lee.

Tanner turned on her laptop and cast the images to the large screen that nearly was as tall as she was. There, Sonya's agent ID picture was on display, with connecting lines going to the pictures of three other men.

"I am aware of these men, except for one. Who is the old man?" she asked.

"Elam is a puzzle piece we are still trying to unwrap, but it is the brothers that I need you to get up to speed with." replied Director Lee. "Let's start with the eldest brother Ronel Jean-Baptiste. Immigrated from Haiti with his siblings and the old man during a daring escape by boat from the Duvalier Regime. Both parents are dead. 12 people lost their lives to sea, 15 others were hospitalized for dehydration, and malnutrition. But, other than a few cuts and bruises, the children and Elam were perfectly fine. Elam adopted them while continuing his seminary schooling, and is now a priest at St. Bedes, in Fort Lauderdale, FL. After being homeschooled, Ronel went on to join the U.S Army, and quickly moved up in rank. Joins special forces and has several confirmed kills. A multitude of solo missions under his belt. He was like nothing they had seen before. His speed, agility, and sense for war is as if it was taught to him from birth. He has mastered an assortment of sword fighting styles, from traditional fencing to variations of Kenjutsu. His weapon of choice is a custom-made machete blade, made from the finest of Japanese steel. He had the type of career that one doesn't just cut short, but he did. He asked for his discharge and disappeared into the private sector. There were rumors of an account made by a fellow militia member. They described an orange-colored aura emitting from him after he killed off half a camp of insurgents on his own. We just chalked it up to PTSD. We can't say for sure how many contracts he has completed, but his renegade biker lifestyle doesn't match up to the life he could be living with the money in his accounts. He stays in contact with his family while he drifts from town to town, state to state. He is well-trained and deadly. Highly intelligent and fluent in 6 languages, other than his native Kreyol. Oh, and he is also a drunk. Everyone has a thorn in their side no matter how remarkable they are.

Speaking of the opposite of remarkable, Judson "Ti Swayze" Jean-Baptiste. He is, as you can gather, a stark contrast to his older brother Ronel. Also home schooled by Elam, but decided that further education wasn't in the cards. He has a criminal rap sheet that would make cartels compete for his services. Grand Theft, robbery, money laundering, assault after assault after assault cases pile up like pancakes. Not to mention, the countless arrests. No gang affiliations though. Almost no accomplices, and he has not gone without making a few enemies in the process while taunting them with his lavish hood lifestyle. Although crime seems to be what he practices best, it's not his strong suit. Underground fighting seems to be his biggest cash cow. A big man that moves like a featherweight. His fight videos have been banned from YouTube, due to the level of brutality and gruesome injuries he has inflicted on his opponents. He continued to fight in the underground circuit even while in jail, cutting the Warden and officers in on the action. He is radical, narcissistic, and loud.

Not even Dana White would sign this guy out of fear for his own fighters. Despite all the negative attributes, he is highly trained in very brutal fighting disciplines, and is also a master marksman. No doubt taught, not picked up like a hobby. He goes out of his way to portray his masculinity with his constant womanizing.

Then there is Sonya Jean-Baptiste, the baby of the bunch. Top of her class, and a natural at Computer Intelligence and military science. Holding two bachelor degrees simultaneously, while serving as an airman officer. No field operations under her belt. You would think, just another extraordinary recruit that could work behind a desk and make millions in contracts, but this one is special. During the Duvalier Regime, Haiti was the number one supplier of corpses for studies completed by several U.S. institutions from education, to pharmaceuticals, and yes, even us. Now that it has been declassified, I can tell you that in one of our projects, we were looking for a particular gene. A gene that could only be found from the descendants of one of Haiti's founding fathers, Jean-Jacques Dessalines. After a few tests, and countless specimens, we were only able to salvage a few test tubes of this concentrated gene. The project was eventually scrapped. Due to controversy stemming from one of the suppliers well publicized exile to the US from Haiti, after the coup against Baby Doc's Regime. That is until, a routine blood sample was taken from Sonya. She was overflowing with the gene, so much so, it was as if she was Jean-Jacques' actual daughter. This, of course, was brought to my attention, which is why we have opened this staged office solely in hopes of getting samples from her older brothers."

"So why not pull up the army records and arrest records, to get samples that I'm sure were taken from them?" asked Tanner

"A good question Agent Tanner. None of their records are available. They have been either destroyed, or lost on purpose. As if someone knew how precious their DNA was," replied the Director.

"How would they have known, and why is their DNA so precious?" asked Tanner.

"Enter, now, Father Elam Joseph. Not much is known about this man. However, he seems to have a level of authority and access to authority that we still are trying to figure out. No fingerprints, or DNA records. His identity seems to have been fabricated and backed by institution and government entity heads that are even above my pay grade. He is a made man in the sense. The only records we were able to find were those related to the Jean-Baptiste children. He was their guardian, and to this day, a parent figure. He has attended every military graduation, and bail hearing. My guess, he is the reason why we have to go through all of this trouble just to get a few more samples without amassing suspicion. The Russian gangsters were hired by us. We knew Judson owed a huge debt, and they were more than willing to carry out the hit. But we knew, there was a huge possibility that we were sending them in to be slaughtered. So now, we are working on other avenues."

"I'm still not grasping why their DNA is worth all of this!" Tanner stated forcefully.

"I can't technically give you more information Agent Tanner. I can, for old time's sake, spark a level of curiosity though. Elam, and the children made it to our shores April, 26th, 1971, a few days after the death of Francois "Papa Doc" Duvalier. Ronel was 7, Judson was 6, and Sonya was 4 years old." said the Director

"That doesn't make any sense. Sonya is 26, our records show that the brothers are in their early 30s. How is it possible that they were alive, or born before 1971? They would be well into their 40s or older,"

"The records were expertly altered, except for one record that no one, not even someone as connected as Elam, thought would exist. The smugglers kept a ledger of who they carried on their boat just in case they needed to track down anyone to further extort them for money. There was a name that stood out and was translated to that of 'Dr. Reginald Jean-Baptiste and his wife, Carline', with three columns below indicating the ages of the children with them," explained the Director.

"But their parents were killed. Their bodies were burned in their home. How is it that he took the children and left them to die?"

"We have no reason to suspect any foul play on his part, no motive to kill the family that took him in,"

Tanner was speechless. Still trying to wrap her mind around

what this all meant. If all of this was true. There was only one other eventual question that had to be asked.

"How are they still….young in appearance?" asked Tanner.

"Our question exactly." said the Director.

Chapter 8:

Not So All Together

What time did you say he was going to be here again?" asked Manny as she continued to cut up onions and peppers. Behind her was an even busier, and highly annoyed Sonya who had enough of her best friend asking about Ronel.

"Manny, if you ask me one more time while I'm cutting this chicken up, I will serve it to you raw!" shot Sonya, as she expertly cut two whole hens into numerous pieces.

"Fine, I won't ask anymore. I just wanna know if he really stuck on Rosa." she said, fake-twerking against Sonya's back. "You know we are going to make you some beautiful nieces and nephews." Sonya mock-gagged at the thought.

"Just stop. He will do what he has always done. Treat you like a little girl, and either mispronounce your name or forget it completely." replied Sonya. Manny could not help but notice the well-proportioned cuts of meat that Sonya tossed into the murky concoction of limes, vinegar, and water.

"Why isn't my knife cutting like that?" asked Manny. "You must have sharpened yours and gave me these dull ass ones just to make me look like I don't know my way around a kitchen."

"I don't have to do anything to make that obvious," said Sonya tossing up a chicken breast to meet her eye-level. With quick swipes of her knife, six perfect strips fell onto a nearby plate. "Grow up a little, and I will be happy to show you," Sonya smiled.

"So, you picked up some ninja Gordon Ramsey shit, good for you sis. Unlike you, I use my God given curves he cut out by hand to get my meals paid for," said Manny, grabbing a hold of her cell phone and pulling up her contact list.

"Look, Cute Meal #1, he cute but not cute enough to go out with, but he got fire taste in food. He gets me lunch whenever I ask. Then there is Chubby Meal Boy #3, now he knows how to surprise me every other week! I almost gave it up off some steamed seafood from this restaurant he had to drive two hours to go get." flaunted Manny.

"And you see nothing wrong with you playing with people's feelings like that?' inquired Sonya.

"I"m not the only one playing with dude's hearts out here. You do the same to Jesse knowing damn well that boy in love with you," shot Manny. Sonya let out a muffled laugh while draining the sink. Turning on the faucet to further wash away the residue before seasoning the meat the classic haitian way.

"Jesse ain't thinking about me like that." Sonya said, wondering if it was a possibility. The thought annoyed her, as well as the fact that she allowed her friend to plant the seed.

"Damn right! I ain't thinking about your short ass. It's a height requirement to talk to ya boy!" said Jesse, poking his head into the kitchen. "Nothing like having women in the kitchen cooking me my dinner. Chop chop ladies!" he said, smacking Sonya's butt-cheek. Sonya, now enraged, took one of her knives and hurled it towards Jesse's direction. He barely made it out of the kitchen. The tip of the blade penetrated the lid of his Miami Marlins fitted-hat, lifting it off of his head. It spiraled into the air, until it lodged into the sheet rock wall. Jesse was frozen in his steps. His fingers shook as he began to mumble under his breath uncontrollably. A slight burning sensation coming from the top of his head. Followed by a warm stream of blood that made it down to his neck from the quarter inch cut. He managed to bring his fingers up from the rigor mortis that had set in to assess the fresh wound.

"Nigga if you EVER touch my ass again, I will cut off your hands, then your balls. Put them in those hands and put my work of art on your mantel to remind you I'm not the one!" yelled Sonya. Manny, in shock at first, began to chuckle. Then outright laughed at Jesse as he retrieved his hat from the makeshift hanger while clutching his head. Jesse, not wanting to appear frazzled, gathered the muster to perk up.

"I was just playing damn! That's OK though. Next time, I will hack your laptop and have it play random porn noises in your next briefing. And I don't know what you laughing at 'thot of the year'! She needs my brains, unlike the dudes you couldn't keep with yours. MAKAK(monkey)!" smirked Jesse as he walked toward the bathroom.

"GRIMACE(clown)!" Manny shot back, throwing a half-eaten apple at him. She waited for Jesse to close the door of the hallway bathroom before speaking again.

"Girl, I didn't know you could throw knives like that. When was you gonna tell a bitch? Better yet, teach me!" said Manny, doing her best ninja impression.

"Lucky throw. I didn't know that was going to happen. I was just trying to scare him a little. Jesse plays too much." said Sonya as she continued cooking frantically after noticing the time. She had one shot to carry out a secret mission of her own. Now that Jesse arrived, it was time to make her exit.

"Don't act like your ass ain't turned on by that. And why are you moving so fast, where do you have to go?" asked Manny

"Not everybody has your libido, Manny. Besides, I forgot to get some bay leaves. I'll be right back, just going to run to the store," Sonya said as she began to undo the ties on her apron. There was a knock at the door that stopped her. The hidden ability to sense the slightest change in smell, motion, and presence engulfed her as she pondered to herself.

"Why is he here early?" asked Sonya softly.

"Who?" asked Manny.

"Ronel." She answered. Manny, in excitement, ripped off her own apron. She hurried to the door, cooing as she swayed her hips. She looked at herself in the mirror on the wall just to make sure that nothing was out of place. She opened the door, and there stood Ronel with his head down.

"Hi Ronel, you ok?" she asked, adjusting her cleavage to sit higher than their prior position.

"I'm more than ok Debbie, cuz I got drinks!!" mumbled a clearly intoxicated Ronel, holding up an assortment of bottles. He stumbled past Manny, who stood confused and embarrassed.

"It's Manny. You don't remember my name?"

"Oh yeah Manny. Take these and put them on ice please. Where is my KID SISTER?!" yelled Ronel.

"Oh dear God, how drunk are you?!" said Sonya, staring him up and down.

"Always observing and learning, Sonya. But I'm not drunk. I'm tipsy, it's a difference. Now, speaking of observing. We need to have a little chat because I have been observing some of these little 'projects' you and Jesse have been 'working on'." blurted Ronel as he motioned to Manny to pour some drinks. Sonya, caught off guard by his comments, quickly grabbed her brother by the arm and forcefully led him toward the bedroom.

"Oh, I wasn't supposed to say that. Sorry Debbie, that was not meant for your ears." chuckled Ronel as they entered. Sonya slammed the door behind them, then shoved her brother onto the side of the bed.

"What the fuck do you think you're doing?" blasted Sonya.

"Exactly what you are doing Sonya! Being reckless!" said a now less intoxicated Ronel. "Did you think that I wouldn't have found out what you and black Bill Gates in there are doing? If I was able to find out, how long do you think it will be before your agency catches onto their list of bad guys dropping like flies?" asked Ronel sternly.

"What I do is none of your business Ronel! I am grown. What I choose to do about the scum of the earth is my decision to make." snapped Sonya

"Doesn't matter. You are way over your head. These are cartels that you are messing with. What makes you think that they won't find out who you are, where you live, and who you care about? I'm sure Manny doesn't know what you are doing out there now does she?" asked Ronel.

"No, she doesn't, but she almost did before I dragged you in here." said Sonya

"I may be tipsy, but I haven't forgotten the art of deception. I was not going to compromise you in front of someone who doesn't know anything about this #blackgirlninja shit you got going on." said Ronel rising to his feet.

"They were all clean kills Ronel. I was careful. No evidence, and nothing traceable. I was sure and efficient." explained Sonya as her elder sibling walked past her towards the window.

"Just like you're going to be tonight? Yeah, I know about

your next target. Tell me, did you and Jesse factor in the spices that you are cooking with? "Maggie" is a very strong and specific spice, traceable," said Ronel, as he took another mouthful of the brown liquor. "They get a big enough dog, they will follow the scent here. This isn't your world, Sonya. I get that you are bored but this is a level of extreme that you're not built for. I'm not always going to be there to snatch you out of the teeth of the underworld." he warned.

"Ronel, I don't need your protection anymore. In case you've forgotten I trained alongside you. I don't get you and Elam still directing and watching my every move. I have proven time and time again I can take care of myself and be more than just a pencil pusher! Now if you would excuse me. Try not to throw up in my room. I have to go" said Sonya, as she put on and zipped up her black sweater. The night was unusually cool.

"Juan Gabriel Perez," said Ronel. Sonya stopped, and slowly turned around.

"Your target's name. Right? Wanted for the murders and sexual assault of two of his step-daughters. He just so happens to be associated with the Juarez Cartel, that has kept him well hidden. Up until now that is. Or should I say up until 20 minutes ago?" asked Ronel.

"What do you mean 20 minutes ago? Did you alert him?!" demanded Sonya.

"Hell no. The prick deserved to die." Ronel said, as he reached into his jacket. He pulled out a plastic sandwich bag that contained a freshly cut off ring finger. Sonya rolled her eyes in disgust, and flopped down on the floor. Aggravate. Ronel knelt down next to her. "Look, I know you are trying to make the world right for what happened. It's not your responsibility."

"Then you tell me whose is it?! These assholes get to run around and there is no justice for their victims. I'm doing something, even if it's my own justice." she said, fighting back tears. Ronel's eyes peered to the ground as he noticed dust mites hovering over the tile floor. They stood still in the light rays coming from the street lamp outside. Suddenly, the particles fell to the ground as if they were weighed down by dumbbells. Clusters of goosebumps formed on his forearms. Elam's efforts to thwart her unpredictable powers were not as effective as he made them. Ronel composed himself before she noticed. Launching into a hastily planned outrage.

"You can't swing the gavel if you're dead Sonya! I understand your pain, trust me. I deal with it by..." he began.

"By doing the exact same thing! I know what I am doing Ronel, and it's about time you and Elam get that!" she snapped. The bed shifted next to Ronel, pushing him forward with the strength of 100 men. Yet, Sonya was oblivious, staring at the ground still. As he struggled to hold back the queen-sized furniture, he had to think quickly. Before his brain could generate its next thought, the room was engulfed in a windstorm, lifting anything loose from its place and sending them into orbit. Grinding at the ceiling's surface.

"Okay Sonya, you're right!" screamed Ronel, as he used his hands to heat the metal legs of the bed to melt into the ground to stabilize it. Ronel couldn't refute the truth. As much as he knew Sonya to be tough and resourceful, he couldn't bear it if anything happened to her. Elam's barriers were barely holding down her power, and despite how he felt about their mentor, he knew Elam needed to know. He wrapped his arms around her, attempting to calm the entranced Sonya. Instantly the objects in the air fell violently to the floor, startling Sonya back to reality.

"Hey are you all ok?" asked Manny on the other side of the door. "I get yall arguing but c'mon nah. Fighting isn't the answer." Ronel sat up and opened the door.

"We are good." Ronel called, as he pulled a confused Sonya closer. Jesse appeared and noticed the debris on the ground behind them. Her friends stood silent as they were familiar with Sonya's emotional episodes.

"What happened? Why is my room a mess again?!" blurted Sonya, assessing the damage.

"So, this has happened before?" Ronel asked, as he loosened his hold.

"Yes, and I can't figure out what it is. I don't want to go to Elam about it. I was waiting to tell you because you would understand," Sonya started. "Tell me what is wrong with me...." Ronel held her close as he felt her break in his arms, and to avoid another indoor nor-easter. The fragility of Sonya was at stake, and he could not fight the urge to keep the most recent news from her. He motioned for her friends to walk away, and closed the door behind him.

"Sonya, I need you to focus on me and nothing else." Said Ronel holding the sides of Sonya's face. "No matter what I am about to tell you, I need you to focus on my voice. Do you understand me?"

"What are you talking about Ronel?" she questioned

"You wanted trust? I am trusting you with what I am about to tell you. Even Elam isn't in on this. At least, I'm not sure to what extent." Ronel started. Sonya looked into his eyes, and it became clear that this was not the liquor talking. She nodded for him to proceed. Ronel's mouth began to stream words into existence that changed Sonya's face from understanding to shock. The knowledge that the commander was alive prompted an immediate transition from screams and tears to anger. Ronel did not break eye contact as his flames surrounded them, to incinerate the flying objects from hitting him. The door flew open as Sonya's concerned friends were met with the force of Category 3 hurricane winds. Ronel yelled to the top of his lungs to regain her attention, pleading with her to stay in the present. Then, calm filled the small apartment. The friends collected themselves and stood in the doorway, speechless over what just happened. Ronel, now holding his sister in a full embrace, rocked back and forth with her as she wept in his arms. After a few moments, Sonya collected herself and tapped Ronel to break from him.

"He lied to us, Ronel, I don't think I want to hear his

explanation," she said.

"Well, we have to get answers. Before me and Judson take out the Commander, we have to know why?" replied Ronel.

"Again with this shit! Already excluding me?" yelled Sonya. Ronel didn't have a comeback prepped. There was no need for one as it sunk in that she had a point. The delicacy of the situation was now even more complex with Sonya up to speed. Yet, Ronel knew that he had to stand in authority to guide the next steps.

"We need to focus on Elam right now and this is how it is going to go tomorrow." stated Ronel. Sonya listened as Ronel outlined how they are going to confront the man that was their father figure, mentor, and friend. The more they spoke about him the more anguish and confusion set in.

"I need a drink." said Sonya, rubbing her temples.

"Now you speaking my language," replied Ronel. He quickly stood, and reached his hands down to help Sonya up. Jesse stood next to Manny who at this point needed another wig. He stepped forward to break the ice.

"Hey Ronel, are you good, bro? Hey if you don't mind, I need to talk to Sonya about something she forgot to get at the store and .." Sonya shot him a stare, as to say that Ronel knew of the ruse. He gazed toward Ronel, who gave him confirmation as he approached. Ronel proceeded to adjust the cap on Jesse's head.

"Hey, I get that you run behind my sister, and that you are a huge asset to her. But make no mistake. If anything ever happens to her on another one of your little missions, I will make that little cut on your head large enough for forensics to know what you were thinking at the time of death. Now, let's drink." smiled Ronel as he patted Jesse on the shoulder, heading to the kitchen. Sonya looked at Jesse in defeat. Like a little girl having to leave a play date early, she followed her brother.

"What is wrong with your family? Are all of you like this? Damn, I hate to know what the priest is like," said Jesse as he followed behind.

Chapter 9:

Sunday Morning

The A.C. was malfunctioning again. There were some who modestly endured the heat to be nice. The programs that were handed out earlier in the mass, turned into makeshift fans for the more than five thousand plus parishioners in the audience. The South Florida heat penetrated the tiles of the ceiling and engulfed the festive atmosphere already occupied with the voices of young and old migrants. There was clapping, swaying, and laughter as they fellowshipped in song. It gripped everyone who knew the words, including Sonya and Ronel, who were dressed in their Sunday best. Father Elam led his congregation in as many old hymns that came to mind. Reminding him of the joy of praise and worship. He lost himself in it purposely. There was nothing like a Sunday at St. Bedes, and no priest like the eccentric Father Elam Joseph. The music concluded to a standing ovation, followed by everyone taking their seats. He stood on the pulpit and looked over the crowd. He noticed Sonya and Ronel sitting on the side pews. He smiled at the surprise of Ronel being there, but was not surprised at the absence of Judson. He opened his mouth to speak, but was immediately interrupted by the sound of an approaching noise. The whole congregation looked around to be sure of what they were hearing. The stained-glass images of Mary, Joseph, and baby Jesus began to rattle, then the glass doors of the sanctuary. The sound of a heavy muscled engine gradually became louder. The younger members of the congregation were familiar with the rumbling baseline to the latest Rick Ross joint. Sonya looked at Ronel, and then to Elam. He looked back at her to confirm their unanimous suspicions. Sure enough, a crimson red donk pulled up in front of the church doors in full view of the patrons. The car door swung open with a large billow of smoke escaping into the humid air, and out stepped a very eclectically dressed Judson. He reached back into the vehicle to turn off the engine taking one last drag of the roach then threw it aside. He began to make his way towards the front doors. The smell of potent marijuana seeped into the church, causing an influx of chatter rooted in disgust and anger. He walked in and gave a nod to the ushers. They attempted to stop him but the bloodshot stare from Judson made them think twice.

"It's ok, it's ok. My other son is here. Like the prodigal son, he has come home!" said Elam as he continued to hold his patented smile. Judson's eyes met Elam's, and he returned a mean mug to him and everyone that gave him a look he didn't like. Many attempted to fan away the fumes as he walked by.

"I can't believe he is not taking this seriously!" whispered an annoyed Sonya.

"What did you expect? Did you really think he would change for this? He is loving this attention." replied Ronel.

"Is that a cummerbund?!" whispered Sonya loudly.

"Oh my God, it is! Did he just raid Little Richard's closet?" joked Ronel.

"Ha ha ha...." said an approaching Judson as he motioned for some patrons to make way between him and his siblings. An older woman did not want to accommodate his passing, which led to a prolonged staring contest.

"So you not gonna move Man Junie?! Fine!" Judson said with frustration. He leaped over her frail legs, knocking away her larger-than-life church hat that caused the congregation to stir louder in their discontent. He then flopped down next to Sonya who did not want to look in his direction. Judson smiled and looked out into the congregation who all had their eyes fixed on him.

"What?!" said Judson in a loud voice as gasps filled the sanctuary.

"Go on back to Jesus yall, I ain't him!" he said jokingly before being pinched by Sonya.

"You know you could tone it down a little." said Ronel

"I don't owe these people shit. You know why we are here.

Now let's get this quiet charade on the road." whispered an obnoxious Judson.

"Now that all my KIDS are here. Forgive me if I indulge myself and your ears as I ask my beautiful daughter Sonya, to grace us with a selection." said Elam, trying to recover the crowd he lost. Sonya, caught off guard, immediately looked in his direction and began to signal in denial.

"Come on baby girl, just one song." said Elam, as he began to clap. The rest of the congregation began to applaud and cheered with encouragement.

"He isn't going to let up. You better get up there." laughed Ronel.

"I hate when he puts me on the spot like this. He knows I don't like it." said Sonya as she reluctantly got up and approached the pulpit. She walked up to Elam and embraced him with a kiss on the cheek.

"You know this is not cool right?" whispered Sonya in his ear.

"What type of proud father would I be if I didn't make you uncomfortable in front of a large group of people?" laughed Elam. Sonya couldn't help but crack a smile at his answer. He then limped his way back to his seat behind the altar. Although she held back the anger in her heart, the frailty of Elam put her feelings in check.

"Forgive me everyone. Father Elam has a habit of making me sing in the most random situations. But I couldn't be prouder

to sing for him and all of you on his anniversary. I love you Pop."
said Sonya as she smiled at him. Sonya took a deep breath,
exhaled, then began singing her mother's favorite gospel song,
"How Great Thou Art".

Chapter 10:

The Cut

"*She is beginning to resemble her mother more and more every day, but she has her father's eyes for sure. They all do.*" *Elam thought to himself. "That fierce, untamed look of determination. I have done all I can to subdue the effects of that day, and it has cost me more than I ever imagined.*"

To understand what happened that bloody morning, requires a venture back to a couple of decades prior. A young aspiring botanist by the name of Reginald Jean-Baptiste, traveled with a seasoned doctor who was exiled to the outskirts of Haiti. They treated the poor towns and villages that did not have access to proper care, using breakthrough medicine supplied by the US to control the spread of disease. The doctor took Reginald under his wing, and the two became good friends. Reginald returned back to school to continue his studies. The traveling doctor would go on to gain fame and support for his bid for the presidency after the regime that exiled him collapsed. The doctor, now President Francois "Papa Doc" Duvalier, went on to rule one of the deadliest dictatorships the Western Hemisphere has ever seen. Although he held a reputation for killing anyone who dared to question his actions, Reginald, now part of his Health Ministry, held favor with Papa Doc. The questions, criticism, and attempted reasoning Reginald levied against his former mentor baffled even his most trusted generals. Instead of a violent end, Duvalier answered with wit, prestige, and stoic humor. He looked at Reginald as a son he was still teaching, which bred jealousy and contempt among his cabinet. One officer in particular, Commander Charles, wanted to have the honor of killing Reginald himself. Unfortunately, he knew the level of retaliation that would come his way if it was not sanctioned by Duvalier himself. However, the relationship of mentor/student was not the only reason Duvalier avoided making an example of Reginald. Duvalier was dying, and although he had the best medical doctors and medicine at his disposal, years of treatment did not slow his impending demise. The shard of legend that gave Jean-Jacques Dessalines power and presumed immortality was in his possession. Duvalier was desperate. He knew that a gifted Reginald could somehow revive the piece of shard that was nearly destroyed in an explosion during the coup against then King Henri Christophe I.

It is for this reason, The Assembly, hired an assassin to

infiltrate the Jean-Baptiste home. They chose me. I had the solo task of killing Reginald if he was to revive the power, they wanted to stay dormant. Reginald was a devout Catholic, opened his home to me as I portrayed a young aspiring seminarian. Reginald worked diligently, knowing that his life was contingent on completing the revitalizing process, and not knowing it was also in danger if he was to succeed. Nothing was simple and cold cut. The closer I became with his family, the more I questioned if killing him was the right choice, despite what was required of me. They were innocent of all the madness around them, especially her. There were no eyes that could avoid the beauty of Reginald's wife, Carline. Gifted in voice, with a level of poise and elegance that made every man envious of Reginald. Then there were the three children; Ronel, Judson, and Sonya who was just a toddler at the time. I was the adopted older brother whom they had no idea was there to take everything they knew to be comfort from them. I made a decision. A decision that came too late. I broke my oath to the Assembly, and revealed to Reginald who I really was. I warned him to discontinue his research and escape the island with his family. He was upset, rightfully so. He revealed to me that he was successful in reviving the shard and created a serum that he handed over to me. In exchange, he wanted safe passage for him and his family off of the island. In keeping with our daily routines, I set out for the cathedral in the morning for prayer. He would head towards work by car and leave his family at home. The plan was, in a few days, to have his family meet me *at a rendezvous point a few miles into the wooded forest behind their home. There, I would hide them in the back of the church's van under discarded palm leaves, and get them safely on a private plane bound for France. He would eventually join us on the tarmac as it was routine for him to pick up newly shipped materials from the airport. None of us could have predicted what took place the very next day.*

April 27th, 1971, Duvalier was dead, and Commander Charles wasted no time. I could not reach Reginald by radio, so I quickly got onto a motorcycle to get to his family. I reached the outside of their home to find that it was surrounded by Tonton Macoute. My approach for a rescue had to be subtle but effective. The last thing they expected was a seminarian who fought back, but combat had to be the last resort. I scoped the area, and found our escape route to the van. I needed a diversion of some kind, and a high-powered weapon within arm's reach just in case things did not go as planned. I walked towards the first set of guards who immediately recognized me, and after a few words, he motioned for me to follow him. I could hear the cries of Carline pleading with her captors for mercy, then there was a shot and her cries stopped. I began to run up to the hill but was restrained by the guards behind me. In my heart I prayed that she was not dead, but my mind knew the truth. In an effort to calm the soldier's nerves, I muffled my raw emotion. They agreed to continue to take me further if I did not attempt anything or I would be shot. I was led through a circle of navy-blue uniformed soldiers, many of them smoking, others laughing as their sweat drenched faces looked on in amazement. Reginald was in and out of consciousness, covered in his own blood as they took turns striking him in the face and abdomen as two other soldiers held him up. Carline's lifeless body laid at the front of the door as Sonya and Ronel cradled her. Sonya innocently sang to her mother in an effort to wake her. I ran in front of them and begged them to stop at which point all guns were drawn and pointed in my direction. Then a voice came from behind me within the house.

"So, we have company I see." said Commander Charles as he walked towards the doorway buckling his belt and zipping up his pants.

"Where is the other child?" I asked, realizing that Judson was nowhere in sight.

"You think that you are in a position to ask me questions, seminarian? That collar means nothing to me. I will have these good men gun you down where you stand!" barked Charles.

"Please, I mean no disrespect to your rank Commander. The children are in my care, forgive me, please have mercy on them." I begged.

"Mercy is very much in my power to give, but not to a traitor like Reginald who had the gall to attack me. All I was going to do was speak to his wife in private to work out the terms of their release. She fought back too, so I had to put her down. I figured the next best thing was to "speak" with his daughter, but none of *my men were able to pry the hands of this young man off of her. So, I settled for the one who showed me the most fear, and if you want him, he is inside. I have gotten what I needed." laughed the Commander as he brushed past me. I was infuriated as it dawned on me what had taken place. Withholding my anger, I asked to tend to Judson and the other children. He nonchalantly granted my request as he walked over to Reginald who heard everything. In a last-ditch effort, Reginald spat blood-filled saliva into the Commander's tan uniform. Silence fell, as Reginald screamed out to his children, I love you. I turned to look in his direction and our eyes met. He smiled and nodded to me, before a bullet exited the chamber of Charles' gun and into his temple. I gripped the hands of Ronel and Sonya as anger and tears engulfed my face. We entered the bedroom where I found Judson sobbing in a corner, without any clothing. I frantically dressed him. He said nothing, looking through me towards the entrance. I attempted to calm the others, until Judson spoke the words that, to this day, breaks my heart.*

"Where were you?" he asked.

I didn't have an explanation, not one that he would understand at that moment. I looked outside to see that the soldiers were passing out Molotov cocktail bombs. Without thinking and to ensure their survival, I took the vile from my pocket and had each of them drink from it. I knew what I was doing would impact their lives forever, but I had to ensure their survival. I led the children outside and was immediately motioned to come towards Commander Charles. There was an immediate pain in my right hand, but I thought nothing of it. As we walked closer towards him the pain intensified, to the point that it felt like my hand was literally on fire. That's when I saw it for the first time. I did not think that Ronel would have a reaction so soon. The air surrounding his slim little frame became blurry from the heat that was generated from his skin. Before I could calm him down and hide it from the soldiers noticing, he let go of my hand and ran towards the commander. Charles began to laugh as he cocked the hammer back on his gun, then Ronel disappeared. It took a few milliseconds for my eyes to adjust to what was happening, as it had been a while since I saw anyone with the ability to move so fluidly. Everyone else's vision could not keep up as I watched Ronel dash towards his father's machete. He appeared in front of the commander and jumped up into the air raising up the blade. The commander's gun was still pointed down at the ground in the direction he initially thought Ronel was running in. Before he could react to the blur above his head, the blade came down, slicing his face in two. Blood particles began to fly, followed by a stream of it coating his neck and tan uniform. As soon as Ronel's feet landed, I had to make use of the situation. I quickly disabled the century next to me and relieved him of his AK-47 and began to fire at the unsuspecting soldiers, killing as many as I could before they could draw their weapons. I yelled to Judson to take Sonya to the back of the house, but he did not respond. I grabbed a hold of

Ronel's shirt, dragging him away as I continued to fire. Ronel continued to stare down the commander that was rolling on blood covered dirt, squealing in pain while holding his face. Judson snapped out of his trance and reached for the hands of his sister and took off into the backwoods. I threw down the gun after the magazine ran out and took up a shotgun from the side of one of the dead soldiers, continuing to fire as we retreated behind them. I looked down at the commander, whom I was sure would die from wounds. I was sure.

We made it to the van, and took off towards the shoreline. Reginald and I agreed this would be an alternate way of escape. We made it to the harbor just as the boat was being untied from the dock. It was filled to the sides with people, but it did not deter us from boarding. Helping each of the children board, then jumping in myself as it departed. I held on to the orphans, as we watched the island become smaller and smaller. It is at this time that I noticed that all three of them had huge clots of blood on their clothing. Gunshot wounds. I reached for Sonya, only to find that there was not a scratch on her. I looked at the boys, and came to the same result. Their wounds were healed. The curse had taken hold and it was all my fault.

It would take years. Multiple, agonizing years to raise such extraordinary children into adulthood. Training them, while keeping them away from who they truly were. I bear the pain each day as old age and injury have ravished my body. A body I wish would finally fail me but God has kept me for reasons I have no explanation. Was it to keep the facade as the man after his own heart for the many who are celebrating me today? As I sit on an altar that should engulf me in flames, I look at the three. Each of them suffering internally with their own demons, while keeping up an image of perfection. Well, maybe not Judson. I fear what is to come. I fear what is to be revealed. I fear everything.

Chapter 11:

Save Us.

Father Elam stood outside the doors of the church greeting every parishioner on their way out. Some embraced him, many shared a quick laugh with him, and the children flocked to hug him when they got the chance. He squinted in pain but still welcomed them to run up to him. The doctors advised him to take it easier on his legs due to his age, but Elam has never been one to adhere to medical advice unless it was absolutely necessary. His gray hair perfectly complemented his dark skin and clean-shaven face. Small moles gathered in threes under each of his eyes, which were next to deeply formed crow's feet. The years have been kind to him, but there was evidence of age finally catching up. There was a slight hump in his back, and his shoulders that were once firm began to slouch. The three stood to the side, and Judson was becoming more and more impatient. He took a step forward but was quickly restrained by his brother.

"Not here," said Ronel. "We have to handle this as calm as possible"

A frustrated Judson fired back "Fuck calm! I need.."

He was quickly cut off, "What you need is to cool down. We have all day to get the answers we want. We still have a lot of people walking around." said Sonya as she smiled in Elam's direction. He limped over to them, and embraced them.

"You have no idea how much it means to me that you all made it. I had my doubts, but here you are." Elam said with a smile.

"We got you something." replied Ronel as he handed Elam a key.

"Now you know I'm too old for that crotch rocket you have, Ronel. That thing will send me to Jesus faster than He intended." said Elam as he examined the key further. Then it occurred to him that the key was familiar, but he could not put his finger on why.

"C'mon Elam, you're....vintage. So, I had to get you something that not only you can handle, but something old school." replied Ronel as he walked over to a covered motorcycle that Elam presumed belonged to one of the parishioners. Lifting the leather cover to unveil a masterly restored motorcycle.

"Is that what I think it is?!" said Elam as he briskly walked over to it, trying not to trip over his vestments.

"A 1972 Suzuki GT380J. It looks so much like my old one,

but brand new!" admired Elam as he inspected the bike further. Even struggling to one knee to marvel at the Ram Air chrome tank.

"It is yours, the original one. It took some tracking down, and some custom work but my guys were able to pull it off. Want to go for a spin?" asked Ronel.

"Not in this. The last thing God's people want to see is their priest riding a bike in full garb." retorted Elam. "Let me change!"

"Well before we do that, there is something that we would like to talk to you about. Can we go somewhere private?" requested Ronel. Elam looked at each one of their faces, and realized that what he suspected was true. Judson didn't even try to put on the façade that Ronel and Sonya did, and he saw right through it. Keeping a smile on his face, Elam motioned towards the Parish Hall, and followed his adopted family to the entrance. They walked through the door into a wide spacious room, with tiled floors. The beams from the early afternoon sun shone through the blinds, and reflected off Elam's robe. He locked the door behind him. The smile was gone from his face, transforming into nothing, an absence of any emotion. He turned and was met with scowls.

"So, it would seem that I have drawn together a family that didn't want to see me just because they missed me. Anger and apathy always has a scent. I thought I taught you better." said Elam as he stared each of them down.

"There he goes. Talking that shit. You got some nerve

thinking you got a say in anything right now!" scolded Judson as he removed his jacket.

"Judson, what do you think you're doing?" asked Ronel.

"You know that this is not going to end well." Added Sonya.

"Since when did it begin well? I'm done with this fake ass reverence for this fake ass Reverend!" replied Judson.

"Oh, so you would like to do this now?" asked Elam as he moved towards Judson's direction.

"I've been waiting for this moment for years. Finally, I get to smack that wise face clean off your head!" yelled Judson as he grounded himself before charging towards Elam.

"Giving away the origin of your attack? You embarrass me Judson." smirked Elam as he stood with his arms at his side. Judson lifted his hands and arms into a Muay-Thai high guard, spreading his fingers in order to crack them, before bringing them into fists. He charged, then swiftly switched his trajectory to the left in hopes of confusing the old priest with a rising uppercut. Elam's body remained still, but his eyes caught the tall stature of his attacker. Judson changed his mind and threw the punch, missing Elam. Met with a block when he threw another. Elam grabbed a hold of his wrist, using Judson's violent momentum to lift his body up, wrapping his legs around Judson's massive neck. Shifting his hips, he brought the angry brute to the ground, hitting Judson's head on the tile floor. Elam then extended the arm to secure a painful submission.

"Choose Judson. A broken pride? Or a broken arm?" asked

Elam as he struggled with Judson's flailing upper body. Judson, angrily lifted his legs from the ground, and kipped up back to his feet, lifting a surprised Elam into the air. Judson looked over his shoulder to an exposed support beam, and ran towards it slamming Elam back first into the steel pole. Yet Elam's grip grew stronger, tightening his hold on Judson's neck, cutting off his breathing ability. Judson slammed him to the ground, but Elam was determined. As much as he hated the fact that he couldn't breathe, Judson's anger would not allow him to stop the devastating slams to the man of God. The slams began to lose their sound, and his vision blurred before fading to black. The old man, not wishing to send his former pupil into dreamland, loosened his hold. Judson collapsed. Elam sat up next to a coughing, bested Judson, rubbing his neck attempting to catch his breath.

"Never enter a fight with the mindset of you winning. Always enter knowing that you may die, so that you do everything in your power to not do so." said Elam as he adjusted his garment and walked towards Ronel and Sonya. Then suddenly, he realized something was not right. The air molecules were shifting, and moving at a rapid pace towards his left, which indicated some sort of attack had been initiated. Before he could react, Judson's fist cracked into his skull, causing his skin to ripple sweat off of his face. Elam's eyes widened in shock as he stumbled down to a knee. He looked up to see no sight of his attacker. Again, his senses were set off by another impending attack as Judson appeared above his head in mid-air, attempting to drive his foot into Elam's head. Elam evades, but is then quickly met with a high knee strike from Judson to the face. It began to sink in that this was indeed a real fight. It has been years since he last tasted his own blood collecting under his tongue, which angered him.

"Practicing I see. Your agility and power have gotten stronger, child. But yet, still an angry child with no focus." stated Elam, as he removed his vestments down to his shirt and pants.

"Ok you two. Stop it! He hasn't struck you once Judson! He doesn't want to fight!" yelled Sonya from the side.

"No baby girl, Judson obviously has a point he needs to prove. Please, give him the opportunity" replied a stern Elam.

"No mercy, OLD MAN!" yelled Judson as he bolted towards Elam. The now bloody mouthed priest closed his eyes, and bowed his head. Judson jumped into the air, and cocked back his right fist for one last devastating blow.

"Elam, MOVE!" yelled Sonya.

"Save your breath Sonya. Judson just messed up." said Ronel as he nonchalantly tapped his fingers against his crossed arms. As his fist got closer to connecting, Elam's eyes opened and caught eye contact with a descending Judson. He then jumped and grabbed Judson by the forehead, forcing him down to the broken tiled floor. He dragged Judson's body forward until it hit the concrete wall, creating a crater. Elam commenced slapping him in the face repeatedly.

"Aprann respeke-m!(Learn to respect me) Aprann respeke-m! Aprann respeke-m!" said Elam with each slap. A helpless Judson could not do anything as each slap sent a numbing sensation through his body. Elam raised his hand again to strike, but it was halted by Ronel.

"I think it's time for this little scuffle to end Elam. I assure you, as much as this is not going to sound right coming out of my mouth. Respect is not something you have from either of us right now." said Ronel as he aided the old man up to his feet and off of his dazed brother. Elam spat out the blood from his mouth and made his way over to a close by sink to rinse out the rest.

"What is the meaning of this impromptu intervention?" asked Elam as he flicked his hands and dried them. He painfully leaned down to retrieve his robe and cover.

"What is the meaning of you lying to us?!" shot back Ronel. "You said he was DEAD. Charles is very much alive! I have seen him with my own eyes!"

"What have I always taught you?! If I say something is dead, it is dead. It does not interfere with your focus and the task at hand. That it does not matter or have value. Charles needed to die so that you can live your lives, each of you! He has not existed since our departure, and he will continue to not exist until I say so! It does not matter what you saw. He is not your concern." replied Elam.

"Not our concern?!" asked Sonya. "He killed my mother! He killed my father! You lied to us and now you think your Jedi mind trick words are going to just make that go away?!"

The priest walked over to her, and stood before her. His eyes, non-threatening, and his lips lengthened to form a closed smile.

"You are the last person that should be pointing fingers, baby girl. I smell the blood that still stains your fingers. You took an oath to never use your skill for any combat until absolutely necessary. I warned you of the dangers of being so well skilled in the deadly arts! But you insist on running around the city as; court, judge, and executioner!" snarled Elam.

"Hey, I'm still alive down here." said a sarcastic Judson as he struggled to get back on his feet. "To tell you the truth old man, we didn't come for your blessing. This is all an unneeded formality that they wanted to do. I don't need no answers. Just Charles' head on a platter will suffice. We don't need you. We will take him down ourselves."

Elam dusted off his vestments without making any eye contact with them. Placing the alb over the chair, then the chasuble, and lastly the stole that he folded perfectly in two before laying it in a prestigious manner over the others.

"So, all of you dare to go against my wise counsel? I put these clothes on not for a fashion statement. This is my life now. I am done seeking blood, and you all are not built to travel down this road. Just because you chop one head off, doesn't mean a thousand won't take its place." explained Elam.

"You talk as someone who is afraid, Elam. Is it because he wears the ring of the Assembly?" asked Ronel. Elam's gaze was cold. For the first time in a while, he was visibly stricken with fear. Coming clean regarding the former organization he once served was now mandated.

"What is the Assembly?" asked Sonya, as she attempted to assist Judson with the cut on his face.

"Yeah, Elam, tell her who they are and who you really are!" yelled Judson.

"Sonya, there are some things that I felt that you weren't ready to know and..." began Elam, as he reached for her hands, which she quickly snatched away. Her eyes began to well up and her lips shuttered violently before her next sentence.

"Well, it wasn't that important enough to keep from my older brothers! Why is it that you keep thinking I am this weak little girl that is so naïve?" asked Sonya as she vigorously removed the gloves from her hands.

"Elam, I think it's the time that she knows. At this point, she deserves to know" expressed Ronel as he took a step closer to his confused sister. Elam's fear crept out of his eyes as he looked at her. The relationship he has with Sonya is that of father and daughter. Having lost everything he knew to be family; this was all that he had left. It was now in jeopardy with the next words to come out of his mouth.

Elam began:

900 years ago.

Three bandits from different sides of the globe came together with the solemn goal of stealing a treasure of legend, what was thought to be the holy grail. James of Bermen, Alexander of Cordoba, and Mayer of Wagadou. They entered the second Crusades playing both sides of the conflict to gain wealth along the way. The three were known for their prowess in battle, and even more for their comradery. After a group of warriors that would come to be known as the Knights Templar managed to capture a particular castle, it was evident that they found something of great value. The comrades wasted no time in penetrating the security forces. They made it to the throne room where they discovered the wooden grail. With the thought of immortality and power flooding their minds, they each took the chalice and drank from it. However, the effects were not what they anticipated at first. There was immediate pain that coursed through their bodies that caused them to fall to the ground screaming in agony. This commotion drew the attention of the unaware knights. They stormed the room, and attempted to restrain and execute the traitors, but all 400+ men that entered would never exit.

The locals recall hearing screams of multiple men set on fire, and seeing massive fields of energy escaping through every orifice of the castle, until it collapsed inward. Three men would walk out unscathed, each holding a broken piece of the chalice that they drank from. The friends, not fully understanding what was happening to them, ran off into the woods as another wave of soldiers were making their way towards the explosion. The three ran until they found cover under a massive tree, where they fell asleep. Mayer was then awakened to a lamb grazing nearby. The lamb raised its head and looked in his direction, then proceeded to walk over to them. Mayer woke the others as the out of place animal began to shake away its wool as if it was sheared perfectly. Then it spoke.

"I cover you because you are naked again. But with this power and youth, comes eternal battle. Your bloodlines will be cursed with madness if this should ever repeat. Men pursue you, until five cuts lay you deep." With a flash, the lamb vanished so quickly that fibers of its wool remained in its shape.

The follicles of wool then entered painfully into their pores, as the wooden shards embedded into the right palm of their hands. The men transformed; adorning armored attire with weapons that formed in their hands at will. The three would soon find the words of the lamb to be true, as power and immortality rested upon them. With their abilities, they influenced governments, battled in conflicts, and reaped wealth to almost match that of Babylon. They made a pack and created an alliance known as 'The Assembly'. A secret group of loyal assassins and soldiers at their disposal. Each of the three controlled their own chapter in their respective regions.

It would be less than a century until James was the first to die. Having watched his descendants age or be hunted by those seeking his power, he hung up his sword. Instantly aging to bones after a season's time. He died at the age of 132. The group under his command would disband soon after. Alexander would suffer the same fate. Hanging up his sword and settling on the outskirts of Spain. As the last yellow leaf fell to welcome winter, he died at the age of 274. Leaving his accumulated fortune to his children who were hunted for generations. Until all remnants of his existence were lost or destroyed.

Mayer, now the sole head of the Assembly, wandered the world teaching and engaging in battles he sought special interest in. He pledged to himself and to the Assembly a vow of celibacy until death, to avert the bloodline curse.

It is rumored that he settled and died somewhere in the Caribbean. Others say that he disappeared out to sea. Nearly two centuries later, The Assembly, now without its charismatic leader, soon fell into disarray. The Candiru assassins would then overthrow the chairmen in a bloody coup. Appointing five Generals of their own while still keeping the traditional business as assassins-for-hire. Each General was given a ring, inscribed with the mark of Mayer. The half clock image, with three swords connected at the center. Each member of the Candiru has this symbol tattooed on their backs by hand. A rite of passage and oath to serve the Assembly until death. The very same, that is tattooed on mine. The Candiru are well trained, deadly, and delight in the shadows. Their pack attacks are swift. The cleanliness of their kills depends on the directive of the contracts set on the poor souls.

Chapter 12:

Kick into Gear

Sonya's eyes welled up. The uncontrollable spasms in her face muscles tensed as all attempts to hold back her anger fell in obscurity.

"The Candiru?! As in the infamous assassin organization?!" asked Sonya.

"I can explain. The Candiru took me in. They raised me, and taught me everything I know. They are no longer my family. You all are." returned Elam. Opening his arms for her, he felt the cold of her eyes tearing him to shreds.

"Family don't lie to each other. They don't tell each other lies about them being an orphan that my father took in. The CIA has files that could fill a library about the Candiru and the bodies left in their wake. You probably arranged to have my parents killed over that stupid serum you gave us!!" said Sonya.

"No, my child, that is not what happened." explained Elam as he slowly inched towards her.

"Don't touch me! I am not your child, and after today I am nothing to you!" hurled Sonya, as she picked up her bag to leave. She turned and faced her two brothers.

"And you two. You could have told me. I hate you both." conceded Sonya

"Sonya, you wouldn't have been able to handle knowing the truth," said Ronel.

"And what is the truth? That I have a liar, a drunken jackass, and a vindictive criminal piece-of-shit brother for a family?! Thanks Ronel for actually respecting my level of intelligence. You can all go to hell." said Sonya, as she stormed out of the parish hall doors. After the door slammed, Judson couldn't help himself.

"Well that went exactly like I thought it would." joked Judson as he continued to pat the dust away from his dress slacks. The tension between Elam's eyebrows could crush a vehicle as Judson's words drove pins into his brain.

"You never let up do you? You always have to be the center of unneeded friction where it is not welcomed!" blasted Elam.

"The next words out your mouth old man, better be how we get to Charles. Or I will turn that collar into a choke and squeeze that bass out your voice!" replied Judson, raising his large, tall frame to his feet. Spitting on the ground to further dig the pins past the surface of Elam's trigger button.

"Choke? Did the dealer become the consumer? I perfectly remember laying you out ten minutes ago!" shot back Elam

"It will take less than a second to put two bullets in your head!" replied Judson, as he cocked back the hammer on a loaded Glock 45 pistol, pointing it at the priest's head.

"Do it! DO IT!" prodded Elam.

Suddenly there was a flash of light, with the sound of metal slicing through air. The barrel of the gun fell to the ground, while Judson held the smoldering other half in his hand. Ronel's machete illuminated in an ember glow began to fade. The frustrated peacemaker stopped emitting the heat that could have scorched away his clothing if prolonged any further.

"Sonya's outburst was an exception. The last thing we need is to go to war with each other." said Ronel as he put away his blade. "Elam, give us the information we need to do what we need to do."

"It is not that simple and cold cut Ronel." Replied Elam. The priest lowered himself slowly to sit nearby, wincing as the adrenaline ran its course. The aged joints and burn injuries decades old sent piercing pain through his nervous system.

"Even if I give you both any indication of where and how to find him, the consequences are more dire than you think." warned Elam.

"I am perfectly aware that killing an old man may seem weak, but we all know that every breath that he takes is borrowed time." said Ronel

"Well if you plan to dig that grave, you need to make room for a thousand more. The Candiru will not stop until the killers, and everyone attached to them, are dead. That includes me. That includes my entire congregation. I cannot risk that!" replied Elam.

"Why would the Candiru kill for him? The only way you can get that level of protection in the Assembly is if you were knighted." said Ronel. Elam was silent, and looked off into space, clearly distraught.

"He was knighted over 10 years ago. The only man to successfully muscle his way to a seat at the table." conceded Elam.

"How is that possible?!" asked Judson.

"Doing the dirty work that the Assembly will not touch. With his eldest son Bello's crime organization, they cashed in on those contracts. On top of that, they are responsible for systematically trying to kill off an entire bloodline. Do you remember the summer of 2008?" asked Elam.

"Yeah, shit was crazy in the streets. Bodies dropping left and right. I thought it had to do with some regular gang shit." replied Judson.

"Twenty-six murders in the span of two weeks, all drive-by shootings. Yes, it would seem like a turf war, until you looked closer. All were of Haitian descent. All with Dessalines' blood running through their veins. Many who were not even criminals, or had any dealings in crime. Just young teens and adults." said

Elam as he did the sign of the cross. "The Assembly no longer holds the honor it once did. After the Candiru's successful coup d'etat backed by the Templars, it is not surprising that they are still seeking the annihilation of the bloodline. It did not take long for Charles and Bello to provide their services."

"When you spoke of Mayer, you often said that he had no heir. Why are they seeking to destroy Dessalines' bloodline?" asked Ronel

"They believe that the shard was somehow activated and ingested by Jean-Jacques, giving him and his men the edge to defeat the world's most respected armies during the Revolution. Their efforts to punish his descendant have been in operation ever since." Replied Elam.

"If that is true, why haven't they come for us?" asked Ronel

"Scratch that! Here is a recurring question he has yet to answer. Why haven't the Candiru killed you for abandoning their order?" asked Judson.

"I don't have an answer that would give either of you satisfaction. I do know that I have taken every precaution so that your names were never brought up in the conversation." replied Elam

"But Charles knows about my abilities. Judson is the only one that hasn't shown any evolution other than the baseline dexterity, strength, and the fast healing we all share." Said Ronel. Elam's head shot up to Ronel, as he struggled to his feet once more.

"Thanks for making me sound like I ain't shit dear brother. Real class act." Intruded Judson.

"Wait! What do you mean by that? Are you saying that Sonya is displaying her power?!" inquired Elam.

"The barriers aren't holding Elam. Somehow, she has found a way to tap into them again. I felt her might, it is unlike anything I have dealt with before." Conceded Ronel. "Maybe we should try Mayer's ritual again and ....."

"I WILL DO NO SUCH THING! You know nothing of the words you speak!" shouted Elam, before composing himself. "We cannot allow Charles to know. Which is why it is best that you both let this gripe with him die. He has let us live in peace, let's not do anything to bring any attention our way. I will deal with the issue of Sonya quietly."

"Well, I ain't trying to hear all that. I may not have the power to spit hot fire like Renegade/Biker Mice from Mars over here, but bullets still kill. I have one for every letter in Charles' name!" said Judson. "Let's Go Ronel, you got your half ass explanation."

"You don't know what you are doing Judson, this isn't the streets. These aren't just local gangs, and mafias. Even if you were to have a chance to take him out, your brashness will get us all killed." said Elam

"Elam has a point, Judson, the last thing we need is any collateral damage from just one kill. So tell us teacher, hypothetically, how should we take him down?" asked Ronel.

"I am no longer an assassin! This is suicide!" said Elam as

100

he turned around to walk away.

"Do you still believe in honor, Elam?" asked Ronel. Elam stopped mid stride and took a deep breath. Remembering the code of the Candiru and what the Assembly once stood for. He was torn in the moment, teetering between repentance and a long dead duty to the group he once served. The clergyman knew that nothing would deter them. Even while making his closing arguments, the path between the orphans and their persecutor was sutured in steel, blood, and fire.

"Julius Augustin." Elam relented.

"Who is that?" asked Judson

"Charles' and Bello's right hand. He handles the books, the money, and the affairs of their organization. There is an annual gathering of the Assembly that Charles will not be attending, as his youngest son, Mathieu, has aspirations for the presidency of Haiti. Charles will travel to Port-au-Prince with his son and a few Candiru. Jude will stand in Charles' stead. The host, Gomez, is the last remaining member of the Assembly who has been secretly dissatisfied with the presence of a tyrant like Charles. The Candiru will not interfere with the killing of an Assembly leader, if it can be proven that Charles has committed treason against the Assembly." said Elam.

"How are we going to convince Gomez to even hear our case?" asked Ronel

"The killing of your parents will mean nothing to him. Gomez is no stranger to families with vendettas against him and the Assembly. But proof that Charles sought the shard for his own gain will definitely spark the reasoning that Gomez so desperately seeks." replied Elam.

"What purpose could the shard serve Charles? The last of its power was drained, remember? You told us that. How do we provide proof? The shard was lost after we escaped." stated Ronel

"Charles has it in his possession, along with the skull of Mayer. The one person that knows their locations and the manner Charles acquired them is Mr. Augustin. He will need some "persuasion", to profess the truth before the Assembly's court, which will be called immediately if Gomez is informed. My hope is that you hold your composure. Augustin was one of the Tonton Macoute soldiers that survived with Charles when you almost cut his skull in two," said Elam.

"Another thing you kept from us!" barked Judson. "Why should we listen to another word, Ronel? For all we know, this could all be an elaborate way to throw us off from getting to Charles!"

"No Judson! For once, kicking down doors with guns blazing isn't the answer." reasoned Ronel. "How do we find Mr. Augustin?"

"I would suggest a change of wardrobe. Especially if you want to blend in with the swap meet crowd." replied Elam after looking them both up and down.

Chapter 13:

So, you want to be a spy?

The cars seemed like blurs passing her by as she weaved through traffic on Interstate 95. With only four more exits to go, Sonya's eyes darted back and forth between the road and the rear-view mirror. The tower of the church was long gone from its reflection, and the tears have dried. She was still panning through Elam's words while approaching her exit, wondering how the man she considered a father could betray her so deeply. She wanted to prove herself to be more than the child they saw. As she approached the red light, her cell phone rang. The name that appeared on the car's dashboard brought her more discomfort. Agent Tanner did not shy away from calling her on weekends. Since Sonya started her position, Tanner demanded more tedious clerical tasks to be performed by the rookie. Sonya gathered herself, and answered.

"Hello?" answered Sonya

"Agent Jean-Baptiste, you are needed. Please meet us at HQ at 1400." said a stern Tanner.

"Ok. But I'm just getting out of church." began Sonya

"Did you pray for a field position, Jean-Baptiste?! If so, I would like to thank you for also inconveniencing my day off too. The Director wants you to run point on an assignment so get your ass in here. I don't care what you are doing. 1400!" Blurted Agent Tanner before a swift click.

The initial sting of the rude demeanor from her superior was suddenly flushed with happiness. Sonya was so elated, that she had no idea what to do next. She wanted to call Manny and Jesse to give them the great news, but she was too excited to think straight. She swerved her vehicle and ran the light, almost hitting the median before whipping a U-Turn at another red light which caught the attention of a State Trooper. As she re-entered the highway, she was quickly followed and the officer's lights went on, but Sonya didn't stop immediately. She rolled down her window, and slowed down enough for the officer to see that she was holding a badge. The trooper, realizing that the car was registered to the government, stopped his pursuit. She reveled in the thought of finally being recognized, and at the opportunity to display her intelligence and skills on an elevated scale. Before she knew it, she was out of the car, into the building, and on the elevator bouncing in excitement. She stepped out of the elevator to an awaiting Tanner in a t-shirt and jeans. This surprised her, as

Sonya felt that Tanner was way too stuck up for regular clothing other than a pants suit.

"Follow me, Jean-Baptiste, we are meeting in here." said Tanner as she opened the door to the conference room.

"Please sit. Deputy Director Lee, you are on with me and Agent Jean-Baptiste." said Tanner as she leaned over the speakerphone in the middle of the long table.

"Sonya, how are you? I do apologize for summons, but the world is the world no matter what day, time, or holiday it may be on our shores. So, I hope you can understand." said the voice from the speaker.

"I have no choice but to understand, Director. Whatever is needed of me, I will go above the call to assist." said Sonya as she tried to contain her excitement.

"Good!" said Director Lee. "I love the vigor. Please open the document given to you by Agent Tanner. Do you recognize these men in the photos?"

One photo in particular caused a cold feeling in Sonya's fingers, numbing them into a frantic shake, which Agent Tanner observed. Sonya kept her composure, but remained silent as she examined the other photos. Fighting the pounding headache, and confusion of why she was staring at her parent's killer. Flashes of her mother and father's faces caused her to close her eyes tightly.

"Sonya?" asked the Director. "Are you still there?"

"Yes. I am here." answered Sonya. "What is the objective?"

"The objective is to infiltrate the Clerveaux Crime Family,

but only to monitor and report. It is well known the disdain that Mathieu Clerveaux has for his father. Although his popularity within the Haitian community is large, his reputation is not completely clean due to his father funding his political campaign. We need you to get close to Mathieu, gain his trust, and give us any vital intel." stated Director Lee.

"With all due respect, Director, why does the CIA want anything to do with a local crime syndicate and an impoverished country? Shouldn't this be the job for the DEA, as this is clearly drug related? Open and shut case." stated a more aware Sonya.

"Fair assessment for a regular detective, but you know that we only get involved in certain matters that threaten National Security. A few months ago, we intercepted communications between Charles Clerveaux, and a Russian doctor that specializes in nuclear medicine." Said the Director as he introduced pictures of an older white male standing next to Charles. "Nickolay Ursov, has been on the watch list of numerous intelligence agencies across the globe for his role in conducting human trials of nerve gas testing. We suspect that he may have struck a deal with Clerveaux and the Assembly to begin testing and production right under our noses in Haiti." said Lee.

"We can't have another instance like the Cuban Missile Crisis repeat itself in American-friendly waters. We need all possible intel without room for any error. Do you understand Sonya?" asked Agent Tanner.

"Understood. When and where do I begin?" asked Sonya

"Find your best gown, you are going to a ball in a few days. A Gala to be specific," said Lee.

Chapter 14:

If I was President

"**O**rder! Order! There will be order!" said Chancellor Janvier as he held his grip on the gavel in anticipation of using it once again. The hostile atmosphere was sure to produce another passionate shouting match within the cold frigid chamber. It was common around election time to hear the bickering echoing beyond the mahogany wood-laden room. "This is a simple candidacy proceeding and Mr. Clerveaux is not on trial for murder! Now, let's do what needs to be done. Mr. Saintpreux, you have the floor."

"He might as well be!" said the well-dressed Joseph Saintpreux standing to his feet. "The audacity of these imposters to come into our country and automatically become candidates for the presidency is insulting! He even has the gall to wheel in his Duvalier worshiping, human rights violating father!" Charles grinned as Mr. Saintpreux became more vexed at the sight of his facial arrangement.

"Senator Joseph…" said Mathieu Clerveaux, as he stood from his seat with his hands raised as if to surrender. "It is not my intention to, in any way, degrade the purpose of this counsel. I consider it an honor to be in the presence of all of you. I know that I have been away from this country for a while, but this is my country. This is where I was born, and this is where I hope to serve my fellow citizens as President. The alleged crimes of my father are by no means connected to my campaign. My name is Mathieu Clerveaux, not Charles Clerveaux. He is my father, nonetheless, but he is only here to support me."

"Support?!" yelled another Senator towards the back of the room. "So, blood money is behind your campaign?! He is not fit!" The room again erupted in agreement. Pointing their fingers at the candidate and his unwanted plus one. Charles wiped his glasses before restoring them back onto his wrinkled nose. He muttered to himself incoherently.

"Please my brothers, that accusation has no basis!" Said Mathieu. "My father is ill, and is not in his right mind. The things he has done were before I was born, and I have said it time, and time again that I condemn the crimes committed by the Tonton Macoute.

"Which are you Mr. Clerveaux?" asked Senator Joseph. Leaning towards a visibly flustered Mathieu. "Devoted son, or hardened criminal like your brother Bello? Do you think that we don't know of your non-profit organization being a money laundering hub of your brother's organization? Even if we were to approve your candidacy, what is to stop the nation from believing that we gave our stamp of approval to a criminal?!"

"What is criminal, is the hypocrisy of these proceedings, and the planned butchering of my son's right as a citizen of this nation." Said Charles as he adjusted his wheelchair. His eyes panned the room as a crooked smirk slowly formed on his wrinkled, scared face. A barrage of shouting were hurled in Charles' direction as he looked into the eyes of all the members. Closing his eyes, he reveled in it, chuckling to himself. The sound of the gavel hitting the heavily dented desk came into focus as Chancellor Janvier once again yelled for order.

"How dare you open your mouth to speak?! Chancellor Janvier, we move to have these proceedings adjourned, and to throw these charlatans out! The nation does not need another stain on a quilt which we can barely keep from detaching at the seams!" said Senator Joseph, now patting away the sweat from his forehead. Suddenly, the doors to the large room opened as multiple men in black tactical gear entered.

"What is the meaning of this?!" yelled Chancellor Janvier. "Who are these men? Guards!!" The men withdrew short blades and held them to the necks of each representative. One of them pointed a high-powered machine gun at Janvier, who gingerly sat back in his seat. The doors closed behind them, as the bodies of numerous Haitian law enforcement officials laid in pools of blood in the hallway.

Charles reached into his pocket and pulled out a folded Haitian flag that he began to undo as silence fell onto the lips of each dignitary. He then laid the fabric across his lap as he stared at it proudly.

"Is it not beautiful? Red and Blue, or even better, Red and Black. Either way, the flag of Dessalines was not just simply two halves of the French flag, but it represented something greater. The separation of any foreign influence. It is for this reason Duvalier refused to change the color black on the flag. It represents the blood that was shed, and the blood that repaid it."

"Father please! There is no need for you to inter-" began Mathieu.

"Shut up boy! We have tried your way. You are speaking in a language they do not understand." Charles interrupted. "The true crime is that every one of you that sits at this table has foreign currency flowing in and out of their bank accounts to keep the cycle of confusion and coup etats rolling."

Charles methodically put on his leather gloves. "Our young are disenfranchised. Our economy has been siphoned for almost two centuries by the elite. Elites like you and your bad French speaking colleagues abroad are the true cancer. Eating away and leaving nothing for the people. No inheritance. No legacy. No life." Continued Charles, as he adjusted the brakes on his wheelchair and braced himself.

"Legacy is everything, and the old order of business has long passed its expiration date. Chancellor, I propose a new vote. I humbly urge the leaders in this room to make a choice worthy of our nation and your lives," said Charles flagrantly motioning his trembling index finger to the knives at their throats. He kicked up the footrests to lay his dress shoes on the ground. "Please, do not misunderstand the blades under your necks. I simply want to have your complete attention."

"It doesn't matter what you do TYRANT! The truth about you and your son will get out. The people will oust you and your puppet son back to the shores of the United States where you have hidden away from justice being served upon you." Said Janvier. The gunman cocked the gun, and readied his rifle. Charles raised his hand to wave him off.

"The truth is very much like a lie. If enough people believe one more than the other, it becomes the truth accepted by all. Unfortunately for you, the dead cannot make an objection to what the people will accept as truth," said Charles. A black aura began to engulf his body as he stood from his chair. The first steps were that of a fawn, before gradually becoming that of a determined man. Walking towards the Chancellor as his visibility faded into the darkness. The men removed their grip from the blades that were now levitating, surrounded by the same black energy. The men began to cry out in horror and for their lives as the dark figure converted into that of an old soldier of the revolution. The energy surrounding him shook the room like a strummed string on an upright bass.

"Spare them Father! Please, this is not the way!" protested Mathieu.

"My ways are not your ways. I am a god among sinners that have rejected me, and a price must be paid" said Charles in a distorted culmination of his and another's voice. Before Mathieu could belt out another plea, the sound of iron cutting into human flesh happened one after the other. The screams became skin crawling gurgles as the men choked on their own warm blood that shot out onto the conference table before running down their chests.

"Congratulations my son. The votes were unanimous. You are now a candidate for the Presidency!" said Charles as he motioned away the gunman who left the rifle suspended in the air, still pointing towards the last remaining man..

"Chancellor, are the votes unanimous?" asked Charles for further confirmation as the safety on the floating rifle disengaged. The voiceless, shivering lips of Janvier struggled to get the words out. His eyes drenched in tears, surveyed the massacre's aftermath. His trembling hands reached for the gavel as he swallowed hard. His fingertips barely touched the wooden handle when the object flew across the room, hovering over the head of Senator Joseph, who was still struggling to breath. The instrument rose and fell repeatedly, banging into Janvier's skull violently before falling to the crimson ground.

"I would say we are adjourned," said Charles as he turned and walked over to his chair. As he sat down, the darkness left him. The men in black exited the room, and his reluctant son stood behind his father's chair white knuckled. Mathieu began to push in horror, rendered speechless, and helpless. They walked past the bodies strewn about and Charles motioned for his entourage to stop as they made it to the hallway.

"Oh, I almost forgot," said Charles as the sounds of machine gun fire cracked into the hollow hallway. Shell casings flooded the floor until the very last one clunked against the tile, followed by the riotous clash of the smoldering weapon.

Chapter 15:

Smash & Grab

The South Florida heat barreled down on the asphalt, cooking the sand and aged gum that regained elasticity when stepped on by the crowd of people making their way through vendor tents. The swap meet was notorious for its foot traffic on a Sunday afternoon. The smell of gyros meat, fried chicken and fresh fruit filled the nostrils of Judson as he made his way through the sea of patrons aggressively.

"Hey! Can you make us anymore obvious?" said Ronel as he grabbed Judson's massive bicep, hanging out of his unbuttoned baby blue shirt. The multiple tattoos on Judson's body were on display, with the exception of his thigh pieces covered by his shorts. "We just need to find his booth and pose as customers looking to buy some food, like it's a regular day. We lure him away from his security detail with an offer he can't refuse, nab him and put him into our "sound-deprived" vehicle and jet. Clean and simple. No bloodshed."

"For a man who carries decades of souls on that machete, you would think that a little of the red stuff wouldn't bother you. Is it beginning to get to you Ronel? Need a drink?" smirked Judson as he continued to force his way through.

"That's low, even for you Judson," replied Ronel following in haste. Adjusting his dreads into a ponytail, he followed his younger brother. His white tee, jeans, and brown shoes were not his style, and neither was it to keep from slapping Judson on the back of his bald head just for making such a statement.

"Speaking of low. Didn't you say we were looking for a Haitian food booth?"

"Yes," said Ronel, still peering around their surroundings.

"I think I found it."

"What makes you so sure?"

"Because I can smell the burnt legume from here and I'm guessing that that dilapidated food booth cannot afford the undercover security surrounding it. Plus, no one is eating."

Judson's eyes focused on the larger of them all who wore gold rings and chains; Bello Clerveaux pulled in the nicotine from his cigarette into his gold grills while surveying everything moving. The thick bonded dreads laid wildly over the upper portion of his large frame. He motioned to his lower-level henchmen to observe a blind spot that he noticed.

"Looks like someone tipped them off," said Judson. Ronel

continued to scour the premises until it hit him.

"I know what we need to do. We need a diversion. Something that will draw their attention away long enough for me to make the grab. I will need you to….Judson? Judson?!" whispered Ronel to his brother who was in a slow, anger-infused daze looking in the opposite direction. Ronel looked over his brother's shoulder to the realization that their afternoon plans were as good as dead. He didn't count on Judson to hold his composure at the sight of Shona in another man's company,

"Hey, we don't have time for this," reasoned Ronel

"Oh, I got a lot of time for this shit! I get put in the box for a short time and this chick think it's open season on what is mine?!" Judson walked towards the unsuspecting couple.

"Judson!" whispered Ronel aggressively as he his shoulders dropped in defeat. There was no stopping him now without drawing the attention of the goons too soon. Swaying his vision between the bodyguards and the back of his brother's shiny head, Ronel had to think on his feet. Shona's laughter came to a halt as her, no longer incarcerated, ex made his way over.

"Hey Shona. Come here baby!" Judson attempted to embrace her but the hand of her male companion grabbed a hold of his arm, imprinting his fingers on the now provoked former lover.

"Not sure who you are but the lady - -AAHHH!" cried out her companion. The mind-blowing, searing pain shot through his side as he felt a few ribs break. Judson had delivered a seismic

117

muay thai kick. Shona's date dropped to his knees, feeling a warm liquid rise up his esophagus then coughing it out onto the ground. Before the sound of Shona's cries for Judson to stop reached his ears, he caught a glimpse of his attacker skipping backwards before launching his knee into his nose. Silence fell, at least for him. The snoring from the unconscious laid out hero drew the attention of camera phones. Shona collapsed down to cradle his head while shouting every obscenity in her vocabulary at the bearded brute. A hand tapped Judson on the shoulder, which caused him to swiftly turn his body to throw a punch. He quickly snapped out of his trance when the hand of Bello caught his fist.

"So, look who it is. Judson I presume?" said Bello while holding Judson's shaking fist. Judson threw another, also surprisingly caught by the much larger Clerveaux. "So, this is the power of the Jean-Baptiste boy that my father had his way with?"

Enraged, Judson swiped his hands free, while in the same motion slipping behind the Bello. Wrapping his arms around his waist and lifting, until Bello's neck met the concrete slab behind them disturbingly. The other bodyguards began to rush towards him, before the sounds of police sirens blared towards their position. A paddy wagon pulled up next to Judson with the sliding door opening as it stopped. He was shocked to find a gagged and bound older gentleman lying on ground fighting the restraints.

"How did you get to him so fast?!" asked a winded Judson

standing at the corridor of the van.

"Get in DUMBASS!" yelled Ronel from the driver's seat. Judson, ever the dirty fighter, stopped to kick dirt into the eyes of both a recovering Bello and his first victim. He then kissed Shona on the forehead which she fought back, before jumping into the vehicle that sped off through the barrier, and onto the main road.

Chapter 16:

Exiles and Reptiles

"You mind telling me what was so hard about following the plan? Now we have Bello, who will alert his Father, and the Assembly before we can get Augustin to speak the truth to Gomez." said Ronel as he struggled to hold onto the speeding airboat. The wind, mosquitoes, and evening mist from the mangrove-infused water assaulted his T-shirt with droplets.

"We got away, didn't we?!" said Judson before launching into a comical impersonation of his seething brother. *"Noooo Judson, keep your strap in the car. Don't go in with guns blazing. If I was strapped, we wouldn't have this problem!"*

"Where are we going anyway? And who is this?" asked Ronel, pointing to the nearly toothless, overalls adorned, slim Caucasian man at the controlling arm of the loud water vehicle.

"That's Country Mike, the grim reaper." Judson introduced.

"Since staying off the streets is imperative, I figured we get a little creative in our interrogation of Mr. Augustin here." Judson patted the kidnapped man on his head as he wriggled away defiantly. "Stop moving around like that, there won't be nowhere for the vomit to go if you get seasick"

Layers of duct tape were wrapped around Augustin's mouth, and the grayed peased hair of his sideburns stuck to the adhesive. The high-ranking official spewed muffled madness into their direction before gulping from the gas battling with the contents of his stomach. Fighting to keep it down, his digestive system failed him. His mouth filled as he began to convulse, before the contents seeped out of his nostrils.

"He's CHOKING!" said Ronel.

"I warned him," replied Judson before cutting off the tape to relieve the accountant of his near asphyxiation.

"You don't know who you are messing with!" coughed Augustin. Judson grinned, and again patted his head before turning his attention to the direction the boat was heading.

"Are they hungry Mike?" asked Judson.

"I haven't fed the guys in a while, so forgive me if they are a little snappy. Is that their lunch?" asked Mike, slowing the vessel to a crawl to gander at Augustin with childlike enthusiasm. As the motor from the propeller winded down, the everglades came alive in nature's symphonic sound. The slow creak of the compound, coupled with the orchestral unity of insects, amphibians, and birds of the night made the moon that shone above them its centerpiece.

"What does he mean by lunch, Judson?" asked Ronel, now standing between Augustin and his unusually relaxed little brother. Judson smiled while assisting Mike in tying the boat to the rickety dock.

"You are embarrassing me, dear brother. You agreed to my way of getting the truth out and for that, I assure you success. I don't plan on doing anything stupid." said Judson as they approached the dark compound. "Would it pain you to be gratuitous with just a little level of trust?"

"Just lead the way," said Ronel as he assisted Augustin to his feet and off the vessel. It did not take long for Ronel to figure out which method of fear his brother had in mind. As they made their way into the one room shack, Mike fidgeted with a switch behind the door until a spider-webbed amber bulb illuminated after a few flickers. Next to it was a hook connected to a long thick manila rope that ran from a rusty, swiveling pulley. Right below it, Mike lifted a hatch-like contraption to reveal a 6-foot-deep silo with two large dark figures resting on a mound of rotted vegetation, bones, and a murky, thick liquid. Without warning one of the figures lunged its nostrils up along the side of the silo, opening its mouth to reveal multiple bone crushing teeth, letting out a deep, long hiss.

"Gators? Nice touch Judson!" said Ronel with elation. Augustin began to contest as the grim reaper lowered the hook and brought it closer to him, taking his bound hands and sliding the hook between his palms and tape. Wrapping the excess slack around his wrist and tying it into a knot that would please the greatest of water enthusiasts. Glancing into the tank, the once tough accountant passed out at the thought of meeting his demise at the jaws of the prehistoric beasts. Judson assisted further by pulling on the rope on the other side of the pulley, hoisting the guilty up above certain death.

"Wait, wasn't there three of them?" asked Judson.

"Well would you look at that?" said Mike as he inspected his larger than before reptiles with a flashlight. "Looks like they ate their baby brother. Family matters my ass!" joked the heavy jawed, tobacco chewing undertaker as he took the rope end from Judson to tie it to a cleat on the nearest wall.

"Wake up Augustin, they like their food alive and kicking!" said Judson, as he threw a foul-smelling bucket of cold fish guts onto the dangling man. Waking up from his brief slumber, the accountant yelled and pleaded with his captors. Gasping for air as he tried to make his words become more coherent.

"Please, get me down from here! You don't know who you are dealing with. Charles will come for you all!" yelled Augustin as he attempted to swing his feet to try and find a solid footing on the silo's edge. "I will defend you; I will tell him to have mercy and he will listen! Please just GET ME DOWN FROM HERE!! You all are dead!"

"Now that is no way to talk to your host Augustin. We went through so much trouble to accommodate your presence," snickered Judson

"Your threats mean nothing. And unlike my brother here, I don't play with my food so I will cut to it. You are going to give us viable proof that Charles has possession of the Skull of Mayer and the shard. Then you will escort us to Gomez' estate." demanded Ronel as he sharpened his blade along a steel post, dangerously near the tight rope that held Augustin in place.

"You two are in way over your heads! The old priest should have given you boys the mercy of suffocating you in your sleep while you were children. He will eat you all alive. And I cannot wait to watch it happen," laughed Augustin in utter defiance.

"It would seem that your little wet dream is in reverse right about now, isn't it" asked Judson. "Hey Mike, do you remember that thing you told me about using gasoline to preserve the integrity of the rope?"

"Why yes," replied Mike, beginning a light chuckle to himself. Ronel then held his blade against rope staring at Augustin as the brown surrounding his pupils faded to amber. Steam began to rise from his arm to his hand wrapped around the grip of his weapon. The metal of the sword became red hot instantly, igniting the rope. The flame traveled to the hands of Augustin, who could not only feel, but hear the sizzling of his skin around his fingers cooking to a crisp.

"OK! OK! Please, I will do it. I will tell you where you can find the items you seek to prove your case to the Assembly. Please take me down!" cried Augustin, fighting between the choices of wriggling out of his oven restraints to become reptilian feed, or giving up the information that the brothers needed as his fingers seared. Judson, in mid-laughter, caught the scent of the burning material and flesh. His eyes widened as his focus on Augustin became more intense. Images of his parents flashed before him, and quickly disappeared, with the constant laughter of Charles echoing between his ears. Peeling back the old layers of skin around Augustin's face in his mind, revealed the face of a young soldier, dressed in Tonton Macoute clothing. The trance became more intense as the vivid memory came into focus. The young soldier ties Judson's child-like hands to his parent's bed post, before opening the door for Charles to walk in. The soldier exited, locking the door behind him. The gaze of Commander Charles released urine into the child pants, resulting in a deviant, sickening alignment of Charles lips and teeth as he began to unbuckle his belt. A flash of light returned to an adult Judson. Back to the calls of his older brother behind him, attempting to snap him out of yet another memory loop.

"It's no time to daydream, J. He will cooperate," said Ronel, lowering his sword and reclaiming his energy back into his body as Mike extinguished the flames to Augustin's relief.

"The skull and shard are with Charles in a briefcase he holds near to him at all times. Augustin will give us Charles' itinerary in exchange for his exile and freedom. We will set him free after he makes the proper introductions to Gomez," said Ronel. Judson walked towards the pit, looking down at the destructive duo pacing and crawling over each other, anticipating a meal that would not be granted to them. He then turned his gaze to Augustin still reeling from the 3rd degree burns on his hands as he hung.

"Sorry boys, no human meat for you today," said Judson, turning to walk away, then stopping. "I remember a song my mother and father used to sing to me. About an innocent bird being warned to not follow a certain path to danger. It was simple and clear. Steer the innocent and young away from entities that seek to devour them. Are you familiar with the song Augustin?" asked Judson

"Yes, I am," he panted.

"Then may I ask why you opened the door for the demon to devour the innocent? Don't we know better through that nursery rhyme being passed down from generation to generation?" asked Judson. As the accountant heard the words, it occurred to him that his true worst fear had reared its head. Judson remembered exactly what happened to him.

"No! You are not supposed to remember! The priest......Please, do not do anything you will regret. I will help you get to Charles." Reasoned the now shaking prisoner.

"The priest?!" began a curious Judson as his brows furrowed.

"Judson, let's get the information and we can address that later," said Ronel putting his hand on Judson's cold shoulder.

"You know what bro, you're right. But I must ask Mr.

Augustin to indulge me before we go," replied Judson as he approached the still restrained man. "Sing the song with me. I'll start and you follow. Ready?"

Judson: *Ti Zwazo kote wap ale? - "Little bird where are you going"*
Augustin: *Map ale kay feyet lalo. - "I'm going to Feyet Lalo's house"*
Judson: *Feyet Lalo kon manje timoun - "Feyel Lalo eats Children"*
Augustin: *Siw ale, lap manje ou tou. - "If you go, it will eat you too"*

"Bird is on the menu," said Judson with a blank stare as he reached for the grip on Ronel's blade before its owner could react.

"Judson, NO!!" yelled Ronel, failing to get to his brother this time. Judson sliced the rope above Augustin, sending the screaming soul into the murky substance at the bottom of the silo. The screams were then muffled and silenced by the overwhelming jaws and chompers of the beasts. Ripping and twisting until he was no longer in one piece.

Chapter 17:

Chill

The boat ride back to civilian land was quiet. The ride back to Elam was quieter. The raucous revving of Judson's donk, blasted through thuds of bug remains smeared on his windshield. Maintaining their speed from Alligator Alley, all the way to the residential corridors of Melrose. Judson drew another tote from the roach blunt hanging from his lips. The bass from his music sent glass-shattering vibrations against each home as they sped past. Ronel, exhausted and annoyed, looked out of the other side of the vehicle, not wanting to engage Judson's gleeful flashing of his gold teeth. Knowing what was coming, he took out a flask from his side and sipped the contents slowly. They pulled up closer to the dark, moonlit entrance of the church, and there stood Elam. Ronel's recount of what happened in the swamp fueled the furious eyes that followed the car until it came to a full stop.

"WHAT was the meaning of THAT?!!" yelled Elam as Judson emerged upward, followed by Ronel from the passenger side. "I gave you specific instructions! He was to only be used as a pawn. You have no idea what you have done!"

"The world has one less maniac roaming free. For once in your life, would it pain you to utter the words "Thank you Judson."? smirked Judson as he leaned against the hood and lit another ganja-filled cigar. Ronel opened the passenger door to interject but hesitated. Although his brother took liberties into his own hands, he envied the mindless decision.

"What is the matter with you? You don't think anything through. Did you not think of the consequences?! Ronel, how could you let this happen?!" said Elam, limping down one step at a time. With a newspaper under his arm, the elderly priest was fervent with each step. Finally reaching the bottom, he threw the Haitian newspaper to the ground. Ronel walked over to pick it up and read the front page.

"Holy Shit!" said Ronel. "8 Senators slaughtered. I highly doubt that we had anything to do with this." Ronel continued to scan the paper but there was no mention of the culprit behind the killings. Elam limped over to Ronel, using his cane to knock the paper out of his hands.

"Your actions, or lack thereof, did not contribute to these killings. They took place before Augustin's death. Charles is determined, and so must you be," said Elam, putting his hand on Ronel's shoulder briefly, before turning his back to ascend the stairs. Judson propped up in anger, spitting the cigar out.

"That's it? No other bright ideas old man?!" yelled Judson as he started up the stairs after Elam.

"The instructions were just given, just not to you, brother. I will intercept Charles and take the skull and shard. You will stay here where your antics will not drastically affect the outcome of our plans again," said Ronel, hopping onto his motorcycle and starting it up.

"So, you are just going to cut me out of this?" asked Judson. "I deserve to be part of this just as much as you do!

"You lost that privilege when you decided to go into business for yourself," yelled Ronel.

"You damn right I did. I did what needed to be done, and that's killing off pedophiles and their various accomplices. Speaking of which, right before the fucker met the jaws of life, he mentioned you having something to do with me not knowing who he was. You care to explain yourself?" demanded Judson. Elam looked to the ground flustered, but picked up his gaze and put his attention back on them.

"Look at him, he can't even look me in the eye. He is still lying! And we are supposed to follow his every word because he is aging and we can't?! This shit is ass backwards!" spewed Judson before spitting at Elam's feet. Elam began to take a step as did Judson before Ronel stepped in between them.

"Ok, ok, let's not do this again," Ronel said. "Look Judson, I promise you that you will have your chance to kill Charles. We all will." Judson slapped his arm away and walked briskly towards his vehicle, getting in and slamming the door shut. Elam's strength left his legs, as he flopped down to sit on the steps.

"I will do what is necessary," said Ronel to Elam. Their eyes met, and a silent agreement was made. Ronel walked over to Judson who raised his middle finger to him while looking straight ahead. The elder brother went to press, but instead shifted his approach to his awaiting motorcycle. Starting, then revving his engine before jetting off into the night's abyss. Judson held the custom wheel as his clenched fist created cracks in the fabric of the material.

"He is better suited for this," said Elam from the steps. "Let him do what he is great at. This will require a lighter touch. I can understand-"

"You don't understand shit about me!" interrupted Judson "You don't know what it is to lose anyone or anything. Fuck this hero bullshit!"

Entering his key into the ignition, the angry brawler fought with the older security feature of the ignition that caused the key to lock into place unless turned in the correct fashion.

"And the worst part is that you think you are a suitable replacement for my father and YOU ARE NOT! YOU WILL NEVER BE HIM! You cannot begin to fathom what we go through trying to get answers that our brains can't materialize. You didn't save us with that serum, you damned us to an eternal hell. Yet somehow you think dragging your old sickly ass to visit me behind the wall, playing chess in silence, then walking off with a pat on the back would make you half the man my father was?!" Judson started his engine, the muscle of his engine growling like a predator to the moon. "I don't answer to you. I will get to Charles, one way or the other."

Elam's voice barely made it to a distraught, yet determined Judson who had now put the car into drive. Elam rose and again hobbled down the steps to get closer, as Judson reluctantly slammed the gear to park.

"I never sought to replace what I could never be," began Elam, now closer to the rattling old school car. "Your father meant the world to me, and he was strong, just like you. But your father had limitations, just like you do right now. Yet, I know that you can break through them, you just have to be patient," reasoned Elam. Judson nodded his head, shrugged, and dragged as much smoke as he could into his lungs before blowing it in Elam's direction.

"You know what is fucked up? You think giving us that serum was saving us but it only damned us to hell. Or purgatory…you have the collar you should know. But something tells me even you don't believe half the shit you say on that altar. Answer me this. What kind of God allows the innocent to be killed in front of their kids? Then as a sick joke, give them the power that could have saved them? I'll tell you. A God that is no good, and if he sits on the throne then there is no good in this world. Just enough assholes who are afraid to do the right thing. Those who take advantage, and a handful of gunslingers who randomly decide who's right and who's wrong. And you are the last person that should be telling me when and how to pull the trigger," said Judson. Shifting the gear on the side of the steering wheel, he peeled off into the night. Leaving a trail of his sound system, cigar and muffler smoke in a cloud behind him.

"If only he was patient, it would all make sense," said Elam leaning on his cane, rocking as each painful step caused his facial muscle to spasm. Slowly making his way back to his quarters.

Chapter 18:

Harmless

S earching the mind was not a task Sonya enjoyed. There was something missing, a component so essential yet foreign to the seeker. As she sipped on another margarita shoved in her direction by Manny, the newly appointed agent drowned herself in another incomplete memory.

"Hello? Earth to Sonya, where are you? It's like you left us and went into another dimension," said Manny after flicking the melted ice water from her drink onto Sonya's face.

"Sorry Manny, I'm just thinking about my next assignment," replied Sonya. Flashing a grin she hoped would put off Manny from asking another follow up question. Before she could part her lips, Sonya took the drink down in one gulp before erupting. "Wooooo! I got promoted!"

"Look who is in the spirit?! There's my best friend! The only reason why I'm in this little nerd spot is because you like singing here. You my girl, and it's all about you. So get out your head and let's drink!"

Raising their glasses, the two longtime friends shared a laugh. It was rare for any of the Jean-Baptiste three to have real connections outside of each other and Elam, but Manny was different. Although she did not know much about Sonya's past or her mysterious, unchanged youth, she never questioned it. At least, not after the first time that Sonya refused to or could recollect a concrete answer. Manny was her constant connection to normal, and so was Jesse. The only man she truly trusted with her life. After the other night at Sonya's, the friends did what they always did; kept silent about the supernatural events surrounding their best friend.

"I knew I heard the thot-mating call. Aren't you two too old to be acting like 20 something year old hot girls?" laughed Jesse as he made his regular, fashionably late appearance.

"I am 29 stupid," said Manny, shooting him a death stare.

"You've been 29 for three years now. We all know you been lying about your age forever," replied Jesse, sitting next to Sonya and motioning for the bartender.

"So how long you going to keep lying about liking Sonya?" pressed Manny. Jesse coughed on the large gulp of rum on the rocks. "Better question Jesse, what color panties does she have on?"

Jesse sat up to look into Sonya's eyes. Their pupils were

135

playing a dangerous game of seduction and goofy, as they often did to mock another of Manny's crazy theories. Jesse took in the sight of Sonya's perfect lips, and the curvature that began at her slim waist. With a slight smile, he submitted his wager.

"I'm guessing maroon," said the confident tech wiz.

"Sonya, is he right?" asked Manny

"Lucky guess. Something tells me I need to keep that lid on my laptop closed," joked Sonya.

"Don't flatter yourself. I'm not concerned about your unmentionables. I'm about my money and it's about time I got myself a raise for my expertise. Besides, if I wanted to see you naked, I don't need cameras. I'm willing to bet my voice is so much embedded in your brain function by now, one word will have you like honey on my fingers," said Jesse as the two again engaged in a tense stand-off.

"I got one word. LAME!" interrupted Manny, as she directed Jesse's attention to the drink the bartender left in front of him.

"Frekan!(idiot)" shot Jesse, as he took down the rest of his drink.

"Lan Merde!(Fuck off)" replied Manny.

"Guys we came to have fun. Now who is going first?" said Sonya playfully.

"I am," said Jesse as he motioned for another round. "Sonya is not the only one here with vocals. I can sing too. Watch and learn Grimace!" Walking towards the organizer of the karaoke event, Jesse made his request. Getting up on stage and beginning his rendition of Alicia Keys' "If I Ain't Got You". Sonya's ear for music was irritated by each note Jesse fumbled over in her favorite song. She tried to maintain a supportive smile. Sonya went for another sip of her drink when her purse began to buzz. Reaching in to retrieve her device, she saw Elam's name and quickly threw the phone back into its housing.

"He's calling again, isn't he? You should pick up. Maybe he is genuinely sorry," said Manny, as she nudged the back of Sonya's arm.

"I don't feel like dealing with him right now. I never thought he would lie to me. My brothers; I understand their asshole tendencies. But it stings more from Elam. The closest thing I have to a father, and he stuck me in that back with a knife he didn't train me for."

"If I could play devil's advocate, you did lie to him too. Two wrongs don't make a right, but not fixing the situation with family will haunt you. Do you really want that?"

"Look at the Ricky Lake on you, Manny. You sound like you need a talk show."

"If I had a talk show, it would be all about finding a man, keeping a man, and how to keep a side nigga invested," laughed Manny.

"Same ol Manny. You're never going to change, are you?" The two made another toast. Turning their attention back to Jesse, who had his focus on Sonya.

"Girl listen, he ain't just singing to be singing. Jesse is

singing to you. I may hate his guts, but I know when a man wants what he is looking at," chuckled Manny.

"Jesse is cool, we work great with each other, and he is funny. But the last thing I need is to turn a good friendship into something disastrous."

"Oh, so you have thought about it?! I knew it was something more between you two," said Manny, tickling her best friend's side.

"Stop! There isn't Manny. Your antenna is off." Sonya playfully slapped her hands away then immediately grabbed Manny's wrist with a firm vice grip. Something had troubled her and entered her space. Something negative but familiar. Manny contested in pain, which took Sonya a few seconds to register. Sonya let go and stood up to look at the entrance. Her fears were confirmed. A woman dressed in an all-black business suit, with red hair draped over her shoulders. Followed by a handful of men who cast a dark energy that caused all chatter in the club to cease. The lead visitor glazed a clear applicator onto her lips as she stopped to look at her reflection in one of the mirrors that lined the bar's walls. Handing over the beauty accessory to one of the men behind her without breaking her black-aligned focus on Sonya.

"There is my Little Bird! It's been a while Sonya," said Banshee while ejecting and releasing the Odachi sword by a perfect inch each time before it audibly clicked back into its sheath at her side. "My how your posture has declined since we last trained together. If I were you, I would have already snapped my neck by now. A demon walks in and you are still assessing."

"I thought you were dead. What are you doing here?" asked Sonya as she reached behind her slowly for one of the hidden blades in her purse.

"I like my prey to think that all is well before death swiftly overtakes them. It is a sweet sight to see my reflection in the eyes of those cut down by my sword. Kind of like the look you have in yours right now."

"I don't fear you," Sonya gripped the handle of her hidden blade with an intense clutch.

"Um, Sonya, who is this bitch? Is there a problem?! Do we got a problem?!" questioned Manny as she joined Sonya at her side.

"A problem that you don't want," replied Banshee, removing her silk red gloves from her fingers as her gaze never broke from Sonya.

"Oh this Bitch!" began Manny before stepping forward and being abruptly pulled back by Sonya.

"Manny! This isn't the time. Seriously, sit back! I have this covered," said Sonya, attempting to calm her down.

"Does she not know that if I were to blow in her direction, her limbs will scatter all over this bar before the bones and tissue remember to bleed?" laughed Banshee resting her hand now on the handle of her sword.

"She is not your business," said Sonya, motioning to Jesse

to grab Manny who desperately wanted a piece of the stranger. Sonya turned her focus back to Banshee and her entourage. "You have yet to state why you are here."

"I have come to issue you a warning, Little Bird. As the new leader of the Candiru, I felt the need to privy you with a visit before just killing you. Abandon your pursuit of Charles Clerveaux. Neither you, your brothers, or the old clergyman can stop what is coming," cautioned Banshee.

"I know nothing of the pursuit," replied Sonya, now exposing the short blade at her side. Banshee quickly noticed and widened her stance. The men behind her would follow suit with blades and guns of their own.

"It is my job to know all threats, even the small, worthless, benign ones. Cut your losses and go back to slitting the throats of mid-level crime bosses and their minions. This luxury will only be granted to you once."

"And if I do not adhere?" asked Sonya with a slight grin.

"Then," began Banshee, as she bolted towards Sonya, swiftly removing her sword from its sheath, colliding it with Sonya's knife. With each slice Banshee attempted to throw her way, Sonya countered. With an upward swing of her blade, Banshee instinctively knew that her rival would defend. She took advantage of the intended distraction, tripping Sonya onto her back. Quickly recovering, Sonya kipped up to go into the offensive, before stopping at the sight of Banshee's blade at Manny's throat.

"Let's hear you put those vocal cords to good use, Little Bird! Or I will cut hers out right where she stands!" belted Banshee.

"No! Spare her Banshee! This is between me and you!" yelled Sonya.

"Just like a good pet," laughed Banshee, lowering her blade as a slight blood droplet began to form on Manny's neck. Slowly they circled back to their original places when Banshee walked in. Never breaking the energy reflecting off of each other's irises. Sonya lunged towards Manny to assess the cut, to find that it was not as severe as she thought. Banshee begins to walk towards the entrance and stops. Taking a blade like Sonya's from the side of her coat.

"Oh, and Little Bird? Heed my words. If you don't stay away? EVERYONE is fair game!" said Banshee, throwing the short knife into the air, and leaping up to follow it. Using the handle of her sword as a bat, she swung at the smaller blade, sending it towards Jesse who was still standing on the stage. Sonya then used her weapon to change the trajectory of the projectile. Lodging it into the wall behind him, missing his head by centimeters. By the time Sonya's attention returned to the doorway, they were gone. Silence still rested on the room, until Jesse spoke over the microphone.

"What the hell? What is it with you attracting sharp shit aimed at me?!" yelled Jesse in Sonya's direction. Relieved that Jesse was not hurt, Sonya attended to Manny once again.

141

"Are you ok Manny?" asked Sonya, using a napkin to pat at the fresh wound on Manny's neck.

"Who was that Sonya?" asked Manny.

"A nightmare. A really bad nightmare that I never thought I would see again. I was twelve when Elam had the motorcycle accident. He suffered some extremely bad burns and cuts, and stayed bed ridden in a Seminary Hospital. He sent me and Ronel to Japan to further our martial arts studies under an old friend of his, while Judson was serving time in Juvie. It's there that I encountered Banshee. By then she was the fiercest combat student the school has ever seen. We have had our share of run-ins, neither of them friendly. "Little Bird" was the nickname she gave me after our last spar ended with her face getting scratched."

The bartender and staff of the bar emerged from their hiding places. With all eyes trained on them, Sonya pulled Manny by the hand and headed towards the entrance. Jesse followed right after them into the darkness outside. The calm of the stars and moon caught their attention shortly after looking around for any remaining threats. Guilt washed over Sonya as pools of tears collected under her eyes as she looked into the distance. Without a word, her friends gathered to console her.

"Looks like I need to see Elam," whispered Sonya. "I can't afford to lose anymore of the people I love to this."

"We will come with you," said Jesse. Manny nodded in agreement.

"No guys, I got this," replied Sonya. "Right now, I need you to take Manny home. Then I need you to pull everything that you can on any recent Candiru chatter. If what Banshee says is true, then it's possible that the mission is compromised. I won't be able to just show my face at that Gala without being made by Candiru foot soldiers."

"I may have a way for you to blend in without a problem." suggested Manny.

"I don't think having my face beat to the gods is going to help me Manny."

"Who said anything about basic bitch makeup?" smirked Manny. "By the time I'm done, you will be another person." Sonya contemplated and weighed the possibilities of now involving Manny after what just took place. She had to take control of the situation. The thought of being powerless enraged her.

"Ok Manny, let's see what you can do. For now, I have to go see the old man."

Chapter 19:

Mission 509

He felt the clouds looking back at him as he peered into the night sky. The buzz from inside the cabin of the Bombardier Challenger aircraft, coupled with the constant radio chatter began to annoy Ronel. Tapping his fingers on the handle of his machete, he gazed past the closed blind. Through the clear stretched acrylic, into the stoic marriage of darkness, gas, and star light.

"10 minutes to the drop point," said Jesse through the com in Ronel's ear. "Now keep in mind, you have absolutely 20 minutes to retrieve the items. Ground recon pictures show an old briefcase that Charles keeps tucked away under his wheelchair at all times."

Ronel sorted through the photos on his phone, constantly zooming to Charles' face. The scar was fading. No longer a memory that gave him solace when the alcohol wouldn't. Pulling back his braids into a knot, he placed the device face down and drank a glass of rum.

"Thank you, Jesse, for finding me a plane on such short notice."

"No problem. I just want to help as much as I can. With Sonya preoccupied with her new assignment, I have the time to dedicate my resources elsewhere," said Jesse typing away inside his dungeon-like office nearly 1000 miles away. Six screens stacked on top of each other reflected off of his glasses. Jesse monitored the sky, and local authority chatter. All while controlling a drone hovering in silence over the Clerveaux family compound nestled on a 15-acre plot of farmland. The thermo video feed of multiple white human figures patrolling the massive home structure played in real time, with one figure he kept great attention on. Charles sat in a wheelchair in the master bedroom, having not moved an inch for hours.

"So, this cripple really has done yall some damage, huh?" Jesse asked jokingly.

"Oh, this shit funny to you, nerd?" yelled Judson through the com in his ear. Sitting in his crimson beast parked in an apartment complex, Judson was also monitoring the live feed.

"I swear I didn't mean nothing by it."

"Sounds like someone should close out their porn tabs and shut the fuck up about things they don't understand!"

"Ok Judson, that's enough. Lay off of him," reasoned Ronel.

"Only reason I asked you to be part of this is because Jesse's eyes can't see movements like we can. So, I need you both to be on your job."

"No prob bro. The only reason why I ain't beat you to Haiti is because you know I hate planes. I don't know why we couldn't just take a speed boat and pop up on that nigga!" said Judson.

"Noise Judson. Noise. Not everything gotta start with a bang. They would have clocked our location miles away if we showed up that way," said Ronel, while adjusting his chute bag, inspecting the rip cord, and his blades' sheath.

"Two minutes to drop point," said Jesse.

"You mentioned that my sister was put on assignment. Let me guess, another observe and report detail?" smirked Ronel while still making the necessary adjustments. He opened the custom hatch, bombarded by the loud night's wind and calm of the atmosphere.

"She isn't on just any detail. She has been tasked with getting chummy with Charles' son Mathieu," Jesse blurted before he realized the secret he let slip.

"WHAT?!" yelled Ronel.

"Well, I'll be damned. Told you about them alphabet boys. Now look at what they got sis doing," joked Judson.

"Shut up Judson! Why in the fuck did you not tell me this from the get go Jesse?" fumed Ronel as the wind whipped at the fabric of his camouflage pants.

"Honestly man, I don't know what is secret and what I

should be making noise about when it comes to yall," started Jesse. "I'm watching my best friend fight with herself internally and now this new threat. Hoping to God that another one of her episodes don't have the refrigerator flying at my head!" Ronel halted his next words. Sympathizing with Jesse's position in enduring Sonya's erratic power for years in his absence.

"My bad Jesse, I'm sorry," began Ronel.

"Oh my God, would y'all two stop with the 'I want your daughter's hand in marriage' soap opera yall got going on?! We get it Jesse, you in love with our sister. Ronel, stop trippin' about Sonya, she got it. We all had to figure it out when you not around, so don't start the protective shit now," scoffed Judson.

"I swear Judson, this is NOT the time..." began Ronel

"Jump! Jump NOW!" yelled Jesse. Ronel shook off the urge to level his brother who, once again, hit the one part of him still bleeding heavily. Taking a deep breath, he leaned forward and allowed the momentum of his weight to propel him out of the hatch and into a free fall. With his eyes closed, the images of Charles standing over his mother and pulling the trigger pinched at his heart. The wind wiped his face as droplets formed under his eyes. The pain rose into his esophagus and breached his nasal cavity. He wanted to scream, but he fought it, and won.

"Wait for the signal to deploy your chute," said Jesse, looking for a sweet spot to slow down Ronel's descent. "Now! Deploy. Deploy!"

Ronel pulled on the cord and a small chute halted his

momentum towards the dark earth.

"You should be landing about 1.4 kilometers outside of the compound. Make your way north and you will see a slight incline on the wall. You should be able to get over it and into the garden. Take out the Candiru on the other side and you should be virtually invisible after I cause the power failure," Jesse explained.

"Good. Thank you, Jesse," said Ronel.

"As long as Sonya doesn't know I'm helping you, keep me out of the crossfire. That crazy ninja girl with red hair really has her worked up. Last place I want to be is between you all throwing daggers around like Gordon Ramsey."

"So, Banshee is back?" asked Ronel after landing safely to the ground and cutting away the chute.

"Funny how all of you assassins know each other on a first name basis. She claimed to be the new leader of the Candiru," said Jesse.

"Interesting," relayed Ronel. "Judson, you have been real quiet. Are you still reading us?"

"Oh, I'm here. Sounds like you two have it under control. I got some shit on my end that requires my attention. Like this new dude that Shona thinks she can start seeing walking up to her apartment," said Judson.

"You have got to be kidding me!" yelled Ronel.

"Judson, I hope to God you are paying attention to that live feed. The Candiru are known for their element of surprise. Only you can tell Ronel if there is suspicious activity. It won't be long until they notice the recon drone," warned Jesse.

"I'm in the car looking at this dumb ass screen, I got it! Besides, can't you just use your flame to see your way through?"

"Sure, use my fire to draw all the attention to me, while blinding the thermo vision you are supposed to be watching. Real good suggestion little brother."

"You're welcome, Jit. I'm watching," insisted Judson.

"Ok, heads up! Charles is on the move. You are going to have to breach that wall a lot sooner than we planned. Go!" instructed Jesse. "Remember, in and out, and back in time to get to the Gala tonight."

"Copy," said Ronel, as he briskly made his way to the wall and launched himself to the top. Just as they expected, a Candiru guard walked below and noticed Ronel's shadow from the moonlight. Ronel pounced, and slit his throat seamlessly, dragging the body into a corner. "Jesse, cut the lights."

Jesse tapped away and within seconds the compound was void of power. Moving over to the controls of the drone, Jesse circled the flying device overhead and captured the thermo motions of numerous Candiru spreading out into the courtyard and the garden. But one was unaccounted for.

"Judson! I lost him, did you see where Charles went?" asked Jesse frantically while spreading the drone's feed to all of his available screens. "All I'm reading is the heat signature left on the wheelchair. Judson?"

"Oh for real?! So this how we getting down huh?" barked

Judson as the door to his donk could be heard slamming behind him.

"Judson? Judson, who are you talking to?" inquired Jesse.

"Judson, what are you doing here? And why are you stalking me?" said a female voice from Judson's end.

"I ain't stalking you technically, I paid the lease to this place three years out! I think I got a say in who comes in or out!" yelled Judson in the background. "Who is this nigga Shona? And what is he reaching for? Doesn't he know what I did to the last one?" The mystery man stepped in front of Shona and pulled out a silver pistol. Shona stepped in between them.

"No, don't do that. He is my EX-boyfriend; he was just leaving," said Shona.

"Judson! I know you are not doing this while we are in the middle of a mission. Get back to the car!" yelled Jesse. Ronel closed his eyes in anger, but did not want to draw any attention to himself as he laid low in the brush.

"Shut up nerd!" said Judson in the com.

"Shut up?! Nigga I will shoot you right here, right now!" yelled Shona's companion. Judson begins to laugh. He stops briefly to look at the man, then his gun, and then to Shona who knew what was about to transpire. Judson launched into another laughing fit while raising his hands to the air.

"Hey my hands are up man, please don't shoot me. But, tell me something. Did Shona tell you I'm a connoisseur of automobiles?" asked a smug Judson looking the man directly in the eyes.

"I don't know shit about you."

"But I can tell a lot about you just by looking at you. Let's see, you're an Audi guy, right?" asked Judson backing up towards three vehicles parked in the direction Shona and her date came from. "Wait no. You look Haitian too, so you might be an Infiniti guy. Nope, maybe you decided to be a different breed and turned into an Impala guy."

"Oh Jesus. Here we go," said Shona under her breath.

"What do you mean here we go? I'm about to lay this nigga out if he touch my car," affirmed her date. Shona put her hand on the pistol, encouraging the oblivious man to lower his weapon.

"You might as well let this play out, bullets aren't going to work here"

"Not going to work?!"

By now Ronel could not take another second of the lover's quarrel happening in his ear. "Judson, I swear to God! If you are about to do what I think you are about to do, I will cut you in half when I get back. Judson!" yelled Ronel.

"Ladies and Gentleman of the settlement known as Clipper Cove Apartments," yelled Judson as his demeanor switched to that of a ringmaster. "My name is Judson, and I just caught my fiancé fucking with a nigga that's not me. So, for your viewing pleasure I will display to you a rare performance of a little number I'd like to call "The Junkyard Overture". Judson cracked his knuckles, then performed a quick stretching routine before

151

taking a few steps back. He ran towards the gray Chevy Impala and impaled the passenger side door repeatedly with his knee before leaping into the air. He lands both fists swiftly into the roof of the car, caving it in completely as glass shattered everywhere. Making his way to the top of the hood, he jumped up and down until the engine and transmission were resting on the asphalt below the wreckage. Judson continued the same rampage towards a black Infiniti, which caught on fire. He then directs his attention to the Audi.

"Now for the crescendo!" said Judson as he grabbed the front bumper of the Infiniti and dragged it toward the white, later model Audi sedan. He walked behind the burning vehicle and cocked his leg back, kicking the burning inferno onto the top of the Audi. He then walked over to the stunned, speechless, and now urinating young man standing next to Shona and motions for his gun. Without breaking the stare down, he points the weapon in the direction of the carnage and pulls the trigger. Sending a bullet into the gas tank of the Audi which explodes into a cloud of fire and smoke. Judson blew Shona a kiss and a wink, and took a bow as he walked back towards his donk.

"Judson! Judson! What the hell was that? Judson!" yelled Ronel. Before he could get another word out, chills seeped into spinal column, reverberating throughout his ligaments.

"Ronel, I lost the feed. Judson do you still have a feed?" asked Jesse attempting to regain control of the drone that was not responding to his maneuvers.

"No, I don't. It's all static on my end," said Judson as he picked up the tablet, hitting it as if it was a TV from the 90s. Ronel stepped out of the brush and noticed that the darkness in the garden was different. There were no stars, no moon. It was as if the compound had retracted a black roof over itself entirely.

"Someone knows I'm here," whispered Ronel.

"How do you know?" asked Jesse.

"Because I can feel eyes," answered Ronel as he slowly unsheathed his machete. "No more technology now, I've obviously been compromised. Time to do this the one way I know how." Ronel takes a flask of rum from his side and attempts to down it when suddenly the bottom of it falls to the ground, leaving a perfectly cut top half in his hand. His pupils go from brown to amber until both eyes are engulfed in flames which then reveals that he is surrounded by multiple members of the Candiru equipped with night vision glasses. A sword fight ensued. Ronel holds his own but suffers numerous cuts to his body. As they rapidly heal, another onslaught of sword wielding assassins flanks him. Outnumbered, yet skilled to engage multiple enemies, he manages to kill everyone in his path, except for one. The last remaining target puzzled him, making his way closer. The vertically challenged assassin readied his trembling machete. Ronel allowed the flames to fully engulf him to get a better look, and the startling revelation made his knees buckle. It was a child, scared out of its mind, and yet confidently stuck in a fighting stance well beyond his years.

"What is this?" asked Ronel "Hey kid, put that down and run away!" The young boy maintained his position as Ronel drew closer. Using his machete, Ronel lowered the child's blade and knelt down to one knee. Before he could speak another word, the child's blade was lifted, applying resistance to Ronel's. Breaking the metal connection, the child stepped back and circled Ronel before making a swipe of his blade at the inflamed veteran. Surprised, Ronel stood to his feet and was met with a barrage of skilled hacks that he defended against. He then stunned the child with a blunt punch to his gut. The child heaved for air while attempting to stand back up.

"Where are your parents, kid? This is not a game a child should play. Run off and save yourself!" yelled Ronel.

"Bravo!" said a voice from the other side of the field. The sound of fresh grass crushing gradually developed as the dark figure's features became clear. The dapper dressed, salt and pepper haired man hobbled to the side of the child. "Funny how you didn't heed the words that just came out of your mouth all those years ago. You look thirsty Ronel, care for a drink?" asked Charles as his frail hands raised a toast with a glass of wine.

"No thank you, coward! I'll settle for your head instead," replied Ronel as he energized his flaming aura, sending the embers to anything that would catch fire to illuminate their surroundings.

"Such Malice for a young man like yourself to still hold for me. A drink will do wonders. I mean, you did drink the serum, didn't you?" asked Charles as his old arthritis filled hand attempted to bring the glass to his mouth, his eyes rolling up to lock in a stare with vengeance.

"Look you hacked face Idi Amin, child-soldier-science-day-project, pedo-fucker! Hand over the case, and I may think about not finishing the job I started on your face," said Ronel pointing the tip of the blade at Charles' forehead. Charles grinned and let the glass fall to the ground.

"You come to my home uninvited. You insult me in the presence of company. Most of whom you have left dead for the cleaning staff to attend to in the morning. You assault a child that seeks revenge for what you did, and now you want to rob me of possessions? You're really not a nice guest," chuckled Charles as he raised his right palm up slowly. The child's eyes became pitch black as he stood up. Ronel stepped back, pondering what he was witnessing. Yet, his focus never left Charles.

"What the fuck are you talking about? I know nothing of this child."

"Oh, but you leave children like him in your wake when a death contract says his parents are evil. Children are innocent, they see nothing past whoever feeds and shelters them. And when some US military bred thug comes and kills their parents because they kidnapped a broken French speaking old twat to provide for said child. Well, you can understand how motivations can be brought into full view. I am simply providing him the opportunity to right the wrong," said Charles

"Right the wrong......the games you play are sick. And it's game over. Now hand over the case!" demanded Ronel. Charles slowly reached behind him and a black object flew into his grasp. He then threw it at Ronel's feet.

"It is yours. I have no need for that hollow relic. It has served its purpose," said Charles. Ronel was taken aback by how easily he parted with the artifacts. Opening the case to inspect its contents, the shard laid in one compartment as pieces of the skull were strewn about. "I am a giver, Ronel. I give to those who ask of me their truest desires. Now in order for me to continue to be as generous as I have been to you, I will need your pursuit to end here. I may even have a place for you at my side. Consider these things as I consider whether you leave here in one piece. Should you refuse."

"Enough!" yelled Ronel as he swiped his machete at Charles. The blade was blocked by the young child's weapon, and the unnatural battle of strength caused the sharp ends to scrape against each other. Ronel stared into the abyss filled eyes of the controlled puppet. Breaking the metal connection, the child launched a barrage of slicing and stabbing attacks as Ronel evaded. The fit of youth rage caused the more experienced swordsman to once again pity him. Looking and finding his opening shot, Ronel knocked the child unconscious to the ground with the butt of his blade.

"I don't want to fight a weakling, I want to fight you coward!" said Ronel, staring back at Charles. Judson's voice came into focus on the com.

"It's about time you pulled out the stick on him! Now kill that muthafucker!" yelled Judson. Ronel took a few steps toward Charles as the flaming wings of a Phoenix engulfed him.

"I will make this quick Charles. You won't feel a thing but a slight sting and then it lights out," assured Ronel as his blade heated rapidly.

"On the contrary, you have no idea how much quicker it will be for you," sneered Charles, adjusting his posture. Ronel charged towards him with rage. Out of nowhere, Charles was quickly engulfed in a dark aura that took the shape of a man clearly holding a sword. Charles and the dark aura instantly disappeared right before his eyes. Ronel looked around. He turns to find the dark figure standing in front of him with a sword to his throat. Ronel jumped back to get his bearings, and advanced again. This time clashing metal with the supernatural being. Ronel is struck in his face numerous times, causing him to do something rare. Retreat to safety to assess his enemy. The fighting style of the being was very similar to that of Elam and the Candiru. The incorporation of sword fighting and strikes were right out of Elam's playbook. He questioned how Charles could have gained such power and ability. Before he could wrap his mind around it, his body was now beginning to give in to the blood loss he had been suffering. Ronel fell to a knee, but plunged his blade into the ground defiantly as he attempted to stand. Still looking around for Charles, he notices the dark figure standing in the distance. Although it was black, the clothing was that of a regal commander. His stance was that of power and prestige. Ronel then noticed the appearance of another figure. An exact replica of the one previous. Then another, and another, until a small militia surrounded him. Mustering the strength he had left, Ronel stood to his feet. Tapping into his power as his grip on his machete shook at the sight of the impending barrage. Bracing himself to attack first, his vision blurred and blood particles drifted in the air. His tongue tasted his own blood. He was hit, but could not see where the strike came from. His sword flew out of his hand into the muddy grass of the terrain. Suddenly, one of the figures appeared in a flash directly in front of him, burying strikes into his confused and fearful face. Ronel fell to the ground and noticed a black boot coming towards his face. And then nothing. No noise, no vision, just a void. Just him alone with his thoughts.

"Am I dead?" asked Ronel to himself.

"No, not yet," said Charles. Ronel shuttered as goosebumps spread throughout his skin. Then there was a light, dimming and shining at the same time as darkness surrounded it. The sound of wind and grass next to his ears startled him to sit up from his temporary knockout. Turning his head to his left, then his right. Then back again where his eyes met the dark figure looking right back at him, face to face. For the first time in a long time, genuine fear set in. Ronel saw no eyes, but knew that his vulnerability was on full display for the dark man to do with him as he pleased.

The dark aura began to peel away from the top of the figure's head, down to his neck, revealing Charles' rickety smile yet younger appearance.

"I'm going to kill you, but I need you to take a message to those who you love so much. Let them know that they too will die should they make the same mistake you have made this evening," said Charles. As another smile formed on Charles' face, the surgical scars around his jaw line began to bleed. Ronel, still stunned, watched as the horrifying figure stepped back and stumbled. Charles held his face, screaming in agony as the skin around his jaw and cheeks stretched and rejuvenated. Charles fell to his knees, struggling to keep control. Then, the darkness returned and covered his face, calming him. The dark aura levitated Charles slightly off the ground. He turned to look at Ronel before vanishing. The other dark copies disappeared as well, along with the bodies of the Candiru Ronel had defeated. Leaving only the still unconscious child laying.

"What was that?" yelled Jesse.

"I don't know," coughed Ronel. Feeling the burning sensation from the air whipping at his flowing wounds. "I need an evac. The bleeding has not stopped."

"You're not healing?" asked Judson.

"No," answered Ronel softly before passing out again.

"Ronel? Ronel!" yelled Judson.

Chapter 20:

Balance

Wiping the sweat from his brow, Elam continued to cut away at another root that was feeding into a cluster of weeds. His wrist shook as age had its way with his joints. Applying pressure to the half-rusted clippers required more strength than he had. Yet the sound of life being cut from menacing greenery gave him solace. Removing his straw hat drenched in hours of hard work, he noticed the familiar blur of Sonya's appearance approaching him.

"To what do I owe this surprise visit my love?" asked Elam, as he reached for the garden's stone chair to use as leverage to stand.

"Somehow I think you already know why," replied Sonya. "I'm going to give you one more chance not to lie to me."

"If you have a question, my child, ask me."

"No, you listen. You took my choice away. All in the name of trying to keep me from getting hurt because you think I'm delicate. I can handle myself just fine Elam! More than I can say about Ronel who is laying up still bleeding from his wounds."

"How did you…"

"Did you forget that I can feel every cut and every gunshot wound my idiot brothers endure?" interrupted Sonya. "Plus Jesse told me everything."

"You will never understand Sonya. Until it is the right time, you can't understand. I shielded you from this not because I thought you were weak. I did it so that they could never get to you. It will all make sense someday. Even if I have to die protecting you from danger, I will do it gladly."

"Still talking in riddles like it's fun. I'm not seven anymore Elam! I can take care of myself. And since Ronel and the other dummy failed to take down Charles, I will." Sonya turned to walk away.

"Revenge solves nothing," said Elam. "It just opens a graveyard for you, your descendants, and the descendants of the ones who wronged you believing they are justified. It took me a while to bury your parents in my mind, since it was impossible to give them a proper burial. I implore you to do the same for the sake of your soul. What sense does it make to lay next to skeletons?"

Sonya closed her eyes in annoyance, and let out a muffled cackle. "Yet, one walks among us in the living now, doesn't he?

Charles has acquired something more powerful than even Ronel could handle, and you sit here clipping at flowers like its sunshine and French horns." Sonya threw down a large folder next to him. Picking it up, Elam looked at the briefing and his eyebrows tensed up.

"Don't tell me you are going to do this Sonya. This Gala is a hornet's nest! Do not let these people with high-level clearances talk you into something way over their heads." Elam attempted to stand, but fell back into his seat before entering into a brief coughing fit. Sonya rushed to his side, aiding him in retrieving the folded cloth that was stained with old blood particles.

"What is going on Elam? I can feel the discomfort you have, but I can't put a finger on what it is," prodded Sonya.

"I'm fine. Just heed my words. Getting mixed up with the Clerveaux family is the quickest way to a death certificate. If Ronel did not heal from his wounds, what makes you think you have a better chance at surviving whatever Charles has become?" Sonya took a water bottle from her bag, and gave it to him to drink. Elam drank halfway before continuing.

"Daughter, I almost lost one of you because I bended at the anger of your brothers. I will not make the same mistake with you. If I lost you I don't know what I would do. I can't lose anyone anymore," lamented Elam. Sonya rubbed his back and embraced him. The droplets from his eyes soaked into the pores of her forearm.

"I have never seen you crack. I wish I had the ability to just not do anything but I can't let this slide. He sent Banshee," said Sonya. Elam quickly wiped away his tears and sat up.

"Did she threaten your friends?"

"Yes. Banshee does not hesitate to kill. The fact that she did not kill Manny or Jesse in that bar scares me more. She gave me a warning, just like you are warning me now. I know too much about her Elam. She is playing with me and the ones I love like we're food."

"An assassin that plays with their prey is wicked. It's past just a job at that point. She has a vested interest in making you suffer."

"You taught me that assassins like this should be cut down at the root. I can't sleep with the possibility of something happening to them, my brothers, or even you. I am doing this mission, Elam. I just came to let you know. Not to seek your permission."

"You are asking for it, but you are too blinded to notice. I do not give you my blessing for what you are about to do, but I understand the motivations. And that is all I have to say on the matter." Elam grabbed his staff and struggled to his feet. Sonya assisted him. They both began to walk towards the entrance of the small garden. Elam stopped and placed his trembling hand on Sonya's cheek.

"When you encounter your brothers, I pray that you find the strength to forgive one another. They chose their paths to glory, and you soon will find that no such thing awaits you if you follow," Elam said as he kissed her forehead and smiled. "Sing my song for me child."

Sonya's shoulder's deflated while letting out a sigh. Elam encouraged her by holding her hands. Sonya began to sing while he stared into the clouds as her voice danced along his eardrums. Sending his mind to her mother, singing the song to Sonya as she slept in a wooden crib. Rocking back and forth, the clergyman joined in with his own raspy voice. At the last note, Sonya released his hands and left him.

As the distance between them widened, she put back on her sunglasses and walked toward her car and entered.

"What did he say?" asked Jesse sitting in the passenger seat.

"He didn't have to say it. Full speed ahead. We are taking this bastard down tonight."

Chapter 21:

Vakabon

The wall's pattern seemed to lift from its surface, staring back at him. Yet another interviewer trying to make a name for themselves. Questions were hurled at Mathieu about the one topic that was causing his poll numbers to slip. Hands sweaty, and trying not to make his next empty swallow audible, he let out a breath to recover oxygen. The nerves on his face were pulsing as he attempted to keep his anxiety and anger at bay.

"What do you know about the murders of our Senate?! Hello?! Monsieur Clerveaux you cannot deny the Haitian people the truth! Monsieur Clerveaux?!" yelled Maxo Pirus of the Haitian Guardian. Mathieu gazed across the room, as his assistant and campaign manager motioned for him to answer. Taking a deep, and almost obstructed breath, he closed his eyes and leveled his angst.

"Fennel, I have pledged to always be transparent since the day my candidacy was unanimously approved by the Senate before their untimely demise. I have reiterated again and again that I barely made it out alive when those terrorists attempted to disrupt yet another institutional process in governing ourselves. I have the wounds to prove that there are those outside of our nation who see fit to disrupt our democracy, and think we should lay down our guard for their interest. I say no! Mathieu Clerveaux says NO! The Haitian People Say No! Join me, my brothers and sisters! Do not feed into these rumors. Make the choice at the polls that will bring about true change for, not only your children, but the descendants that you may never meet. You have the power now! It is in your hands as it should be. Vote Mathieu Clerveaux for President! A vote for forward thinking Haitians tired of the years of misconduct, coup etas, and the special interests of the diaspora. Viv Ayiti!" articulated Mathieu, whose fingers dug into the soft thin layer of wood that plated the top of his desk. Silence fell unto the room as one by one, the faces in the room were caught between invigoration, wonder, and pride. Even the gold-laden teeth of his older brother, Bello, made an appearance between the parting of his dark lips.

"Thank you, Monsieur Clerveaux, for that spirited answer. We look forward to the debate between you and the other candidates. Thank you for your time," relented Maxo.

"It is always a pleasure to speak with you my friend. I thank all the people in reach of this wonderful broadcast. WLQQ, your home for Zouk, Konpa, and all things Ayisyen!" added Mathieu. "I hope I did not butcher the signature of your station Maxo."

"That was pretty good Monsieur Clerveaux! Thank you for the sound bite. Have a good evening," said Maxo.

"You as well my friend. Love and peace to you all," said Mathieu before pressing the end call button.

"How many more of these torturous interviews do I have left, Michelle?" sighed Mathieu.

"That was the last one sir. You did great!" said the assistant.

"Great? That was a mouse trap! I told you to better vet these people before accepting their invitations. I was fucking slaughtered on that one," spewed Mathieu as he flopped back into his chair.

"This is why I could never be clean cut like you brother. One phone call and that boy Fennel is done, and anyone around him," intervened Bello. Mathieu glanced at his brother and took another breath while massaging his forehead. Turning his back to him, Mathieu plummeted his fist into the cabinet.

"Politics like that is what got us here in the first place! And what are you doing here anyway?" asked Mathieu.

"Father is downstairs, and he sent me to fetch your stuck up ass," giggled Bello.

"I don't have time for this Bello. Michelle, please pencil my father in next week for a quick 15."

"Bitch if any ink come out of that pen to that calendar, imma send that lace front flying into the wall with the back of your

167

skull!" barked Bello, aiming a desert eagle so close to Michelle's eyes that the nozzle clicked against her frames. "I said, father is downstairs. Unless you want a whole new paint job on these walls. I suggest you bring yo bitch ass on!"

Mathieu turned around as the whimpers and shaking of his staff became too much for him to take.

"It's ok guys. I will be right back. Just keep working," said Mathieu as he passed his brother at the doorway. He then stopped.

"Just know when this is all over. You are going to pay for this little display of petty power. It's as pathetic as you and your little big gun," remarked Mathieu before heading to, and entering the floor's elevator. Bello lowered his weapon and followed his younger brother, as the trembling personnel in the office looked on. As Bello stepped one foot into the elevator, he shot his pistol into the air three times, raining down debris and fresh asbestos onto his head. The campaign manager and Michelle screamed in fear, forcing Mathieu's eyelids to close into tight squints. The door closed and the two brothers made their descent as Bello put his arm around his brother forcefully.

"Now don't you ever disrespect me in front of these hoes again. You know my ego fragile," said Bello before pushing his younger brother into the elevator wall. Mathieu sank into the dent as his vision remained focused on the tiles and the space between them. Wishing to disappear into the crevices.

As they approached the running Mercedes Van, he could

smell the familiar aroma of burnt skin protruding from the seams of the sliding door. Bello opened it and motioned for his brother to enter. In a large luxury chair lay his father, Charles, as Dr. Ursov tended to the stitches on his jaw. Utilizing a hot ended device to burn the wounds closed. The hair follicles on his head and face were all black. Charles' open shirt revealed more muscle definition than before. The skin below the multiple ECG electrodes that was once covered in wrinkles and kidney rashes, now becoming clearer by the day.

"There he is. My legacy. I heard your last call and I will be sending a few members of the Candiru to make a nice little mess," said Charles as his lips quivered in pain.

"Dear God father. Can you please stop KILLING PEOPLE! With this media storm and the feds poking around, I'm up to my neck in retweets and inboxes from people using memes comparing you and Duvalier!" pressed Mathieu.

"Do not worry about the media. Everyone will eventually fall in line and support Haiti's only hope. And that is you my boy," said Charles, barely flinching as the smoky, amber end of the device fried his skin.

"It's fighting you, isn't it?" asked Mathieu, as the slight smile on his father's face turned into a silent scowl. "How far will you go for power, father? At what cost, your life?"

"My son, a lot more people are going to die before I do. We both know this power is worth seeking in order to turn the tides in our favor. Do you think shaking hands, smiling on TV, and eye contact is going to hold your reign in place?" asked Charles as he motioned for Ursov to stop. "How many times must I tell you boy. Fear is the only way to rule a people who do not fear easily. It's no different than what this land of liberty has done to many since the dawn of history," said Charles as he stood without assistance and ripped away the wiring.

"I'm not going to be another one of your "Yes" men, father. That Nazi doctor of yours knows what we all know. You need more DNA from that bloodline to keep his bones from literally tearing itself out of you," stated Mathieu.

"Step outside with me son," said Charles as he exited the vehicle to stare up at the building that Bello and Mathieu exited. "I love you, my son. You are better than all of us you know. The compassion, the unquenchable need to make this world and those around you better. It is remarkable, and for that you will always have my respect," said Charles as he extended his hand to Mathieu. Hesitating for a few seconds, he met his father's hand with his. Charles pulled him in for a hug, while looking up at the building.

"You know this is exactly why you need me. You gotta have someone in your corner who doesn't care about structure. Especially the illusion of it," said Charles as he rested his hands on Mathieu's shoulders to break the embrace. "The chair I sent for you the other day. How comfortable was it?"

"It was a great gift, father," replied Mathieu.

"And the campaign manager and assistant you have. Have

they been loyal and attentive to you?" asked Charles.

"Yes, they have been nothing but great. I trust them with my life and the campaign," replied Mathieu. Charles let out a slight chuckle, and motioned to Bello to bring over a device. With a smile, Charles pressed the button and the voices of his staff began to bloom from the mini speaker.

"I don't even know what I'm doing here. The pay is great, but this is just another sinking ship for another rich boy candidate running for Haiti's presidency," said his manager.

"Yeah, I planned on putting in my resignation tomorrow but since he actually had a set of balls on that call, why not take another few paychecks?" laughed the assistant.

Charles turned off the recording and threw the device to the ground as it melted into the ground surrounded by a dark aura.

"Look at this building, my son. Structurally sound, with a strong foundation. Years of history burned into its walls and corridors. Yet, it is outrightly rotten from the core behind the vale of "structure". Just like you and your beliefs. You adhere to laws and social constructs of a foreign soil in an effort to be the "likable" option. They don't love you, they disrespect you, and yet you choose them over me?" asked Charles as the particles of sand on the asphalt rose and danced on the ground.

"Father no. Do not do this!" yelled Mathieu as the wind gust picked up. Bello raised the top of his shirt over his mouth and nose to use it as a mask as he looked on.

"I gave you a flimsy chair with a bug in it because I wanted you to see what the difference is between that and a throne. If you wish to sit on a throne, then you must be willing to tear down any and every thing that opposes it. Say goodbye to your structure," said Charles as he lifted his hands and the dark aura draped over him. With the closing of his fingers into his palm, loud sounds of crunching and screams escaped the breaking glass windows. The concrete, glass particles, and humanity attempting to jump to sure death, were sucked back into the semi-skyscraper as it collapsed inward. It was as if the building was being crushed from the outside by large hands from the very top, to the lobby. Mathieu watched as a large cloud of dust and debris came towards them rapidly. Before he could brace himself for the impact, a dark wall rose instantly surrounding them and the van. The thin crushed building began to lean towards the intercoastal that ran behind it with a few boats escaping the inevitable fall. Bursting into flames as the impact shook the earth violently.

"Choose anything or anyone over me again my son, and I assure you they will meet the same fate," said Charles as he re-entered the van.

Chapter 22:

Chance Meeting

The needle on the thermometer trembled at the limit it could not surpass. The glass window's unorthodox frost was evidence of the duel between the temperatures on both sides. The freezing conditions were set out of frustration, as Ronel drifted in and out of sleep. The fresh bandages wrapped tight around his torso were soaked in blood and sweat, as another round of torturous pain consumed him.

"Ronel..." said Charles' voice echoing in the darkness. Ronel's eyelids twitched at each utterance of his name.

"Get out of my head," replied Ronel as he opened his eyes to an empty room. Looking down at his wounds and exhaling in relief.

"Now why would I do that when I'm right here?" questioned Charles appearing next to Ronel. Breathing heavily and chuckling as Ronel stared in horror at his face. Blood streaming from the wound he inflicted as a child.

"Look at you. Not so tough, are you? Stare into what you did. It still didn't save that bitch or your cowardly father!" ranted Charles. The darkness engulfed Ronel, and latched onto his arms and legs, holding him down. Attempting to garner his power, Ronel's bare chest began to illuminate but it was quickly smothered out by the aura spreading throughout his body. Ronel sunk in a bottomless silent void, flailing frantically for something to grab onto. Only darkness and the rush of air under him were present until he violently landed on a sandy surface. Coughing up blood and saliva, Ronel turned onto his side to spit when he was met with the silent waves of sea water. The moon's reflection and the stars that accompanied brought the island shore into ultraviolet view. Making his way to his knees, Ronel looked around, searching for anything that could indicate where he was. Spotting a light in the distance, he stood up and began to walk in its direction. Sweat beaded from his face while he struggled to hold himself up as the bandages disappeared and the wounds began to bleed.

"You're not going to survive too long. I have seen many men die from lesser cuts than that," said the man staring into the dark horizon of the sea. The black hair on his head was woven together and laid on the back of his neck, under an imperial hat with the finest of feathers. The boots on his feet were planted strongly into the shoreline, as the wind caused the swords at his side to click against each other. Three pistols lined the leather sash against his stomach, with a general's coat that had the privilege of sitting on his shoulders.

"Who are you? And where the hell am I?" asked Ronel. The man turned around slowly, to reveal a freshly sutured gash that lined his neck. His thick mustache quivered; his teeth audibly scrapped against each other. Seething in anger.

"Did he send you?" demanded the General.

"Who are you talking about? Again, who are you?" questioned Ronel.

"I am King Jean-Jacques Dessalines, and I have been stuck in this void since I was betrayed by that traitor Mayer! Did he send you to finish the job? If he did, then he is more of a coward than I thought," replied Jean-Jacques. Unsheathing one of his swords, he threw it at the ground next to Ronel. "Let's make this a fair fight."

"As much as I would like to test myself against Haiti's mightiest warrior, this isn't real. You're not real, and I know this is Charles playing games with me." Ronel went to take another step towards the light in the distance.

"You take another step my boy, and I will execute you where you stand. Pick up the sword!" asserted Jean Jacques. Ronel looked down at the blade, then at his new adversary. Picking it up by the handle, Jean Jacques drew his other blade and stood in a stance that Ronel recognized. The two circled the space between them as Ronel held his stomach. At the ready, Ronel decided to strike first to assess Jean Jacques defense, and was met with a fierce counter. Jean Jacques took to the air as their blades met. Landing, then striking Ronel in the chest with his available fist. Ronel stumbled back but advanced with an assortment of sword attacks that were effortlessly anticipated and opposed by the sword of the General. The cadence of hits sang over the water beating against the sand. Counter to strikes, and strikes to counters. The scuffle between the two was more of an exhibition than a fight to the death. Reading each other's movements, the syncing of styles amazed each other. Suddenly, Jean Jacques changed tactics and went for a kill shot that Ronel swiped away. Then, a standoff.

"You are trained well. In fact too well," said Jean-Jacques before falling to the sand and screaming intensely holding the sides of his head.

"What is wrong?!" yelled Ronel who advanced but stopped as the tormented warrior was sucked into the dark sand. His screams were muffled then interrupted by a familiar laugh.

"GET OUT!" yelled Charles, as the ground under Ronel melted away into the same void that landed him there. Falling as Charles' voice and laughter surrounded him. Crescendoing into a volume much too loud for his ears to take. Looking down, Ronel could see Charles' smiling face. As he plunged, the face got larger in size. Charles opened his mouth, and lodged in between his teeth were multiple faces. He immediately recognized a few that sent a sharp cold sensation throughout his body. There was his mother and father, with blunt gunshot wounds to their heads. Elam slumped over on one of the molars. Sonya and Judson face down in the gunky saliva that he was about to plunge into. Hitting the murky surface, Ronel's eyes opened as he rose up in his bed. Feeling his heart beat faster than what was humanly possible. The white noise of the air conditioner working overtime came into focus. Silence once again. He reached for the damp towel that he had been using, and wiped down his face from his forehead to his chin. Once again, steam evaporated from the towel like times before, except this time it caught on fire in his hands.

"What is happening to me?" asked Ronel internally. Watching his fingers jitter, Ronel clenched them into fists. Slowing his breathing to regain whatever control he had left over his body. This was different. The sensation was one he hadn't felt in years. *"Why am I afraid?"* Sitting up, Ronel took another look at his bandages. Peeling them back slightly, he noticed that fresh new skin covered the injuries. The mixture of blood and fluid dried to a light crust that he brushed away while unwrapping the rest of the bandages. Before the surprise of his healing could set in, something drew his attention to the door. He felt a presence, and was unwilling to take any chances. He reached for his blade but was interrupted midway.

"You won't need that," said Elam from the other side of the door. Ronel stood up, still feeling the pain from his midsection. Opening the door, Elam hobbled in with a long wooden case and sat down at the nearest chair.

"Hey Elam, would you like to come in?" asked Ronel sarcastically.

"Unfortunately, we don't have the luxury of time or your attitude."

"What is that?" Ronel drew closer but was halted by Elam's hand.

"Patience. When are any of you going to learn patience?" Elam opened the case, removing the red velvet colored fabric over what looked, to Ronel, to be a very odd looking, extra-large, Cuban link chain. "This was thought to be lost. There are people who would take down an entire government if it meant even claiming to have this in their possession. This belonged to Mayer."

"It looks like it was stolen from a Slick Rick starter kit," said Ronel. Elam paid no attention to the remark. He removed the chain link, struggling to lift it completely from its case. "Why are you bringing this to me?"

"Because fear is no longer surface level for you. Even I can tell when fear has penetrated the soul of a warrior. No gun, blade, or skill is useful when that poison courses through your veins. It renders you vulnerable. Which is why I felt it was time." Elam stood up and attached one end of the chain to his belt, and attached the other end to Ronel's sword. "This will give you the edge you need the next time you fight him."

"And how is this going to help me against what you have

never fought before? You don't even know what I'm up against."
Elam unhooked the contraption, and laid it on the table. Standing
over it, he adjusted the links to line up straight.

"I don't need to know. I just have a feeling," began Elam.
"The best way to conquer one's fears is to master the skill of blind
confidence. Not arrogance." Elam turned to Ronel and without
saying it explicitly, but with his eyes, made Ronel responsible for
its safe keeping. "You have always been taught to handle your
machete in hand, now you will wield it with your heart." Elam
began to walk towards the door.

"This old relic is no match for Charles. You didn't see what
I saw. You didn't fight what I fought. It was pure bad," trembled
Ronel as his eyes darted so fast, that the friction caused instance
redness. Setting his attention to the ground, Elam stepped
forward to comfort him but hesitated. "I don't understand it. Such
darkness. Then there is Dessalines in the midst of it all and…"

"What did you say?" demanded Elam with a slight anger in
his voice.

"Jean-Jacques Dessalines was there. I couldn't put my finger
on the aura that took the shape of a soldier until my questions
were answered in these recurring nightmares."

"No. You know nothing of what you speak. There is no
way!" yelled Elam. The sides of his mouth quivered as anguish
settled on his face.

"Whoa! Where is all this coming from? Is there something
you are not telling me?"

"Show me," said Elam as he made his way over to the table to unhook the sword from the relic. Handing it over to a confused Ronel, Elam picked up his staff and pressed against a wedge on the side. There was an audible click, then a third of the staff fell to the ground revealing an impressive, shiny blade held by the old priest.

"Show you what? We both know you can't raise your arm past the shoulder."

"Never mind my arm, I need you to show me exactly what happened." said Elam, raising the sword that was trembling violently in his hand. "Advance!"

Ronel, slow at first, gripped his weapon and quickly darted towards Elam in the same manner, drawing it midway as he did with Jean-Jacques. Elam leaped into the air and the metals collided.

"Did he counter?"

"Yes, with a strike to my chest then -" began Ronel as Elam displayed the same move as if synced with the battle.

"To the neck, then a sweep to the ground?" interrupted Elam.

"No, I went at him!" corrected Ronel as he and Elam engaged move for move. Sword to sword. Elam took a step back.

"No, he was toying with you," narrated Elam as they both continued the fight. Elam continued to call each metal swing, slice and cut. Ultimately going for the kill strike that was swept away by Ronel arrogantly. Elam fell back in shock. Tears fell as soon as they formed as the elder looked into dead space. His white buttoned up shirt began to turn red as the blood from his old burn wounds saturated the fabric.

"I knew this was not a good idea," said Ronel as he knelt at Elam's side who was in clear agony. "Would you like me to take you to the hospital"

"No, that will not be necessary. It's just been a while since I crossed swords with anyone who still fights that way." said Elam, attempting to get to his feet without assistance. He made it to a chair panting and attempting to regain his breath. "How is this possible? Is this the same technique that you encountered with Charles?"

"Yes, instead Charles had no mercy or honor in it when we clashed," replied Ronel.

"Jean-Jacques was a student of Mayer. A star pupil who mastered the same style and swordsmanship from a forgotten time. I was one of the last students that was disciplined in it before the Candiru moved away from those teachings. None of this makes sense," exhaled Elam. "I have to go."

"Wait. Where do you think you are going bleeding like that?" Ronel helped Elam situate himself in the chair. "Your prime days are over. Just tell me what I need to do."

"I may not be able to engage, but I could try to get to the bottom of this. If what you say is true, then we have a bigger problem on our hands. I watched and listened to the terror of your sleep. Charles has managed to harness the ability to haunt your mind. What Jean-Jacques Dessalines has to do with all of this is a mystery."

"There is something else you should know. I knew he was about to kill me, but something inside fought back. It made him retreat and run before finishing me off. He didn't seem like he was completely in control," said Ronel.

"Interesting," remarked Elam. "Well, I suggest that we find out what this all means before your sister does. Get to that Gala and take Judson with you. I know it sounds odd coming from me but it's better to have that wildcard in your corner than to lose your shirt again. Gamble smart Ronel."

Chapter 23:

Extravaganza

The hiss from each passing vehicle along the rain-drenched A1A played a light white noise in the distance. The night was festive with headlights beaming from Miami's best, luxurious mechanical chariots. Car after car arrived along the driveway of the white mansion sitting at the farthest edge of Star Island. A blue Rolls-Royce Wraith opened its driver door and out stepped Judson. Adjusting his tie as the pastel-colored suit rested on his frame, down to his albino gator-skinned shoes. The buzz of a motorcycle approached, with Ronel arriving in a black suit and tie ensemble. His hair braided into a bun with a crisp line up. The brothers met the first step of a grand stairway to the mansion's entrance.

"Not bad, Jude," complimented Ronel. "A hell of an upgrade from what you wore to church the other day."

"Well don't look for this to be the norm. Shit cost me some stacks," said Judson as he continued to adjust his crotch area. "I don't get it. Do all of y'all who wear these things have no balls?"

"Of course, you would have an issue with dressing dapper when it calls for it."

"Stop thinking you know me bro. You don't. None of you do," replied Judson as he focused on the entryway where other guests were arriving.

"Ok, I tried to be nice but you insist on being a total bitch right now."

"I don't have an issue with you, Ro. You did, after all, invite me out to a ball. Excuse me if I'm a little bitchy for having to pay for my gown, glass slippers, and carriage. I'm used to you not showing up and showing out."

"How many times are you going to throw that in my face?! Let's address it right here, right now!" emphasized Ronel as he removed a small flask from his pocket and took a quick gulp.

"Easy there desperado. If you're not careful, that bottle will kill you."

"This coming from the weed smoker."

"Hey, pick your poison. Mine just happens to be organic. I grow it, I water it, and I can see it die," laughed Judson. Ronel's scowl could not hold after another one of his brother's classic zingers. They both laughed and began the climb to the entrance.

"So Charles stood up out of his chair and kicked your ass huh?"

"Not my greatest moment. It was as if he could see every move I made before I did it. There is so much that I don't understand. The battle itself, his transformation, and the nightmare afterwards. Even Elam got spooked. He usually knows what to say and do. This is the first time I have seen him genuinely scared." The duo were met by security where both siblings presented their authentic invitations. The concierge presented each of them with black Mardi Gras style masks.

"I don't care what he is feeling right about now. He always casted me to the side. I had to learn to conquer my fears on the streets. In prison amongst the sickest, twisted minds human kind has to offer. You guys were sent to the Himalayas for ninja death school. Structure is built on fear, chaos is what breeds it out of you. Fear ain't in my arsenal," said Judson.

"How much do you remember during that time?"

"To tell you the truth. After Elam's accident, I don't recall a lot of it. Just the sound of that sliding iron door. I just chalk it up to the bud. Speaking of which….." halted Judson as he reached for a perfectly rolled blunt and lit it.

"Seriously?!" gasped Ronel.

"Nigga you got a plantation owner's flask in your pocket. Besides, smoking is encouraged." assured Judson pointing to a section where guests smoked an assortment of tobacco commodities. Finding a standing table, the brothers made camp to observe.

"Me and Sonya don't remember much about our time in

Japan. It was only tidbits of memories that remained," continued Ronel.

"Speaking of Sonya, is that her walking up the steps into the Gala?" inquired Judson. Dressed in an all-white sparkling evening gown, with matching accessories, Sonya presented her invitation.

"Yeah. Elam said that she would be here. Apparently, the feds are using our past woes with Charles to get some answers themselves. And like you already know, if it's the CIA, they are after more than just a party recap," Ronel stated. Sonya caught a glimpse of her brothers and huffed towards their direction.

"So, Elam couldn't help himself and sent you two to babysit me? I'm on assignment, which supersedes him and anything you two have going on!" hissed Sonya.

"Whoa. Hold up there, spicy Cleopatra. We are just here to observe and report," smiled Judson.

"I don't need either of you fucking this up for me. You both failed, now it's my turn. I'm on official top-secret business," shot Sonya as she opened her purse to make sure her makeup was still intact in her little mirror. Closing it, she continued to berate them. "Now we have something in common, secrets that we keep from each other."

As she turned away, Ronel quickly reached into his coat pocket. "Sonya, look, we have the shard. We are going to expose Charles to the Assembly. We can strip away the support of the Candiru and take care of him together."

"Where is the skull?" asked Sonya.

"There is no way that we can present it in the condition I retrieved it. Furthermore, I don't think it is authentic," replied Ronel.

"You fought a demon that has two of the greatest fighters I know shook to their core. There is no way Charles could have acquired Mayer's power without that skull being authentic! I have no time for your doubts. Do what you guys came to do without me, it's none of my concern. Just stay out of my way!" threatened Sonya, turning her back to them and getting lost in the sea of patrons.

"Well, that was a great pow-wow. What did you mean by the skull not being authentic?" inquired Judson.

"I don't know how it's possible, and it's too much to explain right now. Let's just put these dumb masks on and keep an eye out for Sonya or Gomez," said Ronel grabbing another glass of wine from a passing tray. Judson chuckled but was interrupted by the sound of man's voice.

"Thank you all for coming, this has been a very successful night," said Alejandro Gomez, the host, to the crowd. His security detail towered above the slicked back gray hair on his head. His suit was a cross between that of an admiral, and Hugh Hefner's relaxed attire. Smoke rose from his pipe, and came out heavy through his nostrils.

"We have so much to celebrate. Rather than bore you with a list of our latest accomplishments, I say we get straight to the orgy.....of festivities," joked Alejandro. The room erupted in laughter as he smiled at those that appeased him. He tapped his cane on the tile twice. "Angelo, please."

A guard turned to open the door and four men bound from their hands to their feet were carried out to the middle of the ballroom. Forced to kneel, the bruising on their faces was overshadowed by the absence of emotion. Judson tapped Ronel on the shoulder.

"Don't they look familiar?" asked Judson.

"Yeah. Augustin's men," replied Ronel.

"These men have failed me. They have failed each and every one of you that serve under the Assembly. And for that, a debt must be paid." said Gomez circling them, tapping them each on the shoulder with his cane. "Thank you for your service."

"Thank you for your service," said the guests in unison. The security detail for Gomez put black bag-like mechanisms over their heads that were equipped with pull handles. The men were not in anguish, they kept their heads high. Disciplined and proud. The handles were pulled, and the heads of the Candiru members fell next to their bodies.

"Shit!" yelled Judson. Slapping his lips but quickly realizing that his outburst could not be returned from the ears in the room.

"It seems like we have visitors. Please step forward," commanded Alejandro. The brother's looked forward as the majority of the eyes focused on them. The sound of sharp metal, safety clicks, and chambers being made ready was palpable. "I would think that if you had the gall to crash our party, you would have no fear in presenting yourselves. Please, everyone show your invitation."

As the siblings reached for their invitations, the sound of shuffling caught their attention. Ice ran through all three of their spines as they were the only ones who did not remove the top portion of their clothing to reveal that mark of Mayer tattooed on their backs. Immediately, they were detained by multiple Candiru members and brought to the forefront.

"You must be Ronel. The beautiful Sonya. And you, the rude one. Do you care to tell me what you have done with Augustin? And please, this is not a situation that is ideal for lying," smiled Alejandro.

"I would say, right about now, he must be reptile shit," replied Judson.

"What a unique way to kill someone. I applaud you for creativity. But just like these headless bodies, a price must be paid," asserted Gomez before tapping his cane again. Another guard brought a clear bowl holding small pieces of paper and handed it to him. "I will give you each a chance to entertain me and my guests. Please select one and do not open until I say so."

Alejandro took his time to approach each one of them. Ronel picked first and held it in a clenched fist. Then to Sonya who chose her piece of paper. Then to Judson picking the last.

"Art and performance go hand in hand. So, each one of you will display or demonstrate the art that is written on your paper, without aid from each other," announced Gomez.

"God, I hope masturbation isn't on one of these," joked Judson.

"It was one of my first suggestions," shot back Alejandro. "Ronel, you go first"

Ronel opened the paper and his face flushed. The blinking rate of his eyes increased as he stared into the ink.

"What is it, Ronel?" asked Sonya.

"Dance," replied Ronel. Judson fell to the ground and wailed in a sea of laughter. Sonya lost control of her facial expression, letting out a slight cackle.

"Damn, I know I said it when we were kids, but you are about to really die by those two left feet!" belted Judson as he held his sides. Ronel smiled.

"Is it too much to ask for a dance partner and choice of music?" asked Ronel to Gomez. The host reached his hand back, signaling to a woman that emerged from the crowd. Ronel dropped his wine glass as his eyes rested upon his former lover Rosa, switching her medium wide hips towards him.

"I see alcohol still hasn't left your lips, Roro." said Rosa

"Roro?!" asked Sonya and Judson in unison.

"I see you still haven't discriminated against cash, no matter who it comes from," Ronel retorted.

"C'mon Roro, we both know you like when I make myself and my assets available for the right reasons. Shall we?" proposed Rosa. Raising her hand, Ronel took it into his. Leading her to the middle of the dance floor. The band began to play a ravishing merengue number that is outshined by the footwork of both Ronel and Rosa. From the enticing rolls of her flawless curves, to the well-coordinated movements that summoned the eyes and hearts off all that witnessed. Sonya's jaw muscles loosened and lowered to that of her speechless brother Judson as they watched Ronel put on a clinic.

"When did he learn all of that?" asked Sonya.

"I don't know, but remind me to scoop a Latin chick later tonight, because clearly I have been missing out," replied Judson. The song reached a crescendo, as Ronel twirled Rosa repeatedly. They ended with her freely falling to the floor but being caught in Ronel's arms. The room applauded ecstatically at the sound of the band's last note.

"Very good. Very, very good!" applauded Gomez as he walked towards them."One talent expressed in superb fashion. Now it is time for the next act." Alejandro looked to Judson. "Big man! If you would be so kind, open your piece of paper."

"I can do that. Unlike my brother, I actually have real talent! Let me see what you got for me," said a confident Judson as he opened it. He paused. "Poetry?!"

"Is there a problem?" asked the host as the Candiru drew their assortment of weapons.

"Nah, no problem. I can do poetry. Mine is just a little unconventional, according to the suits in here. Yo Papi! Can I get a beat?" yelled Judson to the clueless drummer on the stage.

Sonya and Ronel faces contorted.

"I hope he is not going to try to spit some nursery rhyme shit. We are as good as dead," sneered Sonya. The drummer, drawn by Judson's charisma and confidence, began to play a rhythm close to what he thought a hip-hop beat would sound like. Before Judson could speak a word, the drummer was shot in the head by Gomez and dragged away.

"I don't care for Hip-Hop, not in its current popular form anyway. You will do your poetry without the crutch of any percussive instrument but your own vocal chords. Please proceed," said Alejandro calmly.

"Freestyle shit huh? Ok. Look.....

Carpe diem to the season of the shooters,

Ruger on the dashboard, swerving through the graveyard.

Old guard flow, old street legend with the gargoyle pose.

Better yet a vulture,

fuck doing it for the culture.

Must of seen how

these musket beams,

aim at domes to explode their thoughts to pieces of mustard seeds.

Bleed with confidence....

Please Ops, pick up ya common sense,

Dead or alive, the payoffs is definite.

My moves allude like her body, please elude my enemies

from me.

One shot, three shots, fuck shots, BLOUW goes the tool again!

Gun cocks, buck shots, I bust shots like a bloodclot hooligan!

Damn what I would give to see mom's face again,

I'll settle for black suits, hearses backed up to Sunrise like it's 4pm.

Beautiful,

like the eulogy of a criminal, say something nice Jude,

Shit I rather be rude,

blood out my old girl's head got me in a muthafuckin' mood!

Old boy there too,

them Macoutes let one loose into his cranium.

Same as them?

all who align with old Benjamin button will be famous when,

I steam roll over niggaz until the bones bleed out collagen!"

"Ok, ok," waved Gomez. "You're angry and you want revenge. We get the picture. Your cadence was off but true verses create vivid realities in the mind of the listener. You have succeeded in stimulating the mind of the most important person in the room."

The host, with his hands clasped behind his back, walked over to Sonya. His eyes grazed over her figure, from her toes to the red lipstick perfectly applied. Sonya kept a steady grip on her purse that held a small, .38 caliber gun and short hunter's blade.

Deeply she was shaking in fear, but her gaze was that of a predator.

"Now, for our final performance, please step forward young lady," motioned Alejandro. Sonya did as she was told and opened her piece of paper that was damp in palm sweat.

"First Blood," read Sonya.

"How lucky are you?!" exclaimed Alejandro as he erupted in laughter. "You are now fortunate to entertain us with a display of a classic desperado ritual. A knife fight to the death."

"No!" yelled Ronel. "Please Gomez, allow me to take her place. She is not-"

"I will decide what she is or isn't. Right now, she is mine to do what I see fit," replied Gomez. Before he could utter his next words, the aristocratic host had a blade under his neck. It slowly punctured the small cellular fibers of his skin.

"I am no one's property!" yelled Sonya as she dared the slow reacting guards of the host to take another step.

"Trancilo, Trancilo," said Alejandro with a smile as he waved away his security. "You are fast, I like that. However, I am not going to entertain any more antics!" Sonya noticed the multiple sniper lights pointed at her and her brothers. The host lowered the knife away from his neck.

"My old age does not allow for such an undertaking as fighting," said Gomez as he slowly turned around to face her.

"Who is my opponent?" asked Sonya eagerly.

"You are no doubt the most remarkable specimen I have ever

194

laid my eyes on. For you, I have personally selected someone who will match you blade for blade," exerted Alejandro as he walked back to the viewing area. "Bring in the Jamaican devil!"

A side door opened, and out appeared a man with a smile on his face, and a quarter-smoked cigarette between his quivering lips. Dark skin draped his flesh, covered in sweat. The eyes of the man were possessed with a palpable blood lust. His hands were covered in the gore of his latest kill. He walked over to the wall, and wrote the number "234", before smearing the scarlet sap into the short braids on his head.

"Meet Maxamillion. A real baud-mon! A good faith loan from an associate of ours. Our doctors saved his life. So in return, he handles the messy jobs," joked Gomez. "Max?! Nuh take her fa ease. (Don't take her lightly)" Max nodded in agreement, and grabbed a 7-inch serrated dagger from his side and tread slowly towards Sonya.

"Sonya, watch out for--" began Ronel.

"I'll be fine," interrupted Sonya. She then opened her purse and grabbed a small black rectangular object from it. She placed the purse down while pressing firmly on black box that ejected a medium size blade on the end. Kicking off her heels, she used the blade to slit her dress on both sides, allowing her more freedom of movement.

The two circled each other, never breaking the leer into each other's impenetrable minds. Max began to giggle uncontrollably in mid madness. The shaking veins protrude through the skin around his defined neck and upper torso as the blood he wiped in his hair trickled down unto his wife beater undershirt. His eyes widened as he rushed towards the younger of the three, missing his first swipe of his blade as Sonya evaded. She attempted to sweep his legs from under him, but to no effect. Angered by this, Max tried to drive his knife into Sonya, who met his blade with hers. The two struggled for a few seconds as Ronel's and Judson's shouting became muffled as Sonya focused on her aggressor. Releasing her sweaty grip on her weapon slightly, she allowed Max's momentum to cause him to lose control. As his knife lodged forcefully into the tile floor, Sonya flipped his slim frame onto his side. Repeatedly, she struck his face until he suddenly caught both fists. A bizarre look of madness and laughter escaped his swollen face as he regained the advantage. He landed a punch that immediately caused Sonya to lose all breath in her lungs. She rolled her body backwards to gain some distance and kipped up. As her heartbeat raced, she began to feel dizzy, but determined. She took a deep breath and grabbed her hair, wrapping it in a ponytail. Max, hungry for more, attempted to stab her with repeated thrusts that were met with blocks. Now slashing at his opponent, Sonya continued to hold her own until the edge of his knife managed to cut her shoulder, which began to bleed profusely. Sonya immediately reached for the wound and gandered at the gash. She looked at her palm and could hear singing in the distance. It was her mother again. Singing her favorite lullaby.

"Oh no, not again," said Sonya inwardly. *"Mom, please stop! Get out of my head, this is not the time!"* The melody got louder as Max approached again. His tongue lapped at the blood on his weapon, reveling in the taste.

"What is she doing?!" asked Judson. "She is leaving herself open for an attack!"

"We cannot interfere, remember? She has enough time to counter it," assured Ronel.

Sonya, looked to the ground and saw her mother in a pool of blood. Tears began to form between her eyelids. The room became empty as the melody bellowed loudly. Max was upon her with his blade raised in the air to hammer down into her neck. He paused, as if against his will. He struggled but a disconnect was evident. A powerful gust of wind encircled them, becoming a mini tornado that barricaded the fighters within it. Visibility lost to those in attendance. The furniture began to take flight, as did the plates and silverware causing panic in the room. Yet Alejandro, the brothers, and Rosa maintained a strong stance. Suddenly, Max can be heard screaming in agony, before his body is ultimately ejected from the indoor windstorm. The lifeless body slammed into a support beam before falling to the ground. Motionless, with fresh blood flowing from his multiple lacerations.

Chapter 24:

After Party

The violent winds began to recede, and everyone struggled to make out what remained in the middle of the room. The dust settled, revealing Sonya standing dazed and confused.

"What the hell was that?! Was that all coming from Sonya?" asked Judson.

"This was what I was trying to tell you!" replied Ronel.

"Everyone OUT!" yelled Alejandro as Ronel and Judson tended to their sister. "Nobody says anything about what they saw here, or you are as good as worm food." The guests exited. Rosa then walked over to Ronel to whispered into his ear.

"I will see you soon Roro." Rosa kissed him on the cheek, then rubbed Sonya's back to provide her brief comfort before she left through a side door. They were now alone with their host.

"My how you all have grown since the last time I saw you,"

said Gomez as he poured another cup of tequila.

"How do you know who we are?" asked Ronel.

"I know more about you than you currently know about yourselves, but of course, that is by design," replied Alejandro.

"Ok Champagne Papi, answer the Goddamn question!" began Judson as he drew his glock from his back.

"Point that barrel in this direction and your brother and sister will watch their hothead brother's head get a really bad, back-room acupuncture treatment," informed the host as the sound of multiple guns could be heard from the shadows.

"I always knew this day would come. I have played it out in my head over and over for nearly 20 years. It is relieving. The traitor sent you, did he not?" asked Gomez.

"Elam told us that you would give credence to our case," replied Ronel.

"Killing Charles," conceded Alejandro.

"He degraded the remains of Mayer into pieces. But we have the shard," said Ronel.

"The shard?" asked Gomez. Ronel reached into his coat pocket for the artifact wrapped in a soaked red washcloth. Confused at the sight, he reluctantly handed it to Alejandro. Removing the fabric, Gomez pressed against its damp outer layer. The red substance stained his fingers. A short snicker escaped his closed lips.

"I barely escaped battling against his new form. He now seems to have acquired the legendary powers of Mayer," said

Ronel. Alejandro continued to survey, then took another long drink from his cup.

"What is it that you hope to acquire from me?" muttered their host.

"We seek permission to avenge our parents without any further interference from the Candiru." replied Ronel. Alejandro delicately placed the shard back into its covering.

"Are you familiar with "The Tree of Forgetfulness"?" inquired Gomez.

"No. If you are about to suggest that we forget why we came here papi you can kiss my…" began Judson.

"I am," replied Sonya, stepping forward. "It was a tree that the black tribes that sold their own into slavery used to wipe their memories. So that they would not fight to return."

"Good my dear. Memories are powerful. Even those that are most traumatic in nature. They drive even the most cunning of warriors to forget all skill and logic. Willingly running into Dante's Peak with just their sword and no armor in a blind rage," said Alejandro as he sat down on the steps of the stage. "I see the undying thirst to correct what was done in all of your eyes. But you have an equal, undying opponent. One that I won't be much help with I'm afraid."

"Are you refusing to help us?" pressed Ronel.

"Look around you. Am I not the only one you see? I am sure the traitor told you that there were four of us with the power to give the Candiru command if an elimination of one of the seats was justified. I sit alone. The others mysteriously died in their sleep, which you can already tell was no coincidence. The Candiru is torn to a stalemate. Teetering since the arrival of the Oracle. I can't kill him, and he can't kill me due to Mayer's Law. But Mayer's Law also gives the Oracle the power to recognize Mayer if he returns."

"Are you saying that the Candiru believes Charles to be Mayer incarnate?" pressed Sonya.

"You don't know, do you? None of you know?" asked Gomez looking at each of them. "You may need to have further words with the traitor in sheep's wool. The Candiru for centuries held out hope that Mayer may once again walk this earth. It is why the ways of Mayer's minister and hypnotist have been passed down generation after generation within the Candiru. To not only identify him, but have the skills needed to bring back his memories and full power. Since she arrived, the Candiru's alliance has shifted to Charles. So my days are numbered."

"She?" asked Judson

"Yes, the Oracle of Mayer is a woman known to the Candiru as Banshee," said the host.

The three siblings looked at each other in shock and discomfort. Sonya's sworn rival was not only the current Oracle, but stood on the side growing in opposition by leaps and bounds.

"What does Jean-Jacques Dessalines have to do with all of this?" pressed Ronel.

"What about him? He was one of many leaders that Mayer

mentored and befriended. That is the extent of his importance to the Candiru," replied Gomez, tapping his cane lightly at the tile, emitting a frantic tick.

"Charles' form is not that of Mayer. I have the feeling that you already knew that. I fought two men in less than 24 hours. Two, who are truly one. Only separated by who was in control. I was mortally wounded by a man who sought my blood and life. The other fought me as well, except his intentions were different. He was seeking. If my knowledge of Mayer is correct, he is never one to not complete what he has started," said Ronel. Silence rested on the marble walls of the large hall. Sonya's focus darted between her eldest brother and the melancholy demeanor of their host. Judson, not accustomed to being speechless, pushed to interrupt but his lips would not separate. Alejandro emptied his lungs in exhaustion, and went to inhale but stopped short by a clarity made visible by his widened eyes. Releasing a slight crow to a full on, heaping laugh session.

"How could you laugh when your life's on the line?" asked Sonya.

"When your eyes age as old as mine my dear, you understand that finding humor in the inevitable kill shot keeps the blood pressure low," smiled Gomez twirling the bottle between his fingers masterfully. Letting out another long sigh, the smile dissolved as Alejandro motioned for the siblings to come closer. "What you experienced, Ronel, was not a dream. More of a visitation than anything. I keep saying to everyone that has ears to listen that the Haitian people are unique beyond any understanding. The warrior spirit within its people is unrelenting, and it is why so many other nations see it as a threat. You saw Jean-Jacques Dessalines in his spirit form. A spiritual technique that Mayer used in battle to commune with the departing souls of some of his most respected or feared opponents."

"Was what he said true? Did Mayer betray him?" asked Ronel.

"I know that Mayer did not personally take many under his wing. But there was something about the boy with a branch in his hand, mimicking a long-lost fighting style. What was just a venture to the New World, became multiple. The child took to his teachings like fish to water. From combat to military intelligence, it was inevitable that he would lead the revolt. He grew up to be a fierce general who liberated his people, and eventually became King. History doesn't even mention how grandiose the coronation was. The ones writing the books would not dare depict the French, and Spanish gunships forced to watch a parade of foreign dignitaries attend. Mayer stood next to him as he was crowned. He entrusted him with the shard that was the original source of his power. I can't see a betrayal happening. There was nothing to gain, and everything to lose," explained Gomez looking at the wrapped shard before handing it back to Ronel. "You're going to need that. It is said that the wood from the Iroko tree never loses its soul. No matter how much it is chopped down, burned, and left to die. The soul always remains, and always remembers. It will serve you well when the time comes."

"I know Ronel is just eating this history lesson up but I have a quick question. If Elam is a traitor, why has the Candiru not killed him and us?" asked Judson.

"The priest made a deal with the Assembly right after you all washed ashore. A deal I'm afraid will be null and void once I am no longer in the picture," replied Gomez again laughing to himself. "If I'm going to die, then I would do it knowing that the Candiru will choose wisely." Alejandro chuckled slightly as he looked up at the ceiling. "Oh, Great Mayer, even in death, you control all the pieces on the board. It was a joy to be a pawn."

"So, are you going to get to the part where you tell us how Charles is transforming into a very dead Haitian General?" interrupted Sonya. Before either could retort, a sound of a slow clap came from the hallways. Humming came from another, and clanking of metal came from a third. The four were then surrounded by Banshee, Bello, and lastly, an upright walking Charles clapping while being flanked by his younger son.

"Gomez, I see my invitation may have met an uncomfortable demise, being that one never made it to me," said Charles.

"So did the other three invitations for your back up dancers, Charles. As you can see, the party is long over. These are my private guests, and you are not welcomed," replied Alejandro.

"You disrespectful Spanish Fly SHIT! Father! Please allow me to put this imbecile out of his misery!" asked Bello as he cocked back the shotgun. "Then I would gladly pick up where I left off with punk ass Judson over there!"

"No, no Bello, not now. We have an even more crucial matter to attend to. Our good comrade has guests with such blood-spilling, piercing eyes," said Charles as he approached them. Ronel's eyes shifted as the nightmare replayed in his mind, causing his temples to pulse. The tremble returned, but he did not hesitate to cut off Charles' advance, stepping in front of his siblings.

"I am going to kill you," Ronel said defiantly.

"And how did that work out for you the last time we met?" asked Charles as he adjusted the well-tailored jacket to his tuxedo. He motioned for Mattieu who reluctantly provided him a drink from an available wine bottle. As the younger Clerveaux poured the drink, he could not take his eyes off of Sonya. She shook in anger and exhaustion as she starred a hole into him and his relaxed father.

"Wait, is that the middle child? Well look at you all big and grown up. A far cry from the little squeamish boy that I once knew. Tell me, did you fight in prison the way you tried to fight me off when I held you down?" asked Charles as he sipped from his cup. Judson's face sunk into anger as he patted his sister on her back. Smashing his knuckles into each other, he advanced towards his abuser. Ronel stopped him.

"Judson, whatever you are thinking, we have to be smart about this," whispered Ronel. "Don't do anything brash."

"Brash?" asked Judson as he now faced his brother. "Brash would be letting this sick fuck breathe another breath of air in the same space that I am standing in!" screamed Judson as he pulled out an AK-47, firing multiple rounds at a falling Charles. Enraged and screaming at the top of his lungs, he allowed the flashing of the nozzle to guide him closer to Charles' limp body. The Candiru men quickly stood in front of Alejandro, taking him towards the nearest exit. Charles laid bleeding without moving. The Clerveaux brothers ran for cover as Judson fired in their direction, stepping over Charles' body.

"Now was that so fucking hard! I did what you could not do in the three chances you had to kill this sick fuck!" yelled Judson to Ronel as he reloaded the high-powered rifle.

"Look!" yelled Ronel, as he attempted to rush towards his brother. As confidence rested on Judson's face, his eyes caught on to the sight of the blood on the ground now reversing in motion, back into the wounds of Charles. With a low, audible laugh from his lips, Charles rose to his feet without the use of his hands.

"You can't save him now Ronel, just like you couldn't save them before," snarled Charles as he hovered in the air before totally engulfing himself in darkness. The aura began to smoothen and take shape. Jean-Jacques' likeness was now finally on display for all to see and confirm. Ronel stopped in fear as he gazed upon his face. Before he could calculate his next move, Judson pointed the barrel at the figure. Clenching the trigger to let off the full magazine, the nozzle is suddenly cut in half.

"Judson! RUN!" yelled Ronel. By the time Judson noticed the tip of the dark sword held by the anomaly, it was lodged into his abdomen, then exiting clean out of his left side. Judson fell to the ground, attempting to hold back the blood pouring from his almost severed body.

"Gomez!" yelled Charles focusing on the elder and his guards. "It is high time that you join the others and the Great Mayer! Make sure to give him my regards!" The dark being vanished, then reappeared before Alejandro, swiping his sword in one swift motion. Judson, still having the function of his eyes, saw multiple heads fall to the ground, including that of Alejandro staring back at him, with a grin. The figure then turned its attention to Ronel and beamed towards him. Ronel braced for the attack with his flinching eyelids clamped shut. The wind once again picked up. Ronel opened his eyes and the sight of Sonya's small blade restraining the larger black sword of a demon made him buckle at the knees. Sonya, surrounded by a green aura of her own, stood in opposition to the dark matter. Banshee attempted to advance but stopped as bullet fragments ricocheted off the floor in front of her. Judson grinned from across the room, before allowing the high-powered smoking rifle to fall to the tile.

"The girl!" yelled Charles to his minions as he struggled to break from the aura's grip on him. Sonya walked him back on his heels step after step. The tile cracking under the pressure. Her face, void. Her pupils like gorges without a landing, as she slowly gained the upper hand on Charles. Ronel and Judson could not believe what they were witnessing. As she took another step, her knees buckled. The younger sibling suddenly fell unconscious, and the aura's glow dissipated from around her.

"Snap out of it Ronel!" yelled Judson from his now blood-filled mouth laying nearly motionless. "Get Sonya out of here now!" Ronel advanced towards her but all of his muscles tensed up without his control. It was the same numbness he felt in the prior battle with Charles. Ronel's eyes now engulfed in flames attempted to energize his body to break from the hold, but to no avail. He looked down to notice that Sonya was no longer there, and caught a glance of Mathieu carrying her out in his arms.

"Is there something wrong with your extremities?" ranted Charles' voice as he recovered to his feet. "I have a gift for both of you. The sons of that bastard, and insolent pet of Duvalier!" Charles charged his energy but struggled as he moaned in pain. The skull fragments attempted to separate from his face again. Falling to his back and wheezing as his black exterior receded. Bello ran over to lift his father away in retreat, but not before he took a large object with a clock ticking and laid it next to Judson's head.

"Just so that ugly face gets the face lift it deserves!" laughed Bello as he walked away with Charles on his shoulders. Banshee met them halfway to address a semi-conscious Charles.

"Master, it would seem that Mathieu has deviated from the route to the laboratory. Do not fret. They will not get far," spoke a confident Banshee. Charles, visibly upset, yelled for them to pursue his own betraying flesh and blood. Ronel manages to make one step towards his brother lying in a pool of blood. The rest of the Candiru follow their leadership out of the building.

"Judson, stay with me! Stay with me man!" yelled Ronel as the feeling in his muscles returned. He knelt down to his brother's side, attempting to lift his large frame to drag it out before the bomb went off. He struggled with the weight of Judson, inching toward the door before the sound of a large explosion and flames engulfed all around them. The building and ceiling went up in a fury of fire, and force. After a series of loud bangs, to the small cluttering sounds of debris falling to the ground, the flames raged around the ruins of the mansion. The entrance was overwhelmed by a wall of fire, eating away at the concrete and exposed steel rods. Then suddenly, the flame wall began to subside as dirt covered Ronel dragged his brother toward the outside. The eyes of the eldest burned with intense flames as those around them extinguished at each step Ronel took with Judson. Witnessing the power of his brother parting the walls of hell that surrounded them, Judson passed out. All was dark and quiet.

Chapter 25:

Here's to Me

The Miami Heat were down 10 points as Wade stood at the free throw once again. The old television set's display fluttered causing Judson to tighten the grip of his eyelids as the light caused his headache to worsen. Dehydrated and operating on less than a few pints of blood, he opened the top to yet another bottle of Hennessy, taking down another gulp as he leaned on his elbows to sturdy himself on the bar chair. Ronel, sitting next to him, looked into his third glass of Vodka as the reflection from the game played onto it. The silence between them was comforting, as neither sought to address what transpired. Assessing his wounds by running his fingers along the cut to his abdomen, Judson noticed that the burning was less intense and the blood flow stopped. Standing to his feet, he took the rest of the bottle to the head until empty, then slammed it to the counter.

Breaking it. Turning to walk away, his arm was caught by Ronel.

"Where are you going?" asked Ronel, before he felt Judson smack his hand away.

"Doesn't matter to you now does it. Let's skip the formality of you giving a fuck. I'm walking the fuck out of here," shot Judson as he walked to the front door.

"I know exactly what you are feeling. Defeat isn't something I have experienced much of. Honestly, I don't know what to do. I don't even know how you were able to heal. It took me longer to do so."

"Well congratulations Brother, now you have joined the ranks of us common folks. I healed because I have purpose. I drink, I wallow, and I get my ass the fuck back up. I don't sit around and let the drinks drink me." Judson reluctantly turned his attention to his brother. "Unlike yourself, I'm not done with this levitating muthafucka. We take the "L", get back up, and do something about the shit! It's time to reassess oh fearless leader."

"We have to get Sonya."

"Don't insult me. Do you think you are the only one that can sense her energy, and vice versa? Just because I don't have power over fire and whatever the hell Sonya got going on, doesn't mean I don't have the ability to sense when either of you aren't breathing. Which is why I sat here next to you and didn't mention her at all."

"By no means was I trying to imply that you were a weaker vessel Brother."

"Yet you never came to my defense when the old man wrote me off, and prized you and Sonya. Gee, I wonder was that the only time you did that?" Judson exited the bar, leaving Ronel without a word to say. He returned his attention to his comfort.

"Another round please," said Ronel to the barkeep.

"He's off in a hurry isn't he?" asked a familiar voice. Ronel looked over and saw Rosa take a seat next to him with his jacket over the evening gown she was wearing. He didn't notice that it was gone, or that he didn't have it on. "I have never met a snake that injects himself constantly with another snake's venom."

"Venom makes antivenin, so in a sense, my body is simply a conduit for a soothing, healing process," replied Ronel, staring into her brown eyes as he took another sip. Rosa rolled her eyes and removed the overcoat. She called over the bartender and ordered red wine.

"Judge me and then join me huh?" asked Ronel, drawing closer to her, but was stopped by the soft touch of Rosa's hand on his chest.

"I'm worried about you. I'm used to you assessing everything from breach, to an exit plan in a matter or milliseconds. A plan to the backup plan in the stickiest of situations. But back at the mansion, I didn't even recognize you. You froze." Rosa searched her once beau's eyes for anything other than what she observed. "You're afraid of whatever that was, aren't you?"

"I fear nothing."

"Then why are you drinking like a man counting his days? You're seeking an exit plan without finishing the mission soldier."

"You wouldn't understand Rosa!" shot Ronel. "Last time I checked, you were the one that ran off when it got too real between us." Rosa squirmed in her chair as Ronel stared a hole into her temple. She then took another sip of wine.

"You know I know nothing but this life. What you wanted for us could never be. Not if one has to watch the other age and die. I'm not willing to put you through that, and I don't feel guilty. This isn't about us. This is about the moment you have been waiting for all of your life, and you froze. Why?"

"I do not fear Charles, nor do I fear the monster he has the ability to transform into. I fear the deep connection behind it. Call it weird but I felt his pain, coupled with his fighting style. It was like watching someone you love want you dead." Rosa's eyes met his, and as he prepared his lips for another swig, she put her hand over the opening of the glass.

"You have never been one to shy away from a challenge," Rosa continued. "I have seen you kill off a whole militia without breaking a sweat. You need to find that guy and bring him back to the surface."

"There are some things that aren't that simple Rosa. My power, my body and my memory are so out of whack. They have been for a while. Ever since seeing him again."

"And no answers from the old man?" asked Rosa. Ronel

slipped his hand into the side of his dress pants and pulled out the end of the long chain link.

"He gave me this. I'm not even sure what to do with it," said Ronel, getting up from the chair and pulling out the excess metallic yoke that was attached to his blade. He then threw it to the ground. "How is this supposed to help me?"

"It can't help you if you look at it as junk," reasoned Rosa as she stooped down to scan the old weaponry. "Didn't you once tell me that it's not your mind that guides your abilities. Not even sight?"

"Yes, I did."

"Close your eyes."

"Why?"

"Just do it," insisted Rosa, walking over to a rolling tray with an assortment of kitchen utensils. Rosa picked up as many sharp instruments she could hold and placed them on a vacant table.

"Are you threatened by me?" asked Rosa from across the room.

"No," retorted Ronel.

"Good," said Rosa as she skillfully hurled knife after knife at Ronel. Without lifting a hair follicle from his lashes, Ronel reacted to each projectile with agile reflexes. Dodging without moving his feet.

"This is a bad game of dodgeball," snickered Ronel.

"Let's try the kitchen sink then," said Rosa as she launched an abundance of metal objects at him from the full tray. Reaching behind her, she unveils a rare mini-sized UZI that she fires towards him as well. The chain link lifted from the ground, spinning the machete so fast that everything was knocked away. Ronel opened his eyes to see the blur of a forcefield, catching the quick look of his blade in its midst. Reaching out his hand, the spinning stopped and the chain link whipped back. Sending the handle of his machete back into the palm of his hand. Rosa lowered her weapon and walked over to him. Stroking her fingers against his forearm, and up to his bicep.

"Well would you look at that? Looks like someone hasn't lost his ability to handle long weapons at his disposal," winked Rosa. Ronel's dimples deepened as he smiled.

"And to think you were my first."

"Well, you damn sure weren't mine," teased Rosa. "In fact, before all of this is done. You might not be the last guy I have to shoot at." Rosa put his coat back on around her shoulders seductively.

"I need a ride, soldier," requested Rosa.

"Are you sure you can handle the torque?" asked Ronel as he jingled the keys to his two-wheeled rocket.

"You could barely last 5 minutes when I'm dropping the torque of these hips on you," nudged Rosa as she swiped the key from his hands. Swaying her hips to entice him to follow, Ronel took another shot and obliged her.

"That was one time by the way."

"Yes, one time. Then another time. And another, and

another." The duo continued their witty jabs at each other out the door of the bar. Dawn peaked in from the coast. The motorcycle revved and Ronel rolled away with Rosa in tow. Ambitiously steering his bike throughout his path with a renewed focus, and hope.

Chapter 26:

Common Law

"*Ti So-so!(Little So-So) Come here little baby,*" *said Carline, as the child ecstatically ran towards her. Lifting her up and spinning her around to insight more laughter from the toddler. Their eyes met as Carline hummed a melody to Sonya. From humming, to words foreign to them both. Sonya hung onto each note as flight to air. Marveling at the voice of her mother. "You want to go bother Daddy? Let's go bother Daddy."*

"*How long do you plan on staying in those notebooks darling?*" *asked Carline to the back of her husband's short afro. Stopping to wipe his eyes from hours of reading and reviewing his formula calculations, he turned his head slightly.*

"*Just simply reviewing the formula for Duvalier's serum. Although I feel that is complete, I can't help but feel that I may have missed something,*" *replied Reginald, returning his* attention to his work. Carline released Sonya to the floor. Looking up at her mother, then running towards her father and grabbing onto his leg. "Hey So-so! Now why would your mother let you go like that?"

"Maybe it's a soul."

"Soul?"

"He doesn't have one. Maybe that is what the serum is missing," Carline replied candidly. Reginald quickly stood up to place his palm over her mouth.

"It is talking like that that has caused a lot of our friends to go missing. I beg of you to keep such thoughts as only thoughts. At least until we are safe on the plane," interjected Reginald softly, yet stern. "I will get us out, I promise. At least for our children to have a chance for lives not under a regime like this."

"You have only looked at your daughter once," said Carline as she picked up Sonya. Reginald stopped reading to look at the excitement absent from his wife's face. He reached out his hands, and Carline handed Sonya over to him. Bouncing her on his lap, the child chuckled and the smiles returned to their faces.

"Even in utter hell, roses still bloom from the ashes," said Carline, who now stood behind her husband, massaging his shoulders. "As much as you don't like to hear it my love, you are playing with fire. No good will come of this if Duvalier gets his hands on that serum. You know that not so deep inside, your hero is a demon."

"You think I don't know that? I did not choose him; I chose

you and our children. To build a better life than what we had. If that meant signing a deal with the devil himself, I would do it again with my own blood. So do not question where my intentions dwell. It is almost time for us to get away from it all," affirmed a wild-eyed Reginald. Carline stepped back as the vibration from her husband's voice still thumped at her eardrums. Reginald saw her fear, and reached out his hand as Sonya did the same with both arms extended in excitement. Carline took his hand as he pulled her in for an impromptu dance. With each step, Carline rested her head more comfortably on his chest as Sonya toyed with her hair.

"I wanted nothing but the best for us and our family. Soon we will be free. All of us," sighed Reginald with his eyes clenched in slight anguish. Carline nodded in agreement as they held each other. A glass on Reginald's office desk filled halfway in rum, began to form ripples on the surface. Carline lifted her head as the rumbling gained strength with each passing second.

"Where are the boys?" she asked in a trembling voice.

"They should be here by now," Reginald responded while peering out the window into the front yard of their home. Before he could turn away, he caught the sight of his sons coming up the driveway. He smiled in relief but briefly. He then noticed that the boys were running towards the home at top speed. He knocked over a chair and corner table with Sonya in hand and got to the door to open it with haste. Ronel and Judson made it through the threshold of the home and into their mother's awaiting arms. It

was then that the parents saw them. One after the other, pick-up trucks filled with men dressed in navy blue, carrying guns as long as antennas in the distance. The events that would take place next, replayed in Sonya's head as she laid passed out on the damp floor of a dark warehouse. The sun peeking through the cracks and holes in the tin ceiling. Mathieu shook her as she tossed back and forth. As her eyelid's struggled to open, she reached for one of her hidden knives and instantly put it to the carotid artery lining his neck.

"Where am I?!" sneered Sonya as she clinched the back of Mathieu's neck.

"We are safe! I saved you from what my father was about to do to you. I mean no harm. If I did, I would have killed you in your sleep," belted Mathieu gasping for relief. Sonya released her grip and stood up to her feet, keeping the blade at his neck. He rose with her.

"Jesse! Jesse! Do you read me!" yelled Sonya as nothing but static and white noise came through each channel she flipped to.

"I have a phone. You can use it to contact your friend," volunteered Mathieu. Reaching into his pocket, a slight pierce from the blade caused him to squirm.

"Move or interject anything without me asking you to; and it will be the last gesture you make. If I was not so weak right now, I would snap your neck off clean!" warned Sonya as she motioned for him to hand over the device.

"And you're welcome! Saving your life is such an evil act.

Please, do me the honor of being my executioner," Mathieu replied slyly as he pressed his neck against the dull edge of her blade.

"Although tempting as it may, I need to find my way back." Sonya reluctantly withdrew the threat, and presented Mathieu his phone back. "No Signal. Where are we and why did you kidnap me?!" pressed Sonya.

"I am trying to protect you. My father seeks the blood of Mayer's descendants. It's the only way that his transformation will be absolute. I can tell that he took an exceptional interest in you and the power you displayed back there against him and Max. I saw it in his eyes. He wants you and I can't watch him torture and kill anymore souls!" said Mathieu as he flopped back against the wall.

"Your crocodile tears could fill up a well for all I care. If you feel so strongly about your father's methods, you would have done something about it by now."

"I am doing something about it right now by saving you from being another one of his doctor's test subjects. I want what you all want."

"We want your father's head on a stake. Do you expect me to believe that you will betray your own flesh and blood?"

"He betrayed me! He betrayed my trust and used me as a mouthpiece. He is using me to gain the highest office in Haiti. Using me as a front to bring back a dictatorship that will make Duvalier and Castro look like a child's play." Mathieu as he sat to the ground in frustration.

"Castro? Does Charles have nuclear aspirations? That would be impossible, even now. We have eyes in the sky, land, and sea. There is no way he will be able to initiate any type of nuclear program without the government knowing about it."

"How blind are you? Don't you realize that HE IS the nuclear bomb?! What you saw earlier is just an inch of the power he is capable of generating. When I am elected President, he will be the one calling the shots until he no longer has use for me and kills me off too."

"You sound so sure that you will win the election. Did you two buy out the competition?" asked Sonya sarcastically.

"No, I watch him slaughter them all in front of me without remorse or hesitation. I have tried all my life to get from under his shadow. The more I fight, the bigger he eclipses. You have no idea what that feels like," relented Mathieu.

"I do know what it's like to have someone you trust, look at you like a child. Always needing their direction," conceded Sonya. "But enough with exchanging daddy issues. I need to get in contact with my team."

"What if I told you that there is a way to kill him?" proposed Mathieu.

"I would be inclined to listen. What's in it for you?" asked Sonya.

"I want our people and our homeland to be prosperous once again. Without the iron fist of a dictator. He will drain the island for what little it has left. I can't see another innocent child die. Please, I will tell you all that you want to know. Just let me help you," begged Mathieu.

"You can start by telling me where we are and how I can get a signal"

"This is a location off the grid, purposely built to block all methods of communications. I had it built to plot against my father without the Candiru finding my whereabouts. So far, no one wants to oppose him. So, it's just been me plotting for months to stop him." said Mathieu. He walked over to a nearby workstation and picked up a small USB drive, presenting it to Sonya. "Here."

"What is this?"

"A token of good faith so that you know for sure that I am worth trusting. This is all I have compiled on my father's transformation which will be beneficial to you and your brothers. Well encrypted. I did some listening at MIT. All I ask in return is a seat at the table to take him down," requested Mathieu.

"I don't trust anything that comes from that monster, including you. If there is anything valuable on this drive, then we can explore not arresting you on conspiracy charges. Or worse, making you collateral damage," asserted Sonya.

"Fair enough. Just put in a good word for me when you get back to your superiors at the CIA. Trust me, they are going to worship the ground you walk on after you show them the contents of that drive."

"We will see. Now, how do I get out of here?"

"You are remarkable, you know that?" asked Mathieu.

"And you are a son of a Bitch!" replied Sonya. "Again, how do I get out of here?!"

Chapter 27:

The Get Back

"Who is it?!" yelled Judson peeping through the side window of his place. There was something familiar about the jeans on the unknown visitor. The plumpness of her rear end excited him, but he stuck to his raucous demeanor. The door continued to rumble with each knock, which caused Judson to grab the AK-47. He was well aware of the same scenario being played out in numerous home invasions. "I said who is it! I ain't gonna ask again! Next time its lead coming through the door!"

"It's ME!" yelled Shona. "Let me in, we need to talk!"

"What is there to talk about? How much I owe for your little boyfriend's car?"

"That was real fucked up Judson! You left me on the hook for that, but that's not why I'm here. Open up!" yelled Shona. Judson unlocked the door, and looked past his former companion.

Darting his eyes around to scan for anything out of place. He motioned for her to enter before closing the door behind them.

"Shona, I will take care of the expenses," began Judson.

"Is that blood?!" asked Shona as she made her way into his apartment. The stack of clothes on the bed bore the bloody evidence from the night prior. "What mess did you get yourself in now?!"

"I'm fine. I'm still breathing. But that bastard that did it is on borrowed time," said Judson as he sat down on the side of the bed. Unloading and reloading the weapon methodically.

"I have never seen you so much blood, just a few drops before healing. Did you heal right away? Who is this bastard?" asked Shona as she sat next to him.

"He nearly cut me completely in half. I don't understand why it took me longer to heal. I thought that was just happening to Ronel. The bastard in question is Charles," replied Judson, staring back at her.

"You mean the man who," paused Shona.

"Yeah, him. I wasn't afraid of him, but he has Ronel stuck like a rookie. I have never seen him that way," replied Judson.

"I'm sure your brother can handle himself. We need to get you in the shower," said Shona as she grabbed at his arm. Judson reluctantly follows. Fighting another lightheaded feeling, he kept his composure. Looking down at the wound, he noticed that it had now fully healed. Shona opened the glass door to the shower and leaned in to turn on the water to an appropriate temperature.

Judson abruptly drops down to a knee, struggling to get back up. Shona lowered herself under his arm to give him support. Judson points to a bottle of infused water that he was replenishing himself with. She grabs it and puts it to his lips. As he richly drank, their eyes met as the years of love showed up briefly. Fully clothed, she entered under the shower head with him. She held him as they both soaked in the hot water as steam caused the glass to haze. Judson emptied the squeeze bottle and noticed what he had taken for granted for years. As the mixture of dried blood clots and dirt spiraled into the drain, he wrapped his arms around her. Shona's newly done hair was ruined of course, but it was not a priority at the moment as Judson quickly found her weakness. Caressing her back made her moan as she turned away to hide her pleasure.

"This has to stop. You can't be coming in and out of my life like this Jude. There is so much to life than this street shit. There are some things worth living for, instead of this path of destruction you are on," pleaded Shona as Judson buried his lips into her neck.

"I know and I promise I won't leave you again," replied Judson.

"There is something else you need to know," began Shona.

"You're all I need." Judson lifted her drenched, stained t-shirt over her head, then fused his lips into hers. She melted. Losing control of her lower limbs, before suddenly regaining strength. Jumping and wrapping her legs around his waist. She pulled away as a last act of defiance against the man that still made her heart leap bounds. Shona gave into his lips once again. The beaten fighter's hands gripped onto her curvaceous lower cheeks, creating dimples around his fingers as he carried her out of the shower into the hallway. Breaking their lip lock to animalistically glance into each other's eyes. Within a few seconds, apologies, understanding, and forgiveness was exchanged pupil to pupil. Licking her lips as he bit his, they made their way next to a bench near the bed where he lowered her to the ground. She pushed him down to the seat and the duo quickly made their way out of the rest of their wet apparel. She lowered herself onto him and the two let out moans of pleasure and excitement before she rode him with a reckless abandon. Ten seconds later, the damage was done. A release of Judson's delight bred the beginning of Shona's disappointment.

"Really nigga?!" asked Shona as she sat up.

"Um, I was in jail, remember? Nobody told you to get thicker than I remember."

"I'm gonna get in the shower, that was wack as fuck!" said Shona as she grabbed a towel nearby. Finding a mirror, she deflated at the sight of her damaged hair.

"Bet it was better than you had in a while."

"You are delusional," hissed Shona, attempting to see if her hair could be salvaged. Judson, reinvigorated at the sight of her naked body, stood up and pulled her toward him.

"And just like that, I'm ready for round two," said Judson.

Shona looked at him as if he lost his mind, but her attention was quickly taken away by his recovering manhood. Again, their eyes met, and the fire was once again ignited. Lifting her abruptly to a sitting position on his shoulders, her dangling legs and toes told the story of the sensation that began. Her chariot, ever the cocky, paced the room as he held her up. His tongue peaking to the button to her body's intense jolts. Shona trembled in his grasp and nearly lost her sense of gravity when he suddenly lowered her face to face. What took place afterwards would go on to be a few hours of nosey neighbors cracking their doors. Looking out their windows, and stopping in their steps as Shona's screams of ecstasy filled the evening air. Echoing throughout the apartment hallways, and through the thin walls that separated them from everyone else. Then, there was silence. Their sweat drenched bodies wrapped in what was left of the bed sheets. Nothing was left on the mattress but panting human flesh intertwined.

"Did we break the bed?" panted Shona.

"Yeah, we did," replied Judson, pointing out the broken and mangled steel bed frame below the box spring. They flopped back onto the bed after seeing their handy work. Shona laid her head on his chest.

"You have to be better," relented Shona.

"Damn, I thought I did my best work. My stroke game is superhuman, I don't know what you talkin' bout," chuckled Judson.

"It's not that. It's you. You have to be a better man now Jude.

Even with your past coming back to bite you in the worst way. Things are different this time."

"What's different?! That bastard is still breathing. For every amount of oxygen he takes in, it is burning at me like napalm."

"Can you put yourself aside for just one second? Can it not be about you all the time? There are other ways to fight Jude. You could have gone pro, and you still can. There is something you need to know and it's something that we have been waiting to break to you. Father Elam--"

"What does he have to do with anything Shona?! What does he have to do with anything?!" repeated Judson angrily.

"Baby, listen, you have to know--"

"Wait," interrupted Judson as he quickly sat up. Shona wanted to retort but he quickly put his hand over her mouth. Judson smelled the air, and could hear the breathing on the other side of the door. The clacking noise of numerous firearms taken off safety forced him to cover Shona before the door flew open. Multiple rounds began to fire. Judson did his best to conceal what meant most to him. As the projectiles entered into his flesh, he managed to roll out of the bed, carrying Shona into the bathroom. The firing stopped, and a familiar voice yelled out to him.

"Oh, Bitch Boy!? Come on outside. Did you think this shit was over?!" yelled Bello as he loaded another clip into his automatic assault rifle. An angry Judson attempted to stand on his feet, forgetting that he held Shona in his arms who was gasping for air. Looking down at her, he noticed that she was bleeding from her chest. The few bullets that manage to make it pass his shielding attempts, exited out of her back. Judson pressed his hand onto her wounds to stop the bleeding, while watching his own heal; expending the bullet fragments out.

"It's ok Jude. It's ok. You're not as bulletproof like you think you are," smiled Shona as her eyes widened in pain.

"Baby, I got you! I will get you straight to the hospital!"

"It's ok. I love you, and she will too once she meets you."

"What are you talking about? You're not leaving me! Who are you talking about?" asked a jittery Judson defiantly.

"Your daughter. Promise me that you show her how to survive in this world. I'm sorry I never told you," said Shona before taking another deep, struggling breath. She looked into his eyes. Judson's expression and face began to tense in agonizing torture as her life began to fade. Shona's eyes then moved their attention from him to the ceiling above, her body becoming heavier in his arms. Judson continued compressing her wounds knowing she was gone. He looked towards the bullet riddled door that was beginning to collapse from the constant blunt forces to it. With each hit, the temperature to his anger broiled as he stood up. Gently laying Shona's body to the ground. Before he could take another step he felt an overwhelming energy escaping his sweaty pores. The power to the complex was cut off instantly. The power transformers exploded one by one for blocks, scaring his abusers on the other side of the door. Judson's eyes lost their brown hue, becoming infused in ivory. The buzz of electrical static shot from his feet into the floor. The muffled moans of men outside drew his attention. Judson catapulted his body forward through the bullet-riddled door to find multiple masked men standing still as smoke emitted from their bodies. The henchmen fell to the ground in unison once the buzzing stopped. Judson looked down a few stories and peeked Bello entered a vehicle before that sped off into the night. Frustrated, he pummeled his fists into the concrete railing as the white aura around him began to dissipate. Law enforcement and fire sirens loomed in the background as Judson struggled to regain his composure. Looking back at Shona's body, Judson's emotions overflowed. He walked over and dressed himself, then he picked her up. Carrying Shona down the steps, and walking barefoot into the darkness. Although she was dead, he knew that the hospital was only 5 minutes away on foot. His eyes were empty without a speck of energy. Hearing nothing but the beating of his own heart. The twitching of his facial muscles were enacted by the constant questioning, and disappointing answers he could come up with internally. One thing was clear to the grieving father. No cemetery had enough room to accommodate the line of bodies he intended to place in them to get to Bello. An orchestra of artillery was needed, and he knew the maestros personally.

Chapter 28:

Pills

The frigid, empty pharmacy was empty as Pop tuned in to his favorite radio nightly show. Piman Bouk's voice roared through the store speakers, rattling off of the freezer doors in the back. The classic introduction was mouthed and mimicked by Pop, counting a wad money in the open. The tube light began to flicker over his bald head, disrupting his count. He started over, resting his large, hairy forearms over his grandiose stomach, draped with a white apron. Another flicker sent his heavy-set frame to the other side of the counter in an angry haste. Grabbing a broomstick to knock at the light's aging terminals until it remained lit.

As he batted away the dust mites, the bell on the store entrance rang and in walked a young man. He awkwardly walked towards the counter and spoke, but Pop could not hear him.

Turning down the radio, Pop placed the money on the counter.

"Speak up man, I can't hear you," said Pop. The young man's face farrowed at what he interpreted as a rude response.

"I said I want some condoms," replied the lily-skinned teenager looking around to make sure no one else heard his request. A grin graduated into a large smile on Pop's face.

"Oh, so little white boy tryna get Allison to give it up, huh? Yo 'A'!"

"What?!" replied Pop's associate from the back room.

"Get me some regular lifestyles from the back for Steve Wilkos' nephew here!" replied Pop.

"No bro, I want magnums," whispered the customer angrily. Pop sized him up and down, before laughing obnoxiously in his face.

"Who told you that you needed those? Yo 'A', scratch the lifestyle. Give homeboy a Durex!" belted Pop in another laughing fit.

"I'm the customer here, "bro"! My dad has more money than that little chump change you have on the counter. I said I want–." The stunned customer looked down the barrel of an unusually large, exotic firearm that Pop pointed at him.

"I got your magnum bitch! Meet my Maggie, last name Eagle. Gold plated, 6-inch barrel homeboy and that's just the tip. This baby is a classic, and she doesn't like safe sex. She's a lot like your little becky, she gives brains something explosive to think about," sneered Pop, adjusting his grip on the pistol. He pressed the cold end into the young man's forehead who was shaken and wide eyed. Relieving himself into his starched jeans.

"Aww shit, this nigga done pissed himself!" scoffed Pop, holstering the massive weapon to his side. 'A', his associate, would emerge from the back storage area. Sporting his multi-colored braids while cleaning an extender magazine cartridge with a steel brush.

"Why did you have to pull the pistol on him? I ain't cleaning it that shit up," said 'A', taking pity on the boy as he threw a pack of condoms at the boy's feet. "Might want to clean up my boy. Last thing you need is her drying up after smelling piss on you."

Pop snatched the money out of the customer's hand and directed him to the front door. Then increasing the volume of the radio once more. The young man continued to stand waiting on his change.

"No change muthafucka!" yelled Pop. "And there better not be any cops coming in here asking me about shit or me and 'A' tag-teaming your hoe!"

Leaving a trail of urine-laced footprints in a hurry, the young man fled. Before the door could close behind him, it was caught by a blood-soaked hand. A bewildered Judson, breathing through sweat and the stench of fresh blood on his clothing, made his way in. Each step he made had intention, and Pop saw dollar signs written all over the familiar revenge strut.

"Oh, shit Jude! When the fuck did you get out of prison? Where did all that blood come from?" asked Pop, noticing the fresh blood still leaking from Judson's healing wounds. "Fuck, now there is pee and blood on the damn floor. I don't need this shit, I'm trying to run a business here and now my shit is a scene out of 20/20!"

Judson wasted no further breath. "I want a gun. A BIG gun. I know you got it."

"I don't know Jude, you still have the last tab you ran up. I still haven't gotten the money for that," said Pop, continuing to adjust the radio dial as the AM station's distorted audio aggravated him. Judson throws two bloody bags onto the counter filled with cash.

"Like I said, I want a BIG GUN! Something that will air out Sun-Life Stadium! I want bodies, on bodies to pile up," spat Judson who struggled to keep himself from losing control of the tears and anguish that were undeniable. Pop had never seen Judson this way and relented.

"Yo 'A', lock the front. We have a private shopping event that starts now. Come on Jude, I think I got what you need." Leading Judson to the back area while 'A' locked up, Pop opened a steel door hidden behind some storage scaffolding. The heavy set owner attempted to make small talk, but Judson complied with equally short and to the point answers.

"Levitation you say? Well, I got something that will bring anything down to your level." Pop opened a large metal trunk at the far-right corner of the room. Retrieving a sleek, shiny instrument that he handed to Judson.

236

"Modified M60 rifle. Lightweight, but durably encased. It's easy to carry and run with while still packing the punch you need. Comes with two bullet canisters. Running out of bullets with just one of these would be overkill. But since you are fighting a "god", I'll throw in two other canisters. I only have one of these party starters left," pitched Pop.

Judson examined the war machine. "Good. I will take two of them."

"Nigga, did you not just hear me say?" said a contrived Pop.

"I know you have more than one Pop. You always keep the rare shit for yourself. The fact that you are selling this means you got a few more in your inventory," replied an emphatic Judson as he loaded the bullet canisters into a duffle bag.

"I don't know what it is about prison that make people smarten the fuck up." Pop reached for another identical assault rifle in another case nearby. "This wouldn't have anything to do with that Clerveaux crew trying to take over Haiti, would it? I don't want them problems Jude."

"Keep listening to the news. I'm about to make your products really famous," replied Judson stoically. "A" marched in with the bags of cash Judson brought in originally, throwing them at his feet.

"Yo bruh. You're short! Each of those guns are $40,000 with the canisters and ammo. The weight is off?!" yelled 'A' as he went to draw a machete from behind the freezer. Pop raised his hand to halt the tension.

"What was the weight?" asked Pop.

"6 pounds, 9.8 ounces. The nerve of this nigga to pad the top with hundred-dollar bills," replied 'A'. Pop thought to himself, and caught the slight grin on Judson's face as he came to the realization of the mishap.

"Actually 'A', it's $100,000. $50,000 in hundreds, and another $50,000 in twenties. The math don't lie," smiled Pop as he dapped up Judson. "Look at you all grown up and paying off your debt with interest. Whatever is going on, I hope you win. I like this version of you Jude."

"Like I said, keep your ears to the streets and CNN. It's about to be a whole massacre!" stated Judson, preparing to exit the room. He stopped at the corridor, and glanced back at the daytime pill pushers. "A lot of bodies are about to drop.

Chapter 29:

Believe Me

“Where did you get this information?” asked Agent Tanner. “And why did you feel that it was your call to contact the Director directly?”

“We can debate rank another day. This information was too good to pass up. I called Director Lee because he has to be briefed immediately,” replied Sonya. Director Lee stormed into the room wearing a tracksuit, clearly inconvenienced from his Sunday run.

“Will somebody please explain to me why I was awakened at 5:00 AM?!” barked the Director as he sat down at the head of the conference room table.

“My apologies, Director Lee, but you have to see this with your own eyes,” said Sonya. She proceeded to load the thumb drive into the conference room’s workstation, while simultaneously bringing up a video call with Jesse.

"Who gave your hacker friend authorization?! I am already halfway done with your walking papers Jean-Baptiste!" asserted Tanner, crossing her arms. Director Lee motioned for Tanner to allow it. She exhaled and flopped down in one of the swiveling office chairs. "This better be good."

"Jesse, please brief the Director on what we have," instructed Sonya. A series of files and pictures swarm the big screen.

"What are we looking at here?" asked Agent Tanner.

"This drive was secured by Agent Jean-Baptiste during her recent reconnaissance mission, given to her freely by Mathieu Clerveaux. In my opinion, the worst encryption method I have ever seen but who's asking, right?" said Jesse slyly, before highlighting a few files in particular. "These are very detailed records of a particular series of events that took place right after the Death of Francois "Papa Doc" Duvalier. You may recognize Dr. Nickolay Ursov. The Russian doctor was tied to numerous nerve gas plots denounced by the Kremlin. Here he is standing next to a very youthful, but severely injured Charles Clerveaux at a remote medical facility."

"So even while plotting against the United States, these two manage to squeeze in well-wish visits?" asked Director Lee.

"I'm afraid it goes deeper than that sir. There are documents that indicate that Charles was not assisting Ursov with any mission or development having to do with Russian interests. Instead, the good doctor was brought in at the behest of Charles himself to aid his surgical team," explained Jesse.

"How is an exiled Tonton Macoute chief able to afford this top-level medical staff? Something big had to lure Ursov out of hiding to operate so freely right under our noses," expressed Lee.

"Our guess? It probably had something to do with this," said Jesse as another picture slid onto the screen in front of them.

"What is that?" asked Tanner.

"That is a skull," replied Jesse smartly.

"I know dingus! Whose skull is it?" probed Tanner further.

"Jesse, this is no time to be a smart ass, tell her," corrected Sonya.

"This is believed to be the skull of Mayer. You may be questioning what this old worn-out skull has to do with Charles," inquired Jesse.

"No, I am wondering why we are entertaining folklore and legends as opposed to getting down to why these two are all of a sudden the best of friends!" seethed Tanner.

"Brat'ya Zhaka. Translation, "Brothers of Jacques", are a secret society group which traces its origins all the way to Jacques de Molay, the last Grand Master of the Knights Templar. A group of which Ursov is has ties to. As the legend goes, Mayer was one of the sworn enemies of Templar, so it would be fitting that anything having to do with him brought Ursov out of the shadows," informed Jesse.

"Still not understanding. Why would he choose a low-level exiled commander on his deathbed?" asked Lee.

"A vested interest in taking down the organization that has opposed the "Brothers of Jacques" for centuries. That being the Assembly and the Candiru that protect them. Charles not only infiltrated Mayer's organization, he made them believe that he is Mayer in the flesh. Back from the dead," Jesse further expounded.

"How did he manage to fool an infamous, and dangerous international group of mercenaries?" pressed Tanner.

"Show them the footage Jesse. You might want to hold onto your stomachs," said Sonya. The video began to play.

"That is disgusting! What is this?!" fumed Tanner with her hands over her nose and mouth.

"That is Charles with his face split open, and those are fragments from the skull of Mayer being surgically fused to Charles' skull" answered Jesse. "There is Dr. Ursov using a radioactive serum substitute that he is feeding into Charles's arm via an IV."

"It must be some form of nuclear therapy, which explains the use of Ursov's expertise. This couldn't have come cheap," said Lee.

"There are records of campaign funding going to a few Russian shell charities, totaling in millions. Even the blind can see what that is. After numerous surgeries, Charles made a miraculous recovery but there is recent evidence that shows that he is not 100%," continued Jesse.

"Recent? What evidence would that be?" asked Tanner.

Jesse looked at Sonya's stare, and adjusted himself in his seat before answering.

"We aren't prepared to disclose that until we are absolutely sure it is concrete. Sonya narrowly escaped her encounter with Charles," said Jesse. "But we did obtain this footage. It is Charles conducting a field test in a remote, mountainside community in Haiti."

"What is he doing?" asked Lee.

"Please watch," asserted Sonya somberly. In the aerial recording from a drone, Charles stood in the midst of a heavily populated shanty town. Transforming into the dark being, he generated a massive charge of dark energy that surrounded him. Without warning, the dark energy spread flames and ash rapidly into all directions. The drone was destroyed, and the footage ended briefly. The large screen switched to another video clip. The ecstatic voice of Bello could be heard congratulating his father as he captured the aftermath on his cell phone. Skeletal remains lined the pathway to Charles as he marveled at his handy work.

"There were children there. That sick bastard!" levied Tanner. Director Lee sat in disbelief and silence.

"We sent a team to that location. Radioactivity was off the charts." said Sonya.

"So, Charles is essentially a walking nuke that has harnessed the legendary power of Mayer?" asked Lee.

"Not necessarily. We believe that somehow the skull he

retrieved was not that of Mayer, but that of Jean-Jacques Dessalines," inserted Sonya.

"Well, that took a left turn," said Tanner sarcastically. Director Lee suddenly stood up and marched towards the wall at the back of the conference room. Facing away from them. "Are we now entertaining theories of another long dead general? What proof do you have, Jean-Baptiste?"

"We don't have an explanation as to how. Yet, what is pressing is that Mathieu believes that his father has more than domestic political intentions. He intends to make Haiti America's closest nuclear threat," said Sonya. Both of her superiors exchanged looks of severe concern.

"What are the motivations of his son Mathieu?" asked Director Lee.

"He claims to be sickened by the actions of his father, and expressed his desire to follow the Haitian constitution and serve its people," replied Sonya.

"I'm not buying it," inserted Tanner.

"By the looks on everyone's faces no one is, but this is the best intel we could have ever hoped to have at our fingertips. With power like that, he is capable of initiating attacks on innocent American citizens. The power to cause major casualties if we were to engage him by ground, air, or sea. I need to contact the Pentagon," said Lee hastily. "Great work Sonya, but we are going to need more information than this. We need to find a weakness in Clerveaux's ability. Extracted more information out of Mathieu, you have free range to do whatever is needed."

The conference phone began to ring, drawing everyone's attention as the green light flickered.

"Who would be calling our private line?" asked Agent Tanner. Jesse started typing away to investigate and stopped abruptly.

"I don't know. Whoever it is is calling from a burner phone," replied Jesse.

"Put it through," requested Lee.

"This is Agent Tanner speaking, who is this?"

"Oh, you the bitch Sonya don't like. Excuse me but can you please put my dear sister on the line?" requested Judson.

"Judson! What are you doing calling me at work?" asked Sonya.

"How long did you know! I know about my daughter!" persisted Judson.

"My apologies, Agent Tanner. I don't know what is wrong with him. We have been dealing with some family issues and —" began Sonya.

"I can't believe this investigation is in the hands of a rookie that clearly can't even manage a secure conference call. Take care of this! Or I will not only fire you but make sure you and your circle of misfits get probed until something sticks! I want the minutes from this briefing on my desk tomorrow morning before the crust cracks over my eyes." said Tanner.

"It will be printed in a few," replied Sonya. Director Lee

approached Sonya and tapped her on the shoulder.

"I want you to run point on this. All resources are at your disposal. Don't mind Tanner, she has seen megalomaniacs like this throughout her long tenure. I will make sure she is onboard. Washington has to know about this threat, if they haven't already figured it out. Remember to get close to Charles' son. I'm expecting great things at our next briefing," said Director Lee. "As for you Jesse. I will see to it that your clearance is reinstated within the hour."

"Finally, some recognition around here. Thank you Director," replied Jesse.

"Is there anything more?" asked Lee.

"With the exception of some incomplete data on the drive. I don't think so. I've run scans, and they seem pretty benign," answered Jesse.

"Well keep us apprised of any new developments. Let's get this son-of-a-bitch and everyone attached to him," said Lee as he left the room. Sonya and Jesse celebrated in silence as they both mimicked giving each other a high-five. Sonya then returned her attention to the conference phone.

"What are you talking about Judson?! And how did you get through to this line?" asked Sonya. Suddenly, the sound of the 6 AM train rolled by, and the sound could also be heard coming from the open line between them.

"You're here?" asked Sonya.

"Come on down sissy and I will gladly express my

grievances," snapped Judson before hanging up.

Chapter 30:

Exchange

"What do you think you're doing?" blasted Sonya as she made a B-line towards the haze cloud Judson blew into her face.

"So I can't pop up on my baby sister when I need her the most?" pestered Judson.

"I could have lost my job!" belted Sonya before stepping back and holding her nose. "I know the difference between the smell of dank and body odor. When was the last time you showered? And whose blood is that?"

"How long have you known?" pressed Judson.

"I don't even know what you are talking about. Is that shit laced with flakka?" joked Sonya.

"I'm talking about my daughter," replied Judson. Sonya's playfulness left her face when she realized his tone changed.

"Where's Shona?" asked Sonya. Judson took another tote from his blunt and threw it to the ground before launching his face into hers.

"She's dead." quivered Judson. "Bello and his squad ambushed us at the crib. Now you and weirdo hack boy are gonna tell me how to track him down. I know you are getting real comfortable with the politician."

"You're not going to mess this up for me Judson," reacted Sonya. "In case you haven't figured this out yet, this is way over your head! I just became lead on this and unlike you, Elam, and Ronel, I am going to bring justice for our parents. I'm going to do this MY WAY. You come anywhere near this, I will make sure they put you in a box under the jail. I'm sorry for your loss."

"You have a lot of nerve talking to me like that! What I can't figure out is why we are still taking losses. You, and the rest of my so-called family kept me from finding out about my daughter. But I'm the one that needs to be put in a fucking box?!" exploded Judson. "All of you make me sick!"

"Look, Elam thought it would be a good idea not to tell you. He thought that you already had it difficult enough facing yourself in the mirror," conceded Sonya.

"What does he know about me?! What does he know about any of us? You said it out of your own mouth. Do you know what's really messed up? Y'all only see me as a screw up and not even human. The proverbial mirror would crack if any of you looked into it. I am the only one who is truly living their truth!"

said Judson flopping back against his donk car. Retrieving another blunt from his side pocket, he lit up once again. Sonya dodged eye contact as the truth stung, causing her to tap her sandal against the concrete sidewalk. "I want to know where Bello is now!"

"That information is confidential," replied Sonya. Judson without breaking his attention on her, reached into another pocket and pulled out a remote-like device. Pressing a button, the device beeped. "What was that Judson? What did you just do?"

"My insurance policy. I knew you would pull that police ass shit with me," exhaled Judson. "You have 30 seconds until they are collecting your burnt up CIA people from under the rubble. We both know that we are the only ones that can survive the blast. Tick tock dear sister."

"You wouldn't." Sonya hissed.

"Try me!" bolstered Judson.

"I can crush your precious donk in one snap!" winked Sonya.

"Replaceable. 20 seconds. Besides, you and Ronel aren't the only Dungeons and Dragons with power anymore," replied Judson "15 seconds."

"What does that mean?" shot Sonya.

"What I said. 10 seconds. 9. 8. 7…" counted Judson.

"Fine. Shut it off. I will have Jesse give you a com so that you know what we know," relented Sonya.

"Give me yours," demanded Judson. Sonya snatched the ear piece and dropped it in her brother's hand. Judson quickly put it into his ear.

"Punk ass Jesse, do you read?" asked Judson into the mic.

"Loud and clear asshole," replied Jesse. Judson then pressed another button, and the sounds of multiple beeps could be heard from the parking lot under the building.

"Jesse, please call me Jude. Asshole is my government name," goofed Judson. "If for whatever reason I don't get an update or somehow this thing stops working, I have back up bombs near your two masters."

"Noted," said Sonya in disdain. Judson reached out his hand but Sonya ignored it. "By the way. I don't get how something so beautiful can come from you. She is in Atlanta. As soon as Charles appeared. We made sure to keep her as far away as possible."

"What is she like?" asked a choked-up Judson.

"Pure. That is the best description I can come up with," said Sonya.

"Does she even know who I am?" asked Judson.

"Yes, unfortunately she knows her father exists and she is waiting to meet you. But you don't go anywhere near her until all of this is over," warned Sonya. Judson took another draw from his blunt, and nodded in agreement. Sonya turned away and walked back to the entrance.

"Thanks sister," said Judson solemnly.

"Yeah whatever," replied Sonya without looking back.

"Her name?" pressed Judson. "What's my child's name?"

"Carline," returned Sonya. Judson broke down. Falling to his knees and he struggled to control the culmination of everything he tried to keep at bay. The sniffles tore at Sonya as she tried to maintain her cold demeanor. "Remember, don't go anywhere near her until this is over. It's what Shona would have wanted."

Chapter 31:

All in the Family

anshee watched stoically. Particles of saliva were launched as Belllo barked orders at multiple men holding down a seizing Charles. Dr. Ursov attempted to administer yet another emergency blood transfusion, but to no relief.

"You just gonna stand there bitch?" yelled Bello.

"He is Mayer, is he not?" asked Banshee. "Until he is fully regenerated, I cannot begin the ritual to bring his dormant mind back to stop the seizures. He has to ride it out." The dark aura threw the men into the walls, instantly killing a few. Dr. Ursov stood back to his feet. The aura's whirlwind picked up all medical equipment and furniture. The sharp outer bands of the indoor cyclone violently ravished the room.

"Doctor, do something!" demanded Bello as he grabbed her by the collars of his laboratory coat.

"I have tried everything! Charles' body is being rejected by the skull itself!" roared Dr. Ursov. "We are down to our last blood bag. Until we get more concentrated DNA from one of his descendants, he will die. The radiation is rotting away his bones and internal organs."

"Then how do we fix this? It is only a matter of time before those Jean-Baptiste losers zero in on this location," said Bello as he scratched at his neck nervously. Charles' seizure began to recede as the last of the current blood pack pumped into his arm.

"He's stabilizing," panted Dr. Ursov.

"Now why would they know where to look, my brother?" peered Mathieu as he walked into the room.

"Well look who decided to come back to the lion's den? You got some nerve showing your face after running out on us!" pressed Bello. "Did you at least smash the bitch? That ass on her was sitting on an invisible shelf."

"I don't have to answer that," responded Mathieu. "Just like I don't care to reveal that you fucked up majorly by letting your ego get the best of you. That was a dumb move going after Judson. They were off limits, remember?"

"Shows how much you don't know. Father no longer cares what happens with the Jean-Baptiste suckers. After facing your little girlfriend, he wants her blood instead. So, excuse me if I took some liberties to clear out the unneeded trash," lectured Bello, turning his back to him.

"You killed another innocent bystander!" belted Mathieu.

"Unfortunately for you, Judson gave more than a damn about this one. So much so, I wouldn't be surprised if he isn't outside right now with a clear shot to your dirty, dried out, dreaded scalp." Bello turned around, using his palm to send ripples throughout the skin on Mathieu's face.

"Know your place! You are the weak link in all of this!" blasted Bello. Mathieu held his face as his elder brother shifted his focus back to Charles on the gurney. Tasting his own blood secreting from his top gum, reaching into his coat pocket, Mathieu pulled out a powdery substance.

"I've been hit harder than that!" yelled Mathieu now to his feet. Bello attempted to look back in his direction and his eyes were immediately blasted with the substance. Searing pain shot through his cornea, as if tossed onto a skillet.

"Ahhhh!" screamed Bello falling to the floor. Mathieu stood by his head and violently started ramming the heel of his custom-made shoe into the face and nose of his kin.

"Who's the weak ass now?" spilled Mathieu in a rage. Going for another stomp into the helpless, bloodied grill of Bello, his range of motion came to a standstill. Unable to breath or speak, his eyes ventured over to the gurney that was empty. Feeling a presence cast a shadow behind him yet his neck would not grant him motion. Bello looked up and saw his father levitating above them.

"Now now children, stop the fighting," reasoned Charles slyly. "Get up Bello. No one is weak when we are strong together.

Now clean yourself up." Charles then released the unseen hold he had on his youngest son, who planted his hands into his knees gasping for air. Bello stared at his brother, then his father, using the closest piece of clothing to wipe away his shame.

"The prodigal son has returned. A good father always welcomes a child gone astray," said Charles, circling Mathieu until his feet met the ground. "What is it that you have learned boy?"

"Sonya is clueless and doesn't know anything Father. She and her partners at the CIA are still chasing myths. They know nothing about how you became so powerful," lamented Mathieu.

"Lies. Why do you lie to me boy!" screamed Charles as the black aura emitting from his body sent all lightweight objects into the air once again. Lifting his index finger, Mathieu was lifted off the ground and his clothes tightening as he again gasped for air. "When I fought her, I saw her truly. Vulnerable. Scared. Yet determined. You don't get motivation like that from knowing nothing!"

"The first chance she got she took off. She knows nothing, Father! You are killing me!" blurted Mathieu in between breaths. Charles lowered him down, and released his grip.

"I am sure with the time you have spent with her, you managed to form a connection of sorts. I want you to bring her in. I offered Ronel a place at my side, and he declined. With such raw intent in the face of total adversity, she stood. I want that," waid Charles, sitting back as youth returned to his skin. His wrinkles, no longer visible. Dr. Ursov walked over to examine him.

"You must take it easy Charles. The transfusion is only going to hold the seizures away for another week. You need more DNA," pleaded Dr. Ursov.

"Why rest when you are a God!?" joked Charles motioning to Banshee to approach. "It is time, Banshee. I need Mayer's mind to possess his full power. Are you still not convinced to begin the ritual?"

"Not until I am sure you are completely him," replied Banshee.

"And may I ask what is the criteria that you see fit to keep from me?" snarled Charles.

"You know the ways of the Assembly. That is not for you to know until it is time. Worry about stabilizing the skull fragments." stated Banshee. Charles grunted in frustration. Unable to brutalize her due to her value. A smile returned to his face.

"We will see about that," responded Charles. "Tell the Candiru to get my car and my clothing. We need to pay a certain man of the cloth a visit."

Chapter 32:

Hear Me Roar

Mathieu: Sonya.

Sonya: What do you want?

M: I want you….

S: I don't have time for this.

M: I want you to help me poison my father

S: How do you plan on doing that? Isn't he already progressed to a point of no return?

M: I think I found a chink in his armor. Can we meet?

S: I don't know if we should..

M: Please, I swear it will be brief.

S: I will decide when and where. BTW, your brother fucked up majorly. Judson is coming for him.

M: That just might be a good thing.

S: Why do you say that?

M: I will reveal everything. I just sent you something. An invite to a fundraiser that is being held for my campaign.

S: What makes you think I will show up?

M: Because you want answers, we both do. I have a way for us to get what we both want.

S: Will your father be there?

M: Yes.

S: Then we meet now. I am not facing him again until I know for sure that your information is valid. Coordinates have been sent to your phone. You have 20 minutes to arrive or no more talking.

M: Agreed. See you soon.

###

"Something doesn't sit well with me with this politician," said Jesse, as he scrolled through Mathieu's file. He looked up at Sonya as she stared outside the window. Once again, his cohort was lost in her thoughts. Shona was another innocent life gone in the midst of their conflict with Charles. The thought of Judson's daughter no longer having a mother tore her to pieces. She had to stay focused on the mission. Jesse attempted again to gain her attention by clearing his throat and repeating himself.

"When has anyone trusted politicians? I think you are preaching to the choir with that one Jesse," waid Sonya nonchalantly as she walked over to her weapons cabinet. Glancing over the different blades at her disposal, she contemplated the different ways she could go about killing Charles.

"No. It's not that. You and I have been at this long enough to know that no one gives up the opportunity for power. Thugs, legitimate businessmen, politicians; even men of the cloth won't seek to destroy the opportunity for absolute power. I'm just saying, it could be too good to be true,"

"Leave the judgment calls to me. Keep those pretty little fingers tapping away at that keyboard while keeping me informed with facts, not notions."

"Hey, I'm just looking out for you."

"I don't need another man trying to look out for me Jesse! No offense but you aren't exactly the most powerful out of the bunch of men that are on my shit list." Shot Sonya.

"Oh it's like that?" asked Jesse. Sonya realized that she belittled her best friend. She attempted to appease him.

"Don't take it the wrong way," began Sonya, as she rested her hand on his shoulder before Jesse nudged it away. "There are powers at play here that you don't understand or can measure up to. I'm protecting you." Jesse glanced over his shoulder at her, then immediately shot up out of his seat while ripping his laptop and the cords attached to it from their inputs.

"Then why do you need my ass to be in your ear still? Let me know when you and the pretty boy politician are done caking," said Jesse as he made his way into the kitchen of Sonya's apartment. He continued. "For the record, I have never steered you wrong. The least you could do is respect my perspective instead of lumping me in with everyone that has ever let you down. I never have." Jesse suddenly walked towards her, catching her off guard. He reached for her hands, and her eyes met his with intensity.

"And I never will," said Jesse softly. Suddenly there was a knock at the door, breaking their focus. Sonya reached for her blade and made her way over to the front door, looking out of the peephole.

"He's here," said Sonya deflated. Opening the door to the welcome in the summer heat and Mathieu who quickly took comfort in the air-conditioned home.

"Salutations, salutations! You must be Jesse. I have heard so much about you," said Mathieu. Jesse sized him up and gave him a discomforting gaze, before retreating back to the corner.

"What's with him?" ask Mathieu.

"Nothing. So what is it that you have for me?" ask Sonya directly. Mathieu took off his satchel and revealed a laptop. She opened it and began tapping away at the keys, using his mouse to bring up the necessary files.

"According to Dr. Ursov's notes, my father's state is rapidly deteriorating despite the radiation treatments and blood transfusions performed," said Mathieu as he brought up more detailed graphs. "The DNA in the blood is not pure enough to hold Mayer's power under control. The most purest of DNA runs through you and your brother's veins."

"You know nothing about us," protested Sonya as she crossed her arms.

"I knew enough to gather blood samples left behind by you three at the mansion," replied Mathieu

"I'm going to pretend that I did not hear that. What are you suggesting?"

"Sacrifice a pawn to take the board. Judson is hungry for Bello's death more than anyone right now. I say we allow Judson to kill Bello," suggested Mathieu nonchalantly.

"What?! You are willing to sacrifice your own brother?"

"It won't just be me sacrificing. After Bello is dead and your brother is distracted, you take the opportunity to extract the blood from him. I have developed a serum that will halt Judson's healing power long enough to collect what is needed."

"Have you lost your mind?! Judson may be an asshole, but I am not going to betray my own flesh and blood," bolted Sonya as Jesse let out a sarcastic chuckle in the background.

"Judson has the ability to heal rapidly, doesn't he? I wouldn't say you are betraying him, just simply borrowing his DNA for us to poison Charles. Dr. Ursov's research revealed a major flaw in the transfusion method. If my calculations are correct, the potency of the healing element could cause a massive deterioration of the tissue if there is not an activating agent," explained Mathieu.

"What does that even mean?" asked Sonya.

"In layman's terms, your power to heal only works best during extreme cases of adrenaline. My father will be put to sleep for the transfusion and it will kill him if the DNA is given to him in a high dosage. Ursov will have to be eliminated before that time," replied Mathieu

"How am I supposed to believe that this isn't just a trick?" peered Sonya

"You can't seriously be considered this are you?!" blasted Jesse standing to his feet.

"I will show you the experiments run by my team. I have the samples here for you and anyone of your choosing to replicate. I want him gone just as much as you do," said Mathieu. Sonya's eyes spoke volumes to Mathieu. Making it clear that there would be clear consequences if this was a trap.

"Take this to your guy at the lab to verify this," Sonya called out to Jesse.

"Sonya NO! Don't trust this guy!" contested Jesse.

"Like I told you before, this is bigger than you! Now do what I said!" shot Sonya before redirecting her focus to Mathieu. Jesse's eyes opened wide in amazement and frustration. He opened his mouth to object but stopped himself. Realizing that nothing was going to stop Sonya's determination, he turned his back and initiated the call.

"Let's say that this is true, how will I get close enough to eliminate the doctor before the procedure?" asked Sonya

"Good thinking. I have thought that out as well. You will accompany me to my fund-raiser, and we will make my father the offer of Judson's DNA. He is a complicated man and subtlety is not his strong suit. He thinks we have a thing, and I say we use that to our advantage. We gain his trust and good graces, then we make our move," explained Mathieu.

"What about Banshee? She will see right through me and smell the plan before we even make the proper introductions," warned Sonya.

"You have nothing to worry about. Trust me on this one, she is more concerned about the well-being of the Candiru, and preparing for the second coming of Mayer."

"Then we will need to do everything that we can to stop his transformation from coming to completion."

"Now where is your brother Judson?" asked Mathieu.

"I will not reveal anything to you until after this information is verified. Once we persuade Charles that I'm onboard. Then I will THINK about involving my brother," replied Sonya.

"No objections here. We are going to work great as a team!"

"Do not get comfortable. After we rid this world of Charles, I am still contemplating whether or not I should allow his spawn to live," said Sonya as she reached for the blades that she laid out and sharpened them before Mathieu. He raised his hands, playfully surrendering with a smirk on his face. Jesse looked on in disgust as he opened a text window on his screen. Searching through his most recent contacts while running another encryption layer, he located Ronel's name.

Jesse: Ronel, there is something that you need to know. It's about Sonya.

Ronel: I saw the weasel walk into the apartment. Tell me EVERYTHING.

Chapter 33:

Confessions

The congregation looked on as Father Elam cleared the altar after Communion. Although his frail, damaged hands shook with each movement, eyes marveled at the precision of his movements. As he muttered a prayer to himself with his deacon at his side, he stared at his reflection in the gold chalice. Rubbing and wiping the vessel longer than usual as if he was trying to erase what he could not bear to look at any longer. After a slight nudge from the Deacon, he regained focus and handed what was left to him to store away in the Tabernacle. Elam finished the next steps and headed towards his chair as the choir and organist played. Taking his seat, he noticed the presence of multiple people sitting at the back of the church, with one man in particular in their midst. Although his eyes were beginning to fail him, he managed to make out the caliber of guns tucked away.

The rookies from the seasoned. Most of all, a more youthful Charles sat with his eyes closed, feigning being lost in the music. Elam stood and approached the microphone in front of him, interrupting the musicians with a wave of his hand.

"My brothers and sisters. As mass comes to an end today, I will not bore you with the reading of the announcements that have been the same for 10+ years," joked Elam. The crowd returned with laughter which gave Elam permission to add in a chuckle of his own.

"Although the preaching is over. I will leave you with this extra add-on," said Elam as his gaze focused on Charles. "When evil walks into your life, stand up to it. Evil deals well in fear and division. It hates and runs away from those who are firm in their belief. That in the end, good always wins. Go in Peace!"

After ending the Mass, Elam retreated to the rectory, where he removed his vestments as quickly as possible. He then reached for his staff when a booming voice entered the room.

"I never understood how men of God can make such guarantees that they themselves don't really believe," said Charles, advancing slowly as the Candiru and Banshee followed.

"If you know the word, then you know it is God's word, not mine," replied Elam.

"If there is an almighty and all-knowing being, he would have the balls to come down and say it himself. That's the kind of God I intend to be," sneered Charles observing the many religious artifacts surrounding them.

"To what do I owe such a rare visit, Charles? Have you come to erase me like you did those poor souls in that room?" asked Elam. "Or maybe the way you smithed down the last of the Assembly?"

"Oh priest. You dumbfounded me with such a cold welcome. After all, we are associates," replied Charles.

"I am no associate of your kind," darted Elam. "A thousand Hail Mary and weeks of washing could never remove the stench of your hand against mine. I regret it every day that I ever thought that I could reason with a snake like you. Please get to the point!"

"We had an agreement priest. You assured me that the eldest boy would not seek retribution with his limited power, yet I have had to smack that hand, not once but twice," began Charles. "Then the soiled second-born managed to kill one of my closest associates. Now he has tapped into a dormant power of his own. I can feel it awakening in him. Yet, the biggest habitual lie out of your mouth is that the youngest girl would not be a problem."

"She is innocent."

"She was able to withstand my power with quite a defiant force. If she hadn't blacked out, I would have broken a sweat," joked Charles as his henchmen joined him in laughter. "We had a deal, Priest. No interference from you or the bastard children, and I would spare your lives. It would seem that age has not only ravaged you to the point of pathetic deity worship, but to that of a liar!"

"I did what I could do. You're not exactly keeping a low

profile. What did you expect? How long did you think I could keep them at bay?!" argued Elam.

"Long enough for me to complete my transformation. As you can see, it does wonders for the skin." Chuckled Charles.

"Is this all a joke to you? I betrayed my own code and everyone around me by giving you those artifacts. Instead of disappearing with the skull and shard, you re-emerge hell bent on power. You don't know what it cost." Elam ripped his shirt open to reveal his aged, burnt upper body. "Look at me! This is what it cost me. You know nothing of sacrifice!"

"I didn't ask you to set yourself on fire, Priest," jousted Charles.

"What you did to their parents was too vivid. The ritual to erase their memories only amplified their power. I tried to regain control but the incantations could not stop it. We all paid a price. I, with my body, and them with their torched memory," explained Elam.

"Yet the memory we didn't want remained intact. Did you think that a complex ritual like that could work on children?" inserted Banshee as she removed her sword from her side. She advanced towards Elam. "There is nothing stopping us from killing you now traitor!"

"Except me," replied Charles, stepping in front of Banshee. "Priest, this was not a visit to hear your woes. I only hope to warn you of the woes that are to come. The children of Reginald will die at my hand if they choose to interrupt my advances. There will be no further mercy." Charles turned to walk away and his foot soldiers followed.

"You will not win. Even if you kill them, the people will reject you. No matter how powerful you become. No matter how many you kill in your wake," protested Elam. "Duvalier couldn't do it forever. Neither could his own bloodline. Even the skull fragments you have allowed the mad Russian to solder to your head will ultimately reject you. You will never be him. He will never fully accept you." Charles grinned at the corridor and returned fully into the room.

"There once was an elephant that was part of a clan so powerful, legends and even gods were mimicked after it. The Elephant was mighty and large yet the power he wielded made his physical appearance an afterthought. Brutal in battle, yet it preferred diplomacy to resolve wars amongst the multiple tribes of the world. The elephant was highly regarded," narrated Charles. "Utilizing his power to bend the mind's will to his rather than bloodshed. Changing what is seen-"

"-to that which is desired and just," interrupted Elam. "I know the story, Charles. All Candiru must know this story of Mayer. You are not teaching me anything new."

"And therein lies the problem," Charles noted. "No one questioned the Elephant as to why he elected to die. Taking with him the power that could liberate a nation. Why did he allow the circus of Europe to enslave his own species, erasing their memories of prosperity and prominence? The Elephant in the room is dead and I'll be damned if my country and the Assembly continue to breathe in the decomposing fumes of a coward!"

"You are no god," remarked Elam. "What sets Mayer aside from you is that he believed in something larger than himself. All great leaders do. The most powerful man to ever live sat at a table with the very man that would betray him, and another that would deny him." Elam leaned in towards Charles. "A lesser being would massacre everyone that sat at that table to make a point. That's who you are. A lesser man."

Charles tried to hide his disdain. The thought of Elam's bold statement in the presence of his men insulted him. As their eyes locked into each other's, Elam smiled at the confirmed sting of his comment.

"I can smite you right now!" hurled Charles.

"It will prove nothing. My death advances nothing. You are a purposeless General leading a group you will ultimately kill off because your little mind can't stand the fact that no matter what you do, you can never be favored the way Mayer was. Moreover, the way Reginald was. So, what do you have left?" questioned Elam. The room's walls began to rumble, knocking away all pictures and crucifixes. Charles' face lost his resemblance as the dark aura took over him. The face of Jean-Jacques formed as Elam kept his frame.

"Fear!" yelled the combined voices of Charles and Dessalines. Tears pooled at the bottom of Elam's eyelids. The sight continued to break at the mental walls hiding away his vulnerability. Charles laughed as the priest helplessly began to sob while backing away. "That's it traitor, fear me! You should have finished the job when you had the chance."

Elam fell down on his back, trying to create distance between him and Charles. Quickly he covered his eyes and bawled himself into a cocoon, shaking. Charles stood over him as the ground shuttered and debris from the ceiling fell around them.

"Stop it please!" begged Elam.

"Destroy this Temple, and I will raise it again in three days," exerted Charles, lifting his fists to the heavens. "That is what he said in the book, correct? I implore you to call on your God, and gather the children at his feet. Destruction is coming, and there will be no resurrection. All will kneel as the new world power and richest country in the Western Hemisphere ascends to its rightful place."

With an audible sonic burst, dark matter flushed the room as the wind became that of a category 2 storm. Elam, still with his hands over his eyes, reached out to find something to pull himself up on. Within seconds, there was calm. Charles and his men were nowhere in sight. Elam panned the room and saw the resemblance of a hand overhead. Reaching for it, he was pulled up to his feet. Wiping the moisture and debris from his face, he saw the Samaritan clearly. Yet he was not elated at who it was.

"I heard it all," said Ronel, snatching his hand away from Elam's by force. "Of all that was said about you. I still defended you."

"You don't understand," Elam retorted.

"I understand that everything that I think I know is most likely a lie. Judson was right. You are an asshole!" bolstered Ronel.

"Ronel. My son, please!" pleaded Elam.

"You don't get to call me that! My father died with more dignity than you have living. I will find a way to take him down myself," said Ronel as he backed away when Elam reached out to him. "When he gives them permission to finally exact the traitor's rations upon you. Don't look for any of us to come running."

Ronel then left abruptly, slamming the door to the rectory behind him. Elam clutched the rosary around his neck. Belting out an untamed cry as his vocal cords cracked several times in between. Alone.

Chapter 34:

Late Orchestration

*M*ayer observed the aftermath of his ship parting the sea in the night's silence. It was too silent which made him uncomfortable. Still lamenting on the warning he gave King Jacques I a few hours prior about the men he chose as his new generals. Loyalty was far from the impression he had of them, and he made sure to voice this to the freshman Emperor.

"If it bothers you so much Patron, I can turn the ship around," recommended Miguel at the helm.

"Jean-Jacques is smart. He doesn't need me to teach him how to rule," replied Mayer as he sat on the ledge of the steering column. "Believe it or not, traitors are a necessary evil. Cutting the snake's neck publicly guarantees that the behavior will not be repeated."

Miguel chuckled, and was soon joined by the rare timid

laughter of his mentor who still had his eyes in the direction of Haiti. Suddenly Mayer stood to his feet.

"Miguel, the two ships that passed us an hour ago. You said that they were supply ships, correct?" asked Mayer.

"Yes, they bared the insignia with two crossed keys," replied Miguel.

"How many men were on board?" questioned Mayer. Miguel thought to himself. A freezing draft flowed down his back as he remembered the head count. Gripping the wooden helm tightly, he realized his mistake.

"Supply ships never have more than three men aboard. How many men did you count Miguel?!" pressed Mayer.

"15 on the first ship. 12 on the latter Patron," exhaled Miguel.

"It's the Templars! If they are here, chances are they already have moles clearing a path to the shard." Mayer paced back and forth.

"Jean-Jacques doesn't stand a chance. This could be an ambush planned weeks in advance. Possibly to make it look like a coup d'etat," added Miguel. Without speaking another word, Miguel spun the helm to the right with aggression while calling to the deck hands to hoist the sails. Mayer ran to the bow of the ship and pulled out a scope to catch any remnants of the two ships.

"We won't catch up with them in time," said Mayer as he removed his overcoat.

"You're not going to swim for it are you?" asked Miguel.

"I call!" yelled Mayer. Within a flash, the white battle garment formed onto his body, with the numerous blades suspended in the air from their chain links. "I will see you at shore."

Mayer then plunged into the ocean, using the blades chained to him as propellers to push him forward. His head above water as his neck parted the waves. Mayer remained focused on the trail to stop the ambush. Miguel marveled at the Mayer's resolve, before yelling commands at the deck hands to follow the warlord gone overboard. Traveling nearly at the speed of sound, the ships were finally in sight nearing the shoreline. Lunging himself out of the water onto the closest ship, Mayer climbed up the side of the vessel silently. Once at the top, he emerged his gaze slightly above the deck floor level to assess the enemy ship in disguise. The men armed themselves heavily as the ship before them met the beach, unloading a militia of unmarked Templar soldiers. Mayer jumped on-board the trailing ship's deck and announced himself.

"Hello gentlemen. It is my understanding that this was supposed to be a secret?" questioned Mayer as the men circled him.

"It is him. The Formidable One! Kill HIM!" yelled their commander. The men advanced with their swords while others readied their firing weapons. Others entered the deck from down below to join in the massacre of one. Mayer scattered the chains in all directions as the cutting down of doomed souls commenced. Slicing at flesh, metal, and small ball projectiles shot from their muskets; Mayer walked gingerly towards the last remaining man. The chains retreated to his side except one that floated its attached blade above the head of the survivor.

"Who sent you?" interrogated Mayer. The General of the dead regiment spat at Mayer's feet.

"Such power doesn't belong to monkeys and murderous baboons! We are here to reclaim what is rightfully ours. What you stole shall be returned, even if the sands of this beach run red from everyone on this spec of land!" snickered the General.

"Here is the thing about Monkeys and Baboons. The strength of one equals the strength of ten. The way I see it? Ten down, two to go," said Mayer as spotted one more man swimming from the vessel towards shore. Taking his main sword from his side, he launched it towards the escapee. It entered the middle of his back, leaving him motionless in the high tide sea.

"Did you really think we came just for you?" remarked the General. "We now know exactly how to kill you."

"And how can you do away with that which is immortal?" asked Mayer flagrantly.

"By the one flaw every man on earth has, mortal or immortal. Legacy." replied the General, smiling. Mayer returned the smile, allowing his airborne sword to cut down swiftly. The thuds from the General's head hitting the wet wooden floor of the deck caused Mayer to shift his attention to shore. Suddenly, his keen ears caught the sound of a battle ensuing. Using his scope, he finally caught sight of Jean-Jacques holding his own against the Templars and his own men that led him into the trap. Mayer jumped down into the now shallow waters to retrieve his sword only to find that it had been removed. Looking around desperately, he then called out to Jean-Jacques.

"Brother! I am on my way!" bolstered Mayer as he ran towards his direction. Templar soldiers would flank him, but Mayer did away with them one by one with skill, agility, and deadly resolve. As the last of them fell to the mix of sand and seaweed, Mayer was halted in his steps at an unfortunate sight. The number of Templars overwhelmed his former student, pinning him down as he mercifully fought to free himself.

"Oh Formidable one!" yelled one of the men dressed in an all-black robing with the Templar insignia on his chest. Raising the broken shard in hand, he took a fresh wooden chalice from his side. Pouring a mysterious liquid into it, then placing the shard in it as well. "How long did you think you could hide it from us?"

"As long as I needed to!" yelled Mayer advancing before he noticed his sword in the hands of another Templar. It was then put to the back of Jean-Jaques neck. "That shard no longer has any power! You came for nothing!"

"Keep your distance! If that is true, then why leave it in the hands of a common man?" asked the Templar as he circled around Jean-Jacques.

"Mayer! You betrayed me!" yelled Jean-Jacques.

"No. Do not listen to them brother. They speak nothing but lies!" replied Mayer.

"Lies are his specialty, King Jacques." retorted the Templar. "He is the reason you are in such a predicament. The biggest lie of them all is the one he made himself forget."

"What are you talking about?" Mayer demanded.

"Observe." The Templar requested. One of the men kicked Jean-Jacques in one of his badly damaged ribs, causing him to cry out in pain. Another held his mouth open as the main Templar poured the mixture into Jean-Jacques mouth as they continued to strike his midsection. Making him swallow the substance.

"What are you doing?!" roared Mayer.

"Showing you that gods can die," replied the Templar. Jean-Jacques coughed violently while breathing heavily. Suddenly his body tensed and jerked forward. The men struggled to hold him down as the wind around them began to pick up. The sand under their feet darkened and joined the flow of the twister.

"Isn't it glorious?" questioned the Templar loudly over the whirring sound.

"What have you done to him?" asked Mayer. Suddenly Jean-Jacques sent his captors flying into all directions, and stood to his feet.

"You traitor!" yelled Jean-Jacques.

"I assure you brother. I have no dealings with these men," replied Mayer.

"Is this not his sword?" said the main Templar rising to his feet with Mayer's sword in hand. Jean-Jacques, enraged, made his way towards Mayer. Stuck in place, Mayer tried to make sense of what was happening. Before he could draw any amicable conclusion, the Templar men pounced on Jean-Jacques once again, putting a bag-like contraption over his head. A contraption that Mayer knew well. Mayer dashed towards them as fast as he could but what came next was not within his reach to stop.

"A traitor's death and the soul of a god in just one pull of this string!" yelled the Templar as he pulled at the lever on the side of the contraption, instantly beheading Jean-Jacques. Mayer launched himself forward spinning while releasing the chains and blades attached. Instantly killing all in his path. The blood of his enemies drenched his face and uniform as tears rolled down his face. Heavily panting, it did not occur to him that he was levitating. Once he noticed, he landed on his feet. His vision now gray and absent of all color and hue as he stared at Jean-Jacques body. Not understanding the tears flowing so profusely, he continued to wail before abruptly passing out.

"Patron!" yelled Miguel as he and Candiru reinforcements approached. Miguel knelt down next to him, checking him for any mortal wounds as he had never seen his mentor on his back on the battlefield. Miguel stopped as he heard a faint humming. Leaning in closer to Mayer, it occurred to Miguel that a trance had taken over him.

"Get him to the ship now!" yelled Miguel to the Candiru. As the men lifted Mayer up, the humming ceased and his eyes opened.

"No!" launched Mayer as he woke. "Put me down and leave now!"

"But Patron," reasoned Miguel, as the men lowered him.

"I said leave now! Return to the ship and await my word!" exclaimed Mayer. Miguel parted his lips to rebuttal but was interrupted. "Miguel, do as I say!"

Miguel stepped back and saluted his leader. Turning and leaving at once with the confused Candiru in his stead. Mayer laid next to Jean-Jacques' remains. Looking up into the gray darkness of the night. Silence once again.

Chapter 35:

Princess to Queen

The clicks of her heels knocked at the tiled floor in the lobby of the event. The red fabric of her evening dress hugged her shapely frame as security guards fought the urge to look as she passed. Sonya ran her checks and scouted all possible exits just in case something went south hours prior. Jesse silent on the channel streaming into her air. A rare occurrence, but she did not have the time to entertain it. So focused in her stride she didn't see the collision coming at the intersection of the hall. The man lost his cane from the bump, and struggled to reach down and retrieve it.

"I'm so sorry sir. Here let me get that for you," expressed Sonya. The elderly man waved her away as he grabbed a hold of the cane and supported himself to his feet. Sonya stepped back awkwardly. Avoiding eye contact. "Sorry, I didn't realize it was you. It was not intentional."

"If it was your intention. I am sure a hard floor would be the least of my worries, my child," replied Elam with a slight smile. "Your mother loved that color. She loved the way your father looked at her when she wore it."

"Thanks for keeping it all these years. It is the only thing I have left of her," said Sonya.

"You have her eyes, her courage and love. You have her ability to see good and evil," assured Elam.

"You couldn't resist could you?" asked Sonya with a barely held back frown. "You do it so effortlessly without thinking. Still thinking that I am that little girl you have lied to over and over."

"I just wanted to keep you away from the bad of the world. I didn't want you to spiral into an empty dimension that I could not pull you out of," reasoned Elam.

"What makes you think I'm not empty? You don't know what I go through or what I fight every day," mumbled Sonya. She looked around and quickly picked a napkin from her purse to catch the extra moisture that coated her eyes. Elam quickly held her arms, attempting to make eye contact.

"I will never claim to understand. No one could ever know the weight of chains that hold most of us down. We can only hope to build the endurance to carry it to the next step. But I beg of you child. The steps you wish to take here will only lead to more death and confusion."

"That's the problem. You think I don't comprehend when I

do. I have looked into the eyes of the big, bad beast. I see not only evil, but fear. Fear that I will use to vanquish him once and for all," asserted Sonya with strength and determination. Elam applied further pressure to his grip, but deflated as he realized further reasoning would not change the outcome.

"If you must stare evil in the eye, use what your mother gave you. Her song," said Elam as he clasped her hands. "Despite her death, her song lives in all of us. When the time is right, it will serve as a key to all you desire to know and experience."

"If you came here to stop me, it will not go the way you think it will." replied Sonya.

"No. You have been given all that you need. I will not hinder you any further. But please remember this," said Elam as he reached into his evening coat pocket. Pulling out a shiny tiara that left Sonya baffled. It was her mothers. Elam placed it on her head. Sonya adjusting her hair to accommodate it. "It's very rare that a Queen is crowned without a King. But when it occurs as war looms, it is up to the Queen to direct and lead her army into battle. Lead well Sonya. For every decision you make, you have countless lives that hang as collateral."

"Go home Elam." Sonya requested solemnly. "Thank you for her tiara. But it won't change what is about to happen. You don't want to be anywhere near this."

Sonya begins to walk away. Stopping, and returning to kiss Elam on the cheek before heading towards the wine glasses, and the various formal attires that swamped the Gala's floor. Elam looked on until she was out of sight. He grabbed a glass of wine from a server and leaned in to sip when Charles' youthful reflection danced in the liquid. Elam looked up to find Charles raising a glass of his own, expecting the gesture to be returned. Elam slowly and defiantly poured the wine out, before hurling the glass into oblivion on the floor, drawing the entire room's attention. Elam stood as the peering eyes questioned his behavior. He then limped away to the nearest exit with Sonya looking on as well.

"Dance with me," requested Mathieu from behind.

"And why would I do such a thing?" asked Sonya.

"A good amount of donors just saw a priest give my father the proverbial finger. I think it's time we give them a refreshing sight," replied Mathieu as he presented his hand to Sonya. She did not budge. Mathieu leaned in closer to her ear. "Look, I understand the reservations. Half of the people here have heard the rumors that my father was the culprit behind the killing of the Senators. Some who want to be part of the new regime. Others looking for a chink in his armor, willing to open their checkbooks to watch it all burn to the ground first hand. The last thing we need is my father seeing any hope of rebellion that was just displayed by your clergyman. These people are dead if that thought even crosses his mind."

"Fine," deflated Sonya, taking his hand. Mathieu led her to the dance floor as the light dimmed. The remaining spotlight highlighting only them. As the smooth voice of Mikaben over the strums of a hollow guitar, the duo pulled the crowd in with their movements.

"You are very good," complimented Mathieu.

"Don't get used to it," shot Sonya faking a smile to onlookers.

"Humor me, Sonya. You are dancing with the future president of Haiti. You have to admit we are winning over the room," laughed Mathieu as they continued to sway. A tap came upon his shoulder and the room and music went silent. Mathieu turned to face his father staring at Sonya.

"I hope you don't mind if I cut in my boy?" requested Charles as he took his son's place. Sonya, too shocked to move, looked to Mathieu to say something but he had nothing to offer in protest. "Oh, and tell the DJ to play some 'Septan' for us." Mathieu gritted his teeth and clinched his eyes shut but quickly adjusted to a smile. Taking Sonya's hand and placing it in Charles'. He then did what was asked.

"Are you scared child?" asked Charles as they awaited the music to begin.

"It is not an emotion that would help me now, would it?" presented Sonya. Charles chuckled and the music began to play. Pulling Sonya towards him, the two awkwardly at first began to dance. Finding their rhythm.

"You are a spitting image of your mother. Lighting up the room the only way she could with such God-given beauty," commented Charles.

"Was that more of an incentive for you to put a bullet in her head?" pressed Sonya.

"Oh the melodrama," snickered Charles. "Am I on trial? If so, I will not answer your questioning without my counsel present. I believe the two of you have met." Sonya panned the room and caught the visage of Banshee, twirling a blade's end against the side of her own neck while staring back.

"I would prefer to continue the dance we started back at Gomez' estate. You remember that, don't you. I had your number," whispered Sonya. Charles burst into laughter, stopping to elegantly dip her down. He brought her up as the music winded down. Charles adjusted the tiara on her head while staring at her pissed gaze.

"I think a dance like that would better suit enemies. May I suggest we discuss an alternative in my private quarters," suggested Charles.

"Lead the way," challenged Sonya. The music concluded and Charles continued to greet guests as he made his way towards a hall lined with Candiru. Sonya followed behind him. Banshee walked adjacent to her as Mathieu followed on the tail end.

"Banshee," greeted Sonya without eye contact.

"Little Bird," Banshee responded.

"Women and their catty formalities. This is why true leadership is left to the men," joked Charles.

"You sexist murderous bastard," sneered Sonya.

"Well, that didn't take long. In case you haven't figured it out you are walking into the lion's den. I ponder why so willfully?" asked Charles as the Gala was now at a distance. The Candiru men opened the large wooden doors before them. The private party entered as the doors closed just as quickly.

"I have come to make a deal with you. My brother's DNA for you to spare myself, Elam and Ronel from your wrath," bargained Sonya as she looked at Mathieu. Mathieu nodded in agreement.

"This sounds very similar to the deal the old priest made. You have every reason to not want me to ascend to the level of a god. What guarantee do I have that history won't repeat itself?" prodded Charles sitting back in a throne-like chair.

"She won't father," interjected Mathieu. "I have vetted her motivations. She is mortified at what you did to Ronel. She seeks refuge more than she seeks revenge."

"Power like her's does not fear me. Why would it now?" pressed Charles.

"I am the most powerful of us all," pressed Sonya. "Trust me, I come with all the reservations that you can think of. You have experienced firsthand what I am capable of. I am not sure that you will hold up your end out of jealousy. You know, that thing you are the King of."

"That fancy little windstorm you started in the mansion is an inopportune draft compared to what he is capable of now," laughed Banshee.

"Easy Banshee," intruded Charles thinking to himself as his

wild gaze continued to make Sonya uncomfortable with every passing second. "I accept your offer on one condition. You join me at my side or better yet, my son's side. Arranged marriages are not my thing but I can't resist. Think of it as a "joining to avert war". Like the Vikings did all those years ago." Charles stood and extended his hand.

"Sonya. I beg of you please. Do not trust this man! For God sake, he killed your parents!" yelled Jesse into her come unit. Sonya, without expression raised her hand as she walked towards the mad commander. The slicing of flesh and bone can be heard as well as the screams from the on-going Gala. Suddenly the door buckled as a force attempted to kick it in. Thump after massive thump until it stopped all together. All eyes were on the double door as heated beams glowed through the door's cavities. Flames climbed the wooden gateway until fully ablaze, vehemently flying off of the hinges.

"No!" yelled Ronel as he entered the room.

"What are you doing here?! I got this!" Sonya retorted. "I can smell the liquor on you already."

"You are just a child! Acting like a child! I am stopping you from making the biggest mistakes of your life," announced Ronel. Charles huffed and puffed as he could barely keep in his amusement.

"Now this is truly pitiful Ronel. Look what one bout with me has reduced you to. A shell of the warrior you once were," bolstered Charles. Ronel stepped in front of his sister and extended his hand to his side. The chain link brought the machete to his palm instantly.

"Sonya get the hell out of here! Jesse is waiting outside to take you away," commanded Ronel before suddenly clutching at his neck. Struggling to breathe, he dropped his sword and went down to his knees. Clawing at the sight of Charles as darkness draped over his vision, before falling onto his face, unconscious. Charles looked on as Sonya's eyes were now blue, releasing her telepathic hold on her brother's windpipe before it caused any further damage.

"Now, is there any further question as to where my loyalty lies?" asked Sonya looking down at her brother, then to all who stood in the room. "Your condition is accepted."

###

Sonya: Brother.

Judson: Well look who decided to finally reach out. I have been tapping at this detonator button for a bit now.

S: Stop bluffing Judson. The bomb squad found nothing.

J: I had to give you reason to give me Bello. You know I can't resist scaring your ass.

S: Well you got him.

J: Where is he?

S: He's heading up for the Florida Classic. Something tipped him and his crew off. He is mainly staying in well crowded areas.

J: And what's this about you possibly setting me up?

S: Elam got in Jesse's ear. You want Bello or not?

J: You know I do. Doesn't matter to me one way or the other. As long as I get to him. In fact, the Classic is a perfect place for this to go down.

S: Why?

J: You know me sis. I love to put on a show.

###

A blast of cold water drenched Ronel's dreads and scalp, forcing the eldest to awaken. Jesse yelled to him, but sound had yet returned to his ears as he scanned the room. No one but them remained.

"What happened!? Where are they?" demanded Ronel.

"I don't know. Sonya destroyed her com and GPS chip," replied Jesse. "But I got a feeling where they are most likely heading."

Chapter 36:

The Classic

It was different this time. Stunting was the usual this time of
year for him. The raucous rattling of trunks from countless
donk cars and custom trucks vibrated everything grounded as
expected. Yet Judson pulled into the parking lot with just the
audible chopping of air coming from his rims. Adorning all
black, he exited the custom chariot with authority. Grabbing a
heavy duffle bag from the back seat, he proceeded into the flow
of the crowd towards the entrance. FAMU's marching band
began their entrance onto the field to the cheers and jeers of
Bethune's fans across the way.

"He's early," said Mathieu as he watched Judson join the
line going through the metal detectors. Sonya looked without a
response. "He doesn't honestly think that he is going to get
through there without them searching that bag does he?"

"Knowing my brother, he most likely thought of a way around it," replied Sonya. Judson moved to another line, cutting off an older woman in the process. She protested but was quickly quieted by a hundred dollar bill Judson presented to her face. Judson advanced further and took an envelope from his pocket and handed it over to the security guard. After a brief inspection of the cash and some non-verbal queues, his bag was taken and returned to him once he cleared the machine. Spotting his sister and plus-one gandering at him from the top level of the bleachers. Judson pointed at Mathieu and placed his index finger against his lips as the gold grills appeared with a slight smile. Then taking the same finger and dragging it from one side of his neck to the other with a stoic face.

"If it's that easy, I wonder what gets through the most magical place on earth?" questioned Mathieu jokingly. Sonya watched her brother make his way through the crowd until he disappeared under them.

"We have to move and head down below. As soon as he spots Bello, it's go time. He will not hesitate even if there are thousands watching," said Sonya as the two began descending down the crowded bleachers. After a series of turns and steps, they were finally underneath the massive structure. Sonya immediately spotted Bello and his crew drinking and smoking near a support beam. Continuing to scan the crowd, she realized that there was no sign of Judson.

"Where did he go?" asked Sonya.

"I lost him too," replied Mathieu. Sonya continued her search. Stepping on a raised light fixture and removing her baseball cap that completed her casual short pants and t-shirt ensemble. From one face to the other, someone caught her attention. He was familiar, but she did not immediately register him. Advancing closer to Bello's position, she noticed another black male standing in the midst of the festive crowd. The roar of happy children nearby took her attention briefly. A vendor dressed as a clown was trying to keep up with their custom demands. When she looked back, the men began approaching Bello slowly from all directions.

"Quick question. Is there anyone just as pissed off at your brother as Judson is?" asked Sonya.

"Too many to list," replied Mathieu. Sonya then noticed the burnt branding on their necks and realized what was happening.

"That's the GMB Cartel! I saw them in Bello's file. How would they know where…?" began Sonya as further revelation came into mind. "That smart ass bastard! Judson set this all up. They are going to cause a distraction so that he can get a clean shot on Bello."

"So, he plans to shoot from a distance?" asked Mathieu.

"No. He is going to want to do this up close and personal. He has to be close by. This has to be clean. Without any civilian casualties," replied Sonya. The Cartel members appeared before Bello's crew and an argument ensued. Bello blew a pillar of smoke in their faces, insulting them further. The GMB numbers began to grow as more members emerged from the crowd resulting in a shoving match.

"Federal Agent! Federal Agent! Get back! Get back!" yelled Sonya, presenting her badge, and stepping between them. The GMB men retreated slowly as the crowd's attention shifted in their direction.

"Damn. Now I see why Mathieu wants you so bad. I need a Fed bitch on my team for sure. Or maybe I won't have to if you join us on the winning side," urged Bello. As he took another drag from his blunt, the sound of a bullet cutting through air caught Sonya's ear. Bello begins to gasp for air as he holds his side. The sound occurs again and a chunk of Bello's shoulder is blown off of his body. Blood poured from his mouth. The men next to him would all suffer the same fate, suffering traumas to their scalps. The smoking silencer of a multi-colored rifle appears into view as the first of many screams echo beneath the bleachers. The man holding the weapon continues to fire. The clown make-up on his face cracking; revealing the dark melanated skin of a pissed off Judson. Bello fell to the ground, causing the crowd to stampede towards all possible exits. Sonya reached for her brother's shoulder to stop him, but Judson continued to fire into Bello's face until it was no longer recognizable.

"Feel exactly how she felt bleeding out in my arms, you son of a bitch!" yelled Judson. Firing the remainder of his clip until soil, grass, and brain matter exploded with each round. Judson roared at the corpse until his vocal cords were damaged to the

295

point of a wheezy-like groan. Sonya placed her arms around him as the rumbling of an approaching motorcycle was heard in the distance. Ronel sped through the crowd. Maneuvering the handle bar of his speed demon, missing attendees by inches.

"Sorry brother," said Sonya as she comforted him briefly before lodging a katana laced with Mathieu's serum into his neck.

"NO Sonya!" yelled Ronel abruptly applying the brakes, causing him to slide. Judson responds to the immediate pain by dropping the high-powered gun and grabbing at the arms of his sister who was now twisting the blade even more. A sudden electrical jolt surprised Sonya as Judson's hidden power began to manifest. Lightning from his hands caused the stadium light to explode and black out. Mathieu threw down the tarp to collect the blood spewing from Judson's wound. Using her telekinetic power to keep Judson still, the exponential energy from him began to revert to mere sparks.

"I am doing this for us, Jude," yelled Sonya.

"No. There was never an us!! I'm the only one that's been honest about my motivations!" blurted Judson as attempted to fight the hold. "I don't hide behind virtue like you, Ronel, and Elam. Fuck all of you! And for the record….Fuck you too Mathieu. I was gonna put one in your dome just for the hell of it!" Ronel dismounted his motorcycle, and tapped into his flame. Melting the fence links that would have otherwise kept a barrier between them. The tension in Judson's muscles subsided as he passed out from the blood loss.

"I have tried being patient. I have tried protecting you, now look what you've done," barked Ronel. Sonya pulled the blade out of Judson and stood to her feet. Mathieu stood alongside her after pouring Judson's essence from the tarp into a dark, 4-gallon container.

"I did what neither of you have the balls to do. I'm taking care of the problem! Charles' days are numbered, and you're just mad that it's me taking him out," blasted Sonya.

"This all ends right here. Right now. I won't hold back this time. Neither of you are leaving here. Over my cold dead body!" raged Ronel. Increasing the fire that burned around his person, Ronel drew his machete with the chain link attached rattling turbulently. Sonya stepped forward, surrounding herself in a whirlwind as the blue glow infused into her stare. Kicking up dust and ambers, the siblings darted towards each other when they were interrupted by the feedback sound emitting from the Camping World Stadium speakers.

"Ronel! Sonya! Stop it now!" yelled a panting Jesse. "I had to resort to this because you both destroyed your coms. I just picked up chatter from the Candiru. Charles just gave the green light on Elam. They are heading to kill him right after he is done with service. That's if they even let him finish. Put whatever this is aside, and get down here now!!"

"This isn't over. Not by a long shot," expressed Ronel as he extinguished the flames in an instant. "Judson should be healed up by the time we cross into Broward County. Once we make sure Elam is good, we will pick this back up." Ronel picked up Judson from the ground and turned his back to his sister. Opening the passenger side to Judson's car, Ronel placed him in it before hopping into the passenger seat and speeding off.

"Bring the canister, we have to head down there to stop this. When were you going to tell me that he gave the order?" asked Sonya as she and Mathieu began to bolt for her vehicle.

"I had no idea. It serves no purpose to kill the priest now. I'm not sure why this is happening," replied Mathieu. Once in the car, they peeled out of the parking lot. Sonya activated the red and blue lighting with the siren as she whizzed through lanes. They entered the highway and pushed the limit of the gas pedal. Aloof in her gaze.

####

"Jude!" yelled Ronel. The growl of the engine was deafening as he applied maximum pressure to the gas pedal. The smell of sawgrass violated Ronel's nostrils as they sped through the Everglades. Judson's eyes began to flutter until they opened. "Bro, wake up!"

"Stop yelling. I heard you the first time, and stop riding my baby so damn hard," relayed Judson as he attempted to sit up in his seat. Weakened. Ronel peeked over at his brother, and was troubled at the gash still pooling with blood.

"Why aren't you healing?" asked Ronel.

"I don't know," gasped Judson as he attempted to look over at the treasonous blow. Judson began to cough profusely, tasting iron-rich blood as it seeped out of his lips. Flopping his neck back, Ronel pulled the car over to the side of the road, disturbing the bugs that flurried up onto the rolled-up windows.

"Judson. Judson!" panted Ronel as he continually slapped his brother's face to resuscitate him. "You're not dying. You're not dying." Ronel removed his bandanna. Balling it up and pressing it against the wound. Judson gasped into a screech of pain with his eyes opened to capacity.

"Hold this!" instructed Ronel. Starting up the donk and speeding back onto the highway. "We're only an hour out. Just hang in there."

"I'm feeling something I never felt before," began Judson.

"And what's that?" asked Ronel.

"I feel sorry for you."

"Why do you feel that way?"

"I never told you this because I thought it was me being a big pussy…" coughed Judson.

"Don't start talking like that. Tell me whatever joke this is about to be after we get Elam safe."

"Naw. No joke. It must be a lot. To carry what you have had to carry. I just want to let you know that you did the right thing. Don't ask me how I feel about her now, but you were right in choosing to protect her over me," exhaled Judson. "Imagine the damage if you didn't"

"It's hard to think about what you are telling me right now. I have to save you all," blurted Ronel as tears ran down his cheeks.

There was no denying what he was feeling as the life force next to him dwindled with every passing second.

"It's a little too late for me though. Make sure that asshole dies," gasped Judson.

"Stay with me Jude. Don't you leave me too. Don't you abandon me too," mumbled Ronel as his attention danced between the road and Judson.

"Just do me this one solid. Tell my daughter nothing about me. The real me. I don't want her to seek after what got us here in the first place. Promise me," requested Judson raising his hand from the wound. Ronel met Judson's palm with his in a red, soaked agreement. Judson smiled, letting out a slight laugh as he looked into the evening sky. Ronel held on to him as he drove. The pulse dimmed just as the last remnants of the sun disappeared into the grassy plain. Feeling only the thumps of his own beating heart as Judson's gaze was now permanent. Not letting go, Ronel howled as he plunged the bottom of his fists on the wood grain wheel that he once picked out for his brother.

Chapter 37:

Romero

The creak of the aging wooden walls and the muffled thumping of the congregation singing in the chapel tugged at Elam's ears, seeking his attention. Although he noticed, his brows furrowed as the eyes of disbelief blinked underneath. His breathing uneven, he clutched his cane with a grip that caused the instrument to shake uncontrollably under his weight and evident discomfort. Tears filled his eyes. He attempted to take a few steps, only to collapse in a heaping wave of emotion. The altar servers from the outside heard the thud as they patiently waited for Elam to dress in his vestments. Father Elam was never late, and the singing had already begun. The eldest of them decided to inspect, and found Elam face down wailing silently while driving his fist into the concrete.

"Father! Father Elam! Are you ok?!" yelled the concerned

member picking up the elderly leader.

"Please, my child, go. I will catch up. Leave me for just a little while." assured Elam. The server left and instructed the others as to what the priest requested. Elam leaned over on his cane, as the bench below whined with each movement he made rocking. Looking up at a mural of the Savior in the garden, wrenched in pain and knowing his fate. Without looking away, he stood up and dressed himself quickly. Placing his hand on the painting, and making peace with himself.

"I'm not you. I'm not this," admitted Elam to the painting. "I have to be me now to set this all right. When they come for me, I will not go peacefully. I will fight. Tell St. Peter to expect me, and consider this my resignation." Elam hobbled outside briskly to make it to the entrance. Entering with the procession and commencing the late mass as he had done for years. With intent behind each action. Resolve with each word he spoke. Making it all the way to the end of the Eucharistic Prayer. It was then that he saw them enter. One by one until they filled the back of the church. Finally, Banshee entered dressed in her all black garment, with her red hair braided upwards. Making her way down the aisle holding her katana with the blade resting on her shoulder. The congregation fell silent. Elam descended from the altar quickly and met her at the last step.

"No. You don't get to come up here," whispered Elam.

"What's gonna happen priest? Will I burst into flames?" sneered Banshee. Elam grinned. The two conversed at the lowest possible volume.

"I humbly ask that you let these good people leave without a scratch. You don't get to decide the fate of these souls. It's me you want."

"I have no need for any other soul than yours. I will inquire as to if you will let your execution happen willfully, or will you actually defend yourself?"

"Charles doesn't get anything else easy from me. This soul? He has to actually fight to claim."

"Have it your way priest," laughed Banshee as she turned away to rejoin the Candiru. Elam raised his hands to signal all in attendance to rise to their feet.

"My brothers and sisters. The Lord be with you," said Elam.

"And also with you," responded the attendants awkwardly. Elam continued to end with a benediction, then gestured to the altar servers to leave through the back entrance.

"Get to your cars and quickly as possible. Get home to your loved ones, and do not turn back!" requested Elam. The members emptied the parish hastily, leaving the Celebrant alone with his visitors. Elam removed each part of his vestments and folded them carefully, resting them onto the first pew. The masked Candiru henchmen marched forward, lining the walls of the sanctuary. Their backs to stained glass masterpieces that inspired the contrary to what they were about to do. Elam picked up his trusted cane that was as old as he was. Striking it repeatedly until the outer wood cracked and fell away. Leaving behind a very well preserved Takoba sword.

"Any last words?" asked Banshee.

"Are you asking me or the poor devils you have led to certain defeat?" inquired Elam. Doing his best to wield the heavier blade despite his ailments, he braced himself. Banshee is handed the beheading device from one of her cohorts.

"Leave enough of him so that the head is recognizable to the Formidable One," ordered Banshee. The Candiru readied their assortment of daggers, swords, pistols, and clubs. A few stepped forward, and the others followed until there was a full on blitz. Elam impaled his sword fully into the first Candiru closest to him. Before his victim could fall to their knees, he disarmed an approaching gunman. Breaking his arm as he twisted the firearm from his grasp. The clergyman rapidly delivered head shots one after the other until the firing pin clicked. It was then his flesh tasted the first Candiru blade. Undeterred, Elam head butted the culprit, and snapped his neck before dislodging the shank. Banshee took delight at the wounds inflicted on the priest, but descended in frustration as it did nothing to slow down Elam's fighting prowess. The bodies of her men began to pile.

"Not bad for a fossil," mocked Banshee. Dropping the execution device, she presented her katana.

"So you must be the new Oracle. Do your worst!" growled Elam, retrieving his sword. They circled each other and Banshee struck. Elam countered and knocked it away, spinning her around. Banshee returned with an elbow to his temple which briefly stunned him. She sliced upward. Elam stumbled back as he felt the stinging feeling of the burnt skin and thin muscle on his chest separate.

"This is why you should have done a better job of keeping them out of the way, traitor. You're pathetic! Soon Mayer will rise and the world will be his! I will not grant you another moment of mercy so take this one. Yield your neck for judgment!" barked Banshee.

"You serve a weak man that only sees power as his only resource," struggled Elam as his breath was short and his heartbeat beyond control. "He delights in exposing himself as the end all be all. He will be hunted for such power. Day and night. Morning and Leisure. He isn't built to handle the many ways the world will seek his immortality. Knowing him, he will freely use the people of Haiti as a buffer. Further driving the pearl that she is into the depths of the sea if it means saving himself."

Banshee put her blade under Elam's neck. "I think it's time your mouth stops moving," said Banshee. Screeching tires from the outside interrupted her. A black car appeared in her view as she looked out the parish's glass double doors. Out stepped a fuming Sonya staring down Banshee with short knives in hand. As she made her way up the short stairway to the entrance, Judson's donk flew into the crescent driveway. Barely stopping in time before it crashed into Sonya's vehicle. The driver-side door flew open and blood soaked Ronel raised his dark mug into view.

"I was wrong, priest. I will grant you another mercy. I'll allow you to watch them tear each other apart!" sneered Banshee.

"Sonya!" seethed Ronel.

"I don't have the time for this right now Ronel. Take Judson and get out of here. I have Banshee," stated Sonya. Then she felt it. The absence of life.

"Judson is dead. You killed him!" growled Ronel. Sonya looked at the shadowy figure slouched over in the passenger seat. Anguish violated her face as she dropped her weapons. "You are so stuck in trying to be something you are not that you didn't even feel him slip away."

"No...." reasoned Sonya. "He was supposed to heal. He was suppose to-"

"He didn't. And now he's gone. Now I have to put you down so that your actions can't claim any more lives."

"Take me down?" asked Sonya as her eyes glowed blue and the air around them became strong and untamed. Ronel's pupils would then follow, glowing to a golden state. Flames spread around him, burning away any and all debris blown his way. Ronel's outcry caused the flames to spread even more. Rapidly advancing towards Sonya who blocked the inferno, losing sight of her brother. Suddenly Ronel's machete pierced through the flames, but Sonya blocked the swipe with another hidden blade. The siblings engaged with fast combinations of strikes, and counters. Both landing blows while destroying everything in their vicinity. The glass doors and windows of the church cracked and shattered. The broken pieces being kicked up in melee. The parked vehicles were moved and rocked violently from the firestorm the siblings created as they tussled.

"That's it Little Bird. Kill him!" barked Banshee as she chuckled. Elam helplessly looked on, defeated and ashamed. He lowered his head into the glass riddle floor, and began to hum to himself. "Is it too much to handle, priest? Look up at what you have created! They are beasts and you can't tame them anymore." Elam continued to hum to himself which frustrated Banshee. She reached down and grabbed a clump of his gray afro; forcefully lifting his head to make him watch. The humming became louder, which caused Banshee to jump away from him abruptly, confused.

"Sonya!" yelled Elam. Reaching out his hand, he began to sing out the words of Carline's song. The turbulent twister subsided as Sonya and Ronel appeared to be in a stalemate. Both struggled in a test of strength as they levitated at least 15 feet above the ground. Sonya looked over to Elam as she heard the melody becoming clearer and clearer. She started to mouth the words but stopped herself from continuing as the key of the song was different. Ronel broke away from their hold.

"Remember what I said. Don't forget her song!" exclaimed Elam. Banshee looked around for the device she brought initially.

"What do you mean Elam?" retorted Sonya. Elam smiled. Banshee located the contraption and quickly made her way back to the clergyman.

"You know what to do," replied Elam as the bag went over his head and face. Ronel darted towards their position, but stumbled when his feet met the pavement. Banshee pulled the ripcord and the bag's contents fell to the side. Sonya's face broke. As she watched the body of Elam twitch in response to the trauma, her blood vessels broiled. Within an instance, a gust of hurricane force winds pummeled into the church. Cracking the foundation as Banshee attempted to escape with the head of Elam. Ronel stood stoically watching as the church crumpled before him. Sonya's screams of agony blasted away his ability to hear. She descended to her feet and lifted away the debris with a flick of her hand. Unearthing what was left of Elam. She collapsed. Burying her face into the lifeless back while hugging him. Weeping into a riotous fit.

Chapter 38:

LOST

Charles sat on set and observed the audience of young adolescents to adults in their mid-30s that the talk show was famous with. The atmosphere buzzed with whispers and offhand remarks loud enough for him to decipher. He even noticed the silent jeers from the stage hands that stood on the side of the set as Jony Ettiene, the host, was tended to by make-up and wardrobe personnel.

"I cannot believe that you agreed to this interview," joked Jony leaning in. Charles met him halfway. "You do know that nothing is off limits with my show. I will ask the hard uncomfortable questions." Charles brushed at his black facial hair playfully.

"I would have it no other way, Jony. I am an open book," smiled Charles. The intro music began to play as the audience applauded. Jony made the show and guest introductions. Mathieu and Dr. Ursov stood backstage watching the live feed. Ursov departed for the bathroom, leaving the blood infuser with Mathieu. Seeing his opening, Mathieu adjusted the settings on the device and removed the flow sensor. He returned it to its casing quickly. Within a few minutes, Ursov returned.

"I felt the need to take a more active role in supporting my son's campaign. I know there are many misconceptions about me. I figured this once, I would step into the light and reach out to younger Haitians. To help lead them away from mistakes made in the past by former regimes," Charles retorted charismatically. Jony laid back in his seat rolling his eyes. The audience reacted with laughter and hurled accusations at the former Tonton Macoute.

"Monsieur Clerveaux, you are the classic embodiment of the regimes you claim to denounce!" shot Jony as the room erupted once again. Charles grinned and lowered his head. "Yet, you sit here and continue to insult our intelligence. Anyone with WhatsApp or TikTok has seen your murderous tendencies to get your son on the ballot." Charles continued to remain silent while his nerves began to bulge from the sides of his jawline. The crowd began to antagonize him with random outbursts of insults.

"Speechless Mr. Clerveaux?" Jony grilled. "Did you really think that we will just fall in line because you sit amongst us? This is not Haiti, we are in America! You can't commit murder in front of millions watching. We are free and we do not agree with your son's candidacy! Young Haitians are out of work, and homeless. Forced to join gangs with no education or opportunities unless they risk their lives at sea. Do you know how many bodies have washed up on these shores because of people like you?! We want someone better suited!"

"And who is better suited?" inquired Charles

"Anyone but you," replied the zealous host.

"There it is. You elitist runaways crack me up," trumpeted Charles. "This belief that my son's campaign is just a smokescreen for me to take over is asinine. I do not want to be a dictator or president. I seek a higher calling. I will provide something that has not been present since the death of the great Jean-Jacques Dessalines."

"And what is that? The secret to youthful looking skin and a bad dye job?" laughed Jony. Charles clamped his chair without breaking his cheerful demeanor. "I must ask you to introduce me to your dermatologist, you look almost 20 years younger."

"No no." chuckled Charles. Pointing at the map of Haiti behind them, he continued. "I seek to become the living embodiment of our Constitution. An unbiased enforcer of our laws and protector of the Republic. I want you all to look at that island and tell me what you see?"

"I see heritage, tradition and culture. Love and strength amongst our people. I see hope," replied Jony to a loud applause.

"Hope? Hope is a fabricated political lie, and I for one will not insult our people with the suggestion that they should have it.

Our people want guarantees," asserted Charles leaning forward. "I can tell you exactly what you see, young man. Carnival and parties. Your parent's 4-bedroom villa in Cap-Haitien, heavily fenced and guarded by shotgun wielding ex-cops. You see the sexual exploitation of our young girls who know nothing but to seek your illusion of a way out. I've seen the pictures of you flashing stacks of "American" money next to your ear at each Bal(party) you go to. Turning up your nose to those who aren't in your elite circle of friends, and treat the help like a colonizer. You see trips. Lavish week-long escapades and a convenient way back to the States because staying there too long will make you feel too much like a native." The crowd fell silent, short of a few people reacting to the insult.

"You are the fraud Mr. Clerveaux. You and your entire family are fraudulent animals," said Jony.

"Have some sympathy, Jony. I did lose my eldest son recently," mocked Charles, signaling to Ursov to bring out the medical equipment. Ursov proceeded to set up the blood pack feeding into the infuser device as the crowd looked on.

"What do you think you are doing? We are LIVE Mr. Clerveaux," exerted Jony lifting from his seat.

"I really, truly, hate to be disrespected, Jony. I also hate traitors that plot against me," stated Charles as he looked into the camera. Mathieu's skin ran cold as he looked into the oversized eyes of his father on the screen. He knew of the plot. Charles whispered to Ursov, who inspected the device with intent.

Adjusting the settings back to normal. Mathieu excused himself and left the green room. Noticing a few Candiru manning the exits, he looked for another way out and spotted a trash chute near the kitchen. Hoping not to be noticed, he walked over briskly. One of the Candiru called out to him and he picked up the pace. As they gave chase, Mathieu dived into the chutes' opening, sliding out to the outside dump that was thankfully, and painfully empty. He recovered and jumped out the iron enclosure, running to freedom into the bustling Miami traffic.

"You called me a fraud Jony, and that I am not," replied Charles as Ursov injected the IV into his arm. "What I am, cannot be fathomed by somebody so young and un-evolved. I am the new backbone that our nation has been praying for. I am the law. Speaking of which, I have a few amendments and decrees that I would like to broadcast on your platform if you don't mind."

"By all means," agreed Jony. "We are already thoroughly entertained by your delusions Mr. Clerveaux. Please tell the millions watching and listening to your demands."

"Thank you. First, all foreign military and NGOs have 24 hours to leave the Republic of Haiti. All foreign companies and their representatives will be required to exit the country and apply for re-entry to access our work force and natural resources at a price. A visa will be required for entry for all foreign nationals. Second. France will not only forgive the loan but will pay restitution to the island IN FULL. The amount will be set once my son is President. Third, to all the other world powers that attempt to institute any embargo, or sanctions. They will be met with the wrath of our nation. Any hindrance of any kind to our economic growth will be taken as a declaration of war." announced Charles to the silent crowd listening attentively. Jony giggled and slapped his knee. A few joined in with him but the majority of the room waited anxiously for Charles' next words. They have never heard words of power that defied everything they have known. As the transfusion commenced, Charles felt the shackles of limitation melt away. Gaining full control of the power within as it grew exponentially.

"To my fellow citizens. All gangs and local militia will relinquish all weapons at the ruins of our new Palace," relayed Charles as the transfusion completed. He then gave a smile of reassurance. "They will be seized without question, as long as those surrendering them renounce any allegiance to any and all organizations other than the Republic. The kidnappings will stop. All schools, both technical and collegiate are required to open immediately at no cost. All leading professors around the globe and within the country are welcomed. You will be compensated well if you bring your expertise to Haiti, with further incentives if you establish schools in our rural areas. Trade lines will be open to the world for all Haitian made goods, with business loans available for new Haitian entrepreneurs. There will be law and order throughout the land. Any attempts to disrupt, will be met with public executions carried out by our newly rebuilt police and army. To set an example of our new and just laws, my son will serve his term and step down. Allowing for another election that will not be corrupted or meddled with. Coup d'etat is forever banished! The people will choose their new president, and I will simply act as the enforcer. Any protest, criticism, or neglect of this rule will be punishable by death. As for the elite Diaspora. If you are found to have been responsible for contributing to the poverty, violence, or chaos of our nation's past. We will require your immediate extradition to Haiti where you will be tried in our courts, where justice will be served. Kreyol henceforth is the official language of our nation. All literature, and official documentation language will revert to Kreyol and Kreyol only. And lastly, any citizen attempting to flee our shores for another country without permission is an act of treason. Also punishable by death."

"How is it that you plan to pay for all of this? And these demands? We are not a world power, and we will never get anywhere close to it! Do you know what THEY will do to us hearing words like that coming out of your mouth?" warned Jony.

"Exactly what they did back in 1804 when we defeated them all. Slaying naysayers like you." snapped Charles grabbing a hold of the host. Hovering as the host's feet fought to grab hold of his chair. A dark mist flushed from Charles, covering the ground and climbing up the walls of the studio. The Candiru henchmen laid out various sharp and blunt weapons at the feet of the studio audience sitting in the first row. They then rose in a trance. Their eyes darkened. Picking up the available weapons as others advance towards Charles and his hostage. A delighted Charles began transforming into the complete human form of Jean-Jacques Dessalines with the scar on his face still visible. The loyal mob raised their machetes, and those without them scratched and clawed at Jony as he and others screamed in horror. They hacked away with Charles himself withdrawing his own blade. As the bloody corpse of Jony hung, Charles delivered a last clean cut with his blade, leaving nothing below Jony's suit-covered shoulders. Dropping the white-eyed victim, he looked into the camera. "Your king has returned!"

The trance over the studio audience was lifted, and hysteria began to set in when they noticed the aftermath of their deeds. As the confused crowd nearly trampled each other as they fled, Charles embraced Ursov.

"Thank you, good friend." He sighed. "Your services are no longer needed."

Charles plunged his hand into Ursov's stomach cavity. Twisting his hand and destroying every vital organ he could find until the doctor slouched over. Dead.

Chapter 39:

Lily in the Valley

The last of the morgue associates left for the evening. Leaving behind a few security guards barely equipped to protect Sonya and Ronel against the Candiru. The duo avoided eye contact. Choosing to stay on opposite sides of the room. Sonya sat on an aluminum high chair with her head laying on Elam's cold chest. A white sheet draped over his corpse. Ronel stood over the body of his younger brother, also covered.

"He definitely took his hatred of the old man to the grave now, didn't he?" joked Ronel to himself, but loud enough for Sonya to hear. Sonya raised her head while wiping away the fresh tearful streams emanating from her eyes.

"Quite the contrary." Sonya objected. "They loved each other. They just didn't want to admit it. Elam sat with Judson every first Thursday of the month while he was locked up. Judson accepted every visit even though they barely spoke a word to each other. Just played chess. Maybe because they were tired of fighting. Maybe because they felt that what they wanted to say was not worth speaking. Or else the visits would stop if another argument occurred." explained Sonya. She rose from her seat to walk over to Judson's body, but was stopped by Ronel midway. "I don't want to fight you Ronel. I don't want to fight the only family I have left.

"Do you remember your first kill?" questioned Ronel. Sonya looked off to the side wall and nodded no.

"Bullshit!" jabbed Ronel. "You never forget. It stays alive and well in your head. Watching the light leave the eyes of someone's son or daughter as you hold onto yours selfishly. And for what? Virtue? Or even worse, an organization of high prestige says they need to die? That first kill is always the one you remember because it's when you start counting the bodies. You are not fit to handle losing count."

"You know nothing of my motivations." Sonya shot back.

"I know them well. Trying to right the wrong. It consumes you. It makes you erratic and people die because of it. Stop me if I'm not talking about you," said Ronel towering over her.

"I don't give a damn about being civil when it comes to Charles!" exerted Sonya. Ronel huffed at the outburst.

"You sound just like him! You still don't get it. We are all alike in this. Elam dealt with it through religion, Judson dealt with it through chaos. At least his kills had purpose. What purpose was so grand that warranted their deaths?"

"Don't you put that all on me. I did not know that would happen." Sonya challenged Ronel with her piercing gaze. "While you sat back taking swigs like a wounded boy scout, someone had to do something. We both stared into the eyes of the devil. You retreated and I made a deal!"

"You don't get to make that decision." Ronel stated with authority.

"They were my parents too, Ronel!" pushed Sonya. "I have just as much say in what happens to the man that took them away. I'm going down fighting."

"With who, his son? He's played you. I gave you more credit than this," Ronel protested before turning his back.

"Yet it was never good enough for you to lend me one bit of respect as your counterpart," replied Sonya. Ronel took a few steps away but immediately returned his attention to her.

"After what you did? I will never fight alongside you. Consider that an official confirmation to your accusation."

"Neither would Judson. You couldn't even keep him in line. Let alone save him. Twice," said a cold Sonya. Ronel, trembling visibly as anger and heat rose up from him. As his eyes began to ignite, Sonya reacted quickly. Summoning her power to match her brother's growing rage.

"That was real low Sonya. The next words out of your mouth better have the Wall of China in front of them, or I will blast you with the inferno that would make demons blush.

"You will do no such thing!" replied a voice.

"Did you hear that?" asked Sonya.

"Yes." replied Ronel, pulling out his machete. "Show yourself!" Light flickers caused Sonya to present her blades as well. The door to the frigid room flies open revealing the dark hallway.

"I know this is a stupid question…" began Ronel

"The answer is yes. I feel it too. Whatever it is, it's coming right towards us." The sound of heavy breathing filled their ears. A shadow of a figure walked slowly towards them, wearing a red, hooded cloak wet and damp. An aroma violated their nostrils as the unknown drew closer. The hands withered to the bones swayed back and forth as the decrepit, decomposed woman revealed herself in the corridor. Sonya gasped as Ronel pointed his blade in defense.

"What the hell is that?!" yelled Sonya

"I don't know. Bones aren't supposed to walk!" said Ronel as he stepped in front of Sonya. "I don't know who and what devil sent you, but if you don't step back I will set you ablaze!"

"I assure you that will not be necessary, Ronel," said the skeletal figure with her jaws still clinched.

"Wait. How are you able to speak without lips?" peered Ronel looking closely.

"It's like you can hear me in your head. I know. When you have lost as much flesh as I have, you kinda learn to compensate," chuckled the figure as she tossed the hood over her head back.

The gray wet hair on her scalp ran down to her lower back. The sounds of bones cracking escaped her cloak.

"I've seen way too much today. I really need a drink," said Ronel to himself.

"The drinking stops today. I assure you things will become clear. Pardon my interruption of your childish bickering but I'm afraid that we don't have much time," said the figure walking over to Elam's body. Removing the covers from his scarred hands and holding them. She let out a long exhale. "Even in death, you haven't lost your touch. Rest well faithful soldier, your mission is done. Your sacrifice is not vain."

"Who are you? And why do we not have much time?" pressed Sonya.

"It is my understanding that my beloved Mayer has returned. Breaking me from wandering the depths of the sea," replied the being as she presented the coral and seaweed that lined her bones. "He called out to me but my soul is still trapped in these remains you see before you. Something is not right. So, I locked onto the closest energy source that resembled his, and here I am. To find that his plans are still unraveling all these years later. Pardon my manners, I did not introduce myself. I have had many names, but those that know me well call me "The Minister.""

"As in, Mayer's Minister? The original Oracle?" asked Ronel.

"As you said. I am she," replied the Minister. Noticing the fright in their eyes as they took in her visage, she continued.

"Maybe something more soothing to the eyes is in order." The Minister clapped her hands and whispered a few incantations. Suddenly a flash of light blinded the siblings briefly. After a brief adjustment period, a woman they recognized came into view, still wearing the withered clothing. Ronel and Sonya felt weak as the light-brown skin flawlessly covered her flesh. Lips like Sonya's. Eyes like Ronel's. Her smile was as radiant as they remembered. Sonya released a squeal as Ronel comforted her.

"Mother?" trembled Ronel.

"No. I am not your mother. I searched for the most comforting image I could find in your minds. Is it too much?" asked the Minister.

"Yes!" yelled Ronel.

"No." whispered Sonya. "I get to see her again. You will not take that from me."

"Speak. How? What? When? And all that you can fit in between," requested Ronel.

I will try to be brief. My master, Mayer the Formidable, and his friends Alexandre and James angered not only God but the Templars. They were hunted, but the three fought off every assassination attempt, and each declaration and execution of war against them. All accounts of these wars were erased from history because the Templars did not want the losing record. They decided to wait out their deaths to reclaim the shards of the chalice. Another defeat was dealt when they realized that the

322

three outlived them. Hope came in the form of Alexandre's death, then James'. The Templars raided what remained of their kingdoms, but could not find the shards or locate the remains of their sworn enemies.

There was however a weakness to immortality that eluded the Templars. The memories of battles and all that the three comrades killed haunted them profusely. Driving Alexandre and James into madness. After their deaths, Mayer remained.

Ever seeking, Mayer found a temporary solution to the torment. Enlisting a priestess from his homeland who showed him a ritual to void his mind of all memories. The priestess would go on to be his trusted confidant and eventual lover. That priestess was me.

"Wait. I thought he was sworn to a life of celibacy," interrupted Ronel.

"And I thought I was talking." replied the Minister. Ronel raised his hands in surrender.

As I was saying. Voiding his mind also voided him of his power, except for one ability that made him the most dangerous warrior to ever walk the earth. Mayer requested that he be sent to different parts of the world to live as a normal man to further evade the curse and the Templars. These sabbaticals lasted lifetimes, until his dormant mind made him call out. Using a melody that I alone or the Oracles I trained could hear. As you can guess, I aged as my master remained young. This of course allowed his eyes to venture elsewhere. I knew of his many concubines, but never had an offspring been a result, even in his dormant state.

But that changed. He fell in love with a Dahomey warrior that would be sold into slavery shortly after he returned to me. I would then learn that the warrior was with child. This divided us of course. Selfishly, I tried to erase the child from his memory but it only had the opposite effect. He traveled to the new world under the guise of the organization's business. Unbeknown to either of us, he took interest in an enslaved orphan. Freeing and teaching him the ways of warfare as he often does. It was during one of his returns that I searched his mind, and found that the orphan child grew to be King of his people. It was also then that I realized the connection of father and son that neither of them had knowledge of.

"Are you saying that Mayer is Jean-Jacques Dessalines' father?" requested Sonya.

"Yes," replied the Oracle. *"I was enraged, and I did something that I deeply regret in my scorned state. I alerted the Templars of his heir and that he entrusted him with the shards. It did not take them long to infiltrate and swarm the now King of Haiti. The Templars aggravated the situation by forcing the King to drink from the shard Mayer entrusted to him. Jean-Jacques immediately exerted his powerful abilities but was executed in front of a shocked Mayer, who realized the existence of his son instantly. In retaliation, Mayer slaughtered all the Templar men that were sent.*

He took the lifeless body of Jean-Jacques and did something that I'm sure was very painful for him to do yet necessary."

"And that was?" inquired Ronel.

"Man to pursue you, until five cuts lay you deep. If you know the story of how his remains were found, I'm sure the rest will fill itself in," replied the Minister.

"He mutilated his own son…No wonder Jean-Jacques called him a traitor!" said Ronel

"He granted him mercy. He granted that nation mercy. You don't know the extent of the curse," The Minister interrupted. "Mayer knew the news of Jean-Jacques' death would satisfy the Templar's long enough to not further meddle in the young nation's future. Had he not done what he did, the Templars would have raided the King's grave for the remains and destabilized the entire island to harvest what they could. That's if they even got a chance."

"I know you have been wandering the sea for a bit so let me fill you in. Haiti has been poached and ransacked for its resources for centuries to this very day. What mercy do you speak of?" prodded Ronel.

"It isn't the first time that he has had to do it. James and Alexander did not die of old age as the legend says. At their request to rid them of their torment and to deny the Templars the opportunity to harvest their remains, Mayer killed them both." said the Oracle as she walked over to Judson's body. "Only an energized bloodline member of the three can truly kill the other. If death comes from outside the bloodline and the body is not immediately dismembered, the corpse will rise without a soul. Killing and destroying everything in its path mindlessly."

"Is that the reason why Judson did not heal? Is that why I wasn't able to recover from Charles' attack instantly?" asked Ronel. The Minister nodded in agreement.

"Because he was a half-breed, is the reason you are still standing. I am aware of the tyrant who killed your parents. Even now, through you, I can sense him and his absolute power. At his current state, he can deliver a killing blow to any of you since he has the DNA of your brother and Jean-Jacques running through him," advised the Minister.

"Doesn't that work both ways? That means I can also kill him," stated Sonya.

"Even with death surrounding you both, you have yet to learn the lesson. What killed the three friends was their separation. They needed each other. To be vulnerable with each other. If only they did, they would all be alive and well today," the Minister lamented. "You have lost two already. Neither of you can afford to lose one more. So I suggest you find a way to move past this sibling rivalry."

"You don't know how deep this goes," said Sonya. "There are some things that are just unforgivable." The original Oracle walked over to Sonya and reached out her hands. Sonya gazed into the eyes that were not truly that of her mother's but enough to cause jitters. She complied with the request for her hands.

"Child, you may not know it now but forgiveness moves the clock forward on your sorrows. Just imagine the mantle the priest had to carry after what he had to witness. By no means do I say he was perfect and without flaws. There is no denying the great hurt that has caused you to build such tough armor." reasoned the Minister. Sonya loosened the tension in her hands as she took in every word. "There is nothing wrong with being a strong woman. My master once said that not all wounds are inflicted by the enemy. Even your allies can cut you in the process of fighting for you. Ask yourself which of these would you rather? Fighting alone, or fighting alongside someone who knows your weak points well enough to cover you?"

"So, we have a chance if we work together?" asked Ronel.

"Hell no. At this elevated state, he will obliterate your both. He has the skull of Mayer's direct descendant for God's sake," joked the Oracle. Sonya and Ronel looked over at one another. Silently agreeing that there was nothing funny about what was said. "Take comfort in laughter, even when facing certain death. I knew the skull was not Mayer's when I saw it. It was not my beloved. I felt the curse of a traitor flow through my fingers from the bottom of that chest Miguel brought in. I had no choice but to laugh at my karma. His anger was just. I fell ill and delightfully accepted my punishment and final assignment. Miguel disclosed to me that Mayer disappeared into the mountains of Haiti. Not before he entrusted my teachings and secrets to a woman he relinquished the body of his son to."

"You mean Défilée? She is a hero," implied Sonya.

"The very same." replied the Minister.

"Where is Mayer?" asked Ronel.

"I no longer sensed him shortly after his disappearance," She admitted. "Défilée would go on to pass our techniques through generations while keeping an eye on the descendants of Jean-Jacques. Doing whatever necessary to keep the history of the shard away from any of his descendant's knowledge. That is until your father was roped into reviving the shard's power without a drop of Mayer's blood. Although Elam failed to complete his mission, I commend him for his decisions and keeping you all hidden from the reach of the Templars."

"How do you know all of this if you have been roaming the sea this whole time?" asked Sonya.

"The dead can speak, you know. I was filled in on all the details on my way here," chuckled the Minister. "Speaking of which, I will be taking the body of your brother."

"For what reason?" jumped Ronel gripping his weapon.

"It is not safe on the surface. Do not worry, I will make sure that it is well preserved. At least until you defeat that impure evil zombie calling himself a savior," she replied.

"I say we trust her," said Sonya. "We can give him a proper burial if we survive this." Ronel placed his hand over Judson's head as he gazed over the sheet that covered his brother's body.

"Fine. What hope do we have anyways," relented Ronel.

"Hope is what I am selling!" the Minister launched gleefully as she laid down two pieces of wooden chards wrapped in different colored, aged cloths. She grabbed Ronel by the hand and placed his hand over the red clothed shard, and Sonya's hands on the blue equivalent.

"What are these?" asked Ronel.

"Hope," replied the Minister as she rested her hands over theirs. "These hold the essence and strength of the warriors that once cherished them. They will add and enhance your own power. Repairing the potholes in your memories, and granting you full knowledge and true armor. Ronel, I bestow to you the fire of Alexandre. Lord of destruction, and cleanser of souls. Sonya, I bestow to you the air of James. Alchemist of chaos, and calmer of storms." The siblings were confused until Ronel remembered the shard in his possession. As he removed it, he was surprised to see that it was wrapped in a white aged cloth. Placing it in front of the Minister.

"And what do we do with this one?" asked Ronel.

"This one was meant for the one most like Mayer himself. Brash, and unapologetic. Yet wise, compassionate, and without regret. The spark of lightning," responded the Minister. "I will hold onto it for safekeeping until the right time is right." Mayer's first Oracle began to recite incantations as the fabric around their shards began to glow. Darkness filled the room as Sonya and

Ronel lowered their heads, coaxed into a deep slumber as they stood.

"This will hurt but do not be afraid. Focus on my voice and mine alone, no matter what you see or hear," the Minister whispered. In their trance, the duo could hear a loud explosion. Men crying out in agony. Then the pain began. Their skin sizzled as if put to the fire, as strands of the fabric under their hands entered through their pores. Both of them attempting to fight through the torture. "Tell me when you see it."

"See what?" groaned Sonya.

"The lamb. Tell me when you see it!" asserted the Minister. As their eyes searched through the darkness, Ronel felt something brush against his leg. Looking down to see a white lamb looking back up at him."

"I see it," said Ronel. Sonya looked down also as the lamb brushed against her next.

"I see it too," concurred Sonya as the wind began to pick up around them.

"You are now bonded to it, and each other," said the Minister delightfully. "Now say these words with authority and confidence. 'I call." The siblings did as they were told and with a flash, the armor of James and Alexandre rested on them. As they opened their eyes, they were astonished at their attire.

"Are you feeling this?!" asked an ecstatic Ronel, noticing the many blades swinging below the red sash around his waist.

"I feel so alert! No more brain fog. I feel so much power!"

laughed Sonya as she looked down at the sleek, blue uniform. "I even feel my weapons in this suit. How is that even possible?"

"That is because they are now part of you as skin is to muscle. These suits will keep you stocked with all the weapons you are accustomed to or can think of. It will keep you from bleeding out. Working with your natural ability to heal. It can form at your imagination's ceiling. If the old style doesn't work, you can change everything but the color and the emblems of their former owners on your chests." The siblings turned to one another, inspecting each other's glowing attire before embracing intensely.

"With these, you should be able to make a stand against Charles, but you must rely on one another." said the Minister as she placed the remaining shard on Judson's chest. Sonya joined her as she placed a hand on it as well.

"In another life. I hope that you can forgive me brother," said Sonya before kissing his forehead. Ronel rested his hands on her shoulder as his heart became free of contempt towards her. The Minister raised her hands and Judson's body rose from the cold slab.

"Bury the priest. Give him the proper sendoff that a parent deserves." The Minister made her way towards the exit as the levitating body of their brother followed. "I have completed the tasks of my master. To leave the shards in the hands of the capable. I implore you to confront this threat and fight until you can't fight any longer."

"Goodbye Judson. We will see you on the other side, 'jit," said Ronel. The lights return to the room. The Minister and her cargo were gone. The two embraced once more as the armor around them disappeared with the same flash of light.

Chapter 40:

No Time for Emotion

T he white horses galloped as the coachman guided them
around another turn of the procession. Led by the calm of a
large group of priests, bishops, and clergymen of all
denominations. Elam's altar workers carried a cross in front of
them. A sea of mourners marched behind them with an embedded
Louisiana-style street band blaring its horns. The excitement
startled the two large beasts pulling the open-air carriage with
Elam's casket towards the cemetery. Yet they stayed the course.
The upbeat gospel number blasted from the band's horns. The
sound of the snare section, bass drums and tambourines
penetrated the almost sound proof creases of vehicles that
stretched for miles. Those on their feet wore multi-colored,
tailored outfits complete with feathers. Others protested with
Haitian flags and t-shirts with a picture of the slain clergyman,

shouting anti-Charles slogans. Some were in tears, and others danced as the caravan moved forward.

"It's how he wanted to be celebrated. 'I want a second line baby.' He would say that all the time in a really bad New Orleans accent. He wanted a celebration going to and from the burial," said Ronel dressed in a black suit. Putting to rest the inquiry made about the festive nature of the ceremony by Mathieu, who rode with them. The leading black limo followed the carriage at a close and safe distance as they sat inside in a row. Manny laid her head on Jesse's shoulder as he held Sonya. He stared daggers at the additional guest, rubbing Sonya's back as she ventured through strength, weeping, and stories of Elam's hilariously Haitian parenting style.

Reaching the burial site, they watched as the white casket was lowered into the damp brown pit. Ronel held his sister close as they were flanked by flower arrangements and large prints of Elam and Judson. The holy water flew from the aspergillum as the last blessings were made before the dirt was shoveled in. The siblings, now having their memories returned to them, shed tears from their dark shades. One by one, thousands dwindled to hundreds. After a while, a loyal few remained until the dark of the early evening set upon them. Mathieu walked over to Sonya and kissed her on the forehead, then shook hands with Ronel. Walking over to Jesse, he presented his hand that Jesse ignored at first. Putting his hands into his pocket.

"I get it. I'm not asking you to like me but rest assured I am not your enemy," pleaded Mathieu. Jesse felt Manny tap his back, and grit his teeth as he knew what she was trying to get him to do.

"It's not about me or you. It's about Sonya," replied Jesse. He shook Mathieu's hand without breaking eye contact. "I will admit, it took major balls to do what you were trying to do. I can respect that." Just then, Jesse's phone began to ping multiple times, garnering everyone's attention.

"Oh no," quivered Jesse.

"What is it?" asked Sonya.

"It's Charles. He just murdered a few diplomats live over the internet," Jesse responded. "It's bigger fish this time. He just killed the U.S and French Ambassadors by decapitating them using just his hand." They gathered around the small cellphone screen as Jesse replayed the clip with Charles laughing maniacally.

"He's not even waiting for their intervention. He is choosing to strike first," admitted Mathieu. "This is bad, and it's only going to get worse for the innocent on that island."

"Are you still able to contact your father?" asked Ronel.

"Only through Banshee and I know exactly where to find her," Mathieu volunteered. Sonya stood up abruptly.

"Me and her have business to settle. I want her to myself, Ronel. Grant me that," requested Sonya. Ronel stood up as well and agreed. Jesse grabbed Sonya by the hand.

"I'll be where you need me to be. Turn on your com when

you are ready," said Jesse as he hugged her. "I have something that needs my attention. I will take Manny home."

"And I will take Sonya home," said Mathieu with a smile. Everyone paused to suspiciously look at him. "I just want to make sure she knows the layout of what she may be walking into."

"That's not your job!" asserted Jesse as Manny held him back.

"Y'all are not doing this after I just had to put my father in the ground!" bolstered Sonya.

"Yeah boys. This is not really helping either of your cases. I'm not passing out approvals but I will pass out asswhoopings," presented Ronel in his best Judson impression. "Go ahead Mathieu and take her home. We will work out the details to intercept Banshee. Understood?" Ronel gaze jumped from each person as they accepted their duties.

Mathieu tapped away at his laptop on Sonya's kitchen counter. Another "Access Denied" message flashed across his screen. Each attempt at accessing his compound's camera system failed. Sonya stood behind him.

"I don't know why this is happening. They must have blocked me out of my own system," said Mathieu.

"Did you not think to have a master override just in case something like this happened?" asked Sonya. "I will just call Jesse, and he will know what to do."

336

"Wait!" interrupted Mathieu. "There is no need to involve him, I got this. I just need a little more time." Sonya slammed the laptop shut, as Mathieu frustratingly put his hand over his face.

"It's fine. Jesse can take it from here. You have done all you could," assured Sonya as she looked for her com unit.

"I haven't done ENOUGH!" yelled Mathieu as he trembled in his self-loathing.

"First of all, calm down sir. No man has ever or will yell like that in MY house. So, whatever you have going on right now, it's not that serious," said Sonya. Finding the com, she attempted to power it on.

"You all think your vendetta is greater than anyone else's," sneered Mathieu. Sonya stopped and approached him as the glow of her power began to dance in her pupils.

"You want to rethink what you just said to me?" growled Sonya.

"I didn't stutter now did I? I saw how you all looked at me in that limo. As if I am still part of the evil we both want dead. You don't know what he has taken from me," blurted Mathieu.

"A stolen presidency and a Stonehenge chair next to him in the family lair? Get over it! He outsmarted you like he did the rest of us. No time for such emotion," admitted Sonya. Mathieu laughed off the jab the best he could, but the smile could not hold up to the anguish he felt.

"He didn't conceive me alone, you know. As much as it may baffle you I had a mother. You remind me of her. She was young, beautiful, and too good for any of us. My father took her and killed the man she was supposed to marry with impunity under Baby Doc. He forced her to marry him. Forced her to bear his children. She loved us, and tried to keep her mental state of mind for our sakes, but he tormented her. Beat her almost every day. Sometimes half to death," revealed Mathieu rocking back and forth as his eyes burned red. "Until one day we walked in from a day with father, she sat at the table in silence looking out the window. We greeted her and she didn't look our way. My father stomped over to her and delivered a slap so hard that the plates in the kitchen rattled. She turned to him, and smiled. Then she looked at us and did the same. She then pulled father's gun from his waist and shot herself." Sonya attempted to break from her frozen state as regret flushed over her face. She placed her hand on his.

"I still remember the blood splatter pattern in the ceiling. My father wiped his face and walked away like the family pet made a mess. Except she wasn't a pet, she was my mother," blurted Mathieu, letting go of all the strength that he had left. Sonya wrapped her arms around the weeping man and wept with him. She then took him by the hand and led him to the couch where they held each other in silence as the night became dawn.

As the sun climbed on them, the sound of her alarm emanated from her phone, interrupting the missed calls and text message notifications on her screen. Sonya woke and picked up the device. First responding to her brother, then Manny. As she scrolled to Jesse's messages, she felt his hands embrace her again. She turned and parted her lips to speak, but they were suddenly met by the soft press of his. Sonya jolted back.

"I'm sorry," protested Mathieu. Without making eye contact with him and done wanting to pick up another fight, she grabbed him by his shirt to reconnect the kiss. Pulling each other in slowly as their lips massaged one another's pain. Providing a temporary, but needed relief. With each button removed, the goosebumps spread throughout her skin. The draft from the air conditioner vent above them coated them in stages with each clothing removal. Their thirst for one another delayed less and less. His hands explored her curves as she mounted him. Her nails brushed against the dimples of his muscles until penetration caused her to gasp, pressing them into his flesh. With each pop and exertion of her backside, he returned thrusts of his own as their bodies adjusted like a well-oiled engine. Accelerating and idling as their lungs played hide and seek with the elusive oxygen in the air. Sonya's moans played lead, as Mathieu's groans played bass to the percussion of the pelvic bones. Losing themselves to each other. Trusting as the roller coaster of their lovemaking followed an unpredictable route. The thought of restraint would be an insult. From trembles orgasmic in nature, to the flipping over to another innovative satisfying position. Slowly arriving at yet another breaking point, and finally collapsing onto the aforementioned furniture piece. Resting unapologetically on the many sweat and love drenched spots. Connected in pain. Divided no more.

Chapter 41:

The Counter

"You did what?!" blasted Manny's voice through the speaker phone on the conference room desk. Sonya furrowed her brows as she tapped on the wooden surface with a pen, shrouded in embarrassment. "So how was it?"

"I'm not about to get into that. My brain is split in so many directions. It happened. I have no real explanation," replied Sonya.

"It must have been good then," Manny said jokingly. Her tone soon changed. "How are you going to face Jesse? Does he know?"

"Jesse knows what's important. Besides, we aren't together. There's no chance. He is my best friend and I'm not going to complicate that. I need him thinking clearly," stated Sonya as she prepared her final impromptu briefing with Director Lee. Shifting her paperwork until all the pages are perfectly aligned. Right then the door to the room opened and Sonya stood to her feet but deflated at the sight of Agent Tanner carrying a large binder.

"Manny, I have to go," said Sonya as she leaned over the phone and ended the call.

"I don't get why it seems you are always incorporating personal business with matters of National Security. Have you no shame Jean-Baptiste?" prodded Tanner.

"Well, I will no longer be a problem for you," replied Sonya as she laid down her credentials and issued weapon. "This has gotten bigger than I ever thought it would. I don't feel that it would be in the best interest of the CIA if I remained. I have a personal stake in ensuring Charles Clerveaux is eliminated. My brother and I will see to it. This is my final briefing." Sonya presented the report to Tanner who took it from her. The tenured agent looked briefly at the cover before discarding it to the ground. Laying down the large binder, she pulled a confused Sonya in for a hug. Sonya patted her back nervously, as the behavior was unusual from her commanding officer.

"I would say that I will kill you if you told anyone that I did this but I think we both know that will be nearly impossible," joked Agent Tanner in Sonya's ear. Letting her go, she held the young agent's forearms. "I lost my father two years ago. To natural causes, but nothing ever prepares you for when one of your life's constant figures is no longer there. I still mourn him. He is the reason why I'm tough. What I loved about him most was that once the badge came off of his chest, he was my father. I had permission to be his scared, naive, and hopeful little girl." Tanner smiled and motioned towards the large binder.

"What is this?" asked Sonya.

"That is the file that the CIA had on you, and your family. Even Director Lee doesn't have access to this. I have explored my channels, and took measures to not have you or your brother implicated or prosecuted for whatever you have to do. When it comes to Charles, the CIA is willing to accept 'alternative interventions'. Do it knowing that the man you buried did everything possible to shield you all from being science projects. Trust me, once you go through this, you will understand. I have also had the criminal record of your deceased brother scrubbed should his daughter decide to be curious when she is older. Now Director Lee was instrumental in getting that accomplished. He apologizes for not making this meeting."

"Thank you," said Sonya sincerely as she embraced Tanner.

"Unfortunately, Jean-Baptiste, this is where the good news ends," exhaled Tanner.

"What do you mean?" asked Sonya. Tanner walked over the keyboard on the conference room desk and tapped the space bar twice. The large screen flickered on, and a visibly annoyed Jesse stared back at them both.

"I had a feeling that you were coming in to give a resignation performance, so I took the liberty of coming in earlier to get Jesse's findings ready to go. Isn't that right Jesse?" asked an oblivious Tanner.

"Yeah. Always at your service Agent Tanner and Agent Jean-Baptiste," replied Jesse in a monotone voice.

"How long have you been listening?" asked Sonya.

"Long enough to know what's important," shot back Jesse as Sonya looked away shamefully. Tanner ping ponged her attention to each of them.

"I get the feeling I may have missed something here," joked Agent Tanner. "Is everything Ok between you two?"

"Yeah," said a chipper Jesse.

"Yes," concurred Sonya.

"Ok Jesse, would you please bring Sonya up to speed on your findings?" asked Tanner.

"Yes Agent Tanner." agreed Jesse. "The hard drive given to us by Mathieu Clerveaux was essential in understanding the threat his father posed. However, as I stated originally during that presentation of the early evidence, there were some incomplete files scattered about. Something didn't seem right about it, so I ran a re-constructive algorithm to see if anything could be salvaged. Nothing came of it, but something told me to keep at it until one of the scans revealed a deleted encrypted file tied to the scraps. After breaking a very tough yet poorly initiated block, I was able to find more files like it. Please look at this financial record." Jesse aligned and centered the spreadsheet on the screen.

"These look like wire transfers to the same bogus companies that were registered to Ursov," said Sonya.

"Yes, but there are some discrepancies. There is one company that we did not account for. The company was skimming money off the top, and made full blown transactions that were purposely erased. I'll make this short and simple. This new company received more funds from the "Brat'ya Zhaka." That company is registered to one, Mathieu Clerveaux."

"What?" queried Sonya.

"It gets better, Agent Jean-Baptiste. Those funds were spent on medical personnel at an unknown location. Most of it to Ursov himself for services rendered," replied Jesse.

"What services could he have provided to Mathieu?" asked Sonya.

"Agent Jean Baptiste. When you were last with Mr. Clerveaux, did you notice any old scarring behind his ear and underneath his chin?" asked Jesse. Sonya stared at the large eyes of her friend on the screen. Feeling the daggers made for her, Sonya did not answer. "I'm sure you were close enough to notice. Say around, this morning?"

Sonya's eyes darted at the ground as the crisp memory of Mathieu getting dressed played in her mind. Confirming what Jesse was asking. She opened her mouth to answer but she was interrupted.

"Agent Jean-Baptiste, I attempted to reach you multiple times to no answer. I wanted you to watch this video. Please observe," said Jesse. The spreadsheets went away and a video began to roll. Sonya watched as her body buckled and gave way to the visuals of Mathieu undergoing the same procedure as Charles. The bone fragments split through his skin. Falling to the ground as he bled profusely. The medical staff frantically attempted to resuscitate him as he went into shock. Convulsing before being stabilized. It then cut to Ursov pleading with the younger Clerveaux.

"Your body cannot withstand another attempt Mr. Clerveaux. Your father even in old age is a better candidate and has more of a chance of surviving," pressed Ursov. A visibly irate Mathieu knocked over the table closest to him. The video cuts to footage dated the day that Mathieu escaped the Candiru after his father executed a talk show host on live television. Mathieu laid on a gurney yelling at the top of his lungs to the medical staff. They refused to assist him as he attempted to give himself a blood transfusion from the container that held a fraction of Judson's blood. The footage then stops.

"He played you Jean-Baptiste. He sought the power for himself and failed. He recruited you to kill your own brother, and attempted to poison his own father so that he could use the blood for himself," informed Agent Tanner. Sonya closed her eyes and took multiple breaths.

"Where is he now?" asked Sonya sternly.

"After leaving your apartment this morning, he headed back to that same location to meet up with another nuclear biologist. My guess? Probably bankrolled by Brat'ya Zhaka. I would give the coordinates but something tells me you should be able to follow his scent. You know, hunt him down like a certain gender of K-9," blurted Jesse.

"Oh, so we are going there?" asked Sonya.

"Last time I checked, I was my own man, Agent Jean-Baptiste. Not no weazel like the man you choose to sleep with," darted back Jesse.

"OK children! This is a really bad CW show gone off the rails. Let's get back to the issue at hand here!" interrupted Tanner. "Sonya, I'm sure that you and Ronel wouldn't mind eliminating another potential threat. Make him talk, then do what you will with him."

"Understood," acknowledged Sonya.

"As for you Jesse, you will put your personal feelings aside and assist your friend. Is that clear?" asked Tanner.

"Clear as 7-Eleven Sprite, but I have no friends in this business. Not anymore. The coordinates will be sent to Agent Jean-Baptiste and her surviving brother. Please be advised Agent Tanner that after all of this is done, I will be requesting a transfer. I trust you will get it through the proper channels?" pressed Jesse. Agent Tanner looked at Sonya who stared back in shock at her best friend's words.

"I will see what I can do Jesse. Thanks for the good work," said Tanner. The feed went away and Sonya sat in anger and confusion. "Not sure how you are going to fix that kiddo, but that should be the least of your worries. Get to work."

"Yes Agent Tanner," answered Sonya.

Chapter 42:

The Offer

As the compound's structure emerged in the distance, Sonya took another look at her brother who drove the whole way in silence. Jesse advised them of the guard posts, and how many Candiru he picked up on the thermal scans.

"You're about to turn onto a private road. If they don't know that they have company, they will now," advised Jesse.

"Copy," replied Ronel. "We will be ready for them." Sonya pressed the mute button on the car unit.

"Hey um…," began Sonya.

"I already know. No need to get into it," said Ronel with his eyes darting between the road and tree line.

"But I…."

"Let's not discuss what could have been done. We are here now. Let's just fix tomorrow. At least try to," advised the elder brother. Sonya sunk into her seat, forcing the air out of lungs in a controlled release. "By the way, Mathieu and Banshee are all yours. I will offer support when it is needed. I won't interfere in what you have to do."

"Thank you, brother," replied Sonya in gratitude.

"I will offer this advice. Even with this new power and these suits, we have to be careful to not expend too much energy. I suggest we only transform if it calls for it," suggested Ronel as they pulled up to the tall linked fence. Two of the guards cocked back their machine guns and ordered the two to exit the government vehicle. "I'll take out the first two. Let Jesse guide you through that building. Are we good?"

"Yes. See you on the inside," replied Sonya. Ronel offered a smile then exited with his hands up. Slowly walking towards the gate, a burst of shots blasted away dirt and gravel near his feet.

"Don't take another step! Keep your hands where I can see them!" yelled one of the guards.

"Ok. Hands are up. Feet not moving," replied Ronel. Sonya watched as the chain link pulled Ronel Machete slowly from his back. "Can my friend come out though?"

"She can stay in the car," commanded the other guard.

"I wasn't talking about her," smiled Ronel. The blade swiftly whipped in front of Ronel, lodging through the fence and into the chest of the lead guard. The other began to fire but the swordsman's footwork enabled him to dodge each round. He killed the other guard with a similar blow as his bullets flew in all directions. Slicing an entrance through the still locked fence, Ronel stepped through as Sonya exited the car and followed him. By then, the courtyard began to swarm with nearly thirty Candiru henchmen.

"Jesse, how many more are inside?" asked Sonya.

"I counted 10 at the entrance of the building. About 5 others surround a room where Mathieu's cell phone is pinging from. Video surveillance from the inside shows that Banshee is heading your way," alerted Jesse.

"I'll clear you a pathway," said Ronel as he rushed forward towards the awaiting mob. Ronel swung his sword, penetrating the military grade armor of the front line, punching and kicking his way through those behind. Sonya took care of those that attempted to flank him. Launching her blades at those farthest first, then dispatching those that got close enough with her unmerciful combat skills.

"Stand back!" yelled Ronel to Sonya, breaching the front double doors. Firing up a blaze of fire in his hands, he sent it into the darkness. The napalm-like attack exposed the henchmen as they rolled around in their own hellish torment, groaning for relief. Sonya found the power switch for the facility and turned on the lights. The evidence of Ronel's destruction laid smoldering except for one figure that stood as the smoke began to settle. Lowering a fireproof cloak attached to her red ninja ensemble, she quickly tossed it aside and unsheathed her katana.

"I spent a good time having a conversation with the severed

head of the traitor. Don't worry Little Bird, I promise that your head will rest next to his on my mantle," said Banshee pointing to her sharpened steel weapon.

"You're going to pay for that," cried Sonya as she stepped forward with a katana of her own. Ronel stepped back towards the wall, leaning against it as he toyed with a cone-shaped flame on his finger. Sonya launched forward and the two ninjas engaged fiercely. Although intent was behind each swing of Sonya's blade, it was nonchalantly countered by Banshee. The adversary grabbed Sonya by the throat and slammed her into the edges of a nearby staircase.

"What's a hummingbird to a vulture?" growled Banshee as she stood over Sonya. "You fight with emotion only, and that will get you killed. Get up!" Sonya begrudgingly used her sword as leverage to stand back up to her feet. Banshee continued to taunt her, motioning for her to make another attack. As she stepped forward, four Candiru members appeared. Taking their places at Banshee's side.

"Your chances of dying just increase exponentially. What are you going to do now Little Bird?" asked Banshee. Sonya's eyes began to glow. The slow whistling of the air began to intensify as she walked towards them.

"No Sonya!" yelled Ronel. "If you can't beat them without resorting to that, then we have no chance of defeating Charles. Play them at their own game." Before Sonya could register what Ronel said, the fists of grown men pummeled into her face and head. Ronel rooted her on internally. *"Come on sis. Find it."*

Sonya launched herself into the air and delivered spin kicks to the chins of her attackers. Tumbling backwards, she felt the knots growing, which rapidly healed. Glancing as all five attackers circled her, she stood to her feet and closed her eyes, hearing her heart beat rapidly. Humming her mother's song to herself, calm fell over her. Suddenly, she could see the room and its inhabitants outlined in blue. With her lids shut, Sonya was able to visually see their energy waves. Down to muscle and tissue, she could make out what part of their bodies would possibly move next by the flow of blood or nerve stimulation. The attacks came and she was prepared. Cheating physics, Sonya dodged and returned death blows to all four henchmen. Banshee stepped back as Sonya moved towards her.

"Go ahead and tap in sis!" cheered Ronel from the side of the room.

"It makes no difference!" bolstered a surprised Banshee, as she advanced with a flying strike. Sonya blocked, and vanished. Banshee landed on her feet and turned to find Sonya's blade at her neck.

"Here is the thing about hummingbirds. They are a lot like us Haitian girls. We keep our business short and sweet," said Sonya as she began to twist her blade to cut down into Banshee vocal cords. She was immediately interrupted at the sound of her lover's voice.

"Stop!" yelled Mathieu who appeared on an overhead

railing. Banshee kicked and swiped Sonya's feet, turning to run away. With a fluid motion, Sonya sliced. Leaving a large gash on Banshee's face as she ran off into the darkness. Sonya looked up at Mathieu as he smiled back. He descended down the stairs with an assertive stride.

"You know I was beginning to wonder if I was going to get away with this," beamed Mathieu. "I always knew that your computer boy was going to find out somehow and go running to you like a lap dog."

"Big talk coming from someone whose father was right about them the whole time. I saw the footage; you couldn't even handle a scalpel. Neither what I'm about to do to you," replied Sonya as she began to make her way up the steps. "You are and will always be a peon." Mathieu's smile grew larger.

"Who do you think gave the green light on the priest, bitch?" fluttered Mathieu. Sonya stopped as she seethed in anger. "I was your needed distraction. A strong woman with daddy issues was too easy. Something about that makes them prime and ready for some long dick." Ronel stepped away from the wall and reached for his sword. Right then, white powder escaped the vents, covering his skin and face.

"You disrespectful fuck boy!" yelled Sonya.

"Oh I'm King Fuck Boy! I'm also the least of your worries," laughed Mathieu as he motioned for Sonya to look behind her. Immediately, Sonya felt the power level and heat flaring from her brother's direction. Ronel levitated and flew towards his sister.

Bombarding with strikes and the swinging of his deadly weapon.

"Ronel! What are you doing? Stop it!" yelled Sonya as she did her best to repel his attacks.

"Good ol' fashioned Goofer dust. You can thank our ancestors for that," taunted Mathieu. "He is a zombie now. And just like I killed Elam to get back in my father's good graces, I can't wait to handover your bodies as a gift." Ronel stepped back and began to generate a flame blast. Sonya collected her own power to deflect the impending attack.

"Unlike you and your father, my brother has a soul," said Sonya. Ronel released the deadly sun-like hellfire, which pushed against the wind barrier concealing her. *"Don't make me do this brother. Snap out of it!"* Ronel launched another blast, pushing the inferno towards Sonya's face. As she felt her tactical clothing begin to sizzle, she readied herself for her next step.

"I am going to make you kill another brother! Except this one won't die unless he takes you with him. I must say I love your family's dynamic," jeered Mathieu.

"I wonder what your mother would say to you if she could see what you have become?" blurted Sonya under duress, her fingernails began to smoke from the heat.

"The same thing she said to me when I pulled the trigger. Except I didn't let her weak ass say another weak ass thing," joked Mathieu. "But I will extend you that courtesy. Any last words?"

"Yeah, two," Sonya responded as she looked a confused

Mathieu in the eyes. "I Call!" A rush of light surrounded Sonya. The blue garment flowed from her feet to her neck, completing with a mask over her nose and mouth. With a burst of wind, she sent the fireball into the ceiling causing the sprinkler system to activate. The water poured onto Mathieu as he tried to take cover under his arms. He glanced over to Sonya's position and realized that she was gone. Mathieu suddenly caught standing behind her brother who was still in a trance, commanding the air and water to clean the excess caked on powder. Sonya closed her eyes, and hummed to herself. The room went white.

"Ronel. Can you hear me?" yelled Sonya in the empty void.

"I can," replied Ronel. Placing his hand on her shoulder and smiling. "I knew you could do it."

"I'm sorry for everything," sniffled Sonya.

"No need to apologize. The fight is not over yet. We will heal when we have peace. You still have a bastard to catch," said Ronel, hugging her. "It's a good thing you transformed because I wasn't holding back."

"Wait. You were in control the whole time?!" gasped Sonya.

"Hell Yeah! I wasn't going to let that control shit happen to me again. I had to make him think it was real and push you to the limit. Now go get him!" Sonya opened her eyes, and the two siblings returned to their present selves as the sprinklers began to recede. Mathieu was gone. Using her radar-like ability, she saw his blue thermo image making his way to the back of the building. She gave chase but Mathieu barricaded himself in a server room.

Going over to one of the terminals, he began to type away. After a few clicks of the mouse, the software initiated a covert distress call, which was answered.

"Did you and Banshee take care of our little problem?" asked Charles on the other end. Not looking in the webcam as he marveled at his custom made throne.

"The powder did not work Father! I am being hunted, and they are almost here," heaved a frantic Mathieu. "I can't reach Banshee. She has gone dark. Please send the Candiru to rescue me!" Right then the door flew off of its hinges, sending fragments in all directions. One of them lacerated the top of Mathieu's head. He fell to the ground holding his head as red flowed through his fingers. Sonya appeared through the doorway with Ronel behind her. The siblings stood over him, and noticed Charles' face on the screen staring back.

"Please," begged Mathieu as Ronel picked him up by his collar. "I pose no threat to you! Pran pitye!(Give me mercy)" Mathieu looked at the screen as his father nonchalantly waved his hand, bidding him farewell.

"Father please. Do something!" screamed Mathieu.

"I have already done everything for you son. I have nothing left for you," voiced Charles. Mathieu's skin ran cold as his last hope dwindled.

"I have a proposition Charles." stated Ronel. "How about you take some time off from being Dick-wad Dictator, and meet us on the beach to finish this. Grant us this in exchange for your son's life!"

"I like the idea, but what's truly in it for me?" shot back Charles.

"You get us." replied Sonya. Ronel looked over at Sonya as she made the decision for them. "You get us at your side without a fight.

"Well, I must say your offer is very tempting, but at this point I just plainly and simply want you dead. Making you zombies to serve me blindly," said a maniacal Charles.

"You could be right," entered Sonya. "But I want to show you how confident we are!" Ronel, without breaking his attention to Charles, let go of Mathieu. Sonya snatched Mathieu from the back as he attempted to flee. Wrapping her arms around his neck, she raised him while levitating. Charles' remaining son struggled to breath as his feet jerked for a solid surface. "Brother. Hold onto something."

Ronel gripped the nearest support beam he could find. As Mathieu squirmed even more for oxygen, Charles continued to smile. With her pupils illuminated, the wind began to pick up with hurricane force winds. The sidings on the building flew off and joined many other large objects circulating them.

"I want you to feel exactly what Elam felt," whispered Sonya into Mathieu's ear. As she held his neck and raised her body to float horizontally, the victim watched as his dangling body contorted. His shoulders slowly turned clockwise as his neck broke audibly. The spinning of his body continued until bone and tissue under his chin tore away. Leaving only his head in Sonya's clutch. She lowered herself to the ground as the winds subsided. Tossing away what was left of Mathieu to a dark corner, she walked back over to the screen, joining her brother.

"We will be waiting for you at Twa Rivier(Three Rivers), where God meets land. Tonight, this all ends," said Ronel before slicing through the screen. Charles's face remained static as sparks flew from the clean cut through the hardware.

Chapter 43:

Port of Peace

"So. It's alive?" asked Manny as she pressed her fingers against Sonya's armor.

"Yeah. Crazy right?" responded Sonya into the aircraft's headset as Manny continued to fawn over the attire.

"How is it glowing like that?" asked Manny.

"It's my heartbeat. It is truly connected to me," answered Sonya smiling.

"We're 10 minutes out," announced Jesse who sat at the small aircraft's controls. Sonya looked in his direction but he would not make eye contact.

"Remember Jesse. Slow down fast enough for us to jump. Don't even let the wheels touch the landing strip. Take off immediately," directed Ronel. The elder brother noticed Sonya staring at Jesse. "Hey Manny. You want to see MY suit?"

Manny's eyes nearly rolled to the back of her head as the request enticed her.

"Well, well. Look who's come around," whispered a horned-up Manny. She joined Ronel and he quickly transformed before her. Sonya understood her brother's wingman move, and rose up to sit next to Jesse.

"Five minutes out Agent Jean-Baptiste," said Jesse, still manning the controls.

"Can you stop calling me that?" requested Sonya. Jesse sat silent at the helm. "Are you going to talk to me at all? Are you serious about transferring?"

"This ain't gonna be a rom-com ending where you realize, finally, that I'm the man for you. I don't need any pity consolation prize," ripped Jesse. "Do you have any idea how many times I have to sit behind a headset, wondering if this will be the time that you die? Yet here I am flying a plane into yet another warzone. Except this time, I'm not sure you're coming out of this."

"I will," replied Sonya as she turned to him. "I'm sorry for the things I said and the things I have done to hurt you. I don't expect you to stay, but I'm begging you not to go. Give me a chance to fix this." Jesse took a breath and looked at her. Conflicted yet absolute.

"Come back alive," requested Jesse as he returned his eyes to the dark clouds. "If you don't, I'm crashing this shit into him. That I can promise. Talking to you after this is still up for debate though." Sonya silently agreed with a head nod, and stood up to her feet. She leaned in towards him.

"No." stopped Jesse placing his hand on her abdomen. "If you gonna take it there, you better be prepared to take it all the way. I want all the love. All the nasty, and all the freaky that makes that shit with weazel look like a 3rd grade school dance. Anything less? Keep it professional." A speechless Sonya tried to keep focus as Jesse's words almost knocked her down. The ultimatum was abrupt, but weirdly arousing to her. He didn't budge. Not even physically. Sensing every cell in his body defying her advance, she backed away and awkwardly smiled.

"I'll see you when I get back," responded Sonya. Returning to the back of the aircraft to a very elated Ronel who quickly got away from Manny's aggressive hands.

"You two good?" asked Ronel.

"I think we will be," responded Sonya.

"You have to give him the nookie or no dice huh?" joked Manny, taunting her friend to come into her embrace. "It happens to the best of us, girl. We gonna figure it out."

Their feet landed onto the dirt within the plume of dust caused by the single engine of the passing plane. Plain clothed, Ronel and Sonya blended into the night as they made their way to the main road. Remaining in the shadows as they advanced towards the coast line, they noticed the area's desertion.

"Picking up anything?" asked Sonya.

"Nothing." Responded Ronel.

"Why did you choose Port-de-Paix of all places?" asked Sonya. "Twa Rivier is not the most advantageous battleground that will work in our favor. Gravel, sea water, and La Torture is a grim swim away if we need to retreat."

"That is why I chose it. I don't want to make it easy on him either. Peace will be the end result here. We will see to it," Ronel responded. The siblings made it to the shore line and instantly noticed six Candiru awaiting them. Behind them on bended knee was a black hooded man carving his swords into a large stone overlooking a fire pit. The grinding of steel and earth sent sparks and smoke into the air.

"It's rude to keep your host waiting you know," said Charles as he placed each blade into its holster. Turning around, he lowered the hood. Dark black hair on his head tied with a thin gold ribbon at its ends. His goatee expertly trimmed without a gray follicle or flaw, other than the scar between his eyes. Emphatically ripping away the cloak to reveal an expertly tailored version of Jean-Jacques Dessalines' attire.

"Are these men here to bury you, or to join you in your grave?" asked Ronel.

"If anyone will have the luxury of burying my enemies. It will be you soulless voided shells at my command," hissed Charles as a dark barrier surrounded him. The commander's face dimpled and compressed. Bone structure readjusted on his face, and his skin tightened. Charles' full transformation in Jean-

362

Jacques Dessalines was seamless. The dark hue of his skin was now only the result of natural melanin. The aura was no longer needed.

"You desecrate him by wearing his face. Even he calls you an imposter!" yelled Sonya. Before Charles' lips could part to make a rebuttal, Sonya blasted into the air, releasing a barrage of blades made ready by the armor yet to be revealed. The henchmen and their leader struggle at first to hold back the objects. Charles' dark aura deflects each blade, bending and rendering them into smoldering balls of metal.

"Is this a fight or circus knife throwing?! Please tell me that was simply a sound check Sonya," laughed Charles.

"Oh I'm about to play those eardrums like a fatboy in a tight band uniform!" bolted Sonya as she harnessed her power, causing the wind to kick up surf water and dust from under the stones that lined the beach.

"C'mon, put up the fight your family couldn't," sneered Charles as the wind whipped at his garment. Enraged, Sonya beams down from the heights, landing and crushing the earth where Charles once stood. Before the dust settles, she is met with boot to the side of her head. The force sent her small frame skipping across the shallow waves into the rolling swells of the dark sea. Ronel continued to look on as Charles reappeared once again, turning his attention to him. "So are you just going to stand there and leave your loved ones to my hands again?"

"I wouldn't worry about me right now," replied Ronel as he

gingerly inspected the chain link he pulled from behind him with his sword dangling on the end. The nonchalant demeanor made Charles seethe. He motioned for the henchmen to attack the eldest brother. As the men advanced, Ronel patiently tugged at the chain link until the handle of his sword made it to his palm.

"How dare you insult me?!" shouted Charles. "Kill him!"

"She is going for your neck!" warned Ronel before heaving the metal weapon towards the unfortunate henchmen. As the chain link led the blade through bone and guts, a confused Charles pondered.

"My neck?" thought Charles before realizing that a soaked Sonya regained her footing and gracefully wrapped her legs around his neck while falling backwards in a fluid motion. Charles' face met the ground repeatedly as Sonya kept her tumbling death grip. Releasing him, she leapt to the air, releasing a different share of knives. Plummeting them into Charles' back like an oversized pin cushion. An elated Sonya descended next to her brother grabbing him by the hand.

"This is the part where we run!" huffed Sonya as they began to retreat a few feet away behind a large gum tree.

"Why?" asked Ronel who was briefly startled by the multiple explosions from Sonya's new addition to her arsenal which plunged the dictator into the earth forcefully.

"That should do some damage," confirmed Sonya. Both emerging on opposite sides of the mammoth trunk of the grandfathered plant, they peered into the debris. Charles was no longer present, except for the dead Candiru guards lying lifeless.

"Where is he?" fumbled Sonya. Ronel stepped forward to further inspect but stopped as the cold, icy awareness ran down his neck to his sneakers. Feeling the evil energy through his senses in multiple forms. A quiet settled, then the thumps of weighted objects landing on the branches of the tree. The force shook their foundation as they looked up. In the sea of barely visible leaves and nature's shelves stood multiple figures of Charles. All smiling, some even letting out laughter that came and lost their volume in the expanse of the night.

"Anything is stronger in numbers!" yelled one of the entities, presenting two swords in each hand. The other clones would mimic the action, becoming an army against two. They descended violently, surrounding the siblings who now stood back-to-back. The clones advanced, which caused Ronel to tap into his flame power while speeding up the rotation of the chain attached to his machete. Sonya summoned the wind as her katanas made their appearances as well. The clashing of blades mirrored that of great wars as the siblings battled against the onslaught. Evading and countering as many thrusts and swings of surely fatal metal, the duo were formidable. Ronel, engulfed in fire, used his flame throwing energy blasts to ward off the bombardment. Sonya, using her telekinetic energy, threw each Charles copy into oblivion, only for them to return. Less strikes were being stopped as exhaustion set in. The punctures were now lacerating their skins. Retreating briefly, the siblings looked to one another. It was time.

"Can't keep up?" asked one of Charles' clones.

"Let's see if you all can keep up after this," stated Ronel. Sonya surrounded in a blue aura, and Ronel in red raised their hands to the moon lit sky.

"I call!" they both said in unison. Instantly, their issued battle garments dressed them. The wounds healed quickly as they confidently readied themselves for another barrage of attacks. As the clones maintained their smiles and laughter, one looked as if it saw a ghost.

"There you are," noticed Ronel, now with an assortment of chained blades at the ready. He then launched them at the clones. Each of them incinerated with each blow until the true Charles fought off ones aimed at him. Unbeknownst to the tyrant, the attack was a diversion. As he knocked away the last blade, one exited through his chest. Charles looked on in shock as the chain attached tied itself into a large ball in front of him, trapping him like a fish hooked by the gills. Pulling in his prey, Ronel rapidly landed punches into his face. Stopping abruptly to allow Sonya to return a booted favor that Charles dished out earlier.

"We're no longer misguided kids with powers, Charles. We have absolute control now," launched Ronel as he rammed his fiery knee into Charles' back, knocking him to his hands and knees. Charles heaved for air as Sonya approached with knives circulating her. The closer she reached the more the heaving turned into a laughing fit. She stopped.

"And what exactly is so damn funny?" asked Sonya.

"Did you really think a wardrobe change just shifted this battle in your favor?" chuckled Charles. The chain link ball torn to shreds of hot, blackened metal. Charles stood to his feet, ripping the excess metal from his back and healing his body instantly. "Since we are upping the ante. This is how winners play!" Snapping his fingers, an immediate explosion occurred between them, sending sound and nuclear-powered energy in all directions. The blast was so massive that it shook the ground, causing the waves to become violent. Swelling to nearly 10 feet high, attacking the shoreline. The siblings used their energy to shield themselves as trees were set ablaze, and the sounds of people screamed in the distance.

"You fucking psychopath!" yelled Ronel.

"Oh wait, my troubled children. The aftershock is to die for," revealed Charles as another blast was sent out from him, yet it was dark and without sound. The siblings felt the wave pass them without effect.

"What the hell was that?" asked Sonya. Ronel stood at her side and went to respond but could not utter a word. Sonya looked inland as she also felt the faint but massive slow advance of something they could not put their finger on.

"The screams stopped." stated Ronel. The com units in their ears produced some static before they heard Jesse's voice.

"Sonya! Ronel! They are coming! I don't know how but they are packing every single weapon and firearm you can think of!"

367

yelled Jesse.

"He signaled for the Candiru's full force. We will be ready Jesse," respond Sonya.

"Wrong." trembled Jesse. "These aren't Candiru."

"What?" asked Ronel. Jesse exhaled as he tried to gather the best way to explain what he was seeing from ground surveillance.

"It's young. It's Old. Men, women, and children. All converging from all the nearest towns, villages, and communes," fretted Jesse. "They are armed to the teeth. Some with clubs, and whatever they can find. They are on a beeline towards your position, and they are not in control." The siblings lost all sense of strategy.

"Now it's time that you meet the wrath of a nation," announced Charles as the national anthem of the Republic of Haiti blared through hidden but numerous speakers from within the island. The infantry of dark-eyed civilians approached, their feet stomped and crunched the ground. Louder and Louder until they were visible to the siblings. More massive than they thought, many of the civilians had visible injuries from the blast sent out by Charles. The numbers multiplied with each line of the mindless, bloodthirsty mob. "Eat, my children. They are your enemies!".

Chapter 44:

The Destiny Rule

"Any ideas?" asked Sonya.

"Not one," replied Ronel. "I'm not killing innocent people, but I for damn sure don't want to retreat from his cowardly tricks."

"What if we just knock them out?" reasoned Sonya. "The same way you did when he used that kid to fight you."

"That kid he used somehow was able to fight like a mini version of myself. Same skill level. This isn't going to be a walk in the park if he is using the same mind control," pressed Ronel. "But you're right. We don't have any choice. He is going to hide behind them and we are going to have to fight our way through to get to him."

The national anthem repeated again on another cycle as the mob continued to advance towards them. Charles raised his sword and pointed to the Jean-Baptiste duo, speaking the words that caused the march to erupt into a full-on blitz of rage.

"Koupe tet. Boule Kay!(Cut off their heads! Burn their houses!)" commanded Charles. First came the gunfire of multiple guns. Many tearing through the first line of the charging crowd. Seeing this, the siblings began to use their levitation abilities while keeping their energy shields up to deflect what they could. Suddenly the hands of the mob pulled them down and the machete wielders began their assault. Piling onto them while slicing and stabbing away. With a quick blast of energy, the siblings cleared their paths briefly before engaging with a fresh line of new attackers. Holding true to Sonya's suggestion, the pair chose to engage in hand-to-hand combat to avoid any further casualties. Delving knock out blows to everyone, including children.

"I don't want to hit another kid," huffed Sonya.

"You've been hitting them?! I just trip them. Yeah, you should feel bad," joked Ronel before nailing another right hook to another zombie.

"You will eventually tire," stated Charles. "When you do, they will tear you both apart."

"Face us like the enforcer you claim to be, you bitch-made muthafucker!!" bolstered Ronel. "Even from the grave, my brother's words will always be true about you!"

"Don't you worry. I will send you both to meet him," warned Charles before blitzing his way through his own army, killing all that were in his way with his dual sword attack. Reaching the siblings, he engaged them. Taunting as he landed strikes and cuts of his sword to each of them.

"This is what happens when you care. This is what happens when emotion fills your heart for anyone other than yourself!" blasted Charles. Ronel engulfed himself in more intense flames in an effort to repel the crowd and Charles' attack. Yet, he was taken aback by how willfully they walked into sure death. Conflicting him and leaving himself open to Charles' combination of attacks. Sonya stepped forward and produced a whirlpool sending many of the mob flying into each other, and the sea. The brief clearing allowed her to launch an offensive, but she was quickly overpowered by Charles' version of the same whirlpool. The massive twister sent her to the ground. The armor on them now showed evidence of fatigue. The fibers regenerated yet the wounds and trauma to their bodies took longer to do so, rendering them to a constant defensive. Tasting blood rise into her mouth, Sonya clinged to her brother's arm. Ronel increased the flames around them in desperation and defiance.

"You can't do anything by yourself?!" yelled Ronel pointing his machete at any and all that surrounded them.

"Look at you now. The old priest warned you, but you persisted with this so-called revenge crusade!" barked Charles, stepping towards them and pressing his chest on the edge of Ronel's trembling sword. "Men like me do not come from nothing. Circumstance births many like myself. I stand on the side of right, and you stand on the side of right. Join me and become a legend! Join me and sit at the table as the severed heads of the world powers roll below your feet. The red and blue of our nation shall continue to be raised without blemish. Live forever at my side Ronel. The offer extends to you too, my child." remarked Charles, as new clones and an army of the innocent moved in. The tyrant's copies reached and retrieved Napoleon-like pistols from their holsters, cocking back their handles, and pointing them at the doomed siblings.

"We will never fight alongside the motivations of a man like you. We consider it fortunate to die trying to right the wrong you committed against us," grunted Ronel and he slowly applied pressure to the handle of his blade, as the shaking of his arm became firm. "You will have to kill us to get us to stand for you."

"Then it will be my pleasure," sneered a frustrated Charles as he removed Jean-Jacques' pistols from his garment and sent his dark energy into them, pointing each nozzle at their heads. Suddenly a look of concern flashed across his face as an energy source, faint at first, grew and intensified. Charles directed his attention to the sea. The buzzing of a motor in the distance drew everyone's attention. Ronel and Sonya felt the surging power as well. Suddenly, lightning struck the ground, incapacitating the surrounding mob to an unconscious state and shorting out the speakers.

"What is that?" whispered Ronel. A tearful Sonya stepped forward, attempting to hold in a combination of disbelief, grief, and elation. "No, it can't be?!"

"It is!" fluttered Sonya. The motor of a classic Donzi speed boat roared towards the mountainous isle with a tall form standing on at the bow. Pastor Troy's "Vice Versa" blaring from its speakers. The rage burning in the figure's eyes pierced the fog, as if lighting the way to a white hell. The beach shirt on him whipped behind him, as the drunkard redneck captained the vessel, keeping it steady. Sweat and sea water caused his tatted dark skin to shine under the moonlight.

"Mike, take us in hard!" yelled the now smiling and rejuvenated Judson. Raising his hand to display a white, wool-wrapped shard that once laid on his corpse. He belted out the words that sent Charles' facial perfection into pain. "I call!!"

A flash of light beamed from his hands, spreading throughout his body in immaculate glory. Shining briefly, until the attire once worn by the Great Mayer rested on him, with the emblem that was once tattooed on the back of Elam. The hands of the Judson were wrapped in the mysterious fabric, creating matching fighter gloves; an upgrade to the ancient suit. The electrical energy was palpable and Judson reveled in it. He leapt onto the beach before the bottom of the vessel could meet the shore.

"Oh, I'm back bitches!" yelled Judson, concentrating the static-like energy at the remainder of the mob. Charles began to retreat angrily. Stepping backwards with his weapons still drawn, as Judson approached confidently. Reuniting with his family,

Judson checked on them.

"Y'all good?" asked Judson in a serious manner.

"Are you really here?" asked Ronel as he inspected his brother like a concerned, overbearing mother.

"Bro, I'm good. I'm good. Long story short? A very waterboard-like baptism at sea by a woman with mom's face." laughed Judson as he pulled in his elder brother. The two embraced as Sonya stood off to the side with her head down. Judson noticed, and approached her. Towering over her menacingly.

"Judson, I..." began Sonya.

"We will iron it out after we kill him," intruded Judson. "Right now, you are the key to getting to the man behind all of his power."

"What do you mean? " inquired Sonya

"Sing Mayer's song. If you want to reach our ancestor you have to lose yourself in the melody. It's the only way! C'mon, we don't have much time. Me and Ronel will hold him off as long as we can. It's on you now to save us. Don't fuck this up!" inspired Judson as he took Ronel's side. Ronel nodded to her in approval of what Judson commanded. The two brothers charged their power and advanced towards Charles as he multiplied his existence once again. The brothers landed a series of blows with each clone they engaged. Judson pulled out a white and gold version of his gun, firing non-stop as the real Charles evaded.

Sonya closed her eyes, and began to sing. As directed, she

lost herself in her voice, until she could hear it echoing as the sound of the gunfire drowned out. She opened her eyes to find that she was now in a voided white space. She stopped singing, as her voice still continues to echo. She looked around, unable to make out anything but the endless purgatory.

"Hello?" she called.

"Why are you here?" a voice replied. Sonya looked and found a man standing with his back to her.

"I am Sonya Jean-Baptiste, descendant of Mayer the Formidable."

The man chuckled to himself then turned to reveal himself. Jean-Jacques stood before Sonya, dressed in his regal commandant attire with his arm resting on his blade, puzzled. "This nightmare never ceases to amaze me. You are but a child and our language weighs heavy on your tongue. How do you know my mother's song?"

"Because it was passed down to me by my mother, Carline, also a descendant of Mayer."

"Child, what you speak is impossible. Mayer did not have an heir, no one could ever bear such a mantle. Even if he is a traitorous bastard."

"His son did," replied Sonya. "He became a King, one of the greatest to ever live. I consider it an honor to be of his bloodline as well. The king's name outshined even that of his father's."

"If what you say is true, I regret having never met such a man." responded a stoic Jean-Jacques.

"That man is you, ancestor," stated Sonya.

Jean-Jacques laughed. Looking into Sonya's eyes and seeing into her soul. The expression on his face changed as his mind pondered on the possibility. Thinking of the similarities of his training at the hands of his mother and Mayer. The trust and mentorship only bestowed to those of elite stature, was given to him so freely. He thought it to be a circumstance of luck. As he pondered, his eyes welled only to turn into a face of anger. Rubbing the scarred tissue that deformed the skin around his neck, he tugged at the collar of his coat to expose it.

"Why did he leave me to be betrayed?! Why did he allow me to be devoured by the contraptions of foreign men?! He watched me die!"

"Ancestor, I know it is a lot to consider all at once," muttered Sonya. "I don't have the answers to your questions, but I don't have much time as the lives of the ones I love are in danger. Your people are in danger."

"I am aware of the tyrant at the helm of my abilities. I have watched men like him come and go. Ever since I was betrayed and sentenced to this void, I feel the suffering of my people. I thought this curse to be the most extreme, that is until my power returned to me once more, yet not mine to control."

"You can control it. You just need a guide. That is why I am here. I know what it is like to have an elder let you down. But what I have learned is that their decisions, although dire, serve a greater purpose that will not be clear to us when the wound is fresh. Not all understanding can be explained in life, only after death."

"Such wisdom is beyond you. Your power is steps beyond anything I have ever seen. It is as beautiful as you are." Jean-Jacques placed his hands on her shoulders. "It is great to know that my descendants have produced such great warriors. Your brothers are definitely formidable opponents. That bald one seems to have an affinity for foul language." They both shared a laugh.

"Child, I am not sure of what use I can be, but I am at your mercy and direction." submitted the General.

"Sing with me. I know it sounds menial," began Sonya, until a deep humming escaped from his lips. She held his hands and joined him as they both closed their eyes."

Charles struck Judson, sending him into a nearby brush of trees. Judson stood back up for an immediate counter attack.

"I can go all day, Charles! If you want to kill me, you are going to have to do it your Goddamn self!" incited Judson.

"The next time I make contact with you, there will be no resurrection!" ranted Charles as he prepared to charge another negative blast. Yet, it would not amass the force he expected, instead it smothered into nothing.

"What is happening?!" fumed Charles, as he attempted to garner the dark force once again.

"You don't get it do you?" Ronel asked as he prepared a fiery blast of his own, emerging from his peripheral. "You don't win, not this time!"

"It's the girl!" sneered Charles as he realized what was taking place as Sonya hovered overhead in a trance. The tyrant took his sword from his side and lunged it towards her. Ronel directed his blast to intercept it, incinerating the blade instantly.

"No! This cannot be happening!" cracked Charles as multiple burning sensations coursed throughout his body. Specifically in the places where the bones of Jean-Jacques were surgically attached. Falling to his knees, the dark figures at his side evaporated into ash.

"I am free now," whispered Jean-Jacques as Sonya slowly opened her eyes to find her ancestor adorned in all white. White noise garnered their attention to two portals spinning like a whirlpool behind him.

"Where will you go?" inquired Sonya.

"It would seem that I now have a choice to make," replied Jean-Jacques as he stared into one of the portals. "I feel an unbelievable love from the portal to my left."

"Do you see my parents?" asked Sonya tearfully. As he looked into the portal, the answer was clear.

"Yes," acknowledged Jean-Jacques as he looked at the spirits staring back at them. "Your mother says that she sees you. She has always seen you, and will always be at your side." Sonya embraced him, collapsing in his arms as she wept in gratitude.

"What about Elam? Mayer?" asked Sonya.

"They are where they are needed most," replied the fading

King. "We will always be with you. I will always be with my people. Encourage them to continue the fight. The Almighty hears and knows their anguish. Their victory is certain!" Sonya opened her eyes as she watched her ancestor join with those they both held dear before the portal closed behind him.

Sonya looked through the other portal, seeing the battle between her brothers and Charles came to a standstill. As she walked towards it to regain control of her body, Jean-Jacques' voice returned to her.

"One more thing child, he is vulnerable now. Make us proud!" said Jean-Jacques Dessalines.

"Oh, we will Ancestor, I assure you!" confirmed Sonya as she stepped back into the fight.

"Brothers! Mom and Dad give their regards, and their permission!"

Upon hearing those words, Judson readies the crackling energy in his hands until it engulfed him completely. With pupils shimmering and focused on the man responsible for a lifetime of agony.

"Burn in hell!" he belted. Thrusting his forearms forward, the flow of energy hits Charles' chest, seizing all of his extremities. Sonya released every blade in her arsenal towards her awaiting victim below. Charles yells in torment as he is impaled. Blood pooled out of each puncture as the gray spread across his hair follicles. The commander's skin withered, wrinkled, and darkened.

"Do you think this is over?! Because of your power, you will always be hunted! Eternal fire burns for the immortal because man seeks it so diligently! There will always be hell for you all!" boasted old man Charles, quivering as the bones of Jean-Jacques burned away within him. The mob once under his control begins to come to. Many were confused at what happened. "What have you done?! You have stolen away any chance our nation has to stand against the world. You are the real traitors!"

"Why don't we let the people who you had no problem killing, choose!" said Sonya as she stood before the crowd. Slowly, the sounds of multiple materials could be heard falling to the ground. The former mob threw down their weapons in defiance.

"Murderer!"

"He doesn't speak for us!"

"Get him out of here!"

"Traitor!" yelled the people.

"The nation has spoken, Charles," began Ronel as he pointed his father's blade at the defeated commander. Sonya pulled out her katana as Judson reached for a blade of his own. "Time to cut the cancer out!"

As Ronel's pupils filled with flames, Charles' garments were set ablaze as he screamed out. The tough old skin on him began to sizzle, the flames intensifying as Ronel wielded his sword. Falling to his knees, Charles looked up at his executioners. Ronel ran towards him as he did when he was a child. Judson approached from the right, and Sonya from the left. Judson sliced low, cutting through Charles' torso. Sonya inflicted another slice across his shoulders. Closing his eyes, Ronel leapt while raising the blade above his head, clenching the grip in both hands. At peace with his demons, he sliced down along the scare line on Charles' face until his sword met the stone beach. Ending him.

Chapter 45:

Until Then

"You know he was right," said Ronel as Sonya loaded another bag of clothes for her niece in Judson's car. "As long as we exist, we will be hunted. Are you sure you want to be front and center of that?"

"Alejandro had foresight to know that we would prevail. The offer in his will was extended to all of us. We can keep them new enemies at bay better with all the resources of the Assembly at our disposal." replied Sonya as she directed another contractor to the backyard. The ruins of Gomez' estate were being rebuilt under the watchful eye of the new chairwoman. "I get Judson's deal, he has a daughter to catch up with. I would think that you would want to jump at the chance to go after the real evil of the world." Jesse and Manny brought out the last of Sonya's shopping spree, and loaded them into the backseat.

"Jesse, please make sure she doesn't get way over her head. Remember, I'm just a call away," requested Ronel.

"Don't you worry. She is in good hands. We got her," assured Jesse.

"No, I got you," replied Sonya playfully as Jesse pulled her in for a kiss.

"Get a room! I know some really sleazeball places that would be perfect for y'all," said Judson as he brought the last of his belongings from inside the house.

"Love you too asshole," responded Sonya, pulling him in for a hug.

"Opps, she got a knife!" mocked Judson before getting a quick slap to the back of the head by Sonya.

"Send me pictures of my baby girl as soon as you get up there. Remember, she doesn't know what happened to her mother and Elam yet. You gotta be very careful in how you handle her," warned Sonya as she parted from their embrace.

"I got it. I'm going to make sure I take care of her in every way. That I promise you," promised Judson.

"Look at you. Don't tell me fatherhood is going to make you all the way soft," joked Ronel. Judson energized his hand as his eyes illuminated.

"Only for her. But please believe me, if there is an underground fighting scene in the ATL, you will hear some shocking reviews," announced Judson. "But for the sake of my child, I will keep it at a minimum and actually go legit. I might do Real Estate." All that surrounded Judson erupted into laughter.

"You know what? Fuck all y'all and y'all hating asses!" snapped Judson before getting into his vehicle. As he typed in the address in the GPS, Ronel leaned into the passenger side window.

"Go be the best dad ever brother. Elam would be proud," said Ronel.

"I know he will. I wish he was here to see how it all turned out," sighed Judson as he started the ignition.

"I'll be right behind you for a bit until you break off for Georgia. I'm heading up to New York for some unfinished business," said Ronel.

"You mean that chick Rosa?" inquired Judson.

"She is part of it." replied Ronel.

"Well don't scare her off again. She might be good for you to finally stop wandering the earth, and the bottom of liquor bottles. We all need something to ground us," presented Judson.

"When did you turn into Dr. Phil?" asked Ronel sarcastically. Sonya joined him at his side with an inquiring stare of her own.

"I ain't doing this with y'all two. I love you idiots, but I got a little lady that I'm nervous as fuck to meet," expressed Judson. Ronel reached his hand in, as did Sonya. Judson then placed his hand over theirs.

"Zoes(Bones) forever?" asked Sonya, hoping that her siblings would embrace the new team slogan.

"That's terrible," said Judson.

"I agree, that was really bad," admitted Ronel.

"It will come to me. I will figure it out while leading one of the deadliest groups of assassins in the world," said Sonya. The back and forth between the siblings continued awhile until Judson drove away. Ronel shortly after boarded his motorcycle and rode off as well, leaving Sonya and her friends at the entrance of Alejandro's estate. Turning around to assess the much-needed renovations, Sonya smiled. Everything was right in the world.

"Agent Tanner, what was so important that it could not wait?" asked Director Lee as he ran into the office to escape the rain.

"After the death of Charles Clearveux, we were able to pick up on some increased chatter regarding the Brat'ya Zhaka," said Tanner as she presented a binder of evidence. Director Lee searched through, as Tanner stood next to him in anticipation.

"What's this emblem?" asked Director Lee as he stared at an ancient drawing of a symbol.

"That was the symbol that came up periodically during Jesse's investigation into Mathieu. We were later able to confirm that it was what the Zhaka refer to as 'The Arrival'. I started to cross reference the image in our database to see if it came up in any other investigations." expressed Tanner.

"What did you find?" asked Lee.

"Nothing. Absolutely nothing." admitted Tanner. Director Lee placed the binder on the desk and patted Tanner on her shoulder.

"Well let's keep looking into it. Something is bound to come up," said the Director.

"Something actually did, Director." revealed Tanner as she raised a photo of an intricate tattoo with an ancient emblem hidden throughout it. "You want to explain why this is on your back?" The Director stopped and turned around slowly.

"Tanner, I can explain this," pleaded Lee before drawing his weapon and shooting Tanner in the chest. Tanner fell to the ground as Director Lee stood over her, frantically reaching for his cellphone. He made a call and began speaking in German as Tanner struggled to breath.

"I need a clean up crew, and get him on the line now. We have a problem," said Lee as he shot twice into her head, ending her fight. Placing the gun on the conference desk, he sat down on a nearby chair and lit up a cigarette he retrieved from his pocket.

"Yes brother," replied a voice on the other line.

"An agent too smart for her own good found out about 'The Arrival'. It would seem that we need to expedite the plans to wake up the Enforcer. Although Charles' efforts did not yield us Mayer, he did leave in his wake three problems that we need to eliminate." replied Lee.

"The Enforcer has been watching the whole time since you alerted us of three descendants of that wretched Mayer. It may be time that we accept that he is truly dead. We will hunt them down and take back what is rightfully ours." snarled the voice through the receiver.

"Splendid. Long Live the Brat'ya Zhaka!" asserted Director Lee. The call ended on the other end.

Chapter 46:

Arrival

Ronel's motorcycle sped up the shoulder of the northbound, backed up traffic on the interstate. Rosa's hair whipped in the air from under her helmet as she held on tight to him. A click from his in-ear com was heard before a voice he hadn't heard in a few weeks, spoke.

"Tell me you are also feeling that!" said Judson as the sound of his donk accelerating could be heard in the background.

"I've felt it ever since I stopped feeling Sonya's energy. Where are you?!" asked the concerned eldest brother.

"I'm an hour out," yelled Judson.

"Good. We should get there at the exact same time. Whatever this is, we have to be ready," advised Ronel.

"Daddy, do you have to speed so fast?" asked a small voice on Judson's end.

"You brought the baby?!" growled Ronel. "We have no idea what we are walking into!"

"Hey, I couldn't find a babysitter on short notice. Last time I checked, your "Uncle Missing" ass hadn't volunteered. Not once!" blasted Judson. The sun sank into the high rises in the distance as the brothers pulled into the driveway of Alejandro's old estate, now the Assembly's Headquarters. They noticed that a trail of Candiru henchmen laid out at the entrance. The brothers readied their weapons as Rosa stood guard in front of Carline locked inside Judson's donk.

"Did you get anything from Jesse or Manny?" asked Judson as they made their way inside carefully.

"Not even a word or Morse code. This isn't good," trembled Ronel as he launched his flame energy to light up the foyer.

"There!" yelled Judson as he ran over to Sonya's limp body, still adorning her battle suit. With multiple lacerations, the once impenetrable garment visibly struggled to heal over. "Sonya! Say something! What happened to you?" Sonya flinched at the pain as she tried to shake off the stars she was seeing.

"It's, it's," began Sonya before collapsing.

"What the hell could have done this." said Ronel as he continued to survey the heavily damaged area of the mansion.

"Well, it's about time you two showed up," said Banshee strolling out of the shadows. Sonya's archnemesis appeared on the balcony on top of them, dragging behind her Jesse and Manny who were also unconscious. Dropping them to the floor. Right then Rosa ran in with Carline at her side pointing her high-powered rifle at Banshee as she joined Ronel.

"Why are you in here with the child?!" yelled Judson.

"I think you better listen to what Carline has to say," expressed an fearful Rosa. Judson and Ronel turned their attention to the child who stepped out before them.

"Daddy, I thought you said that Grandpa went to heaven? I've been seeing him in my dreams and I feel him near," said the child so innocently. Carline guided their attention as she looked up at where Banshee was standing. Just then a dark figure emerged from behind her. He walked in authority, even as the darkness concealed him. "I see him Daddy, it's Grandpa!"

The siblings looked on as a familiar set of eyes stared down at them. Ronel froze in place as Judson scowled in confusion and anger. Lowering the mask from his face, the man dressed in a black, sleek assassin attire with multiple swords in his utility belt, smiled.

"I watched you die," said Ronel timidly.

"It can't be him, Ronel, Elam is dead!" added Judson, attempting to reason.

"I am the one you know as Elam. Except Elam is who I was in a dormant state," stated Elam as his face began to change in structure. The hair on his head becomes jet black and is laid on his shoulders. His skin is now clearer, and free of wrinkles and scars. As he removed the gloves, they witnessed as the burned and scarred hands rejuvenated. "Do not worry. Sonya will be just fine. We simply had an exhibition."

"Who and what are you?" asked Ronel as he intensified the flame around him. The man, now with a different face, also engulfed himself in flames to match that of a dumbfounded Ronel. He then sent electrical shockwaves around himself as he jumped down to meet them. Summoning the blades from his side to spin around him as those did for Sonya in the previous battle.

"I am the one they call the Formidable. Mayer, the Formidable. Now that you see my true and hidden power, I ask that you put away your clenched fists. We have a lot to discuss, my children," revealed Mayer.

-Fin-

Acknowledgements

To my God. My Lord, and Savior Jesus Christ. You saw fit to not only love me but chased me until I loved you back. Thank you for being you. If I never do another thing in my life, I thank you for your presence in every step I have taken and will take in the future. Thank you for accepting me just as I am. Thank you for giving me this book in my dreams. I did it! Thank you, God!

To my mother and father, Ismarleine Payout and Gilbert Sylverain. Thank you for enduring and sacrificing for me and my siblings. Thank you for your love of music, education, art, theatre, and discipline. I love you both with all my heart. I hope that I made you both proud. To my late grandmother, Jesula Octavien, I miss you and love you so much. Thank you for covering me in prayer and still watching over me. To my siblings. My older sister Marlene, I love you sis. To my Big Brother

Dorcin. It was always me and you enjoying anime, comics, and video games. Who would have thought this day would come? Love you Big Bro! To Jordany, Cheldina, and Wesner. Thank you for your unconditional love and support. You have shown me that being a Haitian geek/nerd is never a bad thing in the Sylverain clan. From Anime binge watching, to hip-hop, konpa, reggae and rock n roll blearing through the speakers. You guys' rock, and I dedicate this to you!

To Vida Orelhomme. My best friend since the crib, to being old AF 30 something year olds! Thanks for being my refuge and confidant. Love you sissy! To Sandra Georges, my adopted sister, and PR General. Thank you for being more excited about this project than I am at times. Your energy inspires me and everything you touch. Keep being you! To my little nieces and nephews. To all my cousins. The talented Givens Francois, Katrine & Jimmy, Keline, Ali, Karen, Betty, and their families and significant others. Devon, and Ashna. The Fleuricin family. Forgive me for not naming you all, you know who you are! To all my aunts and uncles, especially the late Villison Payout. To my other mothers Sina, and the late Marie-Zane. Love you both to death. A special thanks to Kay and Clifford Mitchell for their support, advice, and encouragement.

To my brother Frederick Williams, CEO of 139Designs. Not enough words to say how much you were instrumental in helping me breakthrough when it came to writing this. I stand in awe of your work and talent. Thank you for this book cover! You are one in a million bro. To James & Jennifer Saintolien. I miss and love you both. Thank you for the times we laughed, cried, and kept each other sane. To Charlie Brown, and Timothy Russell. Thank you for not only being my mentors but showing me that hard work and dedication does pay off. To Jacqueline and Bruce Parsons, thank you for giving me an avenue to learn and embrace my creativity through marching band. You guys are the coolest!

To Brennen Jones. Thanks for giving me my first real writing gig for TheUrbanTwist.com, you rock! To Troi "Star" Torrain, for giving me my writing gig at Shot97.com. You are legend! To Dr. Cory Greenspan. Thank you for being tough on me when it came to my writing. You made me see my work differently. To Jenna Moreci on Youtube. Thank you for your many videos and advice on writing novels people want to read. I hope you enjoy your copy!

To my spiritual father, Father Robes "Bebes" Charles. Thank you for not just taking me in during one of the lowest points in my life but allowing me a platform to express my love for music and art through ministry. Thank you for your prayers, and for your friendship. Forgive my cussing in the book. "God knows my heart." LOL.

To Nathaly David, Sister Anne, Se Geralda, and Ms. Marie. Thank you for your support. DMC Drumline for LIFE! Thank you to the countless students that became life-long friends. To my Our Lady's and Queen of Peace Family from the Bahamas. The late Father George, Mr. Frank Riphin, and Father Dorvil.

To my late friend and mentor, Mr. Deen President. Thank you for believing in me on so many levels. I truly believe that you are my guardian angel. You said, "Fuck it! Just do it." And I did it. Thank you for showing me what it means to endure until the very end. Your legacy lives on my powerful brother! Your gift of bringing out the best in all you have mentored has yet to be matched. It was your God-given talent, and man, your teachings still live on until this day. I also dedicate this book to your memory. Rest in Power.

To my illustrator Hackney. Thank you for being patient and available when I needed your gift. You brought my visions to life, and for that I thank you. To Vanica, of Louis Lens Photography. Thank you for making me look like a million and one bucks on this photo shoot! To all the people I have encountered. Friends and acquaintances. Thank you for every encouraging word and well wishes.

To my co-editor, Ms. Marie King. The future Mrs. Marie Sylverain. I can't put into words how much you have been and are to me. My best friend, my true ride or die! Thank you for your prayers. The times you held my head as I slept. For trusting me to carry and lead our family. Thank you for giving me the greatest gifts in the world. Two beautiful little girls. Jakayla Joy, and Khari Rose. I never thought I could ever love one again, but God had plans for me to lose my heart to three. I love you all with all that I am. Daddy did it!

To the country of Haiti. Your beauty has come into question for years. But for those who know you and love you, you have yet to descend past perfection. Perfection because you wear your wounds openly, you never hide, and you never have compromised the essence of who you are. To my people, my blood, my identity. This is my love letter to you. Viv Ayiti!

To the 954! Forever my home! Thank you for adopting me. Broward County stand up!

And to you.....My reader.

Thank you for reading and boarding this rollercoaster ride of a book with me.

You took the time to enjoy my dream. For that, you are more than appreciated.

Hang on, we have a lot more places to go!!

Kingdom's Bones II is coming!! HINT: NOLA

Thank you!!

Merci anpil!!

www.ingramcontent.com/pod-product-compliance
Lightning Source LLC
Chambersburg PA
CBHW050856210726
48290CB00004B/1258